Joseph of Arimathea's Treasure

Joseph of Arimathea's Treasure

By

Ellen Foster

2015

Book Five

The Lady Apollonia West Country Mysteries

Lulu Press, Inc.

Copyright © 2014 Ellen Foster

First published in United States of America 2015

Maps and cover photographs by Louis Foster

ISBN 978-1-312-79598-3

http://blogs.valpo.edu/ellenfoster/

Table of Contents

Foreword

The modern visitor to Glastonbury in Somerset finds an English town in the Levels that retains its aura of great antiquity, religious legend, and a multi-cultured significance that pre-dates the Christian world. My heroine, the Lady Apollonia of Aust, came to Glastonbury in the New Year of 1397 for very personal reasons. She is a scholarly noblewoman but one who must now focus on healing the pain and suffering of her family. Her second eldest son, Sir Chad, has lost his wife, leaving him the widowed father of three young children.

Apollonia of Aust discovered that the painful loss to her family is mirrored by that of a local teenager whom she takes into her household. He is newly orphaned by the murder of his mother, a woman known to be aggressively suspicious of a connexion between the church and a series of robberies of wealthy homes in Glastonbury.

The powerful fourteenth century Benedictine Abbey of Glastonbury exceeded most others in England in its age, its size, and its extensive wealth. Upon arriving in Glastonbury, Apollonia became aware that the sanctity of its Christian ministry was being violated by some whose only motives were greed and personal power.

The Lady could not help being conscious of Glastonbury Tor, the steep high hill which dominates the valley surrounding the town. She explored its religious significance, not only to the Christians who visit the monastery built upon its heights but also to ancient Celtic peoples and their priestly class of Druids. The Druids were long gone from England in the fourteenth century, but I have them return to Glastonbury from Ireland in 1397 to emphasize the importance of the Tor and its surroundings in Celtic religious practices.

The Lady Apollonia West Country Mysteries
by Ellen Foster

Effigy of the Cloven Hoof
Plague of a Green Man
Memento Mori
Templar's Prophecy
Joseph of Arimathea's Treasure

Acknowledgements

We enjoyed an especially good research visit to Glastonbury in March of 2014. Lou and I were able to explore the town, its ruins, and remaining medieval buildings with my cousin and his wife, Paul and Ann Yielding, who visited with us from Coventry. They are not only great company but good observers who helped me become aware of the extraordinary history and legend still resident in this ancient abbey town.

Another real gift to me is the group of friends and family who have been willing to be my early readers. On the English side of the Atlantic, I am grateful to our friend, David Snell, of Exeter, Devon, who has read all of the series.

On the American side, I have used the comments and questions of my PEO sister, Ellen Corley, and those of our good neighbors: Mary Henrichs, Mary Leonard, and Ethelyn Rezelman. The Reverend Nancy Becker, a fellow member of the ReVU Writer's group, offered critical comments inspiring a good deal of essential re-writing. Our friend, Philipp Brockington, has never failed to challenge me with new questions and insightful observations in nearly every chapter. It has been especially helpful to have the purposeful comments of teachers from our community schools, Dennis Norman and my cousin, Annette Aust. Also representing the clergy, I am always grateful to Edward Little, Bishop of the Episcopal Diocese of Northern Indiana, for his well-read understanding of the medieval English church and its unique character. In every case, I am grateful to all of my early readers for their significant assistance.

My family has been endlessly supportive: Ted and Marilyn Foster of Lafayette, Indiana, Charlie and Shelly Foster of Valparaiso, Indiana, as well as my better-half, Lou. Thanks to his computer skills, travel insights, and endless patience, he enables me to discover my most inspired conclusions.

Lady Apollonia's West Country

Medieval Glastonbury

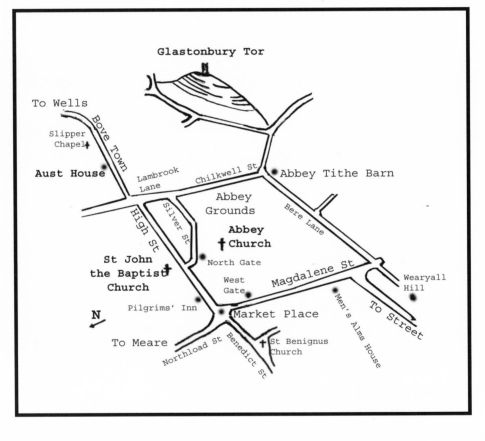

Lady Apollonia's Drawing of the Tor Maze

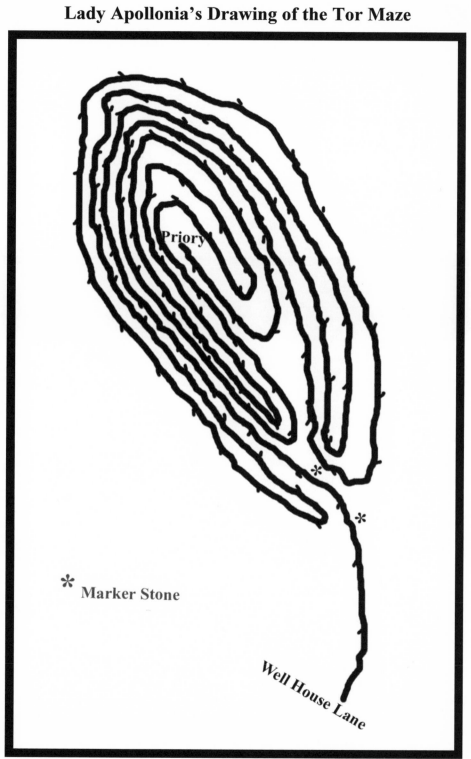

Priory

* Marker Stone

Well House Lane

Prologue

There were few witnesses to their crossing from Ireland into Wales early in February of 1397. A striking couple, they were none the less intimidating and seemed unapproachable to most passersby. They had travelled without a guide to the Isle of Anglesey off the coast of Wales, performed their required ritual, and continued their journey towards England. No one stopped them nor dared to express interest in the purpose of their travels to the River Severn, but once reaching its banks, they were able to take the ferry into Gloucestershire at Aust. If anyone had been observing them, some of their actions, pauses, and even the natural sites where they chose to stop and quietly worship together would have been thought rather strange or, at least, obscure to most Christians.

The deliberate gentleman who was in charge of their journey would have been regarded by any who encountered him as lordly in appearance. He was tall, powerfully built with fierce, bushy blonde eyebrows and deep brown eyes that never ceased to observe critically. He seemed purposed and calm. The woman who accompanied him was slight and slim but sculpted with muscle. Her long hair, once jet black, was now pennoned with white, flowing round both ears as it poured down her back beneath her veil. She was obviously older than the man and aggressively willing to assert her will.

They disembarked from the Aust ferry and the ferryman noticed that the travellers did not go into the village to offer prayers of thanks at the village church or move on to refresh themselves at The Boar's Head. Instead, they both walked away from the village along the bank side of the River Severn and continued walking upstream. Well beyond the ferryman's sight, they paused, carefully locating themselves in a small grove of trees near the riverbank where they could not be seen by casual travellers on the roadway. They stopped in this secluded place and raised their arms in fervent prayer, calling upon all the resident spirits of the region--trees, hills, local animals, and the mother earth--to hear their prayers. Most especially, they called to Sabrann, the Celtic goddess of the Severn River, and made their obeisance to her.

"Hear us, Sabrann, goddess of this mighty river," the man called respectfully to the flowing waters. "We come to you begging that you will grant us Wisdom, Insight, and Guidance."

"In truth, holy Sabrann, we acknowledge that only on the bank of your waters can we find blessing. Here at your side will we find Knowledge and Wisdom granted to us whilst we beg that you will reveal further Guidance in our task." The woman's voice was neither shrill nor even very loud, but it expressed an intensity of devoted confidence.

The man and the woman remained at the river's edge for several hours, watching and praying as the tide flowed inland from the Bristol Channel. When at last the tide-swelled waters of the Severn reached their greatest depth flowing up river past the couple, the man pulled from his robe an elegant golden bowl and hurled it powerfully to the central depths of the river where it sank instantly. Only then did he and his companion leave the river's bank and walk back past the ferry point into Aust to take rooms at the inn.

The couple did not speak together during this last portion of their day's journey. Each of them felt blessed and encouraged of being able to achieve their goal. They believed they could continue on the morrow because they had received the graceful permission of all the resident spirits. Most of all, this man and woman had faith that Sabrann of the Severn had accepted their gift and graciously conceded their prayer requests.

* * *

The man made all arrangements for their accommodation when they entered the inn at Aust. The innkeeper could tell this was a gentleman but one who expressed gracious friendliness in his dealings with the owner. The gentleman made it clear that they required a spacious chamber in which to spend this night and share a good meal.

The innkeeper was aware that these guests were different from others. He frequently hosted members of the upper class. Even nobility had come to his inn for hospitality. This gentleman's speech, however, identified him as a native of Ireland. He told the innkeeper that his name was difficult for Englishmen to pronounce; therefore, he would be known as Maurice of Tyrconnell.

Lord Maurice introduced the lady travelling with him as his mother. She was keenly attuned to all they said, yet she did not utter a word. She barely nodded in response to the innkeeper's greeting and remained withdrawn from their host. He decided that she was very proud and indicated no hesitation to look down upon him. He did not care, he told himself with a shrug of his shoulders. He had encountered great ladies before, and she seemed no grander than any other. "Worse for her," he thought, "she possesses no gentility in her manner, only expresses a demanding force requiring instant obedience."

Maurice and his mother were shown to their chamber to be served their evening meal privately. It was then that she poured out to her son her irritated displeasure with everything. "The innkeeper is a presumptive peasant, Cunomorus, worse yet, an ignorant Englishman. I find this accommodation to be rudely inadequate in every sense." Her complaining was endless.

"Aust is a small village, mother, but located at an ancient ferry crossing convenient for us. We shall bear all that we must to accomplish our task," Maurice said, trying to calm her. "Consider, we shall remain here a brief while. Tomorrow we make arrangements to continue our journey to Glastonbury."

"Cunomorus," she hissed angrily at her son, "you shall acknowledge my estate whilst we complete your father's goal, and you will address me by my name. I am Eponina, namesake of the great horse goddess, servant to none but the gods. I am Druidess and wife to Artur, once arch-Druid, now passed over."

"Indeed, Eponina," Maurice said quietly but with counter insistence in his voice. "I readily grant your estate and degree, yet I tell you that you must contain your aggressive pride until we are finished and ready to return to Tyrconnell. We must not call attention to ourselves among these Angles, Saxons, or Normans. We can not in any way promote ourselves or call attention to our quest whilst we remain in England." As if to emphasise his insistence to her, Maurice walked to his mother's side and towered above her. "We do not wish to be asked to explain who we are or why we are here, Eponina. That is my command as the king's Brehon and Seer. Throughout our journey, you will obey royal rule."

Cunomorus was a gentle and loving son of his parents in spite of his size and position, but in this instant he displayed himself to be more than willing to demand his rank be respected by his mother.

The lady drew herself upward into full height while accepting immediately her subordinate position to that of her son. She clenched her teeth tightly together as she responded to him. "We form a holy triad, Cunomorus: you, I, and the living spirit of your father. This task will be done, and the Christians will know the wisdom and power of the Druids live on. That damnable Patrick and his missionary maniacs not only burnt one hundred eighty learned books of the Druids, he sent his converts to destroy all the remains of our Druidic culture and learning. He was no saint; he was the great ravager of our culture."

"You may say such things to me, Eponina, but to no one else whilst we are here. You know that we have come with the blessing of the gods. We can continue only with the ongoing guidance of the gods," Maurice continued to warn her.

Eponina turned from him and walked towards her bed in their chamber. Maurice could hear her continue to hiss and heave heavy sighs of disapproval at their rural accommodations. He knew, more than any other person, this journey and its task were of signal importance to his mother. She was a fiercely proud woman and even more, she continued to adore her deceased husband.

Artur Amairogen, Maurice's father, had been bard and philosopher to the Prince of Tyrconnell. Artur was known as an arch-Druid throughout Ireland for his expression of divinely inspired knowledge and truth. Eponina would have done anything for him. She longed for only one position in life, that of being his wife, standing at his side. She knew that a portion of her soul had been torn from her when he died, but in true Celtic faith, she believed he lived still.

Maurice turned to wash himself, smiling and sanguine. He could hear his mother sniffing at the inabilities of these boorish English to have any idea of how to entertain guests of great estate. Still, he knew she would maintain quiet and follow his instruction. Their task in Glastonbury was painfully close to her heart and now remained her chief concern in life.

They were prepared for sleep but she came to his bedside and took his hand as he moved to retire. "Forgive my outbursts, Cunomoros. You alone are in a position to understand the significant truth of Veleda's Oracle, my son. Velada is your sister but she also possesses the blessed gift of seeing into the future. She has foreseen a way by which we can encourage the decline of these English and their brutal Christianising of all our holy places. I am truly grateful that you have gained release from the O'Donnell to make this journey with me. Only you can understand how desperately I need your presence. You are my son and, in every way, the son of your illustrious father. Artur began this process; we must finish it."

"Rest, mother," Cunomorus told her gently. "We have days of travel and clandestine pursuits ahead of us which will require our strength and endurance. Thanks to the gods, Veleda's Oracle guides us; father's spirit walks with us. At each level of our journey, we are a sacred triad: body, mind, and spirit. Surely we shall be able to fulfill his dream."

Chapter One

Glastonbury Welcome

The Lady Apollonia could barely believe her eyes as her party entered Glastonbury, nearly completing their journey. They came by way of the village of Street, entered the town on Hill Head, and turned towards Magdalene Street. Below them stretched seemingly endless walls of the local abbey. There was no doubt in her mind that before them lay the grounds of the grandest abbey she had ever seen. It dominated the entire heart of Glastonbury, and Apollonia saw at once that it possessed one of the most colossal abbey churches in England.

She was aware that this ancient place was said to have been founded by Joseph of Arimathea in the earliest days of Christianity in Britain. It was steeped in Christian legend and claimed famous events of Britain's early history had occurred here, including the burial of King Arthur. Apollonia of Aust was an educated woman, and she also knew that many monastic foundations in this year of 1397 were prone to enhance the legends of their establishment. Such things were sure to increase the flow of pilgrims' coin into abbey coffers.

The Lady knew that some monasteries increased the number of saints' relics they possessed or actively sought to encourage the fame of the knights' tombs that lay within them. Some monastic houses also encouraged pilgrims by enlarging the number of miracles claimed by those saints whose altars were built within their walls. Pilgrims were drawn to Glastonbury Abbey from places throughout the British Isles as well as the European Christian world. Most of all, Apollonia was realistic enough to acknowledge that pilgrims' gifts to the monastery enabled the Benedictines of Glastonbury to achieve their ever more impressive buildings, even a palatial new kitchen for the abbot's residence.

"My Lady," her personal maid, Nan, spoke with a childlike sense of gaping wonder in her voice, "surely the monks of Glastonbury have built the grandest abbey in all of Christendom. Are there any others to compare with this holy place?"

"I believe there is one, Nan. Saint Paul's cathedral in London is larger than Glastonbury's monastic church, and one other abbey in London is said to be wealthier. Glastonbury alone can claim to be the place where Christianity first arrived in England. It is even said to have been brought here by Christ's secret disciple, Joseph of Arimathea, who gave his own tomb for the Lord's burial." Apollonia's voice contained a slight hint of skepticism, but until proven otherwise, she remained respectful of church teaching.

"My Lady," her steward, Giles, addressed her doubting tone, "a famous historian who wrote the history of the abbey did not question its antiquity yet expressed little faith in such stories, preferring to leave such disputable matters to others."

Apollonia smiled at her scholarly young steward. "I prefer to call Joseph of Arimathea's landing upon Wearyall Hill, planting his staff there to grow into the Glastonbury Thorn which blooms only at Christmas, an important part of holy legend, Giles. There can be no proof of such legend, but I have no wish to describe it as a 'disputable matter'."

"My Lady, I respectfully quote the words of the historian."

"You are referring to William of Malmsbury's history of Glastonbury, are you not, Giles? I have not read it but perhaps will find a copy whilst we are here. Surely we all agree that this abbey is foremost throughout England. I have also heard that scholars are dazzled by the size and excellence of its library."

"I shall bring my copy of Malmsbury to you, my Lady, as soon as we have settled into Sir Chad's home. It is a learned treatise and will provide excellent background reading as you explore the town," he assured her.

Apollonia sighed deeply. "Thank you, Giles. I can not presume to have much time for reading but will be glad to know that I may have access to Malmsbury's chronicle. My first concern must be my son and his family. Dear Chad is left with three small children to parent since his beloved Cynthia died last December. I fear his grief has disabled him. He needs time and motive to rebuild his life." The Lady spoke quietly but with a sense of intimate knowledge of personal loss.

She had been widowed three times in her life and endured the loss of one of her sons to the ravages of plague when he served with the Teutonic Knights in Europe.

"It will be wonderful to be with my grandchildren, though," the Lady said more cheerfully, "and I am grateful that Chad has decided to remain here in Glastonbury where they will be well schooled."

Nan noted to herself that this was the most the Lady had been willing to speak of her loss since Lady Cynthia's death, even with those closest to her in her own household. The Lady's maid knew that Apollonia had loved Cynthia since the earliest days of her marriage to Chad. Lady Cynthia was a delicately pretty woman of good West Country family. She was sincerely devoted to her husband, and she always expressed warm affection for Apollonia as a personal friend as well as her husband's mother.

Cynthia lost her mother when she was a little girl and welcomed Apollonia with honest rejoicing as her own mother figure. Nan found that little could be done to ease Apollonia's grief when the news of Cynthia's death came to them in Aust. It was not only her anguish for her son's loss but for her personal devastation at the death of one as near to her as a daughter.

Nan Tanner had served Apollonia as the Lady's personal maid since her childhood. She had shared and endured the Lady's tragedies throughout decades of marriages, births, and deaths. She knew Apollonia to be determined that life must go on, and the maid was keenly aware that was why they were coming to Glastonbury. The Lady was convinced that, as mother and grandmother, she had to do everything in her power to help her son and his children begin to heal from their loss and be restored.

Apollonia knew that grief had to be endured but also expressed by the bereaved. Only then, healing could be take place. She was concerned for her son but also for his children, especially her favourite and only granddaughter, Juliana. Now eight years old, Juliana began walking as a toddler with a severe limp because one of her legs was shorter than the other. She learned to walk helped by the aid of a crutch but refused to see herself as crippled in any way. Juliana was small for her age, slightly built, and very bright. Chad had told Apollonia in his recent message that Juliana was assuming responsibilities extraordinary for her age. The little girl announced to him that, as his oldest female child, she would be mistress of his household and oversee the care of her younger brothers: Geoffrey, six, and four year old George.

The Lady's party rode into Glastonbury's Market Place and turned onto the High Street in order to approach its final turning towards Aust House. Nan was not an accomplished horsewoman and always grateful when any ride ended. Just now, however, she was pleased to be riding slowly along the High Street. When the Lady travelled to any town, Nan sought to note the market, the High Street, and all of its shops.

Apollonia's distress for her family was uppermost in her mind throughout the whole of this journey. She remained focused upon reaching her son's town home, and when, at last, she could see they were approaching Bove Town Road, the Lady offered a fervent prayer of thanks.

"There it is, my Lady, Aust House," Giles announced to her at the turning. It stood grandly on the north side of Bove Town Road, the main route into Glastonbury from the cathedral city of Wells. Aust House was the most impressive house on the street, several stories high and surrounded by a walled garden. Chad's young steward had obviously been watching for them. He rushed out in welcome and stood ready to assist the lady's dismount.

"Welcome, welcome, my Lady of Aust. I am John of Glastonbury, steward to the household of Sir Chad. Pray, do enter and allow us to bring you refreshment. Mistress Juliana has been anxiously awaiting your arrival since early this morning."

John helped the Lady from her horse as the small figure of her granddaughter, Juliana, limped carefully down the stairs leading from the main entrance. "Grandmamma, at last you are here," she called. When she reached Apollonia, now standing next to her horse, the little girl tossed her crutch to one side and wound both arms round the Lady's waist to hold her close. Apollonia did not care a fig about appearing emotional in public. She had never wished to be like many noble parents of her generation who maintained lordly distances from their children. The Lady smiled brilliantly while tears poured from her eyes and she knelt to complete their mutual embrace.

"Juliana, dearest child, how pleased I am to be here," she whispered into the little girl's ear as they continued to hold each other.

* * *

Chad's steward, John, first saw that the Lady and Nan were comfortably settled in the hall and prepared to meet the rest of the household. Gareth, the Lady's stablemaster, retreated to the barn with the horses. Giles and Brother William, the Lady's steward and almoner, went off with John to take advantage of his local insights and learn more of Glastonbury. Juliana, using her crutch expertly, seemed to skip into the hall bringing with her the rest of the Aust servants to greet her grandmother.

Apollonia was especially pleased to see Chad's general housekeeper, Martha Manning, once again. The Lady and Nan had known Martha for years as she was from their home village of Aust. Mistress Manning was a mature widow whom they had recommended to Chad and Cynthia shortly after their marriage ten years earlier. The housekeeper was a village woman but one known throughout Aust for her healing skills and loving good nature. Apollonia also knew her to be an intelligent and practical person who soon proved herself prepared to deal graciously with people of all classes in the running of Sir Chad's household.

Martha had also become the major carer to Lady Cynthia in the past two years. Chad and Cynthia's third child, George, was a robustly healthy infant, but his birth seemed to drain his fragile mother of her last fleeting bits of physical strength and well being. Chad's wife grew weaker after George's arrival. She seemed prone to catch every affliction going about as the seasons progressed. Winters were especially difficult for her, and the icy chill of mid-December this past year proved her undoing.

The children were cared for by their nursery maid, Mistress Eleanor Albert, whom Juliana presented to her grandmother with great pride. Apollonia was aware that Eleanor had been part of Chad's household since Juliana was born. The little girl, as the family's first born, felt a strong and loving relationship with her.

Juliana also introduced the Lady to their household cook, Mistress Farber, and to both of the kitchen maids, Amy and Colleen. Apollonia made a point to greet each of them personally, especially because Juliana took such care to introduce them to her. There was no doubt in the Lady's mind that Juliana had taken charge. Apollonia's little granddaughter was not only mature beyond her years, she was prepared to assume responsibility. But, surely, Apollonia told herself, this precious child had been dreadfully wounded by the loss of her mother. She must still be grieving.

Nan left the hall to prepare the Lady's chamber when the rest of the servants were dismissed. Apollonia remained sitting by the fire with Juliana. "As an old woman, Juliana," she told the little girl, "I shall need your help to remember the servants' names and their positions. More to the point, I need to speak with you. May we use this time when we find ourselves alone?"

The little girl assumed that her grandmother had instructions for her, so she gave her full attention. "Of course, grandmamma, I shall do all I can to help you."

"Juliana, my love, you have grown up since last I saw you. I am truly impressed by your ability to take charge of things for your father. You have good relations with everyone on his staff."

"Oh, grandmamma, Mistress Manning sees to it that all the work of the household is done well. I simply try to add mama's words of appreciation to her and all of our servants, as I know mama would have done," Juliana said happily.

"Dearheart," Apollonia said quietly, "your mother's death has been so recent. I am also fearful for you. As your grandmother, I have been worried that the loss of your mama has hurt you deeply. I never knew my mother because she died when I was born, but I know how close you were to your mama. Your mother kept you by her side wherever your parents travelled. Please let me share this painful loss with you, for I miss her too."

Now, Juliana grew quiet, looked into the fire, and took several moments before responding. "Grandmamma, I am grateful that you have come, especially because now I can talk with you. My lady mother knew she was dying, and she spoke with me about it. She told me that her death would make it impossible for us to be together, but she said that she would never leave us, that she would always be with us in spirit. Most of all, she told me that she was depending on me to help Geoffrey and George remember her love. Finally, she said that she needed me to be ready to support and comfort papa."

Apollonia was stunned. Juliana spoke so calmly yet so obviously prepared to do whatever she felt she must. Still, the Lady could see tears forming in Juliana's eyes. The child was struggling. There could be no doubt that she needed help to deal with the very personal loss to her, all the while she assumed responsibility to bring remembrance of her mother to her brothers and comfort to her father.

"I did promise mama that I would do all she asked of me, grandmamma, but I told her I did not know what it meant when she said she remained with us in spirit. Mama smiled and took my hand. Then she told me to tell her what I felt, so I described for her that I could feel her soft hand with its long, cool fingers wrapped around my smaller hand. Suddenly, she pulled her hand away and bent to kiss me.

"Then, mama told me that I had felt her hand and felt her lips kiss me. Yet we both knew there could be no substance to her kiss or to her touch. She told me very exactly, 'When I am gone, Juliana, I shall not be able to take your hand, to hug or kiss you as I just did, but you can remember a sense of my touch and my kiss. In each of your memories of me, I will be with you. Your memory will keep me with you in spirit when I can no longer be here in person.'"

Apollonia took the little girl into her arms again. "Thank you, Juliana; how beautifully you have helped me to understand. I am glad to know all of these things that your mama told you. Do you not see you have just shared her with me, in spirit? You and I must do this every day. Of course, we will continue to speak of her in our prayers, but we can do this at any time during our days together. How good it will be for both of us to treasure sharing our memories of her. She will be with us in spirit whenever we do."

Apollonia continued to sit in the great hall with Juliana in her arms. They talked of the colours that Lady Cynthia especially loved and remembered certain behaviours that she particularly disliked, as well as foods that she always enjoyed. As they sat together, Apollonia could feel an extraordinary sense of comfort come over her, one that she knew had just been given to her by Juliana.

"Oh, Chad, dearheart," she said to herself. "Listen to Juliana. You must allow your little child to lead you as well."

* * *

Chad returned to the house in time for the evening meal. He greeted his mother and politely told her and Nan how grateful he was to have them be with his family just now. "I hope you will think of this as your home and your household whilst you are with us, Mamam. I am truly grateful to have you here."

In spite of his apparent enthusiasm, however, Apollonia noticed deep lines in her son's face, a sense of tension in his conversation, and worst of all, an obvious distance that he maintained from her. She moved to embrace him, and he stepped back from her and bowed deeply. He kissed her hand, then very formally extended his arm and led her to the head of the table in the hall.

The Lady attempted on several occasions during dinner to draw her son into conversation, but whenever she attempted to speak to him on a personal level, he changed subjects. He would refer to some incident on the hunt that day, or ask her what news she could share with him of his brother, Hugh, and his family, or if she had news from his brother, Thomas.

"You know, Mamam," he said, continuing to use her sons' childhood address to her since the days when, as boys, they were unable to properly say madam. "I have not seen Thomas for months. Perhaps whilst you are here, I shall ride over to Axbridge and inquire of my priestly brother how he can find such joy in his celibate churchly vocation?" Chad spoke almost flippantly.

Apollonia did not hesitate at this point in his purposeful diversions. She spoke in a quiet but compelling voice and reprimanded her son. "Indeed, Chad, at this time of loss, you of all people will acknowledge that your family needs you here, in Glastonbury. I respect you as a grown man, but I must insist that you attend personally to the needs of your household. Your children especially are daily forced to face the loss of their mother. They need their father's reassuring love to be present with them."

Chad's eyes, for a brief moment, openly exposed the depths of painful grief haunting his personal life. His flippant tone had returned when he began to speak again, and he admitted that she was correct. "Typical of me, is it not, Mamam, always ready to shirk my chores? Of course, I shall do my duty, but for now, I am off to bed."

It seemed to the Lady that Chad could not wait to be gone from her presence. She longed to take him in her arms and hold him. Instead, he formally kissed her hand once again, begged her blessing, and then left the hall.

Chapter Two

Painful Evasion

There was no doubt in Apollonia's mind that, as the days of February passed into March, Chad continued to find ways to remain distant from her. He made a point to spend time with his boys, reading to them from the stories of King Arthur and even allowing them to examine his armour and weaponry. He was insistent that his boys, even as very young children, recognise these as weapons of war, not toys. He helped Geoffrey and little George feel the weight of his sword and placed his helmet on their heads so that they could feel its ponderous protection. He encouraged them to touch his breastplate while holding it before their chests and made the boys touch the point of his sword and the blade of his battle axe. In each case Chad emphasised that they must be aware of such weapons' deadly potential.

Apollonia was pleased to see that Chad made a daily effort to spend time with all of his children, including his daughter, Juliana. The Lady's son insisted they learn to ride well at an early age and be able to care for their ponies. Geoffrey already demonstrated his talent for riding and a healthy respect for the care of his mount, both of which pleased his father well. George loved to sit in the saddle on his pony while it trotted round a large track through the orchard and made sure, after riding, to take his turn leading his pony to drink. Young as he was, the boy saw that there was adequate feed in his pony's stall, and he liked to bring pieces of apple as special treats.

Chad included Juliana in these outdoor activities with her brothers, pushing her to perfect her riding skills as well. She required assistance to mount her pony, but her father helped her find a way to abandon her crutch. She would balance on the mounting block and spring onto her saddle. Chad also instructed his carpenter to make a pony cart for her to learn to drive. Juliana soon became proficient in bringing her pony to the harness as well as driving the cart.

Chad paused at his mother's side whenever the children returned to the house after spending time with him. He would inform her that he had errands he must run or farms to visit while always making a great effort to express how grateful he was to have her and Nan with them. Her presence was, he assured her, making a very positive difference for his children and was certainly helping each of them to cope. He told her that Mistress Albert, in charge of the nursery, told him that George had ceased to wet his bed, and Geoffrey no longer struggled with nightmares.

Apollonia made a point to tell Chad that all the time he spent with his children was having a powerfully restorative effect in each of their lives. Still, she refrained from speaking of his loss with her son though that continued to worry her most. If Chad noticed his mother's reticence, he chose not to speak of it. Their days continued uncomfortably tense for each of them. Apollonia had never experienced such an artificial separation from any of her sons. She knew the reasons for Chad's awkward restraint with her. She truly could understand it, but she could find no way to correct it. The Lady desperately wished to restore their loving closeness as family.

* * *

Nan was most aware how strained the relationship between Apollonia and Sir Chad had grown since their arrival in Glastonbury. It was very uncomfortable for the Lady's maid, especially because she knew better than anyone how close Apollonia had always felt to Chad and his wife. Still, Nan told herself that she could not mention her concerns unless Apollonia expressed a wish to speak of it with her. It was obvious to Nan that the Lady was trying to use all means available to reach out to her son but was receiving no response from him.

Nan decided to enlarge the Lady's focus slightly in an effort to lighten the atmosphere within the household. This spring day dawned sunny and bright, and as the children were at their lessons, the Lady's maid mentioned that it might be a perfect time to begin their exploration of Glastonbury.

"You know, my Lady, I know nothing of this town or its grand abbey. Do you not think that we might walk into the town whilst the children are spending the morning with Mistress Albert?"

Apollonia looked up from her reading and said almost immediately, "Well, we are obviously not needed at the moment, Nan. Call my almoner to us, and let us benefit from Brother William's knowledge of Glastonbury. He has been exploring the streets of the town regularly in the weeks since we arrived. Perhaps he will have time to be our guide."

"I shall fetch him straightaway, my Lady," Nan said happily. "He is usually gone by this time most mornings, but I saw him in the family chapel as I passed, tidying and gathering altar cloths for the laundress."

"Gramercy, Nan. Pray tell him that I would be pleased to take advantage of anything he can tell us of the town," Apollonia said as she stood and placed her book on the table.

Nan left the chamber to find William and she could see that the Lady's attention was already shifting, for the moment, away from her immediate family worries to other interests. Nan knew the Lady loved to learn and explore wherever they travelled. She was a woman who enjoyed study, sought to inform herself, and was always ready to learn from others' experience as well.

William joined them, and his enthusiasm was contagious. "Ah, my Lady Apollonia, I should be glad to walk with you and share the sites I have discovered in Glastonbury. The abbey and the town offer so much. I find it difficult to say where we should begin."

"Well, William, Giles has lent me his copy, and I have been reading from William of Malmsbury's history of the abbey. Let us begin with a visit to the abbey church. I should like to start with the Lady Chapel, the site of the *vetusta ecclesia*, the oldest part of the church. What say you?"

"Indeed, an excellent choice, my Lady. I can see that you are already aware of the abbey's antiquity, but I must tell you, we shall never see all of the church in a single day," William told her with a nod to her inquiring mind. "Glastonbury Abbey's church is not only one of the great churches of Europe, it is very different from other important churches. I also know it to be the longest church in England."

"Then, let us away, dear friends," the Lady said with a brilliant smile. "Obviously, we have much to learn and even more to see."

Nan rushed off to collect the Lady's woollen cloak, and they were soon walking down Bove Town Road towards the centre of town and the nearest abbey entrance gate.

* * *

Sir Chad returned to his home for dinner that evening to find his mother unable to stop talking of her visit to Glastonbury Abbey and its wondrous church. For the first time since her coming, Chad expressed interested in everything she could tell him. He remained seated round the fireplace in the hall with her, Nan, and William long after their evening meal ended. He was ready to hear each of them describe their impressions of the oldest part of the abbey church and its resplendent architecture.

"I have seen many churches and great cathedrals, Chad," his mother told him. "Yet, there is no doubt in my mind that Glastonbury Abbey has the grandest church I have ever seen. It is not only its extraordinary length, its monumental nave is preceded by an elegant Lady Chapel most unusually placed at the western end and connected through a Galilee porch. I had difficulty leaving the Mary Chapel because of its historic significance, dearheart. It stands on the site claiming to be where Christianity first came to England, brought here by one of Christ's own disciples. William is arranging another tour for us on the morrow," Apollonia said excitedly. "I shall have much more to tell you then."

"Well, Mamam, I look forward to sharing all that you continue to learn," Chad said with a boyish grin at her childlike fervor. For Apollonia, his positive response was thrilling. This was the first time since she had come to Glastonbury that she and her second son shared a subject of conversation which they mutually enjoyed and of which they could speak freely. Monumental architecture was an intellectual interest that excited both of them.

* * *

The following morning broke chilly and blustery. Chad appeared at his mother's chambers very early. He knew she would be up and probably finished with her morning prayers. Nan welcomed the master with a bit of surprise. He begged her pardon and told her he must speak briefly with his mother. Nan knew that her mistress was dressed and ready for the day, so she took him to the window recess where the Lady liked to sit and read.

"Master Chad to see you, my Lady," Nan said with a quizzical smile.

Apollonia looked up with an equal sense of surprise but welcomed her son and bade him to come sit with her.

Chad refused to be seated, insisting that he was preparing to leave. "I do apologise, Mamam. It is far too early to call, but I knew you would be well into the new day. You have always been an early riser."

Apollonia dismissed Nan, urging her to go to the kitchen to break her fast. As Nan left the chamber, Chad begged his mother's pardon again, insisting that he could not linger. "I am riding to Templecombe to be with an old friend, Mamam. I may not return for several weeks."

Apollonia tuned into the urgency in his voice immediately but simply said, "It is a long ride, Chad, but we shall look forward to your return. I do not believe I am acquainted with this friend," she said calmly.

"He is an older man, Mamam, but a comrade in arms who has been a mentor to me." At this, Apollonia felt Chad's voice begin to tremble. "Pray forgive me, I must be away," he said as he turned towards her chamber door.

"Dear son, why will you not share your grief with me?" Apollonia asked him with a sense of urgency in her own voice. "You know I loved Cynthia, surely as your wife, Chad, but also as the mother of my grandchildren and the woman nearest to a daughter of my own."

At that moment, Chad's face crumbled into a deeply wrinkled mask, grimaced round his eyes and mouth. His voice gasped into a mass of heaving sobs, and tears poured from his eyes. He was unable to see anything or respond to her in any way. The young knight collapsed onto a bench opposite his mother's chair.

Apollonia rose immediately, went to her son, and pulled him into her arms. She laid his head on her shoulder and held him tightly, absorbing the quaking his body heaved into hers. Chad could say nothing; his voice was arrested by a sequence of gasping sobs.

The Lady did not speak. She kissed his face, his forehead, his cheeks and continued to hold him close to her. Chad's sobbing seemed unstoppable. It was as if he had buried into the deepest recesses of his heart a lifetime of grief. A painful boulder lay inside him crushing his life's spirit.

"Dear child," Apollonia whispered as tears poured from her eyes, "pray, let it come. I understand your pain and I share it. I have lost a beloved one. I know the searing cruelty of your loss. Weep with me, Chad, and allow me to express my grief as well."

Chad's body seemed flat, emptied, and drained when at last his sobs relaxed into quiet moaning. He continued to lean upon his mother, but neither mother nor son spoke. At last, Chad lifted his arms and, for the first time since she had come to Glastonbury, wrapped his arms around Apollonia and pulled her to him. Their clinging bodies spoke silently but eloquently of crushing anguish and terrible loss.

* * *

Apollonia had no idea how long she and Chad sat together. Eventually she rose to collect two handkerchiefs from her chest and returned to sit next to him. Together they could wipe their tears, dry their eyes, and compose their faces. Mother and son knew they must return to face the world, but Apollonia was inwardly praising God and offering fervent silent prayers of thanks that He had enabled them to share this time together. It had been more than release. She knew that Chad had finally opened to her his months of suffering excruciating grief. In silence, she begged God's guidance for her son, that he could find an avenue from empty desolation to renewed life.

Chad's face was flushed but smiling as he looked directly into his mother's eyes for the first time since her arrival in Glastonbury. "Well, Mamam, you have seen that indeed I am neither a brave nor a valiant knight. I am not strong or manly at all. I collapse into tears like an infant girlchild."

"Precious Chad, pray be fair with yourself. Do not paint such graceless images of human suffering. You, your children, and I have all been wounded. A precious part of our hearts has been torn from us. You and Cynthia shared your love, united your bodies, and became one in your minds. Cynthia's life was cut away from yours. If you had endured such an amputation in battle, how could you avoid tears, moaning pain, or gasping sobs?"

Chad's head seemed to droop for a minute, but then he lifted his lips to her face and kissed her cheek. "Thank you, Mamam. I have taken your love for granted. Most unforgivably, I have underestimated your insight as my mother. Thank you for granting me the grace I could not allow for myself."

Chad began to rise from the bench and took his mother's hand in his as he spoke, "I am going to Templecombe to spend time with my dear friend and counsellor, Mamam. His name is Sir Walter Heath whom I met in Wales. I have always found his presence manly and chivalrous but, like our papa, quietly courageous and heroic. He is of ancient family here in Somerset and has great understanding of human need. I believe at one point in his life, he had considered becoming a monk. I have hoped through him to find a way to deal with my disabling feelings of loss for Cynthia."

Chad's eyes seemed to widen as he spoke. "Dear God, I have just said her name. It is the first time I have done so since she died." Apollonia could hear a gasp of wonder in his voice.

Looking wide-eyed into his mother's face, he continued, "That is the first time I have been able to speak of Cynthia's death."

"These are important firsts, Chad," Apollonia assured him. "The pain will never go completely from you, but you will learn to live with it. We all must do. I am pleased that you seek the counsel of an older knight whom you admire. God go with you, my son, and grant you safe journey. You always remain in my thoughts."

* * *

When Nan returned to the Lady's bedchamber, Apollonia told her that Chad had come to tell her that he would be away for some time, visiting a friend in Templecombe. Nan could sense that things had changed. The Lady was not only smiling, she seemed light-hearted and unburdened for the first time since they had arrived in Glastonbury. The Lady asked Nan what new adventures they could provide for the children during their father's absence.

"You know we are unable to offer insights into the life of a knight, though we can read to them of such things. I would like for us to find some activity for all of us to do together. What do you think, Nan?"

"We can take them riding after their lessons, my Lady." Nan never enjoyed being on horseback, but she knew this was an important time for the Lady's family to be together. "Sir Chad is keen to encourage their riding skills, and my Lady, I know that Gareth would enjoy being with the children. He is the best man on your staff to continue to teach each of them, the boys, as well as Miss Juliana, how best to care for their beasts."

"A brilliant idea, Nan," Apollonia said happily. "You always seem to know what children will like best."

"Are you suggesting that I am arrested in my own childishness?" the petite maid asked with a sly grin.

Apollonia's smiling face twisted slightly into a knowing grimace. "Not at all, impudent one. Now please go off to find Gareth, and ask him to be ready within the hour to help the children saddle their ponies."

"Gareth has already told me that there are some lovely riding trails here in Glastonbury, my Lady. He has been hoping that you might be willing to ride as far as the Chalice Well and taste the waters."

Chapter Three

Called to Court

When Chad returned to Glastonbury later in April, he brought his dear friend from Templecombe with him. They arrived late in the afternoon and swept into the hall with all the energy of great friends anticipating a challenging adventure. Nan was sitting with Apollonia before the fire. Empowered by the thick lenses of her spectacles, she was intent on her needlework. The Lady could see that Chad's friend was considerably older than he, though still fit and strong, tall and straight. His face was deeply lined, his hair greying, and his well-trimmed beard white as snow.

"Mamam, Nan, allow me to introduce my good friend, Sir Walter Heath, longtime resident of Templecombe, Somersetshire."

"Welcome to my son's home in Glastonbury, Sir Walter. It is an honour to meet one regarded by him as an admired friend and counsellor."

"Greetings, my Lady of Aust. Pray accept my thanks for your welcome and willingness to receive me as your guest," the knight said as he bowed to kiss her hand.

Apollonia liked Sir Walter immediately. He was an unassuming and genuine person, one whom the Lady felt possessed qualities of true gentility. She invited him to sit with her by the fire.

Chad excused himself to retreat to the nursery to visit his children. After he left, Apollonia found that conversation with Sir Walter was easily shared. She discovered him to be a man of wide interests and well read. When she began to tell him of her visit to the local abbey church and her desire to learn more of its extraordinary story, he responded with enthusiasm.

"Indeed, my Lady, Glastonbury's claims to be among the first Christian monasteries in England are beyond dispute. Though many of the legends associated with its beginnings may be unproven, the mere fact that such legend is ancient to this place suggests its intrinsic truth," Walter told her enthusiastically.

Seeing that this Somerset gentleman was knowledgeable of Glastonbury history, Apollonia was not the least bit surprised when he mentioned that he had read William of Malmsbury's history of the abbey. "Further, my Lady, you must know that a new history is being written by a Glastonbury monk named Brother James. He has promised that he will save many of his first drafts for me. Given your keen interest, allow me to share with you any of his writings that I receive."

"I would be grateful for your kindness, Sir Walter. James of Glastonbury is known to my brother, Ferdinand of Marshfield, and I have been hopeful of meeting him. If you can share any of his writings, it will be my pleasure to read them. I am always glad to read new historic works," the Lady told him with an equally enthusiastic smile.

Walter was entranced by the Lady's expression. He had never witnessed a more arresting transformation of a mature lady's face. Her teeth were beautifully white and perfectly shaped. "Of course, this woman must be named Apollonia," he thought, grinning to himself. "She has the loveliest gifts of the patron saint for those who suffer toothache. Her smile alone can bless away one's discomfort."

When Chad returned to the hall, he joined their party but continued to stand next to his mother's chair. Apollonia thought that her son behaved as if he had something more he felt he must tell her but she was not certain she wished to hear it. She turned to ask him, "How do you find the children, Chad? We went riding to visit the Chalice Well and have circled the abbey grounds several times whilst you were gone. All three of the children demonstrated real ability in the saddle in spite of their youth. You have taught them well. Each of the boys and Juliana, too, hopes to display improvement for you."

"It will be so good if you and your excellent stablemaster can help them see to the care of their ponies and continue to ride daily," Chad told her.

Again, Apollonia heard more in her son's voice than mere comment. "What is happening now, Chad? Must you leave? Where are you going?"

"Pray, Mamam, you know I must serve the command of King Richard, and I have been called to court. I confess I do not look forward to it, but I have only been excused these recent months because of the death of my wife."

"My Lady, Chad and I will return to court on the morrow," Walter told her. "We may not be gone an extended time as King Richard's plans are unclear. Under normal circumstances, the king prefers his favourites with him, but we must respond to his summons. He may be planning another foray into Ireland."

"No one knows just why, but there has been a radical change in the good nature of our king, Mamam. This year he seems especially vengeful and rules arbitrarily. I am told that when courtiers are with him at court, the king sits on his throne and stares at them. If he catches one's eye, that person must kneel to the king's sovereignty immediately. Everyone in the court is kept on edge except those few to whom he grants particular favour."

Apollonia drew in a deep sigh, but she could not object. "I understand that you must go, Chad. Nan and I will be glad to remain in charge of your household whilst you are gone." The Lady began to bite her lower lip which she frequently did in moments of concentration. "However, I worry that in King Richard the flaws of the Plantagenet character may be overwhelming the virtues. He has never been a warrior as was his grandfather or father before him, and his courage seems to be declining into obstinacy."

Neither Chad nor Walter was willing to comment, and Apollonia understood their reticence. The Lady, however, continued to wonder aloud. "There can be no doubt that the king has been grieving the loss of Queen Anne. I have been told that her death three years ago was a terrible blow to him, but recently he is living with his new wife, a pretty little French princess. She is only eight years old and can hardly be expected to bring a mature balance to his life, but perhaps a degree of comfort," Apollonia said hopefully.

"There are huge problems within Richard's kingdom, Mamam," Chad said quietly. "Folk are struggling to pay increased taxes and forced loans to support the extravagance of his court."

"Oh, yes, my son, the so-called loan that the king's agents came to Aust to collect from me was significant, but I was able to pay it. Such arbitrary rule feeds the growing unrest of the people, and I fear that most."

"My Lady, Chad and I have made it our practice to proceed with caution whenever we are at court," Walter assured her. "For the most part we remain on the side and in the shadows, an obscure young gentleman and his elderly companion in arms from the far West Country. To most eyes, we are of no significance."

"Mamam, I have decided not to take my servant Jeremy with me. I have given him and Steward John specific instructions to see themselves as protectors of our Glastonbury household whilst I am gone."

"Chad," the Lady insisted, "who will serve you? Surely, Nan and I with Gareth, William, and Giles can guard your household without further male protection."

"We have no wish to alarm you, my Lady," Walter intervened, "but Chad and I have been worried by a series of robberies in Glastonbury in recent months. It has largely affected the merchants. Their shop premises have been invaded, especially on the High Street. Of more concern, recently, there have been entries into their homes as well—especially the wealthiest among them. I am served by my good Phillip. He has been with me for years, is well known to Chad, and acquainted with his personal preferences. I promise you Phillip will serve us both very well."

Apollonia understood Chad's wish to leave his family well protected, so she changed her tone and added, "Well, I have known Jeremy Pratt since he was a boy in Aust, and I have always felt him to be a part of the family. All right, Chad, but before you must leave, please take Jeremy out to the barn to become better known to Gareth. God's wrath," the Lady said, "you leave me with much to digest even before dinner. Nan and I shall retire to my solar now but will return to the hall once tables are prepared. I pray you will join us at head table,

Sir Walter. I hope to learn more from your insights into our local abbey before you must leave us."

* * *

When Cunomorus and his mother, Eponina, reached Glastonbury, they did not remain in the town but instead rode out to a small farm called Grove Cottage located near the Tor. They rode through the gatehouse of the farm's sizable dwelling and two men rushed out from the barn to receive them, take their horses, and hold them during the dismount. The Lord Cunomorus greeted them in Gaelic, and their response to him was reverential.

The Druid was a large, majestic man whose significance in the eyes of his servants exceeded that of a nobleman. His person was not only regal, he was regarded as one who knew the secrets of the gods. Once the servants had been acknowledged, they bowed to speak their welcome to the Lord Cunomorus and his mother.

The men's wives came out from the house without speaking. They curtsied silently before escorting the Druidess inside to seat her before the fire. Eponina spoke gently with the women in Gaelic and made her wishes known to them. They did not respond directly to her but waited in silence to receive her blessing and then retreated to the kitchen.

Cunomorus came into the cottage and announced to his mother that they were required to complete their ritual before settling for the evening. "Esteemed mother, we must first retreat to the sacred grove and offer our prayers of thanks to the gods before we may do anything further."

With a small sigh, Eponina acknowledged the propriety of his instruction though she was feeling considerably fatigued after their long journey. She stood immediately, and they walked together out of the house to a large grove of trees on a hill behind the house. Once there, beneath a huge oak tree hung with mistletoe, the Druid and his mother offered their prayers to all the gods of the region and tied Cunomorus's shawl as a gift on a low hanging branch of the sacred oak.

Cunomorus and his mother went back to the house, when their prayers were completed, to speak with their steward about preparation for the evening meal. They wished him to know that it was their intention was to retire early.

The steward begged permission to speak. When granted, he told the Lord Cunomorus that since arriving at the farm, they had been visited by a rent collector from the abbey. "I told him that, as your steward, I would bring the rent to the abbey after you arrived. The man's questions did not end there, my lord. He wished to know precisely who had taken this land and what was to be grown here or how many sheep were to be grazed on the property? I said that all of Grove Cottage Farm had been let to you by the abbey, but as a stranger to this place, I was uninformed of any details."

Cunomorus nodded to the man and congratulated him for handling the inquiries adeptly. "The abbey is the major landowner throughout Somerset, so I am forced to deal with the Christians. My mother and I do not wish to acknowledge any aspect of our true identity to them, and we do not know precisely how long we shall be here. Therefore, whist we remain in Somerset we shall appear to use the land as sheep farmers until we are ready to return to Tyrconnell."

The Druid stayed the arm of his servant before he allowed him to leave. "Privately," he told him, "we shall first remember to honour our forebears, the great tribe of the Durotriges who held this part of Britain. Christianity had not been born as a religion then. Latterly, when the abbey was founded here, they placed their crosses everywhere to override and destroy Celtic Wisdom and the worship of our gods. We intend to assert that they have not destroyed us even though they have claimed our holy places and given them Christian identities."

"We are still recognised by Irish law," Eponina interjected. "Our role as Druids has been diminished, but we shall demonstrate that our power has not gone. These Christians feel they have tamed us, but the gods are still with us."

The steward bowed to both Cunomorus and the Lady Eponina and left them until called to serve them once again. Eponina smiled at Cunomorus, "Is it not good to be speaking Gaelic once again, my son? I find it a joy to stay in the company of real Celts."

Mother and son found themselves alone in the hall, and Eponina asked him to sit with her near the fire. "We have much to do. Let us reason together and lay our plans. How shall we begin, and what must we achieve first?"

"We will begin, mother, but first you and I will ride to the ancient Celtic Lake Village and pay homage to our venerable ancestors. Then, we shall climb the Tor and mark the sites according to father's designation." Cunomorus was very gentle with her, but he made it quite clear to his mother that he was in charge of their mission. He would determine their progress.

* * *

It was early the following morning when Lady Apollonia asked her steward, Giles Digby, and stablemaster, Gareth Trimble, to meet with her in the hall. She had specific assignments for Giles. Especially, she wished to tell him how grateful she was that he had been so considerate of her son's slightly younger steward while they dwelt together at Aust House.

"Giles, I have seen your support of Chad's steward, John. He does admire you, and I have seen that you offer advice to him gently, sharing the benefits of your experience with him."

"Yes, my Lady, I try to be sensitive to young John's position here. He is doing well and knows that I shall merely be in and out of the household handling your affairs in the woollen market. John has come to me with questions, and we enjoy our conversations together."

"Gramercy, Giles, I am truly grateful for your friendship with John. I do not wish to be seen as taking over my son's household. My servants and I must see ourselves as temporary keepers in Chad's absence." Giles wished her good day and begged to be excused that he might return to his work.

Apollonia spoke next with Gareth asking him to accompany her with Nan and Juliana into the heart of Glastonbury. "I do not wish to require you to help with shopping, Gareth, but I am worried about attempting such a long walk for Juliana. She is excited about going into the town, for we plan to visit a skillful local shoemaker who may be able to craft a more enabling pair of shoes for her. If she tires, however, I shall need your strength to lift her and help us carry her back to Aust House. She is a spirited young girl and one who will never regard herself as limited, but I am aware of her painful discomfort when she has spent too much time struggling to walk long distances with her crutch."

"Aye, m'Lady," Gareth said. "Oi be glad to go with ye. Oi've finished chores in the barn, but let me bring round Mistress Juliana's pony cart. She can drive it well enough by erself. We can park it near the Market Square. From there she need not walk far to the shoemaker's shop."

"Of course, Gareth, that is the perfect way to enable her without making her feel handicapped or tired. Why did I not think of it?" Apollonia signalled to Nan who went to collect Juliana from her lessons. The party gathered in the front of Aust House where Gareth brought the pony cart round from the barn.

It was a cloudy day. The spring breezes were constant, but as everyone was warmly dressed, the day seemed perfect for a walk into town. Juliana proudly drove her cart in a stately manner while the Lady, Nan, and Gareth walked behind her into the centre of town.

Chad's steward, John, had told the Lady of this excellent young shoemaker in Glastonbury, Jerryl Cobbler, who was known to be adept in designing shoes to meet special needs. Apollonia decided that her granddaughter should visit his shop and see if specially made shoes could help to accommodate Juliana's slightly shorter left leg. The shop was located on Benedict Street just before Saint Benignus Church, but it required them to walk the length of the High Street, turn at the Market Place, then on to Benedict Street. Gareth's idea of allowing Mistress Juliana to drive her pony cart to the Market Place and then walk the shorter distance to the shoemaker's shop was perfect.

Juliana loved being outdoors and so enjoyed driving her cart that she barely noticed the winds which turned her cheeks to glowing pink beneath her sparkling blue eyes. When they reached the Market Place, she jumped from the seat of the cart and placed her crutch under her arm to walk beside her grandmother and Nan. Gareth remained with the cart while the rest of them walked up Benedict Street.

The young craftsman was busy with another customer when they entered the cobbler's shop. They waited and Apollonia looked round his shelves noting especially the fine quality of his work and the fashionable success of his distinctive designs in examples on display.

The shoemaker addressed Apollonia when he could give her his full attention, obviously pleased that she had chosen to come to his shop. "Pray forgive this delay, my Lady. How may I serve you?" By this time, it was known throughout the town that this statuesque Lady, who had come to live with her son's family, was a noblewoman and titled in her own right.

Apollonia carefully described the difficulty in walking that afflicted her little granddaughter and asked him if some special shoe might be created to help her when she stood and especially when she walked. The young shoemaker gently took Juliana's crutch from her hand and lifted her to a raised counter. "If you will allow me, mistress, I should like to examine the difference in your legs and see how we might compensate for it."

Juliana smiled shyly as she sat upon the counter and extended her legs, whereupon the shoemaker took careful measurements and discreetly examined the muscular development in each of her calves. When he had finished, he turned to Apollonia. "The young lady has well formed legs and might be able to walk more normally if her left shoe was made to compensate for the difference in the length of her left leg."

Apollonia was especially hoping that Juliana might be able to walk without her crutch, and she asked the young craftsman if it might be so.

"I have seen young people employ a combination of raised heel in one shoe and persistent exercise to build the muscles of both legs. It not only improves balance in their stride, but it also enables them to walk independently or, when needed, with the assistance of a walking stick, my Lady."

"Oh, grandmamma, I promise I shall work very hard to strengthen my legs. May we ask the shoemaker to make these special shoes for me?"

"You must not raise your expectations too high, Juliana. Some things do not always work as we hope. If you are willing to try, perhaps we can make a positive difference with new shoes." Then turning to the owner of the shop, the Lady placed her order. "I would like you to create the best shoes possible to compensate for Juliana's needs, Master Cobbler."

With that, the young man began to make drawings of both of Juliana's feet. He asked her age, made some estimates of her growth during the year ahead, and noted all of his measurements. Finally, he promised that he would try to have the shoes prepared in four weeks. He should be grateful, he added, if the young mistress could return to his shop in two weeks to allow him to try the early design of the shoes on her feet and return again later for a fitting as he was constructing them.

Juliana was so excited when they left the shoemaker's shop, she could barely contain herself. The mere thought of being able to walk without her crutch always seemed beyond her wildest dreams, and now it might be possible. "Oh, grandmamma, I can not tell you how happy I am."

"Much remains for you to do, dearheart," Apollonia cautioned her. The Lady, too, was thrilled at the possibilities. Her heart was full of hope.

Skipping along with her crutch under her arm, Juliana reached Gareth before the Lady and Nan.

"Gareth, guess what?" she asked him as she threw her crutch into the back of the pony cart.

"Oi know not, Mistress Juliana. What ave ya planned?"

"I shall soon walk as straight as you!"

* * *

Juliana was sitting in the driver's seat ready to drive the cart back to Aust House when Apollonia and Nan caught up with the jubilant girl. They returned towards the High Street following Juliana. On the way they encountered a noisy exchange from a small crowd that had gathered. The townspeople were surrounding a lonely woman in their midst. Some were shouting and hurling accusations at her. Apollonia sent Gareth into the crowd to question folk about what was happening. No one had any personal complaints, Gareth was told; their charges were against the woman's husband. He was once a wealthy physician of the town who was in charge of the care of a very popular former mayor of Glastonbury. "But the mayor died, m'Lady, and the people be certain that it were the physician's fault," Gareth told her.

"Doctor Medford should ave done more for Mayor Salisbury," one woman said loudly. "Ee were an earty man. Should ne'er ave died."

Another distinguished-looking man told the Lady that many people in Glastonbury were convinced that the physician took the mayor's money but gave inadequate care. "Some say he should have bled him further, my Lady, to re-establish the balance of humours."

A shopkeeper standing nearby told her that he had heard it said that the physician had misinterpreted all of the signs of the zodiac in Mayor Salisbury's case.

Apollonia remained calm and her presence among them caused some of the people to cease their angry shouting. Eventually the Lady unexpectedly spoke up in the woman's defence. "Why is it that you accuse this woman? It was her husband, you tell me, who was the person you blame. Where is he?" she persisted.

"He died six months ago and good riddance, for he grew rich all the whilst his potions and readings of the stars were unable to cure." This damning statement came from a rather large woman who seemed accustomed to having her own opinions dominate.

"Then, mistress, bring your evidence against him. I hear nothing but your opinions," Apollonia continued to insist. "You have no charges against this woman."

The crowd could see that this grand Lady would not accept hearsay, much less gossip, and her words encouraged some of them to reconsider. Indeed, they had no complaint against this woman. They were shouting at her because of her defence against local negative rumours about her deceased husband. Apollonia moved to the woman's side and continued to stand next to her. Slowly the townspeople began to drift away. Even the large, pushy woman who had been so full of accusation muttered that she had better things to do and walked away.

Soon, Apollonia, Nan, and Gareth were standing alone with Juliana seated in her cart beside the woman. The Lady said to her, "I am sorry to find you so unfairly attacked, mistress. Will you tell me your name? We shall be glad to accompany you home."

"I am Christina Medford, widow to the late physician, Rupert Medford," she said very aggressively. "You need not disturb yourself on my account, Lady; I am perfectly capable of dealing with the dunces of Glastonbury. In truth, they killed my husband as surely as if they had stabbed him to death. He died struggling to defend himself against their unjust accusations. I spit on them and rejoice when I find an opportunity to publicly accuse them of murder."

"May I send my servant Gareth to accompany you home, Mistress Medford?" the Lady asked her. "Nothing positive can come of inciting such anger against yourself, and I fear you may need protection."

"I require none of your grace and favour, Lady. I want nothing of your so-called Christian charity. I rejoice in stirring up hatred because all of these wretches know what they have done to me." With that, Christina turned away and walked towards Northload Street.

Suddenly, Nan pushed Gareth to stand closer to Apollonia and moved to her opposite side. "My Lady," Nan's voice was full of shock and disbelief, "why should this woman express such a hateful attitude towards you? It was obvious that you went out of your way to defend her."

Apollonia looked after Christina as she stalked away from them. "I believe she is a badly wounded creature, Nan. She has lost a beloved husband whom she believes was falsely and unjustly accused. Her discourtesy towards me is of no import. I only wish we could help her dismiss her need to hurl judgement towards her neighbours. She needs to rebuild a sense of balance in her life."

Then, turning back to her granddaughter, Apollonia smiled. "We want to express happy thoughts because we have much to hope for in our household, do we not, Juliana? Let us return to Aust House. I pray thee, Gareth, will you remain in hall long enough to share a flagon of ale before dinner? I am especially grateful for your help this day."

Chapter Four

Anchorite's Window to the World

The congregation of Glastonbury's parish church of Saint John the Baptist was growing significantly in recent years because many of its members were attracted by a popular addition to the ministry of the church. A small dwelling had recently been built into the side of the church to house an anchorite. His name was Brother Johanus. Although he was relatively new to Glastonbury, he had been recommended to the town by the Benedictine guest master, Brother Parker. The monk admitted that he had not been long acquainted with Brother Johanus but found his devout behaviour and dedicated prayer life solid evidence of his divine calling. Further, Johanus had come to Glastonbury bringing letters of recommendation from the abbot of Kingswood Abbey.

Soon after his arrival, the members of Saint John's parish found that Johanus extended to them not only a pious and welcoming manner, he expressed sincere concern and desire to minister to folk of all classes any time of the day or night. People began coming to him from different parishes of the town. Some expressed their conviction that Glastonbury was blessed by the presence of a saint. The good brother opened the shutters of his window to everyone, it was said, whether a beggar in the street or a wealthy merchant, man, woman, or child. He dealt with all their questions of faith and their needs for forgiveness. He sincerely sought to express Christ's love to everyone.

The Lady was aware of the hermit's dwelling because she and Nan regularly attended Sunday mass at Saint John the Baptist Church and could not help noticing how popular it was. Apollonia was interested to learn more about this anchorite, not only because he was so highly regarded but because she had long been sympathetic with these religious hermits. Early in her life, the Lady had known the writings of the most famous English anchoress of her time, Mother Julian of Norwich. Therefore, she assumed Brother Johanus to be a similar kind of religious mystic. He had withdrawn from the world into his cell to live a strict life of prayer and penance while continuing to serve those in the world who came to seek his help. Finally, the Lady knew that the Abbot of Kingswood was rigorously devout. If he had endorsed Brother Johanus' piety, the anchorite's devotion must be beyond question.

Chad's steward, John of Glastonbury, told the Lady that, although he had never personally sought the anchorite's advice, he had friends and family members in the town who were full of praise for the kindly brother.

"Johanus has never been known to lead one astray, my Lady. He is always full of good cheer, constantly praising God and offering common sense solutions whilst encouraging those who come to him to be faithful, loving Christians. He freely acknowledges that he is a sinner who must humbly seek God's grace. Chiefly, he is said to have devoted his life to trust in Christ's Great Commandment: to love God with all his heart, mind, and soul and to love his neighbour as himself."

"This is high praise indeed, John," Apollonia said quietly. "Your people must find his advice spiritually meaningful to them, or they could not put such trust in his words."

"Aye, my Lady, Brother Johanus has been able to gain the confidence of all those who come to him."

"Nan and I have noted that there is frequently someone at his window when we pass on our way to church. Oft-times a line of people wait to speak with him," the Lady added.

"People whom I know insist that Glastonbury is blessed to have him resident with us," John assured her.

* * *

The following morning, Giles Digby, Apollonia's steward and overseer of her West Country wool enterprises, made an appointment with the Lady in preparation for his journey throughout Somerset and Wiltshire. He joined her and Nan in the hall.

"Well, Giles, it appears that you shall endure a chilly ride to Wells," the Lady said. She was always concerned for his safety on the roads and was especially anxious that he keep himself adequately protected against the weather.

"I thank you for your thoughts, my Lady. My servant, Carrick, will ride at my side. Further, I have found Mistress Nan's luxurious Christmas scarf, which she knitted as a gift for me, is my best defence against the damp. It is the warmest that Cotswold wool can achieve and so tightly knit that the winds can not penetrate its warmth."

Nan blushed near purple, but her grin told the Lady how pleased she was that Giles would speak so highly of her personally knitted gift for him. Nan knew well how particular Giles was about his dress and the accessories he wore.

"I have made this list of each of my stops, my Lady. I know that Sir Chad has his own carrier pigeons, so I shall take one with me. Then I will notify you when I have arrived at my main stop and thus keep you informed of my progress. Whilst we have been in Glastonbury, it appears that all is going well for your woollen sales. This is past time for my spring visits with each of your managers to oversee their plans for the New Year and examine last year's totals."

"I feel that this is a huge effort for you every year, Giles, and I am sorry that I must ask you to extend your journey somewhat. Would you please carry this rather lengthy message to my brother, Ferdinand, in Marshfield?" the Lady asked, as she placed a folio into Giles' hand.

"Marshfield is not out of my way, my Lady, and I do enjoy calling upon the Lord Ferdinand. I shall assure him that you are well and have been able to offer significant assistance to Sir Chad at this difficult time."

"Please tell him that I do not know how much longer I shall remain with my son's family, but I must stay until Chad is able to return to his home from whatever armed adventure King Richard may be planning. Please assure Ferdinand that Nan and I are content to remain in Glastonbury for the months ahead. I shall send word to him when I decide to return to Aust. God go with you, Giles. We always keep you in our prayers."

Giles bowed to the Lady and then turned to Nan. "God's blessings, Nan, I shall be especially grateful for your gift when the north winds blow," he assured her with a twinkle in his eye. Making a final courtly bow to them both, Giles retreated from the hall and went towards the back door of the house to the stable.

* * *

John entered the hall shortly after Giles had gone, leading a monkish messenger holding an invitation to the Lady.

"My Lady of Aust," John said very sedately as he presented the young monk to her. "This messenger has just come from the abbey."

"Greetings, my Lady of Aust," the lay brother said as he stepped forward. "I bring you greetings and welcome to Glastonbury. Please accept this invitation from my lord, Prior Henry Compton." He extended an impressive looking document with the great seal of the abbey stamped upon it. When the Lady took it from his hands, the messenger remained where he was, obviously expecting to receive a response which he could return to the abbey.

Apollonia broke the seal and unrolled the document. It was beautifully written by one of the abbey scribes in elegant monastic calligraphy. Calling Nan to her side, Apollonia displayed the document to her. "We have been invited to call upon the prior Tuesday next. It seems that my name was recommended to Prior Compton by Chad's childhood friend, Sir Walter Heath."

Apollonia turned to the monk while Nan offered the Lady's thanks. "Pray tell the prior that my Lady of Aust is pleased to receive his gracious invitation," Nan said. "She wishes that you will return her acceptance with thanks to his grace, Prior Compton. Tell him that she looks forward to this opportunity to call upon him on Tuesday next."

"Thank you, my Lady," the messenger said. "The prior asked me to tell you that he wishes to receive you at three of the clock. My name is Michael, and I shall be waiting for you at the main abbey gate just opposite the Market Place." With that, the young lay brother bowed politely and left the hall.

"What an honour, Nan," Apollonia said excitedly. "I never expected to have such high level access to Glastonbury Abbey. It ranks with Westminster Abbey in London among the most important in the kingdom. How kind of Sir Walter to arrange this for me. I had only dared to hope that he would be willing to let me read some of the new history being written by his friend, Brother James. This is exciting,

Nan," the Lady said, "but I pray you will again serve as my spokesman when first we meet the prior. I should like to learn what sort of man he is. Sir Walter knows him as a personal friend from their childhood home, and that speaks very well of him. Still, I will prefer to retreat to my usual silence in public until I may judge him for myself."

"Of course, my Lady, I am always willing to speak in your behalf." Nan Tanner was not only the Lady's personal servant; she was the one human being who had been closest to Apollonia since the Lady's first marriage. Nan also knew that when Apollonia lost her third husband, she made a very conscious decision as a widow to become a vowess, one who adopted a celibate life protected by the church but not required to enter a convent. Apollonia had adopted this rule of silence for practical as well as religious reasons. It enabled her to meet powerful men and yet maintain a distance from them until she felt comfortable to speak in their presence.

At that moment, Chad's steward came back into the hall to find his master's mother smiling as if rather excited about something. John could not suppress a slight smile in response but returned immediately to his dignified role of steward of the household. "My Lady of Aust, you have yet another who wishes to speak with you. This is one from within our household. Sir Chad's personal servant, Jeremy, wants to know if you are free to receive him."

Apollonia composed her demeanour and moved to sit in her great chair near the fire. Once seated, she told John that she would be pleased to speak with Jeremy. When Jeremy entered the hall standing next to John, the Lady could tell that both of these young men were taking seriously Chad's instructions to them that they must be guardians of his household in his absence. Also, she could not help noticing that young Jeremy had grown significantly since leaving Aust village. Though still in his teens, he stood a head taller than John the steward. His muscular build reflected his regular exercise in the tilting yard.

Jeremy had known who the Lady Apollonia was since his childhood, but now in the Lady's presence, he felt suddenly unable to express himself. He forgot every aspect of chivalric behaviour that he had learned in Sir Chad's service and stood silent before her. Nan saw that he found himself suddenly tongue-tied, so she simply got up and went to his side.

"Well, Jeremy, it is clear that you have come up in the world. I do not believe I would have recognised you. You have not only grown significantly taller, your black beard declares your maturing manhood. My Lady, would you have realised that this was little Jeremy of Aust?" Jeremy's flushed face bespoke his embarrassment, but Nan's familiarity with him suddenly brought him back to himself and his purpose.

"My Lady Apollonia, thank you for receiving me. I have been given particular responsibility for your safety whilst you are resident in Sir Chad's household and feel that I must share my present concerns with you."

"Nan and I are grateful to have you serve us in this way, Jeremy. Please feel free to tell us what is troubling you. How can I be helpful?"

"As you may know, my Lady, there has been a succession of robberies in Glastonbury recently. Most of them have occurred in the heart of the town against High Street merchants' shops and their homes. But, two nights ago, Sir Edward Cammel's house, not far from us on Wells Road, was broken into. Significant valuables, the most precious silver plate, and jewels were taken as well as Sir Edward's money box. The money box is normally kept in a special place in his personal chamber."

"Indeed, Jeremy, I brought very little of value with us when we came to Glastonbury. Still, I know that my son has valuables here. Some were treasured gifts from members of the royal family. He also keeps his deceased wife's jewellery here, intending to pass it on to his daughter."

"My Lady, it is especially because the thieves seem so well informed that I have come to you. I believe that we must call Sir Chad's household together to put everyone on watch against the possibility of being spied upon or asked unusually pointed questions."

"A good plan, Jeremy; helping us be alert to a possible threat is our best defence. Please approach John and ask that he gather the household in the hall this afternoon. Nan and I will be certain that members of my affinity will join you as well."

"One other concern, my Lady," Jeremy said quietly. "I would like your permission to accompany you during the day and ask that I be allowed to sleep near your door each night. I know Sir Chad's first concern is the protection of his family, and it has become known throughout Glastonbury that you, his noble mother, are newly resident in Aust House."

"I shall always welcome your company, Jeremy, at any time during the day, but it is unnecessary for you to sleep near my chamber door. Nan is constantly beside me, so I pray that you will not feel that you must go to such extent in my protection."

Jeremy thanked her for receiving him and excused himself to make arrangements with Steward John for the gathering of the household. Nan smiled when he left, as if she was watching not just a son of Aust grow in her estimation but a familiar young lad mature to manhood.

"Our young Jeremy is all courtesy, my Lady, well on his way to chivalrous achievement," she said happily. "It is good to see one of our village lads succeed so admirably."

"No doubt, Nan, Jeremy has grown in Chad's service, but you and I must respect all that he is trying to do just now. We shall meet with the gathering in the hall this afternoon, and please be sure to tell Gareth and Brother William to join us there."

* * *

When Chad's Steward John was certain that every one of the two Aust households had gathered in the hall that afternoon, he introduced Jeremy who stood to speak with them. "It has come to my attention that each of us must be on our guard. Yesterday, there was a serious robbery of Sir Edward Cammel's household which you all know is not far from Sir Chad's home. This is the most recent in a series of robberies within Glastonbury, but its happening nearer to us must be noted. We have to be alert because the thief or thieves seemed to have known where to look for the valuables that were taken from Sir Edward's household."

Apollonia was seated in her great chair in their midst with Nan next to her on a stool. The Lady could see that every one of Chad's servants and her own people were aware of the implications of Jeremy's warning. He was telling them that it was likely that someone within the Cammel household had revealed information to the thieves about where to find things. All of Chad's people began to shake their heads as if insisting that as loyal servants they would never do such a thing.

"The thieves were informed in some way," Jeremy told them, "but it may not have been by an unworthy member of Sir Edward's affinity. It would merely require a clever inquiry or one expressed in strong sympathy with our master to put us off our guard and say something we would never share with an outsider. I have called us together to tell you that we must be on our guard because the protection of Sir Chad's home and family in Glastonbury is in our hands. If anyone in the town, the market, or even one who has come to our door speaks with you innocently enough but seems to ask for private information, bring that person to me straightaway."

At this point, Apollonia stood and said that she wished to add to his comments. "Jeremy is quite right to bring us this warning. You are all faithful servants and well respected by your master and by me. I promise that Nan and I shall do our best to remain alert, and I know that you will as well."

There were several questions from the larger group, and Jeremy dealt with those in a reassuring manner. Then, everyone was dismissed to return to his work. Nan could see that the members of Chad's household were grateful to the Lady for her endorsement of them. They were soon chatting with each other as they left the hall, sharing ideas of how they must always be alert and ready.

The Lady's maid remained seated on her stool, and when they were alone, she leant towards her mistress. "My Lady, these are all good people. Whilst we have been in Glastonbury, I have come to know the members of Sir Chad's household well. Several of them have come into his service with your recommendation."

"I hear what you are saying, Nan, and I agree. Everyone here is trustworthy and devoted. Jeremy's only goal is to warn them of threatening possibilities. Any one of us can inadvertently betray personal information if we are caught off guard. Forewarned is best prepared, dearheart."

* * *

The following Tuesday dawned with threatening storms blowing well inland. Still, there was no way the possibility of rain could dampen the Lady's spirits. She had been looking forward to this visit at the abbey for nearly a week. When the sun broke through the clouds in the early afternoon, the winds also died down. The Lady pointed to the improvement in the weather, but Nan was not to be put off. She insisted that Apollonia dress in a hooded woollen cloak.

Before three of the clock, the Lady with Nan and Jeremy walked through the Market Place to the main gate of the abbey to find the lay brother, Michael, waiting for them. He politely welcomed them and led them from the gate to the lodgings of Prior Compton.

The prior's servant was waiting for them at the door, took their cloaks, and urged them to be seated near the fireplace in the parlour. "My Lady, Prior Henry will be with you directly."

The servant left them and Apollonia began to look about the chamber. Suddenly the door flung open, and the Prior of Glastonbury Abbey came crashing through, flooding the room with his apologies. "I do beg your pardon, my Lady of Aust. Greetings friends," he said to Nan and Jeremy. "I am glad to find you seated comfortably by the fire. As usual, I am unable to maintain a schedule, for I tend to talk too much. There is no doubt that I must consider a vow of silence as my penance. Pray, forgive me."

The prior rushed to Apollonia's chair and took her hand. "My Lady, allow me to tell you how pleased I am to meet you. My dear friend, Sir Walter Heath, has described your grace and charm as a lady but could hardly praise highly enough your intelligence and learning."

Apollonia hoped to allow the prior to take a breath in the midst of his crashing entrance. She looked down modestly and, according to her custom when meeting a new person of significance, sat quietly as Nan told the prior that they had been warmly welcomed by his servant. The Lady's maid went on to say that the Lady Apollonia sincerely thanked him for his invitation.

The prior was slightly taken aback by the Lady's silence, but he settled into a chair opposite to her and encouraged her servants who had remained standing at his entry to be seated with them.

"The Lady Apollonia is truly grateful to her son's friend, Sir Walter, for enabling this meeting," Nan told the prior. "She hopes to learn how you and Sir Walter have been able to remain close friends whilst each of your lives has been dedicated so differently: one to the art of war and the other to the call of faith?"

"Indeed, mistress, our personal callings were not begun so differently," the prior responded politely to Nan. "We were boyhood friends in Templecombe where, during our fathers' childhoods, a preceptory of the Knights' Templar once stood. Walter knew that his grandfather's brother had been a Templar until the order was destroyed by the King of France. Walter's childhood was filled with his father's tales of the religious devotion of the Templars, their great faith, and their highly disciplined courage. When he grew to adulthood, he was unable to see himself a monk but adopted his own personal rule based upon the Templars' moral life of poverty, obedience, and chastity."

"Gramercy, Prior Comptom, it is very kind of you to share these personal insights with me," the Lady now addressed him directly. "You have given me a basis to understand the singular devotion of Sir Walter to the church whilst also serving the king."

The prior was pleased to see that the Lady now looked directly into his eyes. He was complimented by her smiling face that told him she was neither proud nor haughty. Perhaps the Lady is a bit shy, he told himself. "Still, dear Lady, I digress," he said. "Walter told me that you would wish to learn more of Glastonbury Abbey. How may I help you?"

"I can only tell you that in every way the abbey of Glastonbury exceeds my expectations, my lord prior. I have never seen such a grand religious house. The abbey church is beyond description for its size and architectural glory. I have been given tours, yet I find myself returning to experience again the extraordinary antiquity beneath the Lady Chapel."

"My Lady of Aust, you speak of the site of the *vetusta ecclesia,* and I admire your awareness of our history as well as your knowledge of church architecture. I must confess I am no scholar, for I seek only to serve the sacred mission of the abbey."

"Yours is a sincerely chosen vocation, Prior Compton. I have heard of your personal role in the abbey's administration of charity and ministry to the poor."

"You are too kind, my Lady. I merely wish to do God's will. In the absence of our abbot, who is frequently with the court of King Richard, it is my duty to oversee the ministries of all of my fellow monks and lay brothers, as well as the lay servants of our abbey. I seek to be obedient to Christ and an instrument of God's peace," the prior said quietly.

Apollonia found herself drawn to the prior. As a person and a monk, he was sincerely humble. "I have recently read Malmsbury's history of the abbey, Prior Compton, but I understand that a new history is being written as we speak."

"Ah, yes, my Lady. Brother James says it is nearly finished," the prior told her rather proudly. "Our Abbot Chinnock is anxious to see its completion. He feels strongly that the extraordinary history of Glastonbury Abbey must be kept up to date."

"Also, I have learned from my brother, Ferdinand of Marshfield, that the abbey's library is reputed to be among the best in England," Apollonia told him.

"Indeed, my Lady, the Lord Ferdinand is correct, but we do not seek to achieve the largest merely to display our pride. Rather, we hope to possess copies of the best philosophical and theological studies available to improve our understanding."

"Is there any possibility that one might be allowed to visit the abbey library?" the Lady asked him tentatively.

At this, the prior broke into a hearty chuckle. "I confess that Walter emphasised to me your keen intellectual pursuits, my Lady. Of course, I shall see that our librarian is made aware of your interest, and he will welcome your visit whenever you may wish."

"Pray forgive my presumption, prior. I confess I only dared to ask because I have never seen such a large library. Your collection is praised by all of the scholars of our day," the Lady admitted.

"Well, madam, I shall confess to you that I am surprised not by your presumption but by my own. I was certain that you should wish to have a private visit, as do most ladies, to the tomb of King Arthur and Queen Guinevere in the main aisle of our abbey church. I suspect that some ladies have no interest in Arthur's historical reality. They are simply carried away by his romantic story."

* * *

On their return to Aust House, Nan could tell from their conversation that Apollonia was convinced that this day's visit with the prior had completed all her best hopes in visiting the abbey.

"I was so impressed, Nan," Apollonia told her quietly. "Prior Henry Compton is truly a devout monk, yet ever so friendly and welcoming. He made no reference to his elevated status as prior of such an important monastery. He exhibited no pride of place or of birth. Instead, he describes all that he does as merely his desire to serve God. How grateful I am to have met him."

From Nan's perspective, the Lady Apollonia obviously hoped to visit with the prior again soon. The Lady went straight to her solar after they walked into the hall of Aust House and after Nan had taken the Lady's cloak from her shoulders. There, she picked up Giles' copy of Malmsbury's history of Glastonbury Abbey and began to read it through once again.

Chapter Five

Murder in the Market Place

A dreary dawn began to rise over Glastonbury's Market Place, and the earliest peddlers and shopkeepers were jolted away from their preparations setting up the market stalls of the day. Suddenly, everyone stopped. No one knew what to do, but there was no doubt what had happened to the limp body of Christina Medford. She lay thrown at the foot of the Market Cross with her legs splayed and arms akimbo. The bruises around her broken neck betrayed a murderous strangling of all possibility of life's breath from her body.

No one wished to touch her, but someone was sent to find the mayor. Another from the gathering crowd ran off to bring the priest of Saint John the Baptist Church. There was a quiet hush of conversation as if everyone was hesitant to bring notice to himself. General agreement was expressed with nodding heads; there could be no other conclusion. Christina Medford had been murdered, and her body placed to be discovered in the most public location in all of Glastonbury.

Finally, one voice in the crowd called out to the rest, "What about her son? Where is young Paul?" In response, one of the men accompanying the mayor left the Market Place heading towards the Medford home on Northload Street. In a matter of minutes, Christina's son came running into the Market Place. He said nothing when he saw his mother lying at the foot of the Market Cross, being given the last rites by the priest. Paul collapsed to his knees by her side, took her cold hand in his, and crossed himself.

Eventually, when townsmen came to take his mother's body away, Paul stood and spoke to them with more disgust than grief or anger in his voice. "At last, you have done them both in--first my father and now my mother. I shall never allow you to see me weep, for I rejoice that you will all face God and His Truth."

Mayor Arnold moved towards Paul and insisted that no one among them had done this thing. "It was a brutal and criminal act against your mother, Paul. I shall not rest until we find the true culprit."

"Oh, yes, honourable one," the teenager said. "You seek to comfort me just as you have found the robbers who continue to plague our town. My mother knew something about the true identity of the thieves. Certainly, that is why she is dead. Forgive me, but I have lived in this town for thirteen years and have no reason to expect justice in Glastonbury."

The lad began to walk away from the silent crowd but still continued to speak. "I knew something was terribly wrong when she did not return last night. I could do nothing then, just as I can do nothing for her now. Put her in Pauper's Field," he shouted. "I can afford nothing more."

* * *

Chad's cook, Mistress Farber, returned from her daily trip to the Market Place. She could barely contain herself and went directly to Nan and asked to speak with the Lady Apollonia. Nan could see that something dreadful had happened in the town, and she took the cook to the Lady's solar.

Apollonia welcomed her as she entered the chamber and then, seeing how distressed the cook was, begged her to be seated by the fire. "Pray, Mistress Farber, calm yourself. Nan, bring something to put round her shoulders. She is trembling."

"Oh, m'Lady of Aust, it be orrible. Oi ave ne'er in my life eard of such. No one in the Market Place could speak of anythin else. There were a murder in Glastonbury last night."

"This is dreadful news, mistress," the Lady told her sincerely. "Nan, please fetch a cup of wine for Mistress Farber. She has suffered a terrible shock."

"M'Lady, Oi knew er. It were the physician's wife, Christina Medford. Someone strangled er and left er body lyin at the foot of the Market Cross where ev'ryone would see it. What is appenin in Glastonbury? Is this meant to be a warnin gainst us all?"

The cook was so distressed, she appeared to swallow the wine in a single gulp. Apollonia saw at once that she needed time to recover. "Pray, Nan, help her into your trundle in the bed chamber. She has suffered a shock and must be allowed to lie down and grow warm again."

"Oi must not, m'Lady," Mistress Farber seemed near to tears. "Tis not proper!"

Nan was insistent. She took the cook by her hand and walked with her to the Lady's elegant bed where she pulled from beneath it her own trundle bed. Nan stirred the fire, and eventually, well covered and warmed, Mistress Farber began to calm and her body relaxed.

Apollonia stood next to the bed and spoke very firmly with her cook. "I shall go to the kitchen and sort things there whilst you rest awhile, Mistress Farber. I promise you I shall find out the truth of what was discovered in the market this morning."

"But, m'Lady, you must find out what will appen to er boy. Young Paul be in is early teen years. Now ee as no one. Both of is parents be dead."

"Can you tell me where his parents' home is, Mistress Farber? My almoner knows Glastonbury better than any of us. I shall send him to see what can be learned about the boy's circumstances and find Paul."

"Their home be on Northload, m'Lady. You can not miss it for its the biggest house on the street."

"I promise I shall follow up, mistress. Now, I require you to rest. When you feel restored, please join us in the kitchen."

As soon as they closed her chamber door, Apollonia sent Nan to find Brother William while the Lady went to the kitchen to wait for him. She found all of Chad's servants at sixes and sevens when she entered the kitchen. Even Chad's steward, John, appeared muddled. Silence arrested them as soon as they realised that the Lady Apollonia stood among them. Without hesitation, she told them that Mistress Farber had learned shocking news in the Market Place that morning and would join them later.

"I must ask you to avoid provoking gossip. I will send Brother William into the town to bring us the full story of what has happened.

For now, I pray that each of you will set about your morning tasks. I promise you, when we have reliable news, we shall hear it together."

She called Steward John to her side and they left the kitchen as soon as Brother William joined them. They walked into the hall, and Apollonia invited the men to sit with her at the table dormant. Each of them remained silent in her presence, waiting for her instruction.

"John, you must maintain calm in Sir Chad's household, especially when Mistress Farber returns to the kitchen and shares her story with the rest of the staff. She was told that there was a murdered woman, whom she knew, whose body was found at the foot of the Market Cross early this morning. I daresay everyone has heard something by now, but you must put a stop to any idle gossip within our household. Insist that we must first learn the truth of what is known.

"William," the Lady said as she turned to him, "you will be our messenger of truth. First, will you please speak with the mayor? Then, when you are sure of the facts, will you go on to the home of Christina Medford on Northload Street? The physician's wife was found murdered this morning, and her teenage son was brought to the scene of his mother's death. His name is Paul, and I know you will decide on the best course of counsel when you speak with him. I shall remain here until you have returned."

"I will go directly, my Lady. Northload Street is not far from the Town Hall, and I will do my best to see what can be done to help young Paul."

* * *

William returned to Aust House later in the afternoon bringing a visitor with him. Paul Medford was obviously nervous and did not seem comfortable making his way into Aust House, especially because Brother William and he entered through the main front door. He brought a small parcel containing some personal items with him, and when they came into the hall where the Lady and Nan were playing with Chad's children, Juliana stood up immediately to welcome him.

"Greetings, friend," she said to the older boy. "Did you know that Glastonbury has a cobbler so skilled as to make shoes that will help me walk without my crutch?"

Paul was taken aback by the little girl's familiarity but hoped to make a good impression. He responded to her very politely, "No, young mistress, I have not, but I hope you will find his craft very helpful to you."

William moved to Paul's side and led him to the chair where the Lady was seated. "My Lady of Aust, may I present to you our new friend, Paul Medford. He has come to serve your household in any way that he can. At the moment, we are truly famished and would be grateful to be excused to the kitchen."

"Welcome, Paul; I remember well the driving power of a young lad's hunger. I shall be grateful to learn more about you, but we may discuss that later. Pray do go with Brother William to the kitchen. They will find something to sustain you at least till the dinner hour."

"Thank you, my Lady," Paul said with a bow in response to her. Then, he stepped backward to join William and follow him to the kitchen.

"Grandmamma," Juliana said excitedly, "do you think our guest might enjoy seeing my pony cart?"

"I believe we must first allow him to grow to know us, Juliana. Young Paul is facing a great loss in his life, as have you and I. Let us find ways to encourage him to feel comfortable whilst he is with us."

Juliana's eyes seemed to express understanding of what her grandmother was telling her, and she suggested, "Then, perhaps we should go riding together."

* * *

Brother William came to the Lady's solar after the household finished the evening meal. They were seated before the fire when William told her all that he had learned from the mayor and from Paul himself. The boy was still in a state of shock at seeing his mother's body strangled and left exposed to public view.

"I thought you would wish me to bring him home to Aust House, my Lady, largely because Paul and his mother were destitute, even though they lived in a grand house. They have not eaten properly for weeks."

"Indeed, William, you have done precisely as I should have done. Have you been able to talk together? Is Paul able to express his grief? Do you think that we can find ways to help him rebuild his life?"

"I can not say that I know him, my Lady, but I do feel that he has been responsive to my expressions of sympathy and desire to help him. He knows that I am a priest and will expect to begin my day in the chapel with Sir Chad's household. I told him that I would offer special prayers for his mother's soul and would listen to any concern that he feels for his mother or for his own peace of mind. I also told him he must not fear expressing his grief at such a colossal loss, for grieving can help us grow stronger."

"Thank you, William; you are a good pastor," she smiled. "I have always found you to be one who accepts humanity as you find us and instinctively ministers to our human needs."

"Ah, my Lady, you are too gracious. I merely seek opportunities to fulfill my vows."

Apollonia was proud of her almoner, but she would never express that to him. She knew William to be uninterested in accepting praise. She also knew that she was leaning on his spiritual guidance very heavily just now. The Lady's household chaplain, Friar Francis, had been given her permission to go on retreat with his order in Bristol for the past weeks.

"I have yet another favour to ask of you, William," she said quietly.

"Indeed, my Lady, I am here."

"First thing on the morrow, I pray you will return to the kitchen and share with everyone in our households all that you learned from the mayor's office. I have promised that we must learn the truth of what is known and avoid spreading gossip."

"I shall do so, my Lady. Some have begun to ask questions of me, but I have promised everyone a full summary when I received your permission to speak."

"Finally, when you spend time with Paul, would you encourage the lad to feel free to speak with me? I met his mother only briefly on the street, and I found her to be a strong person. I also felt that she had been wrongly judged and mistreated by her fellow townspeople."

"Paul is a quiet lad but very deep," William told her. "He is questioning his faith at the moment and seeks to find reassurance from those whom he respects. I will encourage him to be comfortable in your presence and to feel the special relationship with you that all of your servants treasure."

"Do not hesitate to emphasise my great age, William. I am a grandmotherly figure."

"Indeed you are, my Lady," William began to chuckle. "You are an expression of the best definition of the words, grandly motherly."

* * *

Paul served the Lady's household quietly but very well throughout the days of April. He was willing to do any task from waiting at table to serving as the Lady's regular messenger, to helping Brother William in the chapel. He was respectful of Nan, kind and patient with the children, and more than willing to help Gareth in the barn, especially whenever the children went out for their daily ride.

Paul was in the hall with the Lady, having just returned from delivering her note of thanks to the abbey prior. Apollonia stopped him for a few moments and made a point to express her appreciation of his willing service, as well as to compliment him on his love of books. "All three of Sir Chad's children are enraptured by your reading and storytelling, Paul. I am especially grateful for your positive masculine presence with them, supplementing their father's grace whilst he must be gone."

Paul's face seemed at first to express a kind of discomfort at her words. He quickly realised that the Lady was making a point to compliment him. "I have been without my own father for less than two years, my Lady, but I am grateful to have gained from him a desire to read, to learn, and to understand the value of tenderness. As an adult, I shall always try to be the compassionate man that he was."

"My heart aches for your loss of both parents, Paul. Still, it is especially meaningful for you to cherish memories of your father, his well-educated professionalism, and his service to you as his son and the community as a whole."

"Indeed, my Lady, I treasure all that I know he stood for and pray God that I might someday be his equal." Paul spoke with a strong expression of "regardless of what others might say" in his voice.

"It is a great gift to have good parents," the Lady assured him.

"I had the best," Paul said quietly and began to leave the hall to go to the kitchen. He paused at the door and returned to the table dormant where Apollonia sat.

"My Lady of Aust, may I speak with you about my mother?"

"Of course you may, Paul. I met her briefly and saw immediately that she was a strong woman."

"My mother told me that you defended her against the accusations of people in the Market Place. She was grateful to you, my Lady. By that time in our lives, she had grown so very bitter that she was not the same gracious woman whom I knew."

Apollonia wished to encourage him, so she added, "I could only assume that she had been wounded by the loss of your father, Paul. Her resentment against the townspeople seemed to me to have a legitimate basis. I am sure it was very difficult for her to manage financially as well. Without your father's income, it must have been hard for her to support you, your home, and herself."

"Mother was a good money manager. She brought some money into their marriage which provided a small investment income, but the people of the town never ceased to be demanding of her. When they began to accuse father of inadequate care as a physician, people failed to employ him whilst he lived, and some even increased their accusations against him after his death. Our large house was resented by many, as if father had not earned it. No one acknowledged the truth of mother's struggle. She was required to pay instantly when others were allowed credit."

"Your mother endured significant injustice," Apollonia told him sincerely. "I am truly sorry, Paul."

"Brother William assures me that she is now at peace and reunited with my father. I take comfort in that. However, something drove her into the darkness of every night recently, and it had to do with the robberies that were occurring in Glastonbury. She was never able to sleep well. Long before my father died, she had difficulty sleeping, but

I knew that this was different. She told me that she had discovered something actually going on and would soon reveal all to the mayor and his pompous council. She said that they were missing the thieves' operations under their very noses."

Apollonia knew this revelation was possibly a key to unlocking identities of the thieves. She pointed that out to him immediately. "Paul, you also believe that this might have been the motive for her murder, do you not? What more did she tell you?"

"Nothing, my Lady. I am sorry to say that I know nothing more. Mother said she would tell me everything when the thieves were in gaol but not until then. She had to protect me. If only I had taken her more seriously. She grew so secretive and extreme. I truly feared her rational mind was being overwhelmed. One thing is likely, she was unable to protect herself against someone who realised that she had discovered the truth," Paul said with a sigh.

"Do you have any idea where she was going during the nights she was away from home?" the Lady persisted.

"No, my Lady, but I believe it had something to do with the church. She was very critical of churchmen."

"Was she going to the abbey? Was she disturbed by something she thought the monks were doing?"

Paul grimaced in response to her last questions and put his head down. "I wish I had pursued it, my Lady, but I know nothing further."

The Lady stood and walked towards the lad. "Please know that I shall do everything in my power to pursue the truth, Paul," she said as she put her hand on his shoulder. "I hope you will work with me to find answers to all of our questions. Your mother and father deserve to rest from the injustice done to them, and Glastonbury needs to put a stop to the evil afoot in this town."

"Help me know where to begin, my Lady." Paul's expression was as earnest and determined as Apollonia's. "I shall do whatever you ask of me."

Chapter Six

Terror at Saint Michael's

Cunomorus saw to it that he and his mother were meticulous in their performance of ritual. Their first stop after arriving in Somerset was at the site where the Celtic Glastonbury Lake Village had been, centuries before. They paused at every important natural site, continually offering thanks to the gods and especially the goddesses of the streams, wells, and lakes. They knew precisely where the Lake Village had been located, not far from the village of Meare, amidst a large expanse of pools and reed beds. Eponina and her son arrived there to seek the blessings and guidance of the gods before they began to climb the Tor.

They spent considerable time at the site of the Lake Village to look towards the Tor and acknowledge its majestic grandeur. Cunomorus pointed his mother's attention to its shape. "It is late spring now, but if we had been here at the time of the winter solstice, Eponina, we should have seen the sun rising along that predominant outline of the Tor, as if the rising sun were rolling up hill to its summit."

"The sight that consumes me is the blasphemous presence of the Monastery of Saint Michael crowning the height of our Celtic Tor," his mother sniffed. "The Tor does not belong to the god of the Christians. It is sacred to us as Druids and to our people."

"Eponina, mother, we shall with the help of the gods seek to restore its Celtic identity. We have come here with Velada's oracle to guide us. For the moment, do pause to appreciate the wisdom of our ancestors who built the Lake Village just here, in this location. They could have built the village anywhere, but its position was precisely selected to see the winter solstice sun rising along the Tor."

"I shall only remind you, Cunomorus, there is little left of the Lake Village regardless of its location. These impious Christians have sought to destroy every holy site precious to us. They drain the levels and extinguish the avenues of the gods. Worse yet, they find ways to Christianise those sites they can not destroy. We must respond, my son; we must demonstrate that we Druids still live. We have been limited but never tamed."

Cunomorus heaved a great sigh. He knew well the extraordinary history of their Celtic people throughout the valleys and hills of Glastonbury, and he treasured it. He could see, however, that he had been unable to arouse any of his mother's native dedication to this ancient site.

"We shall carry on, mother. We have much to do before we can return to Tyrconnell, but I insist that you will take some time whilst we are here to rejoice in the greatness of our heritage. It is still vividly evident throughout this tribal region of the Durotriges."

Suddenly, Eponina bent forward, and her face became a mask of pain. "Mother," Cunomorus said as he took her into his arms, "what is happening to you?"

Breathing deeply, Eponina forced herself to smile and waved him away. "It is nothing, my son, a mere twinge. Such things happen because we are being forced to eat this wretched English food."

Cunomorus held his mother close to him and could feel her body sink against his. He knew that his mother ate little enough food of any kind. There was no doubt in his mind that she was struggling physically.

"You are ill, Eponina. You must rest. Let us return to Grove Cottage Farm."

"Yes, Cunomorus, let us return. I shall rest this night and be ready to climb the Tor on the morrow."

* * *

It was a brilliant morning when the shoemaker arrived at Aust House carrying a parcel in his hands. When he was shown into the hall, Apollonia was pleased to welcome him. "Master Cobbler, this is extremely kind of you. I should never have expected a delivery of Juliana's new shoes to our door," the Lady told him.

"Well, you see, my Lady, I must be confident that I have been able to achieve a good fit, but I have also made this properly sized walking stick. When your granddaughter begins to walk in her new shoes, I am hoping she will be able to abandon her crutch altogether. However, she may need a walking stick at first to add a 'third leg' whilst re-achieving her body's sense of balance."

"Pray be seated, Jerryl Cobbler, and allow me to send Nan to bring Juliana to us from her schoolroom. May we offer you a flagon of ale for refreshment?"

The young shoemaker was grateful to have the drink Mrs. Manning served to him. He found that he was thirsty, having forgotten thirst in his excitement over the possibilities he hoped he had created for the little girl.

He lifted the new pair of shoes from his parcel to allow the Lady to examine them. Apollonia expressed her appreciation of the excellent soft leather he had used but asked him especially about the strange cord lacing that began at their toes and continued above the ankle. "I have never seen shoes of this design."

"You will notice, my Lady, the sides of both shoes extend well above the ankle, and the cords laced in each shoe will pull the leather tightly round her ankles to strengthen and support them every step your granddaughter takes."

As he was speaking, Juliana hobbled into the hall with her crutch under her arm, anxious to see her new shoes. She greeted him politely, but could not help asking him, "Are these for me, Master Cobbler? May I please put them on? I have been exercising every day, and there is no doubt that my legs are growing stronger."

The shoemaker asked her to be seated, and he began to loosen the cords on each shoe. He put the shoe on her right foot first and laced it firmly in place, then slipped the left shoe with the significantly raised cushion of leather sewn into its heel onto her other foot. When both shoes were firmly laced and the cords tied, the young craftsman handed Juliana the beautifully carved walking stick he had brought with him.

"Now, when you stand at first, Mistress Juliana, I want you to abandon your crutch. Use this walking stick merely to help you guarantee your balance. It is quite possible that you have bent your body slightly to accommodate the crutch. Stand as tall as you are with your walking stick and try taking a few steps towards your grandmamma."

Juliana went silent as she stood, obviously listening very carefully to everything the young craftsman told her. She remained quietly concentrating as if to get the feeling of standing tall with the stick in hand, supporting her right side. Very cautiously she took one step, then another, then another, pushing ahead every step with her walking stick. She approached Apollonia with a huge smile.

"I can do this, grandmamma. The stick is like a third leg. I do not bend to lean upon it; instead, it helps me to stand tall. And I love my new shoes, Master Cobbler," she said, turning towards the shoemaker. "I can walk in them without leaning upon anything."

Apollonia's heart nearly burst. Seeing Juliana walking towards her, the Lady smiled heartfelt thanks to the shoemaker. "I dare say, Jerryl Cobbler," she told him happily, "you have outdone yourself. We are very grateful to you."

"My Lady, you must urge Mistress Juliana to continue to stand as straight as she can and work to increase her strength. When her body's balance has grown stronger, allow her to attempt steps without the walking stick. I shall be in my shop if you require any further service."

Jerryl began to leave the hall as quietly as he had arrived. Apollonia stood immediately and went to his side. She took his hand in hers and thanked him sincerely for his excellent creation. Then, she placed into his hands a small purse of gold coins.

"My Lady, this is too much. I have made shoes for your granddaughter, not a crown."

"No, my friend, you have offered Juliana a gift beyond price. She will have to continue to walk with great care, but you have enabled her. My son and I are in your debt."

* * *

It had been early in the morning when the Druid and his mother began their climb to the top of the Tor. Cunomorus was not pleased that Eponina insisted upon making this ascent. He was concerned that the effort was too great for her. No matter how she tried to hide the true facts, he could see that she was enduring pain.

"It is truly nothing, my son," she assured him, "merely the indigestion of an old woman. As we walk, I shall occasionally pause briefly, breathe deeply, and soon be ready to continue."

They left their mounts with a servant at the base of the Tor. Cunormorus purposely refused to take the so-called Pilgrims' Path. They departed from the lane on the top of Stone Down and moved off the path onto the lowest of the terraces sculpted around the sides of the Tor. They ascended devoutly on this, a far longer path which moved about the surface of the terraces in a peculiar search. They were looking among the low growth shrubs of the sides for specific egg-shaped boulders, especially those which were more than a foot in diameter.

"There is an eggstone, mother, at the base of that shrub." They climbed to where one of the large Tor burrs lay, and with his great strength, Cunormorus was able to roll it aside and push a thick branch, sharply pointed at one end, into the ground beneath it. Once the branch had been stabbed into the ground, he rolled the heavy weight of the eggstone on top of it. Whenever they found another sizeable eggstone, the Druidess offered prayers to the Great Earth Mother, begging her forgiveness while her son repeated his ritual. Cunormorus employed only the largest of the eggstones, using their weight to intensify his brutal stabbing wounds into the surface of the Tor.

"Forgive us, Earth Mother, for this wound," he would pray at each burr. "We regret to cause you pain. We, your loyal servants, pray that you will express your discomfort, quake the eggstones away, make the Tor tremble."

Again and again, in the midst of his mother's prayers, the Druid forced pointed stakes into the earth and held them in place by the heavy stones. They ceased to complete the climb and turned round when at last he felt they had prepared the entire hillside. Neither Cunormorus nor his mother had any desire or purpose to ascend to the top level of the Monastery of Saint Michael.

The Druids began their descent to return again to Grove Cottage Farm. Eponina tried to be seen as walking energetically but would stop regularly, breathe deeply, then continue until they finally reached the place where their horses were waiting for them. It was then when his mother attempted to mount her horse that Cunormorus saw she was struggling to keep from falling. He led his horse to her side and lifted her into his saddle. He mounted behind her, and held her in his arms. The bondsman trailed her horse behind his mount. They rode as quickly as they could, given the circumstances, back to Grove Cottage Farm. As Eponina lay back in his arms, Cunormorus knew from the wracked breathing in her chest that his mother was seriously ill.

* * *

Later in the day, the monks of Saint Michael's were seated at two of the afternoon in the refectory for their only meal of the day. The shaking began somewhat unnoticed at first, then it began to grow into a sort of loud rumble, and the refectory walls started to shake. The monks looked at each other but continued to maintain their silence until they could feel the entire building begin to move. Suddenly a voice called out in panic, "Run to the church. It is an earthquake!"

By the time the monks were all kneeling in the church of Saint Michael's, the massive trembling of the Tor had slowed, but it was followed by several minor quakes. Their young prior looked around, trying to gauge when the movement of the earth beneath them truly ceased. Then, he lifted a reassuring hand towards his monks and insisted that they all remain on their knees at the altar.

"We must thank God for his gracious mercy," he said, as the chaplain began to sing a hymn of praise and thanks. It became an impromptu but fervent prayer service. All of the monks remained kneeling in the small church until finally one of two lay servants entered the church and announced that all was well.

"It was merely a hearty tremble," the brother assured the rest of the group. "Praise God, all of our buildings survive intact."

At that point, the prior stood while encouraging the others to return to their feet and get back to their chores. "We must return to the Lord's work, brothers. Let us, each one, resume our daily tasks that define the rota of our rule."

* * *

Nan Tanner, the Lady's maid, left the house quietly this morning. She told no one where she was going as she left Sir Chad's home and made her way towards the High Street. It was still fairly early on a sunny morning though the air seemed heavy and clouds in the west threatened as she turned towards Saint John the Baptist Church. Nan did not wish the Lady Apollonia to know that she was seeking the counsel of the anchorite whose dwelling was attached to the side of their parish church. The Lady's maid never did anything to deceive her mistress, but she felt in need of pastoral counsel while they were living in Glastonbury.

Nan was grateful for the chaplaincy of William Fallows to the Lady's immediate household, but as the Lady's almoner, Brother William was frequently gone from their home. He was first required to fulfill his mission in the name of the Lady Apollonia to those in need in the town. Nan missed the presence of their regular household chaplain, Friar Francis, and his personal devotion to follow in Christ's footsteps as a Franciscan friar. Nan tried to be constant in her Biblical studies, seeking throughout her days to live according to the Beatitudes of Jesus. Of all those who wore the Lady's livery badge of English ivy entwined about a pure red heart, Friar Francis made a profound impact on Nan because of his practice of absolute poverty and chastity. All the while they had been in Glastonbury, Francis had been excused from travelling with the Lady.

The Lady's maid hesitated as she approached Saint John the Baptist Church. She could see that there was no one standing at the window of Brother Johanus. Still, she felt uneasy going to speak with this stranger. She had been assured by several in Sir Chad's household that the anchorite was truly a holy man. Nan decided at last that she would simply not reveal her identity to him. Certainly she would never reveal that she served the Lady of Aust.

Brother Johanus opened the window and welcomed her as soon as she approached the street-side opening to his dwelling. "Dear friend," he said warmly to Nan, "I perceive that you are troubled. Let me share your struggle, and we shall take it to the Lord together."

Nan did not respond to him at first. She hung back, still uneasy about approaching him.

Johanus' friendly smile and monk-like simplicity as well as the encouraging tone in his voice seemed to calm her anxiety. Nan walked towards the window from which the anchorite looked out upon the town.

"I am Brother Johanus, servant of Christ and recommended to Glastonbury by the abbot of Kingswood Abbey," he assured her. "I pray you will allow me to speak to any of your spiritual concerns. I perceive that you are a woman of culture and yet well informed of the realities of life."

Nan walked more closely towards him and took the hand extended to her. "I am grateful to meet you, Brother Johanus, but I prefer to remain anonymous for the time being. Thank you for granting me your time and sharing the name of one in Kingswood Abbey who endorses you," she said honestly. "I beg you will call me Foreigner, for I am not native to this place."

The good brother simply knelt next to the ledge of his opened window and began to pray, "Gracious God and Heavenly Father, fill us with a sense of your presence. Forgive us our sins and grant us Your Divine Peace. For Foreigner, my new friend, and for me, teach us to open our hearts to the constant guidance of your Holy Spirit. Amen."

"Amen," Nan said, obviously encouraged by his prayerful sincerity.

"What may I do to calm the turbulence of your heart, Foreigner?"

"Brother Johanus, I am here because I miss the presence of our household chaplain and his willingness to offer me counsel. I know that he will return later, but I find myself unable to refrain from being overcome by my sense of inadequacy. I must make decisions which affect others, and I miss the reassurance his counsel has always given me," Nan said quietly.

"But, Foreigner, you always have at your side the One who counsels, guides, and leads you. You must say to yourself: 'The Lord is my Shepherd, I shall not want.' Repeat these words whenever doubt assails you, and you will feel complete."

Nan stepped back slightly and then said in a questioning tone, "Are you telling me that it is enough for me to repeat the words of the psalmist? I read the psalms every day. Am I to find counsel in that alone?"

"It must become your credo, Foreigner, the daily declaration of your faith. This psalm assures us that God is our guardian, our keeper, our shepherd. When we truly believe that we live in the presence of

God and are shielded by His loving care, we can never feel alone or inadequate."

"I think I see, though it sounds too simple, too easy, and I have never thought of the psalm in quite that way. However, I shall do as you suggest." Nan spoke as she took a coin from the purse on her belt. "Pray, accept my thanks."

"Ah no, Foreigner, leave no coins with me. Surely, you may encounter a beggar on your return home. I hope you will give it then. God bless you and remind you that I am here, ready to welcome any inquiry you may have of me." With that, Brother Johanus stepped back from his ledge and closed the shutters.

Nan turned from his dwelling and began walking back towards the High Street. She thought she could feel a stronger sense of presence with her as she began to repeat again and again as she walked: "The Lord is *my* shepherd I shall not want. The *Lord* is my shepherd, I shall not want. The Lord is my *shepherd*, I shall not want."

When Nan reached the turning, a man standing nearby began to follow her. He, in turn, gestured ahead to a woman begging on the High Street near Archers Way who held a sleeping baby in her arms. When Nan walked near the place where she sat, the woman held out her hand. Immediately, Nan reached into her purse for the coin she had offered Brother Johanus. She placed it in the woman's outstretched hand and then made the sign of the cross in blessing on the sleeping child. Nan continued walking back towards Bove Town Road, unaware that her every move was being observed. When she reached Sir Chad's house, Nan entered through the main entrance which was her privilege as the Lady's personal servant. Jeremy met her at the door with an expression of concern.

"Mistress Nan, I was unaware that you had gone out. It would have been my pleasure to accompany you. Pray, do not hesitate to ask me."

"Ah, Jeremy, you have been meticulous in your willingness to guard our every move, but I needed a bit of fresh air. When my Lady was otherwise occupied, I decided that a brisk walk to the High Street would do the trick. You must know that we women enjoy visiting the shops, even if we do not purchase anything," she said with a grin.

Chapter Seven

A New History

Prior Henry Compton called Brother James to his office to inquire how his new history of the abbey was progressing. "This is not to be interpreted as pressure upon you, James. I freely admit that I have little insight into your academic achievement. It is our Abbot Chinnock who is particularly keen to know how you progress."

Brother James was as typically scholarly as the prior was obviously less than erudite. James was a small, young man whose nose was lined by the eyeglass frame that sat perpetually upon it. His fingers were ink stained, and his shoulders bent as if permanently wrapped round a book. He had come to Glastonbury upon completing his doctorate in theology from Oxford. Abbot Chinnock summoned him shortly after his arrival in Glastonbury and assigned him the task of writing a new history of the abbey. Chinnock was an avid promoter of the legend of Joseph of Arimathea's foundation of Glastonbury Abbey. The abbot restored a chapel containing a holy well beneath the Lady Chapel which he dedicated to Saint Joseph of Arimathea. He adorned its walls with a large mural of the Deposition in which Joseph played a significant role. Chinnock was fired by ideas of how to use the new history Brother James was writing. Chiefly, he wished to establish Joseph of Arimathea's foundation of his abbey as the reason for him, Abbot Chinnock, to have precedence over all other English abbots.

Brother James was encouraged to employ every resource available to him in the library of Glastonbury Abbey to create his new history. He began by using William of Malmsbury's history and that of Adam of Domerham. To these he regularly inserted writings gathered from holy legend and a collection of ancient historical scripts only available to him in the abbey library. James divided his history into sections: it opened from A.D. 63 to the year 1126, part II described the history of the abbey from 1126 until 1290, and the final section from 1290 described events to the present year, 1397. James promoted some reference to the story of Joseph of Arimathea's first century mission to England in each of the sections.

The prior made every effort to reject any suggestion of Abbot Chinnock's wish to pressure Brother James to complete his history. Still, the young monk knew full well that the leadership of the abbey was already making plans to mount extracts from the new history for display at various sites within the abbey church. For James, however, it was not pressure from his abbot which troubled him; the author was being brutally bullied by one of the lay brothers.

"My *Chronica* is nearing completion, Father Prior, and I am grateful to you for your expressions of patience. I was wondering if I might have a new lay brother to serve me?" he asked meekly.

"I shall look into it, Brother James. Does this mean that you wish to have three lay brothers in your service?"

"Oh no, no, not at all, my lord; I simply wish to replace the two I currently have with another," James said as drops of sweat beaded his forehead.

"The abbot has especially assigned Ronan to your service, in part because Ronan and Cadoc were students at Oxford, but, of course, Ronan is the son of the abbot's nephew."

"It is not a problem with Ronan by himself, Prior Henry. It is his friend, Cadoc, with whom I find myself unable to get along." James seemed to tremble when he spoke of the second lay brother. "Would you kindly tell the abbot that I would prefer to have only the lay brother Hubert from the abbey library to serve me?"

"Of course, I shall do as you ask," the prior told him. "But, you must know the abbot will not return to us for several months yet."

"I beg you not to speak of this to anyone else, Father Prior. Pray tell the abbot that it would be a great assistance to me and speed the completion of the *Chronica* if Lay Brother Hubert and his intimate knowledge of the resources of our library could assist me in my work," James said nervously as he turned to leave.

* * *

Brother James hurried from the prior's chamber into the cloister to his personal carrel where he spent most of his working hours. He had only been seated long enough to become engrossed in his recent chapter of the history when the lay brother, Cadoc, came up from behind him and pushed his head roughly to the surface of the desk.

"What is this I hear? Our esteemed author/historian has complained to the prior about his preference to have a pusillanimous librarian serve his scholarly needs. Can this be true, Brother James?"

The muscular lay brother made no effort to be gentle. Cadoc's face was a grimace of wry and hateful amusement. "You know that I could smash your face against this desk until I have broken your nose, scholar. Will that make you feel more superior than you already do, oh doctorate of theology?"

Brother James tried to push his head back from the force leaning upon him just to protect his precious eye lenses, but he could do little against this unexpected attack from behind.

"You see, miserable creep, you can hide nothing from me. I know what you said to the prior about your preferences, and I will see to it that they are disregarded. Ronan and I shall continue to be the lay brothers who provide you with excellent service, as we have done in the past. Do you understand?"

James could only make a muffled word of understanding as Cadoc gave his head one final shove and then walked away from James' carrel. The monk lifted his head slowly from the surface of his desk and took out his handkerchief. Carefully touching his nose, he could tell that, although it was bleeding, it had not been broken. He threw his head back to stem the flow and held it elevated until the bleeding ceased. Once again, he would be seen by his fellow monks with bruises on his face and would have to make excuses for his clumsiness to those who inquired as to their cause. He closed his eyes in silent howls of frustration. What could he do? Where could he go to find protection against this persecutor who pretended to serve him but instead abused him at will within the abbey?

Praying silently, he begged God to grant him any avenue of hope to free himself from these supposed servants. James knew that Cadoc, especially, pretended the humility and the devotion of a lowly parish priest, but it masked a degree of cruelty the good brother had never experienced before in his life.

* * *

It was nearly the end of May when Apollonia was thrilled to see her son, Chad, and his good friend, Walter, suddenly walk into the hall. She was seated with Nan while working with Jeremy and John, the Aust household steward. Sir Chad greeted everyone but walked straight to his mother and scooped her into his arms. "Mamam," he said enthusiastically, "Walter and I are being sent on a mission for King Richard to Bristol. As you, my children, and my household are all *en route*, so to speak, we are able to spend this night with you."

The Lady stepped back slightly from her son's arms, straightened her headdress, and flashed an enthusiastic smile of welcome towards him and his companion. "I can not tell you how pleased we are to have you back, Chad, if only a very brief visit. This is a marvelous surprise. Your children will want to take you directly to the barn. They have much to show you, not only how well they are riding but how much they have learned in taking excellent care of their ponies. Sir Walter, how good it is to see you again. Pray be seated and share with us any news that you bring from the court."

The knight bent over Apollonia's hand and expressed once again how pleased he was to be able to continue their acquaintance. "My Lady, I have no desire to speak of the court when I may share conversation with you. Have you been able to visit with my good friend Henry Compton? I know he was looking forward to meeting you."

"I could never have expected such a grand invitation to visit the abbey prior without your intervention in my behalf," Apollonia said sincerely. "Prior Compton spoke fondly of your boyhood days in Templecombe and even suggested that his admiration of your life's devotion to chivalry inspired him to go into the church." With a slight smile, the Lady suggested a bit of more personal insight, "The prior told me a great deal about you, dear friend of my son, and all of it was truly admirable."

"Compton is a good man, my Lady; though I am told his early life contains secrets. I shall always be proud to call him my friend."

They remained seated around the table dormant until Chad returned to the hall. "You must forgive my delay, Mamam. I have been required to witness an exhibit from each of the children saddling their ponies, brushing them down, and being certain that they were well exercised."

"Chad, I give credit to my servant, Gareth. He has demonstrated an amazing ability to instruct your children. Although we have known for decades that no one of my affinity has his gifts for handling horses, Gareth's willingness to instruct Juliana, Geoffrey, and George has been a revelation to me."

"I shall return to the barns to express my gratitude to Gareth before we leave, Mamam, but I can not tell you how grateful I am to you when I see Juliana walking without a need to use her crutch."

"That is all due to a brilliant young craftsman in Glastonbury, my son. When you have more time, I shall take you to his shop in the town, and you may express your thanks to him then."

"May I seek a great favour of you, my Lady," Walter asked her. "I freely acknowledge that this is a significant imposition upon your time, but as Chad and I must leave in the morning, could you call upon my friend, James of Glastonbury, the author of the current history of the abbey? He told me that he was not free to speak with me today and could give me no explanation. But I could see straightaway that something has happened to him. His face was bruised; he was trembling in the presence of his fellow monks, and would not look into my eyes when I addressed him."

"Of course, I shall call upon him, Walter. Better yet, may I invite him to visit Aust House? Thanks to you, I had a marvelous visit with the prior recently who encouraged me to visit the abbey library. I shall remind Brother James that his reputation is known to my brother, Ferdinand of Marshfield. Both he and you have encouraged me to make his acquaintance."

"I can not say whether James will be willing to leave the abbey precincts, my Lady, but I believe he needs help and may be more able to accept it from a visiting noblewoman in the town, someone who resides outside the abbey. I shall leave a personal note for him. If you can give it to him, it will tell my reasons for speaking with you."

"I shall send a message to the abbey on the morrow, Sir Walter, and will try to visit with Brother James at his convenience during the week ahead."

"My sincere thanks to you, my Lady. I shall leave Glastonbury with an assurance of something positive happening in my absence."

"Pray do. Surely you have already seen how I admire the abbey and its ancient ministry to the West Country," the Lady told him. "There may be nothing amiss with your friend, but I shall personally be glad to speak with him about the new history he is writing."

Chad and Sir Walter left for Bristol early the following morning. Apollonia sent them on their way with her blessings and promised the worried knight that she would visit with Brother James as soon as it could be arranged.

* * *

Apollonia asked Paul to be seated with her and Nan late in the afternoon while the children were being served their evening meal in the nursery. She knew the physician's son was well educated, but the Lady had recently seen several of his carvings in wood and wanted to encourage him.

"Paul, whilst you are with us at Aust House, I hope you will have time to continue your carving. Juliana showed me one of the beautiful little sheep that you made for her as well as the horse and the eagle that you carved for Geoffrey and George."

"They are but children's toys, my Lady," Paul responded with a shrug.

"Indeed, I believe each of your gifts to Chad's children is a work of art. How long have you been carving?"

"Since I was a boy, my Lady. I do it for my own pleasure. In another matter, I have hoped to speak with you about my mother's anger with the church that I mentioned to you earlier."

"Have you remembered something, Paul? Do you have any idea to which church in Glastonbury she was referring, or did she find some concern about activity at the abbey?"

"I think she spent time watching the dwelling of the anchorite at Saint John the Baptist Church, my Lady. She would sometimes mutter about the supposed piety of churchmen, but then she would say no more when I would ask her to explain."

Nan reacted suddenly as she pricked her finger with her needle, but the Lady pressed Paul to be more specific if he could. "Some of my school friends told me that they had seen my mother standing alone, even after darkness fell some evenings, as if she was taking note of all those who stopped to speak with Brother Johanus. I do not believe she knew anyone within the abbey or Saint John the Baptist's Church."

"Well, my Lady," Nan told her with a slightly reddened face. "I must tell you that I have spoken with Brother Johanus and found him to be a sincerely devoted servant of Christ and his fellow men."

"Did you seek out the counsel of Brother Johanus, Nan?" the Lady asked her.

"I did, my Lady, but not to achieve any secret connexion with him. I only wanted to see what kind of person he is so that I might enlist his comments on Holy Scripture. You know that I regularly read your copy of Wycliffe's English text and would normally have spoken with Friar Francis about my questions. However, he remains on retreat and Brother William spends full days on the streets of Glastonbury. Everyone with whom I have spoken is full of praise for Brother Johanus."

"Then, pray tell me your personal opinion of the anchorite, Nan. I know you to be a person of faith who has no patience with those who abuse it."

"My Lady, I believe he is a godly man who speaks knowledgeably of his Biblical studies. He seems to me to be a man of intense faith who seeks to share it with everyone who comes to his window."

"Is it possible that your mother felt some reason to be watchful of Brother Johanus, Paul, or possibly someone attached to Saint John the Baptist Church? We will continue to follow up on that observation." Then the Lady turned to her maid, "Nan, I am pleased that you have met the anchorite, and I hope you will continue to visit his window. Take all of your questions to him. It is understandable that you are missing Friar Francis' presence in our household these past weeks, so please feel free to speak with Johanus. I would be glad to share his counsel with you. Surely it will help us all to know the anchorite better whilst we are living in Glastonbury."

"My Lady, what may I do to help?" Paul obviously wished to be more active in the effort to understand what his mother had discovered before her death.

"As a local resident of Glastonbury, Paul, ask everyone whom you know what they have heard about the robberies, and bring any comments to me. We must first collect information and then try to piece together some understanding. If you have any further ideas of why your mother wished to observe the anchorite or the church even into the nighttime hours, do not hesitate to tell me. For now, Nan, please send Jeremy to me."

When Chad's personal servant came to her in the hall, Apollonia handed him a brief missive. "Jeremy, I would like you to deliver this invitation to Brother James of Glastonbury Abbey. I should like you to wait for his response as well as accompany him to Aust House on the day he agrees to call upon me."

"Of course, my Lady, I shall not return until I have an answer for you."

* * *

Brother James had been able to accomplish little during the afternoon after Cadoc's threatening visit at his study carrel. James enjoyed writing and was especially grateful to have access to the abbey's fine library. On this day, however, his mind could not focus on research, composition, or any writerly activity. He was a study in jumpy, on-edge, fearful anticipation that Cadoc might return and attack him when he least expected it.

James exhibited a massive startle when one of the messengers brought the Lady Apollonia's note to him. "Pray forgive me, Brother James," Michael said in an effort to calm him. "I bring you this message from the town. The courier waits in the gatehouse for your response."

James opened Apollonia's note and shook his head to realise the possibilities on offer. It surprised him to learn that it came from a noblewoman in the town who said that she was the sister of the Earl Ferdinand of Marshfield and a friend to Sir Walter Heath, both of whom recommended her acquaintance with him. She was asking if she might call upon him in the guest reception of the abbey or if he would be able to call upon her at the home of her son.

A miracle of happenstance, the monk declared to himself in a prayer of thanks. This woman was bringing to him, for the first time, a possibility of finding protection against the physical torture he had been enduring for months. Heaving a great sigh of relief, James said to his brother Benedictine that he would speak with the messenger. They walked together to the gatehouse where Jeremy waited to receive his response.

Jeremy had a good sense of people and was surprised to see that the author/monk seemed in a state of nervous anticipation. Brother James smiled warmly in greeting and made it quite clear that he did indeed wish to make the acquaintance of the Lady of Aust. Still, he insisted to Jeremy, she must not come to him at the abbey. He would prefer to call upon her at Aust House. James inquired if it would be possible to be received at three of the clock on the afternoon of the morrow.

"My Lady of Aust is grateful to receive you whenever you may be free, Brother James," Jeremy told him. "I shall return to escort you."

Brother James thanked Jeremy profusely and rushed back into the cloister. Jeremy thought that something appeared to be frightening the monk. He mentioned his observation to the Lady when he returned with his message.

"I have been warned that something or someone is seriously troubling Brother James," Apollonia told Jeremy. "I am surprised to learn that his distress was obvious to you, a complete stranger. Thank you for telling me, Jeremy."

Chapter Eight

The Brunt of Warning

Brother James was meticulous in maintaining his normal schedule throughout the following morning. He appeared promptly in each of the early morning offices of Matins, Lauds, and Prime. After a brief period of reading, he went back to the dormitory and washed before he returned to the church for Terce and the first mass of the day. He met with the rest of the monks in the chapter house to discuss the ongoing business of the monastery. He maintained his usual schedule when, after two of the afternoon, he ate the main meal of the day. Before three, he left the cloister unannounced to anyone, as was his privilege, and went to the gate where Jeremy was waiting for him.

He greeted Jeremy, and they began to walk along the High Street uphill to Bove Town Road. Brother James said little while they walked, but when they approached Aust House, he asked Jeremy if the Lady Apollonia was acquainted with any of the other monks or staff of the abbey. Jeremy could only say that he knew she had been invited to visit the abbey by the prior, but she had not visited anyone in the abbey before that time, only the abbey church.

Jeremy led Brother James to the front entrance of Aust House and then into the hall where the Lady and Nan were waiting by the main fireplace. Apollonia rose in greeting at their entrance, and Jeremy immediately introduced her, "Brother James of Glastonbury, may I present her grace, the Lady Apollonia of Aust."

"This is an honour for me to meet you, Brother James," the Lady told him. "Sir Walter has allowed me to read a few pages of your new history of the abbey. I must tell you that I look forward to your completion of the *Chronica*. Pray be seated and allow me to give you this note from our mutual friend, Sir Walter Heath."

They seated themselves by the table dormant. James quickly read the brief epistle from his friend and then breathed an audible sigh of relief. "My dear Lady Apollonia, I acknowledge your presence in Glastonbury as my one hope of personal protection. Sir Walter speaks to my point. I have not been allowed to be myself for the past months because I am being manipulated and tormented by some of my Benedictine lay brothers."

Apollonia begged him to continue his story. "Walter was certain there was some evil intent causing you much fear within the abbey walls. How can this be so, Brother James? Pray tell us, what has been happening to you?"

Brother James, in the freedom of the Lady's household, was not only able but seemed to need to pour out his entire story. "It began slightly more than eight months ago, my Lady, when I asked to be served by an abbey lay brother. Two of them arrived at my carrel and announced that they were sent to me by the abbot. Ronan introduced himself to me as a member of Abbot John Chinnock's extended family. I was also told that he and Cadoc were former students of Oxford. I was pleased to meet fellows of Oxford, but I could not be comfortable with his companion.

"I soon learned that Cadoc is a brute of a man whose pretended humility as a poor parish priest serving the abbey masks a vicious character. It was obvious that Ronan did nothing but idle about after they began in my service. He remained out of sight most of the day while Cadoc's only purpose was physical abuse of me to achieve his own ends.

"I have been asked to write the new history of the abbey so was given special privileges in terms of my freedom of movement about the town. Cadoc made it clear to me that he would use all such privileges in my name. If I objected in any way, he would not hesitate to beat me in the dark of the night or even in moments when I was working alone in my carrel in the cloister. Cadoc seems to have spies everywhere. He knows everything that is going on in the monastery and, worst of all, has been able to intimidate the other lay brothers and servants into submission to him."

"Brother James," the Lady told him, "this is appalling. I have never heard of such abuse within a monastic brotherhood. How can this Cadoc, as a mere lay brother, achieve such power?"

"He continually puts it about that he has the ear of the abbot through Ronan. To the leaders of the abbey, Cadoc is insidiously humble, yet I know that he stops at nothing to achieve his own will, my Lady. There is no doubt that he is using the abbey as cover for his own activities and those can not be in the service of the church."

"This can not be allowed to continue," Apollonia said. "I shall see to it that Cadoc will have no further access to you or to your special privileges. Tomorrow morning I will speak with Prior Compton and expose the evil of this lay brother. If we can at least guarantee your protection within the cloister, that will be our initial step. Then, Cadoc must be interrogated to determine how and why he has used your special privileges."

* * *

The moon was rising when Cadoc and Ronan strode up to the main gate of the abbey and demanded to be allowed to go into the town. "Open the gate," Cadoc shouted to the gatekeeper. "We must be allowed to deliver messages in the town for our resident scholar."

"It is a most unusual hour, lay brother," Cadoc was told by the gatekeeper. He had received instructions from the abbot to allow such freedom of movement to the servants of Brother James, so he opened the main gate. They strode out towards the empty High Street.

"Stay alert, for I shall return," Cadoc shouted backward, "and I will not wish to be delayed trying to waken you."

The gatekeeper knew this particular lay brother and his reputation. As required of him, the gatekeeper acknowledged that he would be watching for their return. "That should keep him awake the rest of the night, Ronan," Cadoc sneered.

The two lay brothers walked along the empty High Street until suddenly a hand pulled Cadoc into a small alley between the shops.

"What have you got for us, Crewyn?" the lay brother asked roughly.

"She be the servant of nobility. Oi followed er ome."

"Nobility, are you certain?"

"She be stayin with er mistress's son at Aust Ouse on Bove Town Road. Oi've not been able to find out much, only that the Lady be the daughter of an earl and rich as Croesus."

"Then, dunce, Aust House should be our next site. Have you begun to speak with the servants? Let us be working on it straightaway. I have heard that Sir Chad, the master of the house, is currently away at court. Find out how many men are normally in residence as well as how many servants, you know, the usual."

"This one be different."

"In what way can it be different, for Christ's sake? You said yourself it is a knight's household. How does that differ from our job on Sir Edward Cammel's home?"

"Aye, but ain't nobody in this ouse will talk. No gossip, no stories of the master or is lady's preferences. And the Lady's maid would not e'en use er own name, though ev'ryone in town knows who she be."

"Then, you have your work cut out for you, do you not? Use every possible source for information. If the maid does return to the anchorite, see that someone is in place to listen. Check on the other servants, especially any of those who might be Glastonbury folk. I do not care what you tell them; just find a way to get specifics from the Aust household whilst the master is away."

* * *

Before seven of the clock on the following morning as the monks were completing the office of Prime, Lady Apollonia, accompanied by Nan and Jeremy, was being shown into the prior's chamber. The Lady was determined that she could not wait to expose what she felt was an evil corruption within the brethren of the abbey and, in the absence of the abbot, decided she must speak with her new acquaintance, the prior.

Prior Compton was surprised by her early morning call but was told that the Lady of Aust had returned to the abbey with significant personal concerns that she felt must be discussed with him. Just the set of her face told him of aroused anxiety. When she began to speak, however, her description of the abuse of Brother James by the lay brother, Cadoc, was meticulously detailed. The prior could also see that she believed every word of what had been told her. He called to his lay servant and sent for Cadoc immediately.

There was no conversation within the prior's chamber while they waited. Apollonia was determined that they concentrate on the correction of a serious wrong. The time seemed to drag silently into nearly half an hour. The prior's servant finally returned to his master only to report that neither Cadoc nor his friend Ronan could be found anywhere within the abbey walls. Both of the lay brothers were gone.

By this time, Prior Henry was angry. It appeared that everything the Lady told him about the lay brothers' gross misbehaviour probably happened as she described it. Worse yet, it happened on his watch during these recent months when he had been in charge in the absence of the abbot. He announced to Apollonia and her party that he would begin a complete investigation of this grotesque incident and would get to the bottom of it. "I assure you, my Lady of Aust, I shall begin by speaking personally with Brother James. In the interim, if Ronan or Cadoc are found anywhere in the community, they will be thrown into the abbey gaol."

The prior was painfully embarrassed but had to express his appreciation to Apollonia. "My Lady, I am grateful that you have brought this episode of vice and abuse to my attention. Such things can not be tolerated in our monastery. I shall ask you to be with us when Cadoc is interrogated and bring you a complete report of my findings."

* * *

Prior Henry called Brother James to his chamber after the Lady and her party were gone to ask him for a complete description of what Cadoc had done. This time, James felt free to speak his mind and told the prior everything that he had been suffering at the hands of the lay brother.

"I do not charge Ronan, for I never see him, Father Prior. He has neither served me nor harmed me. It was his companion, Cadoc, who has made a point to display my weakness in the face of his brute strength."

"What is it that Cadoc wants from you?" the prior asked.

"I can not say precisely. My suspicion is that Cadoc has used his residence in the abbey to conceal himself for some purpose beyond our walls and capitalised on the special author's privileges granted to me to give him freedom of movement in the town."

"The lay brothers take simpler religious vows and attend fewer church services than the choir monks," the prior said, "but Cadoc claims to be a lowly parish priest. From your description, he is nothing more than an evil persecutor. Worse yet, if you are correct, he has only remained in our monastery to achieve cover for ulterior motives. Pray, Brother James, why did you not come to me sooner?"

"I confess I was terrified of him, Prior Henry. Cadoc seemed to know every word I spoke with you and would torture me in some new way if I dared to complain of him in your presence." Brother James went on to tell of his recent experience of Cadoc's attack and suddenly seemed unable to hold up his head. He knew he had acted in a cowardly and unworthy manner.

"How could he be so well informed?" the prior demanded. "This Cadoc has never been in my personal service nor even in my chambers."

"Perhaps we must look to your servants, Prior Compton. Cadoc seems to have control over many of the lay brothers," Brother James suggested. "Possibly one of them has been his informant?"

"Then, I shall see to that straightaway. If any of my servants have abused my confidence, they will be sent to the grange and manual labour. I must have assurance that my counsel and leadership decisions remain private until I choose to speak."

* * *

Juliana came to Apollonia's solar after her lessons. The Lady was pleased to see her granddaughter and especially to watch her walking so well. "I say, Juliana, you are obviously finding your new shoes to be a great help. I can see very little hesitation in your step."

"Yes, grandmamma, I do so love to be able to put them on each morning. These special shoes help me to stand straighter because I no longer lean on my crutch. I do use my stick to be certain of my balance when walking as Master Cobbler directed."

Apollonia could not help smiling and pulled the little girl into her arms.

When Juliana moved to sit on a stool near to the Lady, she said that she wished to ask for a favour.

"Of course, dearheart, you know I will grant you anything if it is in my power."

"Will you go with me to the abbey church? I want to visit the Lady Chapel," Juliana told her.

"That is easily granted, Juliana; I have been especially fascinated by the ancient site of the first church of the abbey. When shall we plan to do it?"

"I was hoping we could go this afternoon, grandmamma."

"Well, I see no reason why not. Nan, please call Jeremy and collect our cloaks."

When Nan returned, she brought capes. "It is a damp day for May, my Lady, and it will be best if we are prepared for rain."

Jeremy joined them promptly, and to Apollonia's surprise, Juliana insisted that she would not take her pony cart, that she was able to walk to the church. It was not a long walk from Aust House to the north abbey gate, and the western entrance to the Lady Chapel was a brief walk once inside the walls. In spite of a few raindrops, Apollonia was pleased to see that Juliana walked well with her stick. It seemed no time at all that they entered the church.

Once inside, Juliana quietly asked her grandmother if they might visit the Lady Chapel first because she really wished to go downstairs to its underground level. Apollonia could see that Juliana had some specific purpose in mind. After they descended, the little girl went directly to an arch in the south wall. The opening in the wall beneath the arch gave access to a holy well. Apollonia stayed with Juliana and watched silently as the little girl spoke with the monk who stood in attendance at the well. Kneeling before the well, the child bowed her head in prayer after which she gave the monk a coin and asked if she might have a cup of water from the well. The monk smiled at the very serious little girl and brought up a cup of water for her. Juliana took it reverently from his hands, drank it slowly, and after returning the cup to the monk, bowed her head in prayer once again.

Apollonia moved to kneel beside Juliana to offer her prayers for God's blessings upon her precious granddaughter. Nan, too, assuming that the Lady and Juliana must be praying for healing, added her own silent plea to God as she and Jeremy stood near their mistress and her fervent little grandchild.

When they left the abbey and began their return to Aust House, Juliana said very quietly to Apollonia, "Grandmamma, may I come back to the abbey every afternoon?"

"I think that would be possible most days, Juliana. Let us speak with Mistress Albert. If I am unable to accompany you every afternoon, she will surely try to make it possible for you on days of good weather."

"I have learned that Saint Joseph of Arimathea brought two cruets containing the sweat and blood of Christ to Glastonbury. Do you think that the waters of this holy well might have received some drops of Jesus' sacrifice for us?"

"There is no way for us to know, Juliana," Apollonia said to her. "I believe Jesus' sacrifice offers healing to all people."

* * *

Next to a huge marshland lake, the abbey had built a fish house to be home to its head fisherman. It was not far from the village of Meare, three miles to the west of Glastonbury. The abbey was dependent upon an endless supply of fish from Meare Pool. Over 5000 eels and endless numbers of other fish were taken from it every year because it was required for the monks' meals. On every Friday, Lent, and holy days spread throughout the church calendar, meat was forbidden them.

The fish house was actually a comfortable residence with its entrance on the upper floor of the building. It had a hall with fireplace and a separate bedroom including its own garderobe. On the ground floor, the head fisherman had his kitchen with large storerooms.

Ronan and Cadoc were well acquainted with the fish house because it was run by Cadoc's uncle, a wily curmudgeon of a man who preferred his solitary life but had no desire to be celibate. Jestin Mallot regularly made disgusting comments as to the waste of a monk's male member. Unknown to the abbey officials, Jestin kept a young girl in the fish house, whom he called his personal wench. Erild was less than a slave and forced to satisfy Mallot's sexual needs any time of the day or night. The girl hid away if ever a stranger came to the fish house door. When Ronan and Cadoc arrived, Jestin felt no such need. They knew she was his. The only thing he demanded when he learned that they had run away from the abbey was to insist that they be gone by the end of the week.

He told his nephew that he and his friend could sleep on the floor in front of the fire. He would feed them for the days ahead but then they must be gone. That night, as Cadoc and Ronan lay before the fireplace, Ronan began whining. "Where can we go, Cadoc? We do not have enough money yet."

"We will stay in Glastonbury until we do. For the days ahead, we will let Jestin feed us and provide our shelter. The fuss over our running away will begin to die down, and at the end of this week, we must be off. Then, I say we remain in Glastonbury under the abbot's nose where no one will think to look for us. We shall only go about during the nighttime hours until we have collected what we are sure is enough to sustain us in Bristol."

"But, where will we stay, Cadoc?" Ronan whined, "I do not wish to sleep rough."

"I have stolen a key to the abbey's tithe barn, Ronan, so we shall be able to get inside. We can hide in the upper level of the barn through the days and use its straw to make our beds. We shall find Wort in the town after we have settled, tell him where to find us, and make certain that he brings us food regularly. It will not take long to complete our plans, and then I vow we shall be richly prepared to make our getaway."

* * *

Cunomorus hovered over his mother's bed during the weeks since they returned from their expedition to the Tor. He struggled to bring all of his years of study to aid him in finding the best hope of healing for her because the Druid had no desire to bring any sort of local Doctor of Physic to care for her. Cunomorus knew that his mother must not be bled and weakened further. There could be no doubt that Eponina was struggling. In spite of his regular soothing potions, her chest pains increased and her breathing became irregular. He left her side only to walk out to the sacred grove late in the afternoons and offer his prayers for her recovery. The sun was beginning to set when one of the household servants came rushing out from the cottage to him.

"My lord, we believe that you must return. The Lady Eponina is failing, and she is begging you to come to her."

Without another word, the Druid ran past him to return to the cottage and did not stop until he knelt next to his mother's bed.

"I am here, Eponina Amairogen," he said very quietly. "I will remain."

"Cunomorus, my beloved Artur is here as well. He tells me I am dying, but he insists that I must tell you that we have interpreted Velada's oracle incorrectly. We have created a massive wrong on the Tor. There was no reason for us to try to destroy Saint Michael's monastery. That will not enable the return of the Druids to England. You must undue all that we have done to cause pain for the great earth mother on the Tor."

"Hush, mother, try to rest," Cunomorus said as he wrapped his mother in her robe. He gently lifted her into his arms from her bed, and as if led by an invisible hand, he took her outdoors to see the brilliant light of the sunset. He sat holding her in his lap. "Breathe slowly, deeply, and inhale the healing warmth of the sun, mother. I shall hold you here until its light is faded."

Eponina's breathing became more and more uneven, but a lovely smile filled her face and lighted her eyes as if she were truly rejoicing in the beauty of the moment.

"I was misled by my pride. Forgive me, my son," Cunomorus' mother whispered to him. She died in his arms as the sun set behind the hills. The Druid carried her back into the cottage, howling a wailing lament for his loss.

Chapter Nine

Intimate Threat

Paul went to the market early in the morning. He decided he would speak personally with anyone on the Market Place who might have something to tell him about the recent robberies in Glastonbury. It mattered not if it were based on fact or speculation. He felt strongly that he must begin to collect any ideas that might, as the Lady said, provide pieces of the puzzle surrounding his mother's death.

He entered the shop of the local tapisser and found the owner and his wife in the front of the shop with several of their weavers busily working at their looms in the back room. Paul was not interested in purchasing textiles, but he needed to speak with the owner directly.

"Good morrow, Master Tapycer, and my greetings to your good wife. My name is Paul Medford, and I have come to ask you for information. I am aware that you are a local merchant who was recently robbed. Could you tell me how and when it happened?"

At first, the owner of the shop seemed suspicious and unwilling to answer Paul's questions. He did not seem to want to talk about the incident. His wife, however, moved to the counter where Paul stood and made it quite clear that she would speak with him.

"I know who you are, young Master Medford, and I am truly sorry that your mother was taken from you in such a brutal way. I also knew your father as a good physician who restored me to health after a long illness. It is important that you know that not everyone in Glastonbury blames Doctor Rupert for the tragic death of our mayor."

"Your kind words mean more to me than I can ever express, madam. However, I suspect that there is some connexion between the recent series of robberies in Glastonbury and my mother's death. I would be very grateful to you if you could share any details of your experience with me."

The woman paused to consider and then told him quite frankly, "My husband will tell you that we have gone over it many times. The robbery happened in the dead of night, in the middle of the week, the last Wednesday of December. It was a cold, dark day, and we had closed up shop promptly to hurry home and return to our fireside. Levan and I are certain that we locked all of our doors, front and back, before we left. When we returned the following morning, the shop was open and stripped of every valuable in it. The thieves knew where to find every finished tapestry, and they also knew where to find our money box and the shop key that hangs in a secret place. Thank God we had not let the profits of the day remain in the cash box--took them home with us."

At this point her husband joined in. "That was just it, lad. No one outside the shop knew where I hid the cash box or the key. I immediately charged our local tapissers, every one who had knowledge of the shop, even our charwoman. After quizzing them, it became obvious to me that they are all good people whom we have known for years. They are faithful workers, not thieves."

"From all you are telling me, sir, it was obvious to you the robbery was committed by those with inside knowledge of how to make entry and where to locate things normally kept hidden from common view. Is that correct?"

"Yes, lad, and it troubles me to this day. I have been a maker of tapestries since I was first apprenticed and in the business of selling them for nearly twenty years. I can not understand how it was done and, more to the point, how did they achieve such insight into our private lives?"

"I am very grateful to you for speaking with me," Paul said. "If you should think of anything else, do not hesitate to send a message to me. I am presently in service to the Lady Apollonia of Aust House on Bove Town Road."

* * *

Paul spent the rest of the day visiting the shops where a robbery had occurred. Each of the merchants who had suffered loss was willing to speak of it with him. "I can not guess what you will be able to discover from my tale, lad," the elderly furrier told him, "but I shall be ready to take action against anyone whom you think might have a reason to abuse the commerce of Glastonbury in this evil way."

Late in the day, he returned to Aust House and asked to meet with the Lady Apollonia. He was shown into her solar where they could speak privately. He told her and Nan that he had been able to talk with most of the owners of the shops where robbery had taken place, and all of them had been willing to describe to him what they found when they first entered their shops after the thefts. "No one can remember such a major outbreak of crime in Glastonbury, my Lady. Each of the shopkeepers with whom I have spoken says that recently minor pilfering has been transformed into major crime."

"Have you noted any particular part of their descriptions of the robberies against them that seems to relate one robbery with the others, Paul?" the Lady asked.

"The only reoccurring comment from all of those with whom I spoke was that the thieves seemed well informed of private information. They knew where to find things of value and if such things were kept in special places in the shops or the homes above the shops. The thieves took everything of value that they could carry because they seemed to know where to find it."

"You are performing a real service for those who have been robbed, Paul," the Lady told him, "also for those who wish to bring the thieves to justice. It is important that the shopkeepers who were attacked share their stories to see what they have in common. You have been able to demonstrate that the thieves found ways to learn important details from each site that only someone from within each household could know. This pattern has to be a major piece of our puzzle."

"My thanks, willingly, my Lady. I am grateful for your encouragement, but what do we do next?"

"We have to find the conduit, Paul, the person or persons who are channelling such private information to the robbers."

"Well, my Lady," Nan said with emphasis, "I have to insist that it can not be Brother Johanus. I have now visited his window three times, and he has never asked me a personal question. On the contrary, when I struggle to study your copy of Wycliffe's Bible, Johanus helps me understand Holy Scripture, especially the difficult books of the Old

Testament. He is always willing to pray with me. I find him to be the most devoutly religious person I have ever known."

"I think it is good that you continue to take your questions to the anchorite, dearheart, especially because he is helping you. Still, we must all remain a bit reserved with everyone we encounter just to be sensitive to the possibility of how a thoughtless revelation might be used by unscrupulous people listening to our conversations."

* * *

It was before shops were open on the High Street the following morning when Paul left Aust House to visit the shop of a local mercer on Magdalene Street. Not long after dawn, the day had barely begun to brighten at this early hour. Paul knew he could easily find his way. He had been told the day before that this dealer in textile fabrics had recently suffered a burglary. Paul entered the shop and was able to speak with the owner just before his opening. The mercer told him that he was already aware that Paul had been gathering information from other merchants and shopkeepers.

"These thieves know what they are about, my lad. They knew precisely which of my fabrics are the most expensive and where to find them. They carried off nothing but the finest: silks, cashmeres, and high quality woollens."

Paul thanked the owner sincerely after their conversation. "I hope to gather enough information about these robberies to lead us to the thieves, sir. You have been very helpful."

"God give you good day, lad, and blessed insight," the mercer called after him.

It had grown into a darkly cloudy day when Paul left the shop and turned to walk north to return to the High Street. Suddenly, without warning, powerful arms seized him by his neck and pulled him from behind into the doorway of the almshouses' chapel. A deep voice growled into his ear, "Stop askin questions or ya will be dead." Then, Paul was struck on the back of his head and left lying unconscious.

Young Medford had no idea how long he lay there before he became aware of the allmshouse priest kneeling over him, begging him to speak. "Come, young man, please say something to me. How came you to be here? What has happened to you?"

Paul sat up slowly, holding the back of his head in his right hand. "I shall be all right, father. I managed to bump my head in a nasty way and lost consciousness. Can you bring me a moist cloth to wipe the dirt from my face and the back of my head?"

Paul remained seated on the upper step to the chapel while the priest had one of the women in the almshouses bring him a bowl of water and a cloth. After he was able to clean his face, hands, and the back of his head, he stood slowly and assured the priest that he was recovered, all the while apologising for causing a barrier to the chapel door.

"Pray, forgive me, father. I am feeling better and shall return home." He began to walk away and put a coin into the poor box before he headed back onto Magdalene Street. He found the Lady at work in the hall when he got to Aust House. She was startled to see his pale face and made him be seated at the table dormant with her.

"What has happened, Paul? How have you been hurt?" she asked as she sent Nan to the kitchen for a beaker of ale.

"My Lady, I believe I have gotten in over my head."

Apollonia was in no mood for puns. She could see that Paul had been badly shaken, but she waited for him to explain.

"I do not think there can be any doubt that my mother was murdered because she learned too much about the recent robberies, my Lady. I was attacked this morning as I left the mercer's shop. I went to see him because I was told that he, too, was among those who had been robbed."

"Dear God, lad, what was done to you?" Apollonia asked as she stood and went to look more closely at him.

"I was walking back towards the High Street when I was pulled from behind into the doorway of the almshouses on Magdalene Street. My Lady, I could not see my attacker, but he was powerful and spoke with the accents of the lower class. Before I could say anything, he told me I must stop asking questions or I would be killed. Then, I must have been struck with some sort of cudgel. I was lying across the entrance to the almshouses' chapel with a throbbing head when I returned to consciousness."

"Oh, Paul, this is my fault. Without anticipating the consequences, I have put your life in danger. Pray forgive me, lad. I should never have encouraged you to question anyone regarding the robberies." By now, Apollonia was looking more carefully at the wound on Paul's head. "Nan, send Jeremy to fetch the local doctor. This wound must be seen to."

"It is nothing, my Lady," Paul insisted, and he began to stand up.

"Indeed, it was a nasty blow and has broken the skin beneath your hair," the Lady insisted as she forced him back onto his chair. "You will remain here until the physician examines you, cleanses this, and tells me that you require no further treatment."

"Well, my Lady, perhaps we are closer to understanding the purpose of the 'conduit', as you called it," Paul said to her. "The mercer told me that the thieves took only the most expensive items from his shop: silks, cashmeres, and fine woollens. Either these robbers have been in Glastonbury long enough to know consistently how and where to find only the best, or someone is channelling the facts to them."

* * *

Cunomorus did not sleep. He remained at the bedside of his dead mother throughout the night and into the early morning hours. He seemed consumed by his grief and no one in his household dared disturb him. Each member of his household made a point to protect his mourning. He emerged from his mother's chamber by the middle of the day and spoke with the steward.

"We shall bury the Lady Eponina in the sacred grove at sunrise on the morrow. You will bring men with us today to dig the grave swiftly and be prepared to disguise all signs of its having been done, once her body is at rest. I have things I must do before we can leave Glastonbury. When they are accomplished, we will return to Tyrconnell."

"Yes, master. Young Connal and I shall go with you to the sacred grove and have the grave ready to receive the lady's body on the morrow. Is there aught else that we may do to serve you?"

"Have the women come to Eponina's chamber. They must bathe her and dress her in her finest gown whilst we are away."

Cunomorus wasted no words. He spoke little for the rest of the day. Once the women were set to their task, he went with the men to the sacred grove. The men were digging while the Druid prayed to the gods for his mother's soul, begging that she may be rejoined with her beloved husband.

He dismissed the men and sent them back to Grove Cottage when the grave was ready. "I shall not eat this day. Pray inform the women. Also, tell them they must be ready to accompany us back to the sacred grove before sunrise for the service of remembrance."

After the men left, Cunomorus began his personal prayers of supplication that the great mother earth goddess would receive his mother's body in spite of the mistakes and wrongs they had committed. He confessed their sin and promised that he would repair, in Eponina's name, all the pain they had caused on the Tor.

* * *

The entire household of Grove Cottage Farm gathered to walk beside the body of Eponina Amairogen to her burial in the sacred grove before dawn the following morning. It was a brief ritual of remembrance, and as the sun's beams broke the darkness, the body was lowered into the grave. The men filled in the grave, levelled its surface, and covered it with sod. The members of Cunomorus' household made every effort to express their deep respect for their lord's loss but most certainly for him. He was certain when they left the sacred grove that within a matter of weeks the gravesite would have returned to its natural state.

The Druid ordered a hearty breakfast as he walked back into Grove Cottage. He knew that some heavy labour would be required of him in the days ahead.

* * *

Nan was making an early morning habit to walk with the cook and Jeremy to the High Street shops and the Market Place. As the Lady Apollonia's personal maid, Nan was not required to do shopping for the household, but she always enjoyed seeing what was on offer. Chad's cook, Mistress Farber, was very particular about the foods she chose for the Aust table. Most of the shopkeepers, the butcher, the fruiterer, or the baker always promised their best to her. Nan moved from shop to shop with the cook until her purchases were complete.

The Lady's maid frequently remained in the town while Mistress Farber returned the shopping with Jeremy to Aust House. Faithful to his master's instructions, Jeremy conscientiously returned directly to accompany the Lady's maid home. He knew where to find Nan when she remained behind, and he knew that she would wait for him to accompany her home to Aust House.

Nan had grown fond of speaking with Brother Johanus as her friend as well as pastor. She used every opportunity when she was near the High Street to walk to his dwelling attached to Saint John the Baptist Church. She would wait patiently if anyone had preceded her to his window, but when she approached, he always welcomed her enthusiastically.

"Ah, I am blessed this day by a visit with my most friendly foreigner. Greetings, Mistress Nan, will you pray with me?"

After a brief prayer of mutual thanks and praise, Brother Johanus and Nan would say the Lord's Prayer together, and then she would bring her questions to him. "Brother Johanus, I bring only one question to you this morning. How am I as a Christian to understand the ways in which God is described for us in the Old Testament? I have tried to read from the Book of Kings but find I understand very little of it, especially not the description of God's cruel anger against his disobedient people."

"How is it that you are able to read Holy Scripture, Nan?" the anchorite asked her cautiously.

"I know that copies of Wycliffe's Bible are regarded by some as heretical, Johanus, and I can share this with no one but you. My Lady Apollonia has had a copy of Wycliffe's English translation for several years and allows me to read it and study it."

"I shall never reveal your source, Nan, and I promise that knowledge of your study is safe with me. I, too, have a copy of Wycliffe, and I must admit, dear friend, it is difficult to see the loving Father of our Lord Jesus Christ in Old Testament descriptions. In the Book of Kings especially, God is often described as angry, vindictive, and even destructive of those who disobey Him. But we must remember that such writing was addressed to an earlier age and was trying to promote devotion to only one God whilst discouraging the worship of pagan gods. The ideas of punishment of evil and the rewards of obedience ring like bells throughout the Book of Kings. We must see it as punishment when God's creatures are disobedient, but we are always welcome when we return to Him repentant."

"In that spirit, I shall try to read it again. Thank you, Brother Johanus. Your insights are helpful to me, for I have little understanding of ancient times. Ah, here comes Jeremy to collect me. I must hurry home."

"I am always pleased to speak with you, Foreigner Nan. By my troth, I find your thoughtful questions challenge my study of Holy Scripture. The day is yet young. Have you no more questions for me?" Johanus asked her with some sense of hope in his voice.

"Pray forgive me; I must be back before mid-morning. Today it is my responsibility to mind the Lady's jewel box. My mistress, the Lady Apollonia, never wears more than a simple silver or gold cross. But whilst her son, Sir Chad, is away, she feels a need to personally guard the family jewels being kept for her granddaughter in her chamber."

"Benedicite, dear friend. When you are able to return, I shall be here," Johanus called after her as Nan walked back towards the High Street with Jeremy at her side. Nan did not see a figure slip from the door of a space outside of Brother Johanus' anchorite dwelling and the wall of the church. On this occasion, she was not followed home to Bove Town Road, but everything that she told the anchorite had been noted.

* * *

Cadoc and Ronan stayed out of sight inside the upper level of the abbey barn throughout the day. After sunset, they looked forward to Wort's arrival with food. When Cadoc saw Wort finally making his way down Chilkwell Street, he opened the door to the barn wide enough to allow the bulky Wort to squeeze inside. Cadoc locked it once again after Wort came through, all the while complaining to him, "Do you not see the hour of the clock, dunce? It is evening, and we have not eaten most of the day. I am ravenous." Cadoc grabbed the parcel from Wort's hands and took the bread from it first to break off a large portion. Handing the rest of the loaf to Ronan, he tore chunks of it with his teeth and seemed to chew madly, all the while pulling from the sack pieces of cheese and taking large bites from a storage apple. He literally stuffed his mouth until his stomach felt full.

Wort said nothing, merely grunted his pleasure at causing them discomfort. "Oi'm to tell ye that she be waitin to talk with ye both. Ye are to find er at the usual place well after midnight when the town be sleepin. She not pleased that ye ave run away from the abbey."

"We have served her needs and gathered information for her from the confessional as well from the abbey," Cadoc said petulantly. "What does our leaving the abbey mean to her? We had enough of abbey life."

"She says she not be certain that she still needs your elp."

"Then, we shall spell it out for her when we see her this night," Cadoc told him. "She is supposed to be working out the arrangements for our next major theft. Is she really ready, does she have a plan, has she decided upon when? Perhaps we are the ones who do not need the bitch. What say you, dunce?"

At that, Wort reached out his powerful right arm and snatched the neck of Cadoc's robe in his fist, lifting his left arm threateningly. "Ye be gracious in your talk of Calevera an treat er with respect or Oi shall beat the ell out of ye."

Cadoc's attitude changed dramatically, and Ronan could see real fear in his eyes.

"Let Cadoc go, Wort," Ronan shouted weakly while he remained seated on the ground well beyond Wort's reach. "We shall meet with Calevera at the hour appointed, according to her instructions."

The burly henchman twisted the collar of the robe round his fist so tightly that Cadoc's knees grew weak. Wort pushed him backward and ordered him to open the barn door. Cadoc staggered to the door and held it open just enough to allow Wort to squeeze through. Once Wort was outside, he quickly locked it shut.

Ronan came running to his side, "Did he hurt you, Cadoc?"

Very strong and well built, Cadoc always enjoyed beating on others. Now, however, the bully was breathless and near to tears. "Damn and blast! I shall get my own back from him, the filthy bastard. One more profitable robbery and we are out of here, Ronan. I have had enough of Glastonbury," he said as he pulled the collar of his robe to loosen it from red lines round his throat. "So where were you when I needed help?"

Ronan began to whine, "What could I have done, Cadoc? You know she uses him to keep us in line, and he never hesitates to do her bidding, no matter how cruel or brutal."

"Be quiet and let me think," Cadoc said as he continued to rub his neck. "Perhaps we can see to it that she and her favourite tormentor will find themselves in the hands of the sheriff after you and I are gone."

"Do you mean that we should turn them in? How can we charge them and not involve ourselves?"

"Simplest of all, Ronan. We do not accuse them of robbery; the charge will be murder. For now, we shall meet with Calevera and respond graciously to all her demands of us, as if we are ready to serve her every whim. When we have our share in hand from our final theft, we will complete our vengeance--anonymously of course. My version of what happened to Christina Medford will be sent to those who can enforce the law against Calevera. We shan't actually see her and her ugly brute hang, but I will rejoice in the thought."

Chapter Ten

Relics Revealed

Brandon Landow was in a good mood as he rode his faithful horse, Absolution, towards Glastonbury on a glorious morning. Landow was a highly successful pardoner, and he was certain that here within this, one of the wealthiest abbeys in all of England, he was about to make a huge profit for himself. He had in his saddlebags what he would describe as the most important relics in all of England. He only needed to arrange an appointment with the abbey prior who, he was sure, would wish to buy them.

Landow knew well that the current abbot of Glastonbury was striving to promote every aspect of the tale of Joseph of Arimathea's journey to England. Abbot John Chinnock especially emphasised Joseph's founding of Glastonbury as the first Christian monastery in all of England. To remind everyone of this miraculous foundation by the legendary great-uncle of Jesus Christ, Chinnock was anxious to collect every relic that might relate to Saint Joseph. The abbot was currently serving at the court of King Richard, but the pardoner thought he had left instructions with Prior Compton to complete the purchase in his absence.

Landow rode down Hill Head entering the town from the south towards a glorious view of the abbey and Chalice Hill beyond. The pardoner was a rapacious human being who, having entered Glastonbury, decided that he would not wait another day to meet with the prior. He went straight to the abbey to announce his presence. He continued down Magdalene Street towards the Market Place and entered the abbey grounds through the grand new abbey gateway.

He dismounted from Absolution and proudly announced to the lay brother at the gate that he was the pardoner, Brandon Landow, who had come to speak with Prior Henry Compton. After this announcement, he demanded to be shown immediately to the prior's quarters.

"I must beg your patience, Master Pardoner," the lay brother told him, "but the prior is presently with the community in the chapter house. This morning's chapter may take considerable time, for the prior has been forced to discipline several of the brothers. May I suggest that you return after three of the clock this afternoon when the prior will surely be in his chambers."

"How dare you waste my time in this manner?" Landow grumbled. "Have you no idea of the significance of my call upon the prior? Surely, Abbot Chinnock will not be pleased to learn that you have thwarted me from completing a vastly important purchase by the abbey," Landow said in a distinctly nasty tone to the lay brother.

"Again, I beg your pardon." The now trembling lay brother seemed to be searching for any way to solve this dilemma. "If you could return before two of the clock this afternoon, the prior will be returning to his lodgings for dinner. Perhaps he will be able to speak with you then?"

Landow climbed back into his saddle and looked down upon the lay brother as if he were a creature of no value whatsoever. "I shall tell the prior, when at last I am able to speak with him, how I was frustrated at every turn. What is your name, lay brother?"

"My name is Justus, sir, but I beg you to consider the hours of our daily routine of prayer at the abbey. We are known as an abbey devoted to prayer and service. I can not interrupt the prior when he must be in the church or in chapter."

"Well, Justus, if I have my way, there will be no such grace extended to you," the pardoner said as he rode through the abbey gate leading into the market place. "You have wasted more than half of my business day," he exaggerated, "and those in power shall know of it."

* * *

Landow was able to arrange accommodations for himself at The Pilgrims Inn on the High Street, but being intensely self-centred and vain, he could not settle. Instead, he continued to mutter to himself, "How dare a lay brother thwart me?" Landow decided he should not only be reprimanded for his action, Justus must be punished. The pardoner knew a number of abbeys and priories where the daily routine of prayer was not so rigidly maintained. But, he reminded himself, they were not so ancient, so hugely wealthy, or historically important as Glastonbury Abbey. He knew he needed to remain in Glastonbury, but he continued to complain and swear at his frustration.

Landow walked to the Market Place to look at the stalls, sniffing to himself that he could find nothing of good value on offer here. When he stopped at the stall of the haberdasher, Gareth Trimble was returning to Aust House from the blacksmith's on Northload Street and saw the pardoner standing there, arguing about the suggested price for a new woollen liripipe.

Gareth did not know the pardoner personally, but he was well aware that his Lady of Aust and especially her maid, Nan, had no desire to be in his presence. When he reached Aust House, Gareth went to the barn by way of the kitchen to tell Nan whom he had just seen in Glastonbury's Market Place. As he suspected, she was not pleased to learn that the pardoner was in Glastonbury. Nan Tanner was suspicious of everything Brandon Landow practised, preached, or especially sought to sell.

"This is not good news, Gareth," the petite maid frowned as she looked up to his face. The Lady's stablemaster was a powerful man but one of very few words. Whenever he spoke within the household, everyone, especially Nan, listened to him.

"I shall have to tell my Lady Apollonia that he is in Glastonbury, Gareth. No doubt he has come to promote his own profits by the sale of something to the abbey. He will surely be up to no good."

"Aye, Nan, you shall ave to tell er," Gareth said as he left through the kitchen door to the barn. "Oi be certain. It be im."

* * *

Nan went to the Lady's solar where she found Apollonia reading by the window. "Ah, dearheart," the Lady greeted her, "I visited the school room this morning to see how the children are doing. I can not tell you how my heart rejoices to see our Juliana growing straight and moving about with only the use of her stick."

"Indeed, my Lady, Juliana's progress has been wonderful. The little girl is so determined to work for improvement; she must be given all the credit."

"She continues to go with Mistress Albert to the Lady Chapel to drink the waters of the Holy Well. There is no doubt in my mind that

Juliana quietly hopes for a miracle," the Lady told Nan. "Perhaps a miracle will be granted her in response to her own hard work."

"Pray forgive me for bringing unpleasant news when you are obviously enjoying a happy moment, but Gareth has just returned from the Market Place. He said that he observed that wretched pardoner, Brandon Landow, probably attempting to swindle a stall holder out of his fair price."

"Oh, God save us," the Lady said under her breath. "Does Gareth think that Landow recognised him as being of my household?"

"Gareth does not believe that the pardoner knows who he is at all. In fact, Landow was being so obnoxious that Gareth did not think he noticed anyone but himself."

"I think we must believe ourselves forewarned, Nan. It is unlikely that he will wish to call upon me even if he knows we are in Glastonbury. However, I feel certain that his being here must have some purpose relating to the abbey."

* * *

Before two of the clock, the Pardoner returned to the gate and demanded to see Prior Compton. He was shown to the prior's quarters and told to sit while the prior finished his meal. Landow never waited patiently and proceeded to stalk in circles around the room until the prior entered.

"Ah, my Lord prior," Landow said as he swept a grand bow before him and nearly touched the floor. At this point his tone changed completely from that of demanding bullying to whining supplication. "No doubt Abbot Chinnock has communicated to you that I, Brandon Landow, Pardoner of the Holy Church, have come to Glastonbury on an errand of great importance."

"Yes, pardoner, the abbot told me that you wished to sell us some sort of relic."

"Gracious prior, pray forgive me, but I have in my possession not just 'some sort of relic', but authentic survivors of the day when Joseph of Arimathea came to Glastonbury after the crucifixion."

"How came you by these extraordinary relics, pardoner?"

"I can say nothing more than they were brought to my attention by a Celtic monk on the far coasts of Cornwall. He expressed guilt at having kept them so long, for he knew they should reside here in Glastonbury. Sadly, I can tell you no more as to how he obtained them, but he did include with them this certificate of authenticity granted by the Holy Father in Rome."

"Well, man, get on with it," the prior said. "What have you brought us?"

Landow took a parcel from a large pocket in his cloak. Breathing a great sigh and moving with the drama of high ceremony, he began to unwrap two vessels from a beautifully embroidered linen cloth. At last, he announced to the prior, "These are they, my lord prior, the original cruets Saint Joseph of Arimethea brought to England from the Holy Land, containing the precious sweat and blood of our Lord Jesus Christ. Having lain hidden away in Cornwall for centuries, I bring them to you to be returned to their rightful place in the Chapel of Saint Joseph within your abbey church," Landow said triumphantly.

Prior Compton was obviously taken aback. There could be no doubt in his mind that the survival of these cruets, which had contained bodily fluids of Christ from the first century after our Lord's death, was extraordinary. Their endorsement of Glastonbury Abbey's historical story would draw pilgrims by the thousands. No wonder Abbot Chinnock sent this pardoner to him, but the prior knew in his heart that he had no basis or background to judge the validity of such relics. He looked closely at the elegant certificate of authenticity signed by Pope Saint Leo the first and dated in the year of our Lord, 445.

"Dear God," the prior thought to himself, "this document alone dates back to the earliest days of the Christian Church in Rome. It must be regarded as significant evidence."

Prior Henry, being a cautious man, acknowledged to the pardoner his appreciation of the importance of these relics. "In behalf of Abbot Chinnock, I am very grateful to you for bringing these cruets to us, Pardoner Landow."

"They are yours for the mere fee of three hundred pounds to cover the expenses of my research on your behalf and the journeys that have been required of me," Landow said very piously.

Prior Henry was forced to swallow. After recovering his breath, he announced to the pardoner, "Do you realise that you are asking a price equal to more than two year's salary for the abbey's lay treasurer?"

"But dear prior, I have brought to you relics worth thousands of pounds of pilgrims' offerings in the years ahead. I daresay there is no way to put a price upon the sacred value these cruets will bring to the abbey's Joseph Chapel. Pilgrims will rejoice to see themselves in the same chamber with them, be able to touch them, or be allowed to pray through them to the suffering Saviour. How can you put a price upon access to such blessing?" The pardoner's face seemed to express an attitude of disbelief hurled against the prior as he began to place the cruets back into their linen wrapping.

"Now, now, Pardoner Landow, let us not be hasty. I can not make this decision without consultation with the chapter. Will you leave these extraordinary relics with me until they can be shown during our chapter meeting on the morrow? After they have been seen by all of our brother monks, the decision of the community will be returned to you with our payment of your expenses."

"I make this effort only for you, my lord prior. You may keep guard over the cruets until the chapter's examination is complete on the morrow. Then, I shall wait no longer. Certainly Wells Cathedral's canons will not refuse them."

* * *

The pardoner had barely left his chamber when Prior Henry called one of his lay servants to him. "I need you to carry this message into the town. Ask to see the Lady Apollonia personally, and deliver it *into her hands*," he emphasised. "No one else must see it, and you are to bring her answer directly back to me. If the Lady is not at home, return the message to me unopened. Do you understand?"

The lay brother nodded as he took the missive from the prior's hand and left his chamber to walk towards the north gate of the abbey. It was not a long walk to Aust House, and when he arrived, he asked for a private interview with the Lady Apollonia to deliver a message to her from the abbey.

Apollonia received him after dismissing the rest of the household from the hall. The lay brother offered his greetings but said little. He placed the prior's message into her hands and then stepped back to wait for her answer.

The prior's message was very brief but obviously urgent:

My Lady Apollonia,

I pray you will allow me to take advantage of our newly established friendship. Could you please call on me within the hour this afternoon? My messenger will return with you or your verbal response to me. I truly need to speak with you soon.

Sincerely in Christ,

Prior Henry Compton"

The Lady read the note through and said to the lay brother, "Pray return my answer to Prior Compton as follows, 'I shall be there as you request, accompanied only by those who serve me.'"

"Aye, my Lady, I shall deliver your response in your words," the lay brother said. Then he bowed to her and left Aust House directly.

* * *

Jeremy was called to the hall to be ready to walk with the Lady and Nan. It was another wet day, so Nan felt compelled to fuss until she was certain that the Lady was protected against the damp.

"It seems a miserable day to be making this walk to the abbey, my Lady. Can it not be put off until later when the sunshine may return?"

"I have no idea why the prior insists upon speaking with me so soon, Nan, but I am confident that he must have good reasons. Let us away, and all will be answered," she added with one of her especially reassuring smiles to Nan.

They walked quickly due to the weather. Apollonia was grateful that Nan had urged her to dress well, and she found herself pulling her rain cloak closely to her body. They finally reached the north gate of the abbey, relieved to be within the protection of its walls. They found themselves taken directly to the chamber where Prior Compton waited for them because their call was expected.

"Ah, my Lady of Aust, you are most gracious to come at such brief notice. I am truly grateful to you and shall always be in your debt. If you will trust me with your promise of secrecy, may I ask you to accompany me alone into the adjoining chamber?"

Apollonia looked to Nan and to Jeremy, and they accepted her implied suggestion that they remain behind. Nan, however, could be seen by Jeremy to be distressed at the strangeness of the prior's request. As Prior Compton escorted the Lady into the adjoining chamber, Nan seemed unable to sit quietly and paced the room until Apollonia returned to them. The Lady's maid could think of no proper reason for this separation. If she could have seen what was set out for Apollonia, she would have been truly amazed.

* * *

"My Lady, I do not wish to take advantage of our acquaintance," the prior told Apollonia in an unusually insecure voice. "You know how I value your intelligence and well-studied convictions. I am being asked to make an extremely costly decision for the abbey, just now in the absence of Abbot Chinnock, and I would be eternally grateful for your opinion."

"Prior Henry, as one who respects you and your friendship with my son's mentor, Sir Walter Heath, you know that I would gladly do anything in my power to help you."

"Then, as my friend, would you please examine these and give me your opinion of them?" When he finished speaking, the prior pulled away the linen covering lying over two very simple metal cruets, each with its narrow neck covered to keep within it some valued liquid.

"Am I to assume that these are relics of some sort?" the Lady asked cautiously.

"They have been brought to me as the original cruets carried to Glastonbury by Saint Joseph of Arimathea. They are said to contain the sweat and blood of our Lord Jesus Christ from the time when His body was removed from the cross."

The prior was a bit taken aback as he could sense hesitation in the Lady's acceptance of the cruets' miraculous survival. Apollonia asked if she would be allowed to examine them more closely. When he nodded his assent, she lifted each of the small pitcher-like containers from the table and looked at it carefully. She lifted the lid of each and sniffed the disgusting odours issuing from the liquid inside them.

"I must tell you, Prior Henry, I feel inadequate to offer any scholarly opinion as to the age of these cruets, the metal from which they are made, or the place of their manufacture. Surely, I can not identify the true nature of their contents. Would you be willing to tell me how you have come by them?"

"I received them today from someone who was sent to my chambers by our own Abbot Chinnock. The abbot is most anxious for Glastonbury to place these miraculous survivors in the Saint Joseph Chapel in the lower level of our Lady Chapel. He is certain they will not only enhance the chapel, they will provide endless possibilities of promoting Saint Joseph's story to pilgrims from all parts of the Christian world."

"Can you tell me from whom you received them?" Apollonia pressed him.

"He is a man of the church, a pardoner by the name of Brandon Landow, my Lady. He tells me that he must be paid for his expenses in recovering these relics from farthest Cornwall and demands the huge sum of three hundred pounds."

At this revelation, Apollonia's facial expression was transformed immediately into one of obvious denial. "I can not judge the manufacture or the date of the cruets, Prior Henry, but I can offer you significant knowledge of the life and behaviours of Brandon Landow. I have been acquainted with him since he was a child, and I know him to be capable of lying, stealing, cheating, and deception."

"My Lady, he has brought with these relics a document verifying their authenticity, signed by Pope Saint Leo the first dated in the year of our Lord, 445."

"I must suggest to you that such documentation can be forged," Apollonia insisted, "and I also know Pardoner Landow to be capable of selling forgeries."

"Then, what are you implying that I do?" the prior asked. "Abbot Chinnock truly wishes to have these relics."

"My suggestion to you is that you must not pay any money to the pardoner. Tell Landow that the abbot would be pleased to receive these cruets from him as the pardoner's personal gift to the abbey."

"My Lady, do you think the pardoner would do such a thing?"

"Brandon Landow is a pardoner motivated by profit, not religious faith or devotion to the church. No, Prior Henry, it is unlikely that he would make such a gift unless he felt it promised pardon to him for attempting to defraud the abbey. You might remind Landow that these so-called relics have such meaning to Glastonbury that they can grace the chapel of Saint Joseph as replicas, not relics."

* * *

On the following day, when the prior presented the cruets for examination to the morning chapter meeting, he allowed the monks to examine them carefully. All of the monks agreed, these relics would surely multiply the number of pilgrims to the abbey. They could be elegantly presented behind an altar in the Saint Joseph chapel with the document signed by Pope Saint Leo the First displayed next to them. Later, after their discussion of the value of the relics, the prior added to his presentation a report on the character of the pardoner who had brought them to Glastonbury yesterday.

"The Lady Apollonia of Aust, sister to the Earl of Marshfield, is currently residing in Glastonbury at the home of her son, Sir Chad. She has seen the cruets and understands their meaning as valued relics to the abbey. She understands their very existence would promote the antiquity of our abbey and significantly increase the number of pilgrims. When I revealed to her the name of the churchman who brought them to us, however, and his exorbitant price for them, she told me that it is typical of Brandon Landow to sell fraudulent relics and forged documentation at covetous profits for himself." At this revelation, the chapter was abuzz at the crime being attempted against them.

Chapter Eleven

The Pardoner's Gift

Brandon Landow was in a state of shock. He had returned to Prior Compton's chamber fully expecting to collect an extraordinary amount of money from the abbey. He was so certain of his anticipated enrichment that he nearly swaggered into the prior's chamber. He could see sitting on the prior's table the combination of cruets next to the beautifully inscribed document signed by an early pope of the Christian Church. Obviously, he thought, the prior was pleased to have it on display and perhaps was working on ideas to present the cruets and papal document dramatically within the Saint Joseph Chapel. Landow's ego nearly swallowed his greed as he could see himself counting the number of coins about to be given him. When the prior spoke, however, he presented a totally unexpected offer.

"On behalf of the chapter of Glastonbury Abbey, pardoner, I am authorised to thank you for bringing these replicas to our attention. I assure you that our chapter will be pleased to receive them as your gift to our Chapel of Saint Joseph."

A bewildered Brandon Landow found himself speechless. "Prior Compton, you can not have...Surely you misunderstood... Who calls these holy relics, 'replicas?'" Landow stumbled dumbly towards the nearest stool and sat next to the table without so much as a by your leave.

"I received a visit from a noble friend to the abbey who told me that she has known you since childhood. She is well informed of your side business of creating 'replica' relics which you attempt to sell at extraordinary profits to yourself," the prior said very calmly.

Landow's face flushed deep red, but he knew immediately to whom the prior was referring. "I had no idea the Lady of Aust was resident in Glastonbury," he moaned. "Have you shown the cruets to her?"

"Indeed, as I am no scholar and she known to be a truly learned woman, I asked for her opinion of them. I also asked our local smith to examine them, and he assured me that they are of recent manufacture. So, the Lady suggested that you may well wish to give them as 'replicas' to our abbey chapel, dedicated to Saint Joseph of Arimathea. We shall acknowledge your gift publicly and press no charges of possible fraudulent behaviour against us."

"Indeed, prior, you have anticipated me. I had every intention of bestowing this gift to Saint Joseph in the name and memory of my blessed mother." Landow was sweating when he stood up from the stool, ready to be gone from this most uncomfortable encounter.

"With our thanks, we shall note your gift and its dedication," the prior said. "We shall also keep this forged document. I have been told by the monks of our scriptoria that the parchment upon which it is written is of recent scraping, but we can surely use it again."

"You are too kind," Landow muttered as he hurried towards the door.

"Benedicite, Pardoner Landow," the prior called after him with a smile.

* * *

It was raining, and the winds were howling when Cunomorus ascended the Tor for the second time. A powerful man, well over six feet tall, the Druid was able to ignore the force of the winds, and he maintained in his memory an exact picture where each of the eggstones was located. Cunomorus knew that before he left Glastonbury, he had to heal the wounds that he had made into the earth. Beginning near the top of the Tor, he found the first of the Tor burrs and knelt to push it aside. He had purposefully chosen the largest of these eggstones, and the first of them was more than three feet in diameter. He rolled it aside and began to extract the sharp dagger of a branch which he had driven into the earth beneath it. He offered his prayers begging forgiveness of the earth goddess, promising at each site that he would restore healing balm to soothe her. The Druid poured crumbled dried manure into the hole, once the stake was removed, to fill it with healing potential for growth as the rain softened the manure and filled the wound left behind.

He repeated this process again and again, all the while engrossed in his prayers and the urgent sense of need to correct a great wrong. He did not notice one of the monks of Saint Michael's who had become aware of his presence and his decidedly strange behaviour. The monk, hiding behind small trees as he moved, followed the Druid from one Tor burr to the next and watched as Cunomorus repeated his ritual. The rains continued, and the winds on the Tor grew stronger. Both of the men became soaked through. But Cunomorus was unaware that he was being watched and could not stop until he had corrected and healed every location where he and his mother had brutally wounded the earth goddess. At last, the Druid was certain that every one of their stabbing branches had been pulled out from the earth and healing manure packed into the wound. He sat down to rest beneath a low shrub for protection while he held his hands into the pouring rain to wash them.

Cunomorus remained seated on the Tor while pausing to rest and cleanse himself. The young monk of Saint Michael's hurried back to the monastery and gathered several of his fellows, telling them only that he believed there was someone on the Tor practicing evil magic against them. The four Christian monks went down to the place where Cunomorus still sat. They came up to him and the first monk made the sign of the cross while shouting aggressively at him, "You will come with us, evil doer. I have watched you call upon the powers of Satanas against us."

Cunomorus raised his right arm in a sign of peace, but the most aggressive of the burley young monks grasped his right arm and pulled it behind his back. There was no doubt the monks were taking him prisoner and began to push him up the hill to the monastery on top of the Tor. The Druid did not fight them. He said nothing and simply waited to see where they were taking him. When they reached the compound around Saint Michael's church, they pushed him into one of the underground storage cellars of the monastery and locked the door over him.

It would have been dark in the cellar, but strips of daylight shone through the openings between wooden slats of the door. At least, the Druid said to himself, he was out of the wind. Cunomorus looked around him and found a small chest storing several large linen altar cloths and candles. He began to strip himself of his wet robes to hang them from various hooks. He took the longest altar cloths from the chest and smiled to himself as he wrapped his body within the embroidered Christian Cross now turned to rest upon his chest. His outermost woollen robe was soaking wet. He knew it would take forever to dry unless he could stretch it for drying inside the cellar. It was white wool and he decided it could serve a purpose while drying. He was able to stretch the entire robe across the length of the door to cover the openings between planks of the door. It blocked the whistling draughts of wind while blowing the wool dry, but not blocking the little sunlight that could filter through the white wool.

Cunomorus was very good at lighting fires and was able to ignite a number of the candles just to bring small flames of light to the depths of the cellar where it was warmer for him to sit. As nearly as he could tell, he was left in the cellar throughout the late afternoon and the nighttime hours.

The Druid expected that the monks would come to tell him what they planned to do with him when the first light of morning came. No one came, and he remained seated in the cellar while the sun rose up to the top of the Tor.

Fortunately, the new day was bright and warmed by the summer sun in spite of the constant winds. Cunomorus told himself he would continue to focus upon drying his robes so as to be properly dressed whenever the young monks came to tell him his future.

Two of them opened the door roughly holding large pitchforks threateningly towards him when they finally unlocked the cellar, A third monk placed a loaf of bread and a jug of ale into his space. Then, they locked the door once again and went away.

* * *

The leader of Saint Michael's sent a messenger to their mother house, the abbey in Glastonbury. He reported to the prior that they believed they had captured a devil worshipper in the act of practising demonic magic against them on the sides of the Tor. In truth, the monks did not know what to do with their captive and they knew they must call in help from the abbey. Until they received some word from Prior Compton, they continued to keep Cunomorus locked in the cellar. Slowly the Druid's garments dried, and as he was fed basic foods twice each day, he found himself spending most of his time in meditation and prayer to the earth goddess and the gods of the Tor streams. Cunomorus promised to accept punishment for the wrongs he had done and begged their blessings that he might be allowed to return to Ireland.

* * *

Brandon Landow had spent the last two days in a state of drunken stupor. He was deflated and angry at his loss of significant wealth in Glastonbury. He simply wandered from one drinking establishment to another, continuing to drink until they closed or threw him out because of his foul language. Then he would stagger back to his accommodation at The Pilgrims Inn. On this night, when he attempted to go to the inn, he was refused entry because of his drunken rowdiness. With nowhere else to go, he wandered back to the Market Place where he was approached by a woman whom he assumed to be a whore. She was accompanied by a powerful male companion who was obviously her protection.

Landow tried to walk away from her, but he realised that he had no place to hide. She walked up to him and told him to stop. "I want nothing to do with you, woman," he shouted. "I do not require your services, and I have no reason to remain in this wretched town."

"Are you a man of the church?" she asked.

"Of course, bitch. I am Brandon Landow, Pardoner of Holy Church."

At the use of his word "bitch", the male with her seized Landow by the neck and turned him round to face her. "Ye must ne'er address Mistress Calevera so. Oi'll kill ye for less."

Landow was a coward of the first magnitude and began to weep. "Pray, Mistress Calevera, forgive me. I meant no harm. I am drunk and have been thrown out of the inn."

"Then, pardoner, you shall come home with us," she said.

"Gramercy, I pray you will forgive me, but I will simply sleep here on the square until morning. You see, it is not chilly. We are now entering the first days of August and this summer's days have been warm."

The more strongly Wort pushed him to follow her, the more Landow objected. Before he knew what was happening, the pardoner had been forced to turn onto Archers Way and follow the woman into the house where she was quite obviously at home and in charge.

"This is very kind of you, Mistress Calevera," Landow began to object as soon as they entered the main hall of the house, "but I truly do not mind sleeping rough this night."

The woman had Wort push him onto a stool next to the table dormant. She had said little to him up to this point but now began to press her questions while Wort hovered over him. "You told me that you are a man of the church, is that correct?"

"Yes, mistress, I am Brandon Landow, Pardoner of Holy Church. I am licenced to sell papal indulgences from the papacy's bottomless resource of spiritual capital to achieve remission of the temporal punishment of purgatory by drawing upon the Treasury of Merit accumulated by Christ's superabundantly meritorious sacrifice on the cross and the virtues and penances of the saints," Landow recited word for word.

"Hmmm," the woman muttered, "it is not precisely what I had in mind. But tell me, in your ministry as pardoner, are you invited into the homes of local people?"

"Aaaah, well, mistress, it is not always necessary...," he began to say but then noticed her eyes narrow as if she had decided his services were not the ones she wanted. "Of course, I do go into people's homes to deliver pardons, prayers, or holy relics."

"Would you be invited into a wealthy merchant or nobleman's home?" she pressed him.

"Oh, yes, surely, but can you tell me more exactly how I could help you?" Landow was sweating profusely now and only wished that he could get out of this building and leave Glastonbury by the quickest route possible.

"Could you achieve your ministry in a grand town home such as Aust House?" she asked tentatively.

"Indeed, mistress, I am well known to the Lady of Aust and her family," Landow exaggerated. "I have been her guest in several of her homes."

"Then, I shall have an errand for you on the morrow," she said simply. "For now, Wort will show you to your bed. You will sleep here tonight. I need your drunken mind to return to sober clarity and will give you my instructions in the morning."

Wort stood and pulled Landow up by his arm to lead him to another level of the house. Landow was terrified by this massive creature. The effects of his excessive drinking had nearly been worn away by fear.

"Hold, mistress, I assure you I will return in the morning. You must not trouble yourself on my behalf this night." His whining was nearly more than she could tolerate, so Calevera simply gestured to Wort who dragged Landow up the stairs and locked him into a chamber.

* * *

Early the following morning, Wort opened the door to his chamber and pulled Landow by the arm back down the stairs into the hall. The pardoner was desperately alert in spite of not having slept a wink. Calevera greeted him and urged him to sit with her to break their fast. Landow was hungry but so anxious to be away from this place that he tried to refuse eating and insisted that he must leave.

"No," she said definitively to him, "you will accomplish a task for me before I can allow you to leave Glastonbury."

"Anything, anything, I shall be happy to be of service to you," Landow whimpered.

"Eat and I shall instruct you, pardoner."

Landow did as he was told, and the food was obviously very well prepared, even if he had to struggle to swallow it.

"You will call upon the Lady of Aust this morning and beg her to grant you her hospitality for the night ahead. I care not how you explain your visit, but whilst you are there, I require you to memorise the layout of the household, as much of it as you can see, upper floors as well as downstairs. You will take one of my henchmen as your servant. He will say nothing but will guarantee that you return to me tomorrow afternoon."

* * *

As Landow left Calevera's house and began to walk back to the High Street, he knew that he was not experiencing any sort of liberation. He may have escaped from her home, but her young henchman, Crewyn, watched him constantly with a significant warning in his eyes and a dagger at his belt. Landow did not know where Aust House was located, but Crewyn did. The walk to Bove Town Road was not a lengthy one, and Landow desperately wished it was considerably farther. He did not know where to begin, how he should explain this call upon the Lady, or how he could ask her for hospitality through the night.

When Crewyn walked with him towards the main entrance to Sir Chad's home, Landow literally tried to drag his feet but was physically pushed into position to ring the entrance bell. The door was answered by the steward, John of Glastonbury, and of course neither he nor Landow knew the other. Landow simply asked him to be announced as Brandon Landow, Pardoner of Holy Church, wishing to call upon the Lady Apollonia of Aust.

Steward John led Landow and his servant into the hall where the Lady and Nan were seated. As soon as Nan could see Landow was calling upon them, she expressed an automatic gasp of angry recognition.

"My Lady of Aust, Brandon Landow, Pardoner of Holy Church, wishes to call upon you," Steward John announced.

Apollonia was not a woman to be impolite with anyone, and as soon as she recognised their caller, she spoke to him. "Ah, yes, Brandon," addressing him by his childhood name as she always did. "I have heard that you are in Glastonbury. No doubt you have come to ask something of me. Out with it. What do you want me to do for you?"

Landow made a low bow before her and rose to greet her with an expression of how glad he was to see her. "My Lady Apollonia, it is my pleasure to be in your presence again. Always one with a grand sense of humour, you tease me, of course, all the while you know that I would never miss an opportunity to call upon you. I only learned of your presence in Glastonbury this week."

"Indeed, Brandon," the Lady said, "my friend, the abbey prior, has told me that you have come to Glastonbury to make a significant gift to the Chapel of Saint Joseph of Arimathea. Is it so?"

"Ah, yes, my Lady, Prior Compton expressed his appreciation of my gift of replicas of the cruets Saint Joseph brought to Glastonbury. He is already making preparations to place them above the centre of the altar of the Joseph chapel. The prior is certain that they will enhance the importance of the chapel to pilgrims." Landow spoke without obvious bitterness in his voice, but the Lady could see that his "gift" had been given at cross purposes to his original intent.

"Then, not to put too fine a point on it, Brandon, why have you really come to call upon me?" Landow knew that she always suspected him of ulterior motives, and of course, this was reliably the case.

"As you have granted me hospitality in the past, my Lady, I have come to beg to be allowed to remain with you one night only. My servant, Crewyn, and I have discovered there to be 'no room at the inn', so to speak. We shall remain quietly out of the way until we leave early on the morrow. What say you? Can you help us in this way?"

Apollonia could hear Nan grumbling her disapproval under her breath. The Lady knew that she had been the cause of Brandon's exposure as an attempted fraud at the abbey. She also knew that it was because of her intervention that Brandon had lost a significant amount of money.

"I dare say we can put you and your servant up for one night, Brandon. It will not be luxurious, but you will find space in my son's servants quarter."

"Oh, how full of grace and goodness you are, my Lady," Brandon seemed to simper. "Crewyn and I are truly grateful to you for your kindness." In all the years the Lady had known him, the pardoner had never seemed more ingratiating.

* * *

In the evening after dinner was finished in the hall and Brother William dismissed the household with prayer, John showed Landow and his servant to the servants' bedchamber. Apollonia called Chad's manservant, Jeremy, to her side before anyone else in the household had been dismissed. The Lady spoke with Jeremy very frankly and with a sense of warning in her voice, "You must note these two guests that I have allowed to lodge with us this night, Jeremy. I am suspicious of their purpose in being here. Will you take counsel with Steward John to put all of our servants on their guard throughout this night? Brandon Landow is not dangerous, but he is completely untrustworthy. I pray you will alert everyone against any suspicious behaviour. If anything happens to cause concern during the night, call me at once."

No one in the Aust household slept well that night. Past midnight in the earliest hour of the morning, Landow sat up in his bed and began to look around the chamber where the servants slept. He had only moved slightly, as if to stand up, when Paul Medford lifted his head to question his purpose. "May I help you, Pardoner Landow? Do you wish to go somewhere?" he asked politely.

"Ah, no, lad, I was merely looking for somewhere to relieve myself."

Paul rose from his bed and quietly pointed out two chamber pots, one at each end of the long room. He remained sitting on his bed until he could see the pardoner return to his cot.

Several hours later, just before dawn's first light, the pardoner's supposed servant, Crewyn, silently slipped from his cot, and managed to leave through the chamber door. He had no more than entered the hallway leading towards the stairs when Jeremy approached him with a lighted candle in his hand. "How may I help you, Crewyn?" He questioned their guest politely but with a strength of purpose which caused the servant to return to his bed. "Pray forgive me, sir, Oi be prone to occasional sleepwalkin."

At sunrise, both Landow and his servant, Crewyn, appeared in the kitchen, ready to move on in their journey, they said. They were hospitably given food to break their fast and then accompanied to leave through the back entrance to Aust House. Landow explained that they must move on to the Glastonbury stables to collect their mounts. They were wished a pleasant journey but never left unaccompanied until they were beyond the garden wall of Aust House and began to walk down Bove Town Road back into the town. Even then, John and Jeremy continued to observe them until they were well out of sight.

When Landow and Crewyn walked back into the house where Calevera awaited them, she was keen to hear all that they had learned about the interior of Aust House. Landow said little. "We saw the main floor, great hall and the servants' bedchamber, nothing else."

Crewyn simply shrugged his shoulders. "We were ne'er allowed to look at anythin but the all and the servants' chamber. Oi swear, nobody in the ouse sleeps."

Chapter Twelve

Prior Compton's Dilemma

It was mid-August when a troubling message came to Prior Compton from the monks of Saint Michael's Monastery at the top of Glastonbury Tor. They had captured a man on the Tor who they were certain was practising black magic against them. He was a most unusual person, however, surely not a peasant but a grand gentleman who insisted that he was a visitor to Glastonbury from Ireland. The monks told the prior that they were keeping this man locked in a storage cellar because there was no other accommodation in the monastery at the top of the Tor. As a daughter house of the abbey, they told the prior that they needed instruction. "What should we do with this man?"

Prior Compton had not the slightest idea what should be done, but he knew he must do something just to protect the mother house against a significant wrong which may have been committed. A devoted churchman, the prior accepted his leadership role in the abbey willingly. "But why, Lord, in Your Mercy," he prayed earnestly, "can you not send me simple problems of disobedience or blatant immorality?"

It was an extraordinary experience for the prior when the monks of Saint Michael's brought Cunomorus to him. The prior found standing before him in his chamber not a low-born fellow at all. Instead, the stately gentleman was richly dressed, tall, well built, and handsomely impressive. His face was framed in a massive head of blonde hair, beneath his fashionable hat. Blonde eyebrows half-circled his dark brown eyes, and his smile of greeting was that of a highly educated gentleman.

The prior saw immediately that he must deal with this gentleman from Ireland respectfully. There could be no doubt that he was of the nobility and well aware of his station in life. He dismissed the monks from Saint Michael's and then turned to ask the man his name. "I am

Henry Compton, prior of Glastonbury Abbey, and I should like to know how I may address you, sir?"

"Greetings, Prior Compton, my name is Cunomorus Amairogen, but as my name is frequently difficult for Englishmen to pronounce, please call me Maurice. I have come from Ireland where I serve as the chief Seer and Brehon to Prince O'Donnell of the Kingdom of Tyrconnell. You will find the rest of my household residing at Grove Cottage Farm which I have let from the abbey whilst I visit in Somerset."

At this point, the prior knew he was well beyond his depth. "I do not understand why we of the abbey have been unaware of your presence in our country, Lord Maurice. I sincerely apologise for the ignorance of our monks of Saint Michael's, but they were overwhelmed when witnessing your behaviour on the Tor."

"I was forced to come quickly to Glastonbury on family matters where my mother became seriously ill." Cunomorus stretched the truth to meet current needs, but he went on in the hope of bringing closure to this adventure. "She has since died, and I would be grateful for your assistance to return to Grove Cottage so that I may gather my household and return to my country."

"I hope you will accept the hospitality of the abbey this night. On the morrow, we shall do all that we can to help you return to Grove Cottage Farm. May I ask why you were seen in the pouring rain planting things on the Tor?"

Cunomorus began to laugh, as if to downplay a misinterpretation of his actions. "Indeed, I see at last why my behaviour appeared so very suspicious to the monks of Saint Michael's. I promise you as a gentleman, Prior Compton, I was not planting anything, evil or otherwise, in the thunderstorm. I had dismounted to search for shelter in the pouring rain and lost hold of my horse. I fell to the ground trying to gain cover under the low scrub of the Tor. I respect the Tor, prior, and am fully aware of its ancient meaning in Celtic History."

Prior Henry breathed a sigh of relief. "Ah, it was an obvious misunderstanding. You must forgive our young monks of Saint Michael's, Lord Maurice," he said, shaking his head. "They have been distressed by a recent earthquake on the Tor, and I fear their imaginations must have overcome their reason."

"We shall think no more of it," Cunomorus told him. "I shall happily accept your hospitality this night and be gone on the morrow."

"Then, I hope you will join me for dinner this evening," the prior said.

"With my thanks, if I may first be allowed to retire to my chamber to tidy a bit before dinner?"

"Pray do, sir, for I plan to invite a noble English Lady to join us this evening. She is a recent friend to me whom I know would *not* be pleased to learn that I allowed you to return to your country without making her acquaintance." Prior Henry was smiling, hopefully pleased that he had been able to find a way to correct this disastrous social and possibly political affront that had been done to a foreign guest.

* * *

Apollonia was surprised once again to receive a brief but urgent invitation on very short notice from the prior. "This is unusual, Nan. Prior Henry has just invited us to dinner this evening to meet with a high born minister from the Kingdom of Tyrconnell. It is short notice, but I have never met anyone from Ireland. I should enjoy such an opportunity. I shall speak for myself on this occasion, Nan, but I hope the gentleman speaks Latin at least, for I have no competency in Gaelic."

"Aye, my Lady, I must be silent if either is the case," Nan told her. "Let me call Brother William. He and Jeremy will accompany us."

The party from Aust House gathered in the hall after the Lady dressed and then began their stroll to the abbey. The summer evening was still light after sundown and the evening walk seemed especially pleasant. Apollonia and her servants were shown into Prior Compton's chambers within the abbey walls. They found it already brightly lit and welcoming as if a major event had been planned. When the Lady and her party were led into the prior's hall, however, she could see immediately that they were the only guests beyond one tall, distinguished man who stood beside the prior.

"Ah, my Lady of Aust," the prior called to her, "pray do come hence and meet our guest from across the Irish Sea."

Apollonia walked to join their host with her affinity at either side. Prior Compton was determined to make their small party into a truly memorable one. "Allow me to present to you, dear Lady Apollonia of Aust, our guest. This is Cunomorus Amairogen, the chief Seer and Brehon to King O'Donnell of Tyrconnell."

Apollonia found it hard to believe that this important visitor should be received with so little ceremony, but she was pleased to be part of the occasion. Their host was speaking in English. She responded to the honoured guest in English as well.

"I am pleased to meet you, Lord Cunomorus. Allow me to welcome you to Somersetshire, especially on such a glorious summer's evening."

"My Lady, it is my pleasure," Cunomorus said as he bowed over her hand, then led her to the table.

It seemed to Apollonia that the prior was more than willing to allow her to lead the conversation with their guest. In fact, Prior Henry seemed to prefer to listen.

"I am impressed by your titles, Lord Cunomorus," she told their guest. "To be the official Seer of the King of Tyrconnell, I assume refers to your valued gifts of insight as an advisor. Brehon, I believe, designates your position as judge. Could you help us better understand what you do?"

"My Lady, you have summed up my roles in a nutshell, I believe the English say. I serve my prince of Tyrconnell as his counsel and the chief judge in his courts."

Cunomorus enjoyed being with this noble lady. She was considerably older than he, nearer to his mother's age, he thought. She was slim, tall, and stately and made no attempt to hide what some would say was her unfeminine height. It was her face which captured Cunomorus' attention, however. The Lady's fair skin was elegantly unlined and her large blue-grey eyes expressed keen insight and intellectual achievement. Most of all, he admired her lovely mouth with cherry lips framing her perfect teeth.

"These are positions of importance in any royal court, my lord," the Lady went on. "How is it that you have come to Glastonbury?"

"I was released from my duties to attend to serious family matters. My mother was, as I have told the prior, seriously ill and has since died." Cunomorus did not wish to express falsehoods to the Lady, but he very carefully sculpted the truth.

"Pray, accept my sincere sympathy in your loss. I will offer my prayers for her soul, Lord Cunomorus. As the prior will surely agree, we would have preferred to give you a proper welcome to Glastonbury. I personally hope that you might remain as our guest for a longer while." Apollonia's curiosity was fired by this aristocratic Irish visitor to England, and she felt no hesitation to tell him so.

"My Lady, your grace and kindness are beyond expectation. If Prior Compton will enable me to return to Grove Cottage Farm to make arrangements for our return to Tyrconnell, I would be glad to return to Glastonbury town to call upon you before we must depart."

"All of Aust household will be pleased to welcome you at your convenience, Lord Cunomorus," Apollonia told him sincerely. Her purpose was not only to see him again, she hoped to be able to extend her conversation with this unusual visitor. The Lady described the location of her son's home within the town and told Cunomorus that she would look forward to hearing from him soon.

* * *

A message came to Aust household three days later that the Lord Cunomorus would return to Glastonbury within the week. Apollonia sent a return messenger to Grove Cottage Farm inviting him to be her guest. From that time forward, Aust household grew to a pitch of excitement. Everyone was involved in preparations for the equivalent of a state dinner on Friday evening as well as preparing a chamber for the great lord to rest through the night before his departure.

The Lady and Nan were impressed by his simplicity when the Lord Cunomorus appeared at their door alone. He came with no personal servant or any man servant who had accompanied him to England. There could be no doubt that he was a proud man of noble descent but one who exchanged friendly greetings with all members of her household. Cunomorus expressed his appreciation for the Lady's hospitality when they gathered in the great hall. The Lady Apollonia extended her hand to him and walked with him to the head table. She seated him beside her and they were joined by Prior Compton, the mayor of Glastonbury, her almoner, Brother William, Steward John, and the priest of Saint John the Baptist Church. The rest of the Aust

House affinity was seated in lower seating levels at the surrounding tables. Cunomorus could not help smiling at his singularity within this obviously Christian gathering, but in true chivalry, he acknowledged to himself that hospitality was a blessed gift, regardless of the religion of the giver.

Apollonia had hired musicians to play for them throughout the evening. Their gentle tones of viol, harp, and flute seemed to enhance the conversation which continued brilliantly round the table. Everyone wanted to express a Glastonbury welcome to their guest.

The prior opened conversation by speaking of the great antiquity of the abbey. Brother William, of course, was keenly aware of Glastonbury's ancient formation as a town built around the abbey walls. Cunomorus surprised them all by describing the far greater antiquity of the communities that had been built by the Celts, long pre-dating the coming of Christianity. Apollonia noted that King O'Donnell's Seer was more than just a political adviser. He was a significant historical scholar who could describe a history of Somerset unknown to any of them.

Late in the evening after the other guests and the musicians had gone, Apollonia, with Nan and William, sat in front of the fireplace with the Lord Cunomorus before retiring. The Lady was still trying to organise her thoughts about their extraordinary guest. She continued to be impressed by his intellect and widely informed knowledge of Britain. Quietly looking towards him, she finally asked a question which had been forming in her mind throughout the evening.

"I understand that you may be unable to reveal to us your true purpose in coming to Glastonbury, Lord Cunomorus. I am especially grateful for your willingness to share your extraordinary insights into the culture of the ancient Celts with us. It has made my time in Glastonbury far more meaningful. May I hope that you will be willing to extend our friendship after you have returned to Tyrconnell? I should be grateful to hear from you once you are home."

"My Lady," he said with sincere feeling, "I recognise you as a woman of striking intellectual curiosity and one who possesses insight beyond many. It has been my pleasure to know you. Indeed, you have made my visit to England an unforgettable one. I shall look forward to corresponding with you after I have returned."

Cunomorus smiled to himself as he spoke with her, for he was aware that Apollonia had just told him that she knew he must have had more than family reasons for his activities here that he did not wish to share. He bowed to kiss her hand as they bid each other good night, but he promised himself, "When I have returned to Tyrconnell, I shall tell her all and will await her comments with interest."

* * *

Later that month, Apollonia was pleased to have her son, Chad, and his good friend, Sir Walter, return to Glastonbury for a brief visit. On this occasion, she was immediately aware of a tension in their manner. It was obvious from their demeanour that all was not well in the Court of King Richard.

Chad made a point to tell her why he was mightily disturbed by the king's recent actions while Walter remained quietly concerned and said little.

"Earlier this month, Mamam, the king deceptively held a feast to which he invited his royal uncle, the duke of Gloucester as well as the earls of Arundel and Warwick and others. Several refused to attend, for they were suspicious of the king's true motives. The duke was ill and begged to be excused. As soon as the meal was over, the king had the Earl of Warwick arrested and taken away. That was not all, however," Chad continued fretfully. "The king has since had the Earl of Arundel arrested and personally took the Duke of Gloucester into royal custody from his castle at Pleshy. Dear God, Mamam, the court is full of nothing other than talk of our King Richard fulfilling a long-desired hope to revenge himself upon the Lords Appellant."

Apollonia was stunned by Chad's news and could think of nothing to say at first.

"We do not wish to frighten you, my Lady," Walter told her, "but Chad and I feel that you as a noblewoman must be forewarned. No one knows what will come of this. Some say that King Richard is merely trying to show the German Electors that he should be made their emperor because he is able to demonstrate royal sovereignty over all of his subjects, no matter how mighty they may seem to outsiders. Others in the court speculate that the king only seeks to demonstrate his royal power and then will release the prisoners. For now, the king has summoned a parliament at London in September where all of his prisoners will be put on trial."

"Mamam, I fear for the king's person. His detachment from the world seems a self-absorbing sickness within him."

"Oh, my dears, this is frightening news indeed, yet I must be aware of it. Gramercy, Chad, you know that I am always grateful for your willingness to keep me informed of events at court. My thanks to you as well, Walter. I daresay we shall know more at summer's end. The portents of these arrests may foreshadow calamitous events. I, for one, do not wish to speculate. King Richard is my sovereign lord, and I owe to him my loyalty and obedience. Gloucester, Warwick, and Arundel were leaders of the party that had Richard's favourite ministers dismissed and executed more than ten years ago. I pray God that the king is not seeking revenge for them. Reprisal can not motivate positive rule. I have heard some say that our king seems to declare only his kingship, not his responsibility to his people."

* * *

Near the end of summer, the Lady's steward, Giles Digby, and his servant, Garrick, returned to Glastonbury. Giles was pleased with their West Country journey largely because the Lady's woollen sales had reached new heights. In addition, he was truly pleased to bring an excellent report of the last year's profits as well as positive anticipation of 1398. When he presented his reports, summaries, and totals for her inspection, Giles was obviously pleased with them all.

"You bring such good news, Giles. I must thank you again this year for your excellent managing skills. In spite of the increased wool duties granted to King Richard for life, the success of English wool sales abroad continues to grow, and local consumption has never diminished. This past year we were doubly blessed by good weather and lack of disease, and you encourage me to anticipate another profitable year ahead. I am daily grateful to God but must also thank Him for you. Well done, my good and faithful steward."

Giles chest seemed to expand as the smile on his face spread. The Lady's praise was welcome and valued by him. Giles knew that the Lady had several private points of inquiry to discuss with him, and he was invited to her solar where they could speak alone. After the door was closed and both were seated near the window seat, Giles took from his pouch a letter to the Lady from her brother, Ferdinand.

"Carrick and I were received most hospitably by his lordship," Giles told her as he handed it to her. "The Lord Ferdinand asked me to bring this letter to you when we returned to Glastonbury."

"Gramercy, Giles, I look forward to reading it, but may I ask you to share with me what you learned from my brother?"

"My Lady, Lord Ferdinand told me very simply that he was acquainted with the family of the monk called James of Glastonbury since his childhood. Young James was the son of one of the tenants on Lord Ferdinand's manor of Marshfield. As James was a bright and promising young lad, your brother was instrumental in encouraging James' education and eventually making it possible that he be sent to Oxford."

"That is good news, Giles," Apollonia nodded. "Ferdinand has little personal interest in scholarship, but even he knows the wisdom of investing in the education of young people on his manors."

"Lord Ferdinand's response to your questions regarding Brother Johanus was a bit more complicated, however, my Lady."

"How so, Giles? Does my brother have any reason to be suspicious of the character of Glastonbury's anchorite?"

"I do not think Lord Ferdinand is suspicious of Brother Johanus, my Lady, but he has learned some troubling aspects of someone in the family of the anchorite. I believe he has described these in more detail in his letter."

"Does my brother know where the anchorite originally came from?"

"Oh, yes, my Lady. He says that Brother Johanus came originally from Bristol," Giles told her. "No one knows precisely how he made his way to Kingswood Abbey. Once there, the good brother so impressed Kingswood's abbot of his sanctity and scholarship that the abbot encouraged him to continue his ministry by becoming an anchorite. Kingswood's abbot was responsible for Johanus' attachment to Saint John the Baptist Church. It was he who introduced him to Glastonbury Abbey's monk, Brother Parker."

At the end of their conversation, Giles stood to leave the Lady's solar with a happy smile still filling his face. He enjoyed bringing good news to his Lady because he knew that his work as her steward and overseer made a significant contribution to the success of her woollen concerns. Perhaps it was a bit of the boy still living in him, but Giles was grateful for her praise because he knew that he deserved it. He bid her good morning and quietly left her presence as she began to read the letter he had brought from her brother.

Ferdinand began as he normally addressed her in the diminutive to express his superiority as her elder brother:

Dear Polly,

Glastonbury is blessed to have the presence of Johanus the Anchorite within the town. Abbot Theodore does not miss an opportunity to comment on the sincere devotion of Johanus to his faith and his desire to serve God. The abbot told me that Johanus was already a priest when he fled to Kingswood to give his life to Christ more fully. However, Johanus found that he was unfulfilled being a monk. He needed to have contact with community to serve his fellow humans. That is why Abbot Theodore sent him to Glastonbury to become an anchorite and recommended him to the priest of Saint John the Baptist Church. No one knows details, but earlier in his life whilst still living in Bristol, Johanus as a priest was thrown out of his parish church because of accusations of witchcraft against some member of his family.

Your loving brother, Ferdinand

Chapter Thirteen

September Trials

Brandon Landow remained in Glastonbury until September, far longer than he had expected. He could not claim three hundred pounds of increased wealth, but his earnings from the sale of indulgences were moderately successful. Several people in the town were encouraged by Calevera to come to him seeking pardon. A number of the wealthier merchants, once they learned of his being in Glastonbury, invited him to their homes above their shops to buy indulgences, some in exorbitant numbers of years. Landow would lick his lips as he left each place, counting his money and revelling in the shameful secrets confessed to him. Many of them involved activity at the whorehouse on Wells Road owned by a woman called Faith Morgan. Landow could hardly keep himself from bursting into laughter when one or another of the merchants would confess to visiting Faith's girls.

The pardoner especially enjoyed the confession of one of Glastonbury's most upright men, the mayor's justice of the peace. The man and his wife lived together above the butcher shop on the High Street but for the past few years had shared no marital relations. The wife insisted that as a mother of five grown children, she had done her duty to her husband.

"Great God in heaven, Pardoner Landow, how can one express his manhood without being given some hope of sexual joining? My wife's breasts still excite me, but she will not let me touch her. She is as cold as the Devil's bum, but, Chara, one of Faith's girls, lets me put my fingers where'er I want. Better yet, she ne'er stops me holding her breasts. She even puts one into my mouth and lets me suck on her till I come."

Landow, who always preferred the company of men, suppressed the disgust that he felt in merely imagining this description of such copulation. He found it easy to respond to the magistrate and hypocritically called down judgement upon the man's struggle to remain faithful. The man insisted that he loved his wife and did not wish to leave her.

"But, sir," the pardoner told him self-righteously, "you have broken one of the Ten Commandments of our Lord: 'Thou shalt not commit adultery.' Do you know the punishment for committing a mortal sin?"

"Surely, you can help me." The man was nearly reduced to tears. "Can I not buy pardon? Tell me what I must do."

"It was so easy," Landow chuckled each time he thought of it. He had been paid fifty pounds by the Justice of the Peace, a huge sum, to buy an indulgence for ten thousand years remission of temporal punishment in purgatory. "So, with many thanks to Faith, a satisfying visit to Chara, and a generous payoff for me, our local magistrate is enabled to visit his favourite prostitute when he wishes and sleep in peace every night."

* * *

Landow had not the slightest trouble sleeping once he had been allowed to return to the Pilgrims Inn. He continued to feel uneasy about his grudging but on-going relationship with Calevera and her henchman, Wort. They had not demanded more of him, but he found they were frequently nearby, noting his movements in the town. Calevera posed as the begging mother with a drugged, sleeping baby and Wort stood guard. They often asked him if he had returned to Aust House.

The pardoner was grateful not to have reason to encounter the Lady Apollonia again. He simply wanted to make easy money and then clear out of Glastonbury as soon as his purse was full. He would learn, however, that Calevera had other plans for him.

In the afternoon, Landow could sense that days were beginning to grow shorter. He would best be moving south soon. Still, Glastonbury had proven to be a reasonably profitable visit for him. He was pleased with himself as he left the Draper's Shop. His smile ceased immediately when he encountered Wort waiting for him on the street outside the shop.

"Mistress Calevera wants ya," Wort told him, and to be certain he took Landow's arm and pushed him along the High Street towards the turning.

"You must beg Mistress Calevera's pardon for me, Wort," Landow insisted. "I am leaving Glastonbury within the hour," Landow lied. "I have commitments in Wells and must be on my way before sunset."

"Calevera wants ya," the henchman repeated more forcefully and continued to push Landow towards her dwelling.

When they entered the house on Archers Way, the pardoner found Calevera seated behind the table dormant in the hall.

"Ah, yes, pardoner," she said in welcome. "I am glad you have come, for I have a job for you."

"Pray, forgive me, Calevera," Landow whined. "You know that I would gladly serve you in any way, but I must leave Glastonbury within the hour."

"No, you shan't," she cut him off. "You will first fulfill your role as a dedicated pardoner according to my instructions. When you have completed the task I wish of you, then you may leave Glastonbury."

Several rough looking men stood within her hall. No one touched Landow, but the gang standing round and the mere presence of Wort, his powerful arms crossed over his breast, was enough to terrify the pardoner into total submission.

"How may I serve you, Mistress?" Landow asked meekly.

"This is where you will find Glastonbury's most successful house of prostitution," she said as she handed him a small piece of re-used parchment. You will go there and ask to be received by the owner. Her name is Faith Morgan, and she is expecting you."

* * *

If Landow could have had his way, he would have left Glastonbury immediately. Wort remained at his side, however, and led him back to the High Street. Calevera's henchman was taking the pardoner to a house on the far side of Wells Road. It was a significant stroll, but all along the way, Landow could find no hope of diversion, no avenue of escape, no chance for him to get away.

They approached the house, and Landow could see that it was sizeable, built with many rooms on several floors. They went inside and walked into the main hall. Landow was immediately aware that it was filled with women. The pardoner hesitated. He knew he did not want to be here. Still, Wort pushed him into the hall, and one female who seemed to be in charge came towards them and began to stroke his cheek.

"Nay, Flora, this be business," Wort said, pushing her off. The pardoner's reaction was to take refuge behind Wort.

"Well, it be my business, Luv," she said to Calevera's servant.

"Back off, woman," Wort shouted at her. "Calevera sends us to meet Faith."

Flora turned away in a huff and walked out of the hall. She was not gone long, came back, and told Landow to follow her.

Now, Landow did not wish to lose Wort's protection and said as much. "Surely, Wort, you will not leave me here, alone, with all these women?"

"Flora will take ya to Faith. That is what the mistress said ya must and ya will do it," the henchman said threateningly.

Women on various sides of the hall cast suggestive smiles towards him, made filthy gestures, and sang dirty little ditties at him. Landow was at least relieved to walk out from the hall and be led up a flight of stairs by Flora. The pardoner saw nothing inviting about this place. He looked frantically as he walked, longing to find any door to escape especially now that Wort was gone.

When he walked into the solar, the pardoner was taken aback by its luxurious decoration. Yet, the solar seemed simple by comparison as they continued into a bedchamber where a large old woman sat upon a gilded bed, framed with hangings of silk and velvet. Everything in the bedchamber was gilded, painted, or covered in luxurious fabrics. The floor was tiled as if it belonged to a nobleman's family. The draperies at the windows were made of imported fabrics from the East. Landow had never seen such an elegant place in his life.

"Are you the pardoner?" a husky voice called from the bed.

"I am Brandon Landow, the pardoner, mistress," he said in a trembling voice.

"Speak up man. Calevera said that you would be coming to me this day. I have a task for you, and it must be done soon."

"Anything at all, mistress. How may I serve you?" Landow cringed before her.

"You will create indulgences of twenty thousand years for me and for each of my girls."

"Mistress, I am Brandon Landow, *quaestores* of the Holy Church. What you ask is unheard of. In each case, there must be personal confession of your sins, repentance, and absolution. Do you and all your girls plan to transform your lives from that of mortal sin to that of nun-like purity in all your living?"

The husky voice roared with laughter as suddenly a forceful woman, more than a foot taller than Landow, slipped off the bed and came towards him.

"I am Faith Morgan, and I run the richest whorehouse in all of Glastonbury. If you want to remain in Calevera's favour, pardoner, you will do as I say."

Landow stopped speaking immediately and stared at this giant of a woman.

Faith moved closer until she towered above him. "I say that you are in no position to judge me or my girls. We will do whatever you require of us, and then you will grant us indulgences. I want the full remission of our temporal punishment for twenty thousand years each."

"Mistress Faith, the church requires that I can only do that if each of you makes a confession and receives absolution," Landow whimpered.

"Then we shall start straightaway." Within minutes, after ringing a bell next to her bed, Flora reappeared and Faith gave her specific instructions. "Have the girls, when they are free from other 'commitments', be ready to meet with the pardoner in the corner of the hall. They should be prepared to make their confession and receive absolution. Pardoner Landow will be with them shortly."

Flora left once again and Faith pulled Landow to sit near her table. Then she knelt beside him, bowed her head, and began to speak, "Forgive me, Father, for I have sinned." The pardoner seemed stunned into silence and simply sat across the table from her. The description of sexual activity that was being recited before him was beyond belief. When at last Faith finished confessing, Landow automatically made the sign of the cross over her. She stood up again. "Now, you are to go down to the hall and hear the confessions of the other fourteen girls. Then, you will complete the certificates of indulgence for each of us, and I shall pay you in full."

In all his days, Landow had never worked in this way before. He soon felt benumbed by the girls' stories of extraordinary sexual demands made upon them by the men who bought their services. To his credit, however, Landow heard every confession and then offered absolution. He finished the last of Faith's girls and asked Flora to tell Faith that he must return to Glastonbury to write out this large number of certificates of indulgence.

Faith had given him a list of the names of her girls and asked that he return with the indulgences on the morrow, each personally inscribed and bearing the seal of the pope. It was well into the evening when he finally left Faith's house, yet Landow was not terribly surprised when he found Wort waiting to walk with him back to the inn.

Wort did not say a word on their return to the inn. As he left Landow, he spoke very specifically, "Soon as ya gets ev'rythin done that Mistress Faith needs, Oi will go with ya on the morrow to make the delivery." Landow knew he would be watched until he had completed his task. He neither ate nor slept that night. By candlelight, he completed all fifteen of the indulgences for Faith and her girls and only slept when he knew the documents were ready for delivery in the morning.

Wort was waiting for him when he left the inn and they walked together to Wells Road. Faith Morgan had to be awakened when they arrived, but she was very pleased to see the finished products. Before she returned to her bed, she asked Landow his price.

"Every document is done as you requested, made out personally for you and your girls. I ask merely ten pounds for each."

Faith did not flinch at his exorbitant cost. She called Flora to bring her purse and counted out a hundred and fifty pounds into the hand of the pardoner. When she had paid him, she began to return to her bedchamber.

"Mistress Faith," Landow called to her meekly, "why is it that you have felt such immediate need to do this?"

"It is a matter of protection," she yawned. "I buy it regularly from Calevera, and she suggested I do this. The black monks of the abbey wish to close me down. I care for my girls, pardoner, and we shall keep our indulgences with us at all times. The monks can charge us with no offence against the church, for we are now protected by the seal of the pope."

* * *

Paul Medford found comfort in his carving. It was not diversion that he sought but some means to keep his hands occupied and his mind focused. The passing months of summer had not helped him feel as if any progress was being made in solving his mother's murder. It was always hanging over him, creating turmoil in his thoughts. The physician's son had conceived a more complex project than the little animals he carved for Sir Chad's children. He was trying to carve a statue of Saint Apollonia as a gift to the Lady in thanks for her hospitality, her support, and her obvious willingness to help him through this recent trauma in his life.

When he sought advice from William, the Lady's almoner, the clergyman was immediately enthusiastic about his project. "I believe our Lady Apollonia would be thrilled to have a wooden statue of her patron saint, especially one carved by a member of her household, Paul. How can I help you?"

Paul was grateful to think of himself as a member of the Lady's household and smiled at the thought. "Can you show me any images of Saint Apollonia, Brother William? I would especially like to see how the saint is presented in church art."

"Then, you must come with me to Saint Benignus Church, Paul. In the beautifully carved choir screen, there is a small painting of Saint Apollonia holding in her hand a tooth in pincers as the symbol of her martyrdom."

"I shall bring the things that I need to make a sketch. Do you think that the church will object?"

"Nay, lad, Father Flannan is always glad to encourage people of the town to admire his beautiful church. I shall introduce you to him as a member of the Lady's household. He will be pleased by your interest in studying his painting of their saint."

* * *

Giles Digby was shocked. He could not believe that the September parliament, led by the king, could allow such revenge and merciless redress of grievance. He was so badly shaken the following morning that when he appeared before the Lady, she required him to be seated.

"Giles, what has happened? Have you experienced some dreadful news? What may I do to ease your distress?"

"My Lady, I have interviewed a messenger from London, and he could speak of nothing else. Archbishop Arundel has been exiled. The earl of Arundel was declared guilty of treason and then taken to the tower for execution. The earl of Warwick broke down, sobbingly confessed his guilt of all charges, and is now to be exiled to the Isle of Man. Still, that is not the worst of it. The Duke of Gloucester, a princely son of King Edward III, was being held prisoner in Calais. He has been declared dead and many say he was smothered to death by royal order, as a traitor."

"Have you been able to verify this frightful report, Giles? Is it not possible that such things are merely the abuse of evil tongues seeking to confuse these troublesome times in which we live?" Apollonia was hoping to discover any chance to deny the messenger's news.

"Ours is a civilised nation built upon and protected by a system of parliamentary laws," she said. "What you describe is arbitrary kingship and vindictive sovereignty. These lords were the nobles most resented by King Richard, but would our king seek such vicious abuse of his royal power? Pray God that it might not be so."

"My Lady, I have been given this news from some who serve his court favourites. Those closest to the king say that he has only now truly begun to rule. King Richard's royal rule demands unquestioning devotion by every citizen to him as their sovereign. His power is not subject to question."

"Oh, Giles, do you not see?" The Lady's foreboding was visible in her face. "You and I, Englishmen of all classes, are now forced to accept without question this September's parliamentary trials and their murderously arbitrary judgements. If our king is determined to rule absolutely, then, God save us. We have no avenue of redress."

Chapter Fourteen

Merciless Minions

Cadoc and Ronan continued to use their hideout at the abbey tithe barn throughout the summer. Its interior space was cavernous and its walls so filled with niches, they could always find places to hide whenever wagons arrived to unload tithes from the abbey farms' harvest. Calevera insisted that they keep out of sight since they had run away from the abbey. She knew that Prior Compton maintained a watch for them.

The prior had been horrified by the description of Cadoc's beatings of Brother James and commanded that if these two lay brothers should be found anywhere in Glastonbury, they must be taken prisoner and thrown into the abbey gaol. Calevera's spies had also learned that the prior was determined to discover the extent of their criminal activities. She knew that the prior had been informed that both men abused their positions as priests and lay brothers of the abbey. It was critical to Calevera that Cadoc and Ronan's connexion with her never be known. If they were caught, they could incriminate her and betray her to the sheriff.

Calevera was leader of Glastonbury's best-organised criminal gang. As such, she never risked being seen on the streets except in disguise. Surely, she would never come to the tithe barn to speak with the lay brothers. She sent Wort to summon them to her, and she was always obeyed. No one could object to her being a mere woman. In every sense, she was a physical force with Wort at her side. Her second in command worshipped Calevera, and Wort made it clear that he would give his life for her.

On this September night, Calevera called together all of the members of her gang, within the town as well as her spies from the abbey servants. She was angry and made no effort to disguise it. Cadoc and Ronan remained standing against the back of her hall, as if trying to retreat into the shadows. They both knew that she was particularly angry and displeased with them.

"We have not had a successful robbery amounting to anything more than petty thievery in months, damn it to hell. The abbey is roused against us, and the burghers of the town are keeping pressure upon the mayor. There are citizens' groups patrolling the streets every night; townspeople are on the defensive in their homes, some armed and prepared to defend themselves. Even our pusillanimous mayor struts about with a sword on his belt. The reason that the call has gone out against us lies directly at the feet of our two runaway abbey lay brothers."

Now all eyes turned upon Cadoc and Ronan. Cadoc folded his arms across his chest in a gesture of defiance while Ronan slipped further into the shadows behind him. "You have no reason to blame us," Cadoc insisted. "All of your early successes were built upon the information that we collected for you from endless confessions made to us in the town..." Here Cadoc paused for he knew he must be very careful in his choice of words. He truly hated Calevera and would have called her every disgusting name for a female that he knew. Now, however, he was aware that Wort stood aggressively beside her, so he ended his sentence by addressing her as, "Mistress Calevera."

"And what value to me are you now as two runaway priests being searched for throughout the town?" she sneered. "Worst of all, no one has been able to tell me why Christina Medford was killed. She was an irritant to us, nothing more. To the people of the town she was a loud annoyance, always hurling the charge of murder against them. We had no need for her death, so who did and why was it done?" After posing this question, Calevera looked straight into the eyes of Cadoc.

"Who do you think you are, mistress," he asked sneering back at her, "some sort of judge and jury?" With that, Wort began to move towards Cadoc, but Calevera took his arm and kept him by her side.

"I have not the slightest concern for the law, monkish fraud," she spit at him, "but I will have answers. I command all of you as my henchmen," she said to the larger group, "to search through the town for information. Find out who was aware of Christina Medford's prowling the streets at night and who had any sort of grudge against her?"

"When are we going to do our next job?" Cadoc asked, purposefully changing the subject.

"There will be no new robberies planned until all this commotion dies down."

"Damn and blast, woman, we need the money. Let us finish with Aust House. The master is away, and surely we will find plenty of value there. Once done, we will be rich and able to be gone from this bloody place."

When Cadoc swore at Calevera, Wort went directly at him and slammed his fist into the lay brother's mouth. Cadoc's body flew backwards into Ronan, and they both fell to the floor. Cadoc's nose was bleeding and his mouth a bloody mess. Coughing, he spit onto the floor pieces of his broken front teeth.

"If you will not close your mouth, Cadoc, Wort will help you find a way," Calevera derided him. "Nothing will be stolen, smuggled, or broken into in Glastonbury until I say it will be done."

* * *

Ronan helped Cadoc back to their hiding place in the tithe barn that night after Wort had struck him. Cadoc was a vicious man who had no hesitation to injure others, but he never fought back if a more powerful attack was made against him. Instead, he became a weeping infant when he was hurt. Ronan pushed him into the hay loft where they could lie down, but they found little rest through the night. The tithe barn offered protection from the wind, and its hay warmed them. Cadoc's pain increased through the night from his broken nose, and his swearing at Calevera grew more disgusting. His face continued to swell even after the bleeding ceased. Cadoc was in agony, and Ronan knew he must do something more. "At least I can get some cold water to help cleanse your face, Cadoc. Still, you must be quiet. There will surely be activity below when daylight comes."

Both of them were unable to sleep a wink during the night. Before the first light of morning, Ronan took a small bucket that he found in the barn with a rag hanging on its side. He left the barn to walk to a nearby stream where he dipped the bucket, filled it, and splashed the rag in the flowing waters to rinse it.

He returned as quickly as he could to the tithe barn but could not enter. One of the nearby farm wagons had arrived, and its driver and the abbey lay brother, who opened the barn for him, continued to talk long after they had stored their delivery. When his entry was possible at last, Ronan carried the bucket up to the place where Cadoc remained hidden. Cadoc was furious with him but suffering too seriously from his battered face to do more than swear.

"It is not my fault, Cadoc. You have to know one of the abbey farm workers was here, and I could not be seen entering. Please take this cloth and wash your face."

Ronan dipped the cloth into the bucket and handed it to his friend. Cadoc's face was swelled to such an extent that speech was uncomfortable for him so he said nothing. He grabbed the cloth from Ronan's hand after he had dipped it in the bucket of cold water and laid it upon his face.

Cadoc's damaged nose and lips were cooled by the moist cloth which, for the first time since Wort's massive blow, felt some bit of soothing. Cadoc did little washing; he simply let the cloth lie over his face until it warmed from his body's heat. Then he gave it back to Ronan, commanding him to rinse and cool it once again. They continued this process throughout the early morning until the water in the bucket was used. Cadoc pushed the bucket into Ronan's hands and ordered him to get more.

After darkness fell in late evening, Ronan had made six more trips to the stream and was beginning to resent Cadoc's behaviour towards him. Later than his usual hour, Wort arrived at the barn with their food. He made no secret that he enjoyed seeing the damage he had done to Cadoc's face.

"Ya must ne'er swear at Calevera," was all he would say. Then, he threw the sack of food into Ronan's hands and left them.

"God damn and destroy you," Cadoc muttered after Wort was gone. "When I can, I shall slice every hanging thing from your body starting with your balls."

"Cadoc, we have to work with him," Ronan whined. "What else can we do?"

"Hell no, Ronan. I will never work with that piece of shite, but we will use him. Let Calevera and her gang think we will do her bidding. I wish to leave this God-forsaken town, and to do so, you and I shall rob Aust House. We know, thanks to the listening closet at the anchorite's dwelling, there is a large jewellery box stored there. First we must find where it is kept and then we shall steel it. Once in our possession, we shall be gone from Glastonbury, having left behind our accusations. Anonymously, we shall declare to the sheriff that Wort is the murderer of the Medford woman and Calevera the evil organiser of all the robberies against the good burghers of Glastonbury."

* * *

On the next morning Apollonia asked Nan if she might accompany her. The maid planned to walk into town to visit the dwelling of the anchorite. "I would be pleased to have your company, my Lady, and to introduce you to my friend, Brother Johanus."

"I should like to meet him, Nan, and spend a few moments speaking with him privately, if I may."

"Of course, my Lady. The children are busy in the school room. I am certain we will not be missed if we make a quick walk into town. Shall I call Jeremy?"

"Yes, please do. Jeremy must be bored to death with our walks into the town, but he is so good and endlessly willing to assume his responsibility for our protection."

Jeremy, dressed to walk with them into town, came into the hall to meet the Lady and her maid. The sun was shining, and the lack of dark clouds promised a bright day. Still, sharp breezes told of the coming of autumn as they left Aust House.

They reached Saint John the Baptist Church to find Johanus' window closed against the wind. But, the shutters opened quickly when Nan knocked upon them as if the anchorite recognised her gentle knock. Johanus opened it with his greetings, "Benedicite, Nan, I was truly hoping that you would visit with me this day."

"I have not only come to speak with you, Johanus, I have brought with me my mistress, the Lady Apollonia of Aust."

"Welcome, my Lady of Aust. Everyone speaks of your presence in Glastonbury, and I have hoped for an opportunity to meet you."

"Brother Johanus, it is my pleasure to make your acquaintance, especially because I know you are offering the best of spiritual guidance to my Nan," Apollonia told him. "She has been my servant and dear friend since her childhood."

Nan's face flushed deep red when Apollonia spoke of their personal relationship. It was unusual for someone in Nan's position to have such friendship declared publicly. She knew that their difference in class alone created significant distance between them.

"My Lady, I can see at once that you are gracious towards those who serve you," Johanus said sincerely. "You also seek to express Christ's commandment that we love all those who live in our world."

"Thank you for that, Brother Johanus. I do indeed love my Nan, and I should be very grateful to you if you could allow me some time to speak with you privately."

"Of course, my Lady, Nan will surely understand that most folk come to my window with questions of a very personal nature."

Nan stepped away and told the Lady that she would wait inside the church with Jeremy until she was called. Apollonia looked directly into the anchorite's eyes once they were alone. "I admire your mission in life, Brother Johanus, and I have long been a disciple of the anchorite, Mother Julian of Norwich. On this occasion, I must be completely honest. My questions of you are not those of faith or Holy Scripture. I wish to ask for more personal information about you."

The Lady could see a brief startle in the anchorite's posture. After only a brief pause, however, Johanus answered her quietly but very sincerely. "I shall be completely honest with you as well, my Lady. Pray what are your questions?"

* * *

When the Lady finished speaking with the anchorite, she went into the church of Saint John the Baptist and found Nan and Jeremy. "I know that you wished to speak with Brother Johanus today, Nan. He is waiting for you; pray go to him. Jeremy and I shall wait here till you return."

"Gramercy, my Lady, I shall not be long," Nan said as she hurried out from the church.

When Nan left, the church was empty save for the Lady and Jeremy. "I pray you, Jeremy," Apollonia said to the young man who felt he must stand at her side, "sit here with me. I need to speak with you privately."

Jeremy took a place next to her but the Lady could see that he was not comfortable sitting on her level or so near to her. She had told him that she must speak with him alone and he could not do otherwise.

"I have a very special favour to ask of you, Jeremy," Apollonia said quietly, "and I hope you will be willing to help me."

"In any way, my Lady, I am ever ready to serve you."

"You must know that I am concerned for the safety of young Paul Medford. As you have been told, he has recently come into my service at about the same age you began to serve my son, Sir Chad. I know that he is younger than you and far less experienced than you, but could you please make an effort to befriend him?"

"I do speak with Paul at our evening meals, my Lady. He sits below me at table, but I have found him to be well read, and though a quiet person, he has expressed insightful opinions."

"Most specifically," the Lady said, "I want to ask you to feel assigned to watch over Paul whenever you are together. Your duties are significantly different than his, and I do not ask you to consider yourself a household servant as he has come to be. Allow me to be frank, Jeremy," the Lady said. "I know that there are people in Glastonbury who have threatened to harm the lad. He was attacked when on an early morning errand in the town. He says it was nothing, but it tells me that someone in the town feels threatened by what his inquiries might do to them."

This was news to Jeremy, and he sat back to take it in. "I was unaware that anyone in your household had been attacked, my Lady. When did it happen? Where was Paul, and can you tell me what was done to him?"

The Lady carefully described for Jeremy the day and approximate time in the early morning when Paul was grabbed from behind while walking along Magdalene Street towards the High Street. "Paul was not able to see his assailant, but he knew he was held from behind by a powerful ruffian. The most worrying thing about the incident, Jeremy, is that the creature told him that he must stop questioning those merchants who had been robbed. Otherwise he would be killed. Then, he was struck on the head and left lying unconscious in the doorway of the almshouses."

"Dear God, my Lady, this is deadly serious. I pray you will tell Paul not to venture out alone again."

"I have told Paul precisely that, Jeremy. He is young and somewhat willing to take risks if he thinks he might discover any information concerning the murder of his mother. I have blamed myself again and again, for it was I who first encouraged him to visit with the shopkeepers to collect their stories and see if we might find some facts in common from each of the robberies. Paul suspects that his mother had learned something about the identity of the robbers, and that is why she was killed."

"Would you be willing to assign Paul to be my helper whilst you are here in Glastonbury?" Jeremy asked her. "I shall see to it that Paul's responsibilities will be assigned more specifically within the household, my Lady."

"Gramercy, Jeremy, I have been grateful for your excellent ideas of how to maintain security but, more particularly, I have hoped you would find ways to keep young Paul safely at home."

* * *

Jeremy accompanied the Lady and Nan's return to Aust House and then sought out Paul Medford to tell him that the Lady had assigned him to be his helper. "It is simply because I need more hands at my side, Paul. Master Chad left me with a very specific assignment whilst he was required to be away from Glastonbury. Simply said, I am to protect Aust House and all of the members of the household, especially those who are required to journey into the town."

"I will gladly do whatever I can to support you, Master Jeremy," Paul told him, "though I confess that I am not certain how I can be helpful."

"We shall begin when you meet me in the yard to develop your skills with the dagger and sword," Jeremy said. "Once I have been convinced that you are prepared to handle these weapons, I will lend you both. The dagger must be worn on your belt at all times."

"I fear I have no experience with these weapons, Master Jeremy, but I promise I shall work hard to learn from you."

"You are strongly built and well schooled, Paul. That is your best preparation in handling any weapon. Whilst you are developing your skills, I shall ask you to accompany me on my rounds. You must be aware of the key places within Aust House, that require protection: from the ground floor as well as the garden and the barn. We will speak with Gareth and inform him of your assignment."

"I pledge to do my best," Paul told Jeremy, "and shall strive to give all that I can for the protection of the Lady Apollonia and Sir Chad's household."

"Your commitment will prove your desire, Paul. When a member of the household goes into the town, I shall have to go with them. Whenever I am gone, you will fulfill my role here. It sounds a simple task, but it is full of responsibility."

"I promise I shall be attentive to your every command."

Jeremy could see that Paul sincerely wanted to take up this new assignment. He, more than anyone else, understood the reasons for the threat, and it had a great deal to do with his residence there.

"Come along then; we are off to the yard, lad. You have much to learn, and we must begin straightaway."

Sir Chad's squire found himself impressed once they had weapons in hand. Paul Medford obviously needed instruction in how to handle a dagger and a sword, but he brought to his use of the weapons a strong body and lithe, well-coordinated limbs that moved about the yard trying to anticipate Jeremy's next move. Jeremy could tell that Paul was smart, but not merely book-smart. He was physically adept, and best of all, he was willing to practise and improve.

* * *

Calevera was speaking with Wort very privately. They were alone, and her servants had been told that she was not to be disturbed. Calevera knew that of all the people who feared her, worked with her, served her, or pretended to respect her, Wort alone was hers to command. In every way possible, Wort had not only stood at her side for the past decade, he had consistently been her devotee and defender. He made no effort to hide from her that he loved her. She would allow no expressions of affection to her by any man, not even admiration for her person. Calevera was an embittered, angry woman who trusted no man.

"We can not trust Cadoc, or the silly creep, Ronan, who follows meekly in his every footstep," she said to Wort. "We did benefit by the information they provided us, but they did it for their profit and were well paid. Tell me what can I do, Wort? They are of no value to me any longer, and they know far too much. If the prior of the abbey fulfills his vow of taking them prisoner, they will surely betray us."

"Shall Oi kill em, for ya?" Wort asked her hopefully. "Alls we needs is to take some of the lads out to the tithe barn at night and Oi'll cut their throats. That'll surely buy their silence."

"It is tempting, Wort. Shall we consider it this evening's sport?"

"It'll be sport for me whene'er thee wants."

Chapter Fifteen

Sub Rosa

October filled Glastonbury with all the shades of autumn, and still Chad and Walter were not able to return to Aust House. In their absence, Juliana had a particular request of her grandmother. She appeared in the Lady's solar after her studies were completed that morning,.

"Grandmamma, the day is cloudlessly perfect, the colours of autumn are approaching their peak, and I would like to walk to Saint Michael's Monastery at the top of the Tor to see as far as I can see. Would you feel able to make the climb with me?"

Apollonia was completely taken aback. At first, she was stunned to think that Juliana would wish to attempt such a walk, but then she felt slightly irritated that her granddaughter would think her unable to do such a thing.

"Truly, Juliana, I have reached my fifty-first year, but I am not yet disabled, child. If you should wish to climb the Tor, I will be delighted to walk with you."

As soon as the Lady finished her sentence, she could hear Nan let out a noticeable gasp. "Oh, my Lady, it is a fine day, but surely you can not wish to walk all the way from Aust House to the top of the Tor. Can we not find some less energetic way to achieve a beautiful view?"

"I think that you should have Gareth saddle up our mounts, Nan, and we will ride to the abbey tithe barn. We shall leave the horses there with him and walk to the monastery at the top of the Tor." At this point in their discussion, Apollonia decided that she would have to display how fit she was in spite of her age, but she was more concerned for her granddaughter.

"Juliana, you must remember to carry your stick with you as we ride," the Lady said. "We can not risk your falling."

"Of course, grandmamma, I shall take it. When shall we begin?"

"Call Jeremy, Nan, and as soon as we can change into riding dress, we will report to Gareth in the barn."

Juliana hurried up the stairs to her bedchamber, obviously very excited about their anticipated adventure. After she left the solar, Nan said to the Lady, "Are you quite certain that this is a good idea? I do not wish to suggest that you are disabled by your age, my Lady, but our years are telling."

"Well, Nan, I shan't speak for you. Obviously, Jeremy will accompany us, and you may remain at home until we return."

Now it was Nan's turn to feel a bit put off. "I shall not put too fine a point on it, my Lady," she said with a slight huff, "but I am nearly ten years younger than you."

Apollonia began to smile at her maid as she said, "Well, dearheart, nine years younger possibly, but I am determined to do this with my granddaughter, and we can do it together with Jeremy. I do not wish you to make this effort if you feel your years are telling."

"Indeed, I shall go with you, my Lady. It is my duty, and I shan't be seen as a slacker."

Apollonia said nothing further, and the two of them retreated in silence to change their clothes.

* * *

When they entered the barn, Jeremy was waiting with Gareth, and Juliana had already mounted her pony for the ride to the tithe barn.

"Come along, grandmamma, the days are already beginning to grow shorter, and we must use the sunlight."

"Of course, Juliana," the Lady told her as she mounted her horse. Soon the entire party began their ride towards the tithe barn. Apollonia was an accomplished horsewoman. Nan was not, but the Lady's maid was determined to do this ride. They rode out from the barn at Bove Town Road, then completed the turning down Chilkwell Street which took them directly to the corner where the tithe barn was located on the edge of Glastonbury. Leaving their horses there with Gareth, the rest of the party began their walk towards Glastonbury Tor, the most remarkably distinguished natural hill in the landscape.

"Is it not beautiful, grandmamma?" Juliana asked happily. "I am so happy that we could do this today. It has been my hope since I received my new shoes."

Apollonia noticed that Juliana had brought her stick with her but was not using it for support; she carried it under her arm as she led the group with a quick walk. They reached the base of the Tor and began to follow the Pilgrims' Path uphill, joining a steady stream of pilgrims already underway towards the top. While Juliana continued to lead their group, her stick never touched the ground. Apollonia was thrilled to see how straight and strong Juliana's stride had become, but she said nothing. Perhaps, she thought, Juliana would use her stick on the return journey downhill.

The climb continued, and the Lady noticed that she was becoming somewhat breathless. She was determined not to slow the pace. Throughout their ascent, the surrounding waters of the Somerset Levels and the hills in the distance grew more beautiful, and their path took them upwards towards an ever-enlarged landscape view.

"I may be an old woman," Apollonia told herself, "but I shall breathe deeply and focus myself on the beauty of the countryside."

Nan said nothing but made herself match the Lady's climb, step for step.

"Come along, grandmamma, we still have a way to go," Juliana called.

Both of the older women simply nodded and kept moving silently with Jeremy following them. The group of pilgrims on the path with them was making the climb in different attitudes of penitence. Some were walking in their bare feet; some were achieving the climb on their knees. At the sight of these humble, penitential creatures, Apollonia felt her defensive attitude when discussing her age had been unworthy. She knew in her heart that Nan had always been first to express love and concern for her. Apollonia turned to Nan and took her hand.

"Forgive my silly pique, Nan. I have always depended on you," she said. "I hope you know that I thank God daily for your gifts of service and friendship with me throughout my long life."

Making a point to emphasise her long life, Apollonia smiled in the hope that Nan would see that she knew her earlier behaviour with the maid had been petty. Nan smiled back and kissed the Lady's hand. Walking briskly in step together, they seemed to reach the top of the Tor in a matter of minutes.

Juliana became more determined once within sight of Saint Michael's Church. She obviously had come for a purpose. "Pray, grandmamma, let us go into the church. I wish to say a prayer and obtain one of the pilgrim's badges to declare that I have truly climbed the Tor."

"I think that is a lovely idea, Juliana. I shall kneel with you and offer my own prayers. This has been a wonderful day for me, and I too have much to thank God for."

Apollonia, Juliana, Nan, and Jeremy quietly entered the heavily buttressed, crowded church and walked the length of its narrow nave towards the altar. It was a well-appointed, if very narrow church. Its interior was gloriously lit by the rays of the sun streaming through its stained glass windows, filling the chancel and nave with jewel-like colours while the floor became a sparkling surface of brightly coloured tiles. It was filled with pilgrims and travellers from all parts of England, but the church of Saint Michael was reverently silent.

The Lady and her party completed their prayers. At that moment, Juliana reached out to take her grandmother's hand and placed her stick into it. "I no longer need this, grandmamma. My body has been blessed by Saint Joseph of Arimathea."

At first, Apollonia was not certain what she should do. She was afraid to take Juliana's stick from her in case the child should need it walking down from the summit of Glastonbury Tor. Yet, the Lady could see that her granddaughter was being completely serious. Juliana had ascended the Tor on her own two feet, never using the walking stick. She believed she had been given a blessed gift of healing.

Apollonia took Juliana's walking stick and placed it against a wall of the church porch where walking sticks, crutches, and a collection of supportive braces had been left behind. Each represented the sign of an individual miracle received in this place. The Lady also made certain that everyone in her party received a bronze pilgrim's badge to wear as they left the church and began the descent back to the town. Everyone of the Lady's party had been witness to Juliana's victory. And for the little girl the journey downhill became a glowing triumph as the sun's rays haloed the autumn glory from Glastonbury Tor.

* * *

Cadoc's face grew more brightly bruised, purplish, and yellowed as days went by, and his anger at Wort and Calevera multiplied. "We have to get out of this place, Ronan," he said. "I refuse to remain anywhere near Wort without a weapon in my hand. Let us abandon this damned tithe barn. The summer is over and it affords us little heat through the night."

"Where can we go, Cadoc?"

"We must return to the fish house at Meare. My uncle Jestin is a disgusting old fart, but I will tell him that he must keep us until we have completed our next robbery. We have to remain out of sight, but I shall say that if he helps us, we will pay him handsomely. I know how greedy he is. If we bribe him with the promise of significant reward, he will keep his mouth shut and house us for as long as we need."

"Do you suppose he still keeps that girl, the one he calls his personal wench?" Ronan asked casually.

"I do not care in the least, Ronan; he will keep her out of our way. Best of all, no one will ever be able to find us in Meare. This morning, I noticed there are two horses regularly kept in the barn below. We shall take them and be on our way. Even though the afternoon is still bright, pull up your hood, and we will make it look as if we are local monks on abbey business. With our growing beards, no one will recognise us."

* * *

Late that evening when Wort went to the tithe barn looking for Cadoc and Ronan, he approached from a different direction than his normal approach. He brought with him two husky henchmen of Calevera's and went directly inside as there were still several large farm wagons at the open front doors. He asked the drivers if they had seen two abbey lay brothers near the barn, and they insisted that they had seen no one.

"Do ye mind if Oi take a look round?" he asked the drivers. They encouraged him but remained skeptical. "We've seen no one from the abbey, and this has been a busy day," one of them told him. "Two orses were stole from ere," another driver told him. "think they might ave done it?"

Wort grunted and shrugged his shoulders towards the drivers. He did not leave the barn until he had peered into all of the niches and corners where Cadoc and Ronan might have hidden when the large doors of the tithe barn were opened to receive the harvest. Wort found no one, but he could tell that the lay brothers had been there recently. Some remains from the meal that he brought them the night before still lay in a corner. Wort was not only frustrated, he was angry. He knew he must return to Calevera with word that the lay brothers had escaped him. They had probably stolen the horses to escape farther away and remain out of sight. "The bastards must be found," he grunted to the men when he rejoined them. "They knows too much."

* * *

Calevera could tell by his face that he had been unable to kill Cadoc and Ronan. "Tell me everything, Wort. Why are they not dead?"

"The bastards be gone, run away from the tithe barn. Worse yet, they stole orses, probably to elp them get out of Glastonbury. They might be anywhere, Calevera. Where do we start? Ow do we find them?"

Calevera grimaced and swore mightily. She had been sitting at the table dormant in her hall in the house on Archers Way. Now, she put her head into her hands and continued to swear. Cadoc and Ronan must be shut up, and she had trusted Wort to get it done speedily. Suddenly, she lifted her head with a smile and told her henchman, "This is beautiful, Wort. We shan't have to look for them. They will come to us. You and I know that they are probably planning to rob Aust House before they leave Glastonbury for good. We shall be there watching for them whenever they arrive. Then, we shall finish the job. When their bodies are found, they will be reported to the prior as the defrocked criminal priests from Oxford who took confessions throughout the town to use them to enable *their* robberies."

"When do we start, Calevera?" Wort asked. "Shall Oi go with the lads to Aust House this night?"

"Yes, begin the watch, Wort. It is dark now, and the town sleeps. Assign the most reliable of the lads to be on Bove Town Road every night. Crewyn is best with the dagger. It is not likely that Cadoc will want to appear in Glastonbury soon, especially if they have a safe hiding place nearby. Whenever they try to break into Aust House, we shall be watching for them."

* * *

Cadoc and Ronan arrived at Meare Fish House and Jestin Mallot was not pleased to see them. "Ye can not remain ere; ye must be gone. Monks from the abbey come regular to collect the fresh eels and fish they needs every week. Oi can not ave ye ere when they comes," he shouted at Cadoc.

Ronan said nothing, but Cadoc tried to sound a family connexion between them. "Come, Uncle Jestin; you know that I have been coming here since I was a lad. You are my mother's brother. How can that be suspicious?"

Jestin refused to listen. "Ye must go. The monks will be at my door early on the morrow. If one of them recognises ye, it will be worse than suspicious, for I shall have to tell them ya be my sister's son. The prior wants ye both in gaol."

"Grant us a hearing, Uncle Jestin. If we can remain near Glastonbury for another few weeks, I shall be able to make you rich."

"Ye must go," Jestin said again. Yet, his eyes expressed interest, and his tone suggested that he was listening.

Cadoc could see that he had captured his uncle's attention, so he continued. "There is a knight's town house in Glastonbury that is standing alone without its master in residence and undefended. The master of the house has been called to court for months. The house on Bove Town Road is somewhat isolated. Best yet, it is being governed by one old woman, the knight's mother, with a small household staff."

Jestin could see that Cadoc was well informed of the situation at Aust House. "But, ow is that going to make us rich?" he scoffed at his nephew.

"We know that the Lady in charge of the house is a daughter of the old Earl of Marshfield. We also know that she keeps a large box in her chamber full of family gold and jewels. I only need some time to get into the household to find out precisely where she keeps it."

"If ye can not be seen in the town in daylight, ow can ye be seen on Bove Town Road?"

"Look at my face, Uncle Jestin. Thanks to the bastard, Wort, my front teeth are broken, my face is scarred, and I have allowed my beard to grow long. You will help me colour my hair and get some workman's clothes. No one will recognise me if I appear at the servants' entrance begging for a job."

Now it was Ronan's turn to question him. "You can not be serious, Cadoc. Are you really planning to go to work there as a servant?"

"It will be a matter of working my way inside, Ronan. I will be using every opportunity to map the house, mark where everything is done, and especially make note of the Lady's solar, bed chamber, dressing chamber, everything. Just grant me enough time to prepare, Uncle Jestin. When I have scouted the house carefully, I shall be able to go directly in the dark of night to steal the best and bring a portion of its treasures to you."

"What am I to do?" Ronan asked as if feeling left behind.

"You will stay here with Uncle Jestin. Then, later in the week when I have gotten into service at Aust House, you will come to meet me at the back gate in the wall. I will give you my drawings, and other information will be noted for you to bring back to Meare to study. On the night we decide to do the robbery, you will be waiting for me at the gate with my horse and yours tethered nearby ready to make our final escape back to Meare. We shall make the split with Uncle Jestin and be on our way."

"Well," Jestin said as he stroked his beard, "best laid plans gain more. Ye must know that no one is to be told where either of ye be stayin. Oi will give ye place and feed ye, but if anyone comes to inquire, Oi know ye not."

"Ronan and I will begin here, uncle. We will change our hair colour and steal enough clothes to burn these robes. If anyone from the abbey asks you about the extra horses stabled here, you are to tell them that you are stabling them temporarily to earn a few extra pence."

"Oh, aye, but if any asks bout Cadoc or who ee be, Oi know ya not."

* * *

The Lady Apollonia and Nan were sitting together in her solar early the following morning when Paul came to her door and asked to be received. "Of course, Paul," the Lady called towards him, "I am always glad to speak with you."

As soon as Paul Medford entered the solar, Apollonia noticed how muscular his young body had become, having worked out daily in the tilt yard with Jeremy. The Lady was also aware that he now wore a dagger strapped to his belt and seemed prepared to use it. His arms showed well-defined development even through the sleeves of his tunic, especially because he carried into the chamber a rather heavy parcel draped in fabric.

"I say, Paul," Apollonia smiled at him. "I believe you have grown during these months with us."

"Ah, yes, my Lady, Mistress Farber is an excellent cook, and I have gained weight, thanks to her daily preparations for your household. Would you allow me to place this on your table?"

"Indeed, you stirred my curiousity as soon as you entered the chamber with it in your hands. What have you brought?"

"It is a gift, my Lady, and I sincerely hope that you will accept it from me."

Nan's curiosity was roused as well. She got up from her stool and moved more closely to the Lady's side while placing her spectacles on her nose for the best view of Paul's surprise.

The Lady seemed hesitant, not certain precisely what she should do. This was not a special occasion where gifts were expected. "Truly, Paul, you must not feel required to give gifts to me," she said. "You have served me very well during these past months. Nan and I have been grateful to have you with us."

"My Lady of Aust, I pray that you will accept this from me as an expression of my gratitude to you." Without another word, Paul pulled away the cloth and revealed a beautifully carved wooden figure of Saint Apollonia, nearly sixteen inches high. Paul had chosen to slightly enlarge the painted image he had seen in the Saint Benignus Church screen and carve a beautiful young saint dressed in a floor-length gown whose extended hand held a delicate tooth clasped in pincers.

Nan gasped at the work of art sitting before them, and Apollonia seemed more than surprised. "Dear God, Paul," she exclaimed. "Can this be your work?"

"I fear it is the best I can do, my Lady. I have never had any training in the carver's skills."

"Your artist's gifts are obviously God given, Paul, and I shall treasure this work. It will remain with me in my personal chapel wherever I dwell and will always receive my prayers for you whenever I stand before it. Gramercy, Paul, my sincere thanks for this beautiful gift," the Lady said as she took his hand. "I can think of no words adequate to express my heartfelt thanks. With your permission, I should like to place my personal Saint Apollonia on the table dormant in the hall this evening, so that everyone in our combined households will be able to see and admire it. How have you been able to achieve all this sub rosa, done in secret from all of us?"

"Brother William was my enabler, my Lady. It was he who encouraged my idea; it was he who helped me obtain the wood and took me to Saint Benignus Church. There, he introduced me to the parish priest who allowed me to sketch the painted image of Saint Apollonia from their quire screen. Finally, it was Brother William who helped me slip away every early morning to work on the carving behind the altar screen of the chapel where the light was best. I could not have done it without his help, my Lady."

Chapter Sixteen

Malignant Servitude

The priest, William Fallows, served as the Lady Apollonia's almoner, the official distributor of alms in the Lady's name. Wherever her household was in residence, the good father sought out persons in that town or village in particular need. Brother William returned to Aust House from his usual rounds of Glastonbury that afternoon and found that the Lady had left word for him to stop by her solar before returning to the chapel. She was obviously excited and anxious to speak with him as he entered her upper chamber. Immediately after his greeting, she stood from her chair and led him back into the hall downstairs. There, presented in all its glory, standing upon a linen cloth over the table dormant, was Paul's hand-carved figure of Saint Apollonia.

"I have received an extraordinary gift this day, William," the Lady told him, "but I learned from Paul that you have been involved in its creation since its conception."

William knew precisely what the Lady referred to. He had watched Paul's Saint Apollonia literally emerge from its block of wood. Now, however, William was pleased because he could see that the Lady was truly moved by Paul's gift. It occupied her thoughts and had been on her mind since the lad first presented it to her this morning. The Lady was determined to find the most meaningful ways to thank Paul because, in her mind, the lad had created a significant work of religious art. She wished for the entire household to celebrate it.

"Please help me, William, and grant me your insight. Paul places little value on his carving. To him it is merely a way for him to express his gratitude to me. I feel that I must be able to turn my thanks to him into something far more--a grateful celebration of his art. You have always been sensitive to the ways that events can become instruments of encouragement to young people. Would you please share with me your ideas of how we may do this for Paul?"

"My Lady, you of all people need not ask me how to encourage young people. You have done so all of your life. I merely look back to my own youth when you were witness to my disgrace within the church and lifted me from the depths of despair. It was far more than simple encouragement. You saved my life."

"Ah, but that was an extreme case of betrayal and false judgement against which you were allowed no defence. I simply stepped in where the church should have been in your case, William. Now, however, you must tell me how I can thank Paul for his gift to me and encourage his artistic talent at the same time."

William thought for several moments as he looked at the lovely carving of Saint Apollonia. He walked around it to examine it from all directions, and then returned to the place where the Lady waited for him.

"My Lady, I suggest that you place this lovely statue of your patron saint in the family chapel, but in a special place. Let her stand upon a low pillar just inside the entrance. I shall put the holy water stoup at her feet. In that way, our Saint Apollonia will welcome each of us to chapel as we enter every service. She will be exhibiting her martyrdom whilst pointing our way towards the Virgin and Child on the altar, our hope of God's salvation."

Apollonia could see in her mind's eye that her almoner was creating the perfect presentation of Paul's carving. "Yes, William, I like that," the Lady said encouraging him to go on.

"Every member of your household will be able to view all of the beautiful detail of the carving. And, by elevating Paul's saint to a position of visible intercession for all of us, he will surely grasp your appreciation of the saint's spiritual meaning to you as well."

"Gramercy, William, I knew you would think of a perfect celebration for Paul. Pray, dear almoner, can you have my Saint Apollonia in place when we find our way to chapel this evening?"

"Shan't be very complicated, my Lady. Will you allow me to take the carving with me temporarily? I shall see to it straightaway."

"With all my thanks," Apollonia said as she gently placed the saint's figure into his hands.

"We shall make a special service of dedication over it this evening," William grinned. "Then, Paul will truly see the extraordinary sense of gratitude and appreciation you place upon his gift."

* * *

Nan noticed that the Lady was more quiet than usual but obviously excited as the household gathered for chapel service that evening. She greeted each staff member and servant with a smile, as was her habit, and then turned to lead them into the chapel. Brother William was waiting for them and everyone could see at once that Paul's beautiful figure of Saint Apollonia stood upon the pillar guarding the holy water stoup lying at her feet.

William asked the entire household to gather around the pillar for the dedication of the Lady's gift from Paul. Young Medford was somewhat taken aback by this focus upon him, but even he could see that the Lady wanted everyone to know how she treasured his gift to her.

"Let us pray together," Brother William said. They bowed their heads while the priest began his prayer. "Gracious God and Heavenly Father, accept our prayers of praise and thanks. Receive and dedicate this work of Paul Medford's hands, now to be set apart for your worship. Accept this gift that we dedicate and consecrate to the praise and glory of your Name." The prayer was closed with a unanimously joyful, "Amen"; the, everyone crossed himself and followed the Lady to his place at the altar.

William continued to celebrate the rest of the vespers service, but he saw an intensity in young Paul's worship that he had not seen before. When the household filed out from the chapel, the Lady waited for Paul to join her.

"It would never have been enough for me to merely thank you, Paul. You must know that my personal Apollonia will always occupy a place in my heart as well as my worship."

"My Lady, I pray you will know that you have been the source of healing, restoration, and hope in my life. Saint Apollonia will always represent your gifts to me."

* * *

It was early on a dreary October morning when Cadoc approached the servant's entrance to Aust House. His appearance had been transformed to that of a very different man. He was still tall and well built, but he no longer resembled the abbey lay brother or the humble parish priest he had impersonated. His hair had grown long and was recently coloured to a deeper black. His face was now full-bearded round a broken-toothed smile, and his dress appeared to be that of a travelling labourer. When John of Glastonbury opened the door, Cadoc assumed the demeanour of a very submissive human being who had come to ask for a job.

"What is it that you do?" Steward John asked him.

"Whate'er is needed to earn my way, master."

"What is your name, and where have you served previously?" John wished to have some sense of reference before taking this man on.

"My name is Glebb, master, and I be working my way from Cornwall to Bath to be nearer my sister, newly widowed. I have had no steady employment for months, master, and never been in Glastonbury before," he lied.

"I will give you a trial, Glebb, first in the barn with the stablemaster. You can sleep in the kitchen, but whenever you enter the household, you must first stop at the well and take time to wash thoroughly. It is the Lady's absolute requirement that no one enters Aust House until he has washed."

"Yes, master."

"Well, then, you should know that I am John, the steward of Sir Chad's home in Glastonbury. Your work here will be observed critically, and I shall not keep you on unless you perform your tasks to my satisfaction."

"Yes, Master John."

"Go to the kitchen for food. As soon as you have eaten, report to the barn and offer your services to Gareth, the Lady's stablemaster. You remain on trial, Glebb," John told him. Cadoc, now Glebb, knew that if he were to be accepted into the household without references, he must begin at the bottom.

* * *

Glebb appeared at the barn immediately after breaking his fast and told Gareth that Steward John had sent him to do whatever Gareth asked. The stablemaster put him to work immediately. He was made to do everything from cleaning out the stalls to replenishing the feed and water. He exercised the beasts and brushed them down when they returned to the barn. None of this was difficult for Cadoc. He knew he was good with horses.

At the end of the day, John made his way to the barn to speak with Gareth. "How did you find your new helper, Glebb?"

"Ee don't say much," Gareth told him with some sense of approval in his tone.

"Was he able to do the work?" John pressed Gareth. "Glebb is on trial with us, Gareth, and comes with no references. Tell me what you think of him."

"Ee andles the beasts well and finished ev'rythin Oi asked of im," Gareth said.

"Would you be willing to have him with you the rest of the week and give me your best opinion then?"

"Ee be useful, Steward John," was all Gareth would say. John knew that Gareth's long-term approval would have to be earned, and that would recommend Glebb for permanent hire.

* * *

The bells of Saint John the Baptist Church peeled the twelfth hour after the fires were banked and the household gone to bed. Cadoc remained awake, pulled a small candle from his pocket, and lit it to help him explore inside the darkened Aust House. He was particularly interested in the Lady's solar and her bedchamber beyond, but he knew he must not be seen above stairs because he could claim no purpose in being there. If ever he heard anyone stirring while he wandered about in the early hours of the morning, he would rush back to the kitchen so as not to be found outside the limits proscribed for him.

Cadoc had a good sense of proportion and estimation of size. He was creating a drawing of the interior of Aust House on a small piece of parchment. He believed he knew where to find the Lady's chambers, but he desperately wanted to be able to check his map during the daylight hours.

The week that he served in the barn flew by. On the following Monday, the steward asked him if he would be willing to work within Aust House in the kitchen. He would be needed to feed the fires, scour the great kettles, and help to serve the main meals. "This," John told Glebb, would help him to learn the daily schedule and the names of the household staff.

Cadoc quietly nodded his head, indicating that he was prepared to serve in any capacity required by the master. "Then," Steward John told him, "as a part of the inner household staff, Glebb, you will now be able to sleep in the uppermost chamber shared by the male servants. Move your blankets from the kitchen near the fireplace up to the top floor of Aust House tomorrow night."

Cadoc was pleased to move to the upper floors of the house. That had been his intention from the first, but he knew he would have to be far more careful when trying to explore while everyone was assumed to be asleep. His movements must not be regarded as suspicious.

The night before he moved his things, Cadoc waited outside the gate of Aust House until Ronan came. Cadoc quickly told him that he was being moved to reside inside, and he would no longer be able to sneak out at night. "You must remain at the fish house until I can find my way round all of the inner rooms, Ronan. It will probably not take more than another week or two. For now, I am pleased that your disguise is growing with your beard. Stay with my uncle, out of sight, until the time comes when I shall need you to bring the horses into town to set up our escape."

"Oh, Cadoc, Meare is a beastly place, and it is so boring. There is nothing to do out there, and I despise your uncle. He is a disgusting old bastard who complains constantly."

"Ronan," Cadoc said as he grabbed his collar, "it will not be much longer, dammit. Stop whining and grow up. Remind yourself that when this robbery is complete, we shall be rich enough to move on."

"I have always done everything you asked of me, Cadoc, but you never seem to care when you ask too much," Ronan pouted.

"Oh, shut up and stay at the fish house, fool. I am taking all the risk." With that, Cadoc stomped back towards Aust House, leaving Ronan standing in the road.

"Do not push too far, Cadoc," Ronan muttered to himself. "I am no fool. You say that you are taking all the risk, but we both know that you can achieve nothing here without my help."

* * *

The Lady Apollonia became aware of the new male servant on the staff when Chad's steward reported to her that the fellow had appeared at the back door, begging for employment. His name was Glebb, and John added that he brought no references from earlier service. "I took him first to work with Gareth in the barn, my Lady. His humility and willingness to do anything required of him has been impressive. Even your servant, Gareth, not one to praise highly, found his work acceptable, so I decided to transfer him into the household as a general dogsbody."

"What do you think of him, John? You know that I am always ready to employ new help if they are truly needed."

"Sir Chad's household has been short of staff since you arrived, my Lady, and this Glebb has been able to do whatever I have asked of him. So far, he has performed well in the barn to Gareth's satisfaction. He has lent his hand to Mistress Manning in housekeeping by chopping wood as well as building and stoking the household fires throughout the chambers and the kitchen. I shall try his serving at table this evening."

"It is troublesome that he comes to us with no previous experience to endorse him, John. I am glad to know that you will keep an eye upon him."

"Thank you, my Lady, I shall do all that you ask." The steward bowed to her when he left the hall.

"I will also try to observe this Glebb, my Lady," Nan said. "It is Steward John's role to supervise the household, but I enjoy becoming familiar with the staff. I will find occasions to speak with him and learn what others think of him as well."

Apollonia smiled at Nan. "I do believe that you are able to read my mind, dearheart. I was about to ask you to do the very thing. Most especially, I need to have confidence when we bring new people into Chad's home that they be trustworthy in every sense, especially near my grandchildren. See what you can learn about Glebb."

"I will note everything he tells me, my Lady. We can discuss it further this evening."

"Oh, bless you, Nan. You are always my first avenue to household insight."

* * *

Nan joined the Lady later in her solar and they sat together before the fire. "Oh, my Lady, how good the warmth of the fire feels to my creaking bones." Nan put her hands toward the fireplace and rubbed them together vigorously. "There is no doubt these October days are growing shorter and certainly more chilly."

"Please warm yourself, Nan. When you feel comfortable, tell me, were you able to speak with Glebb? What do you think of him?"

"Well, my Lady, the main thing I discovered is that he does not speak much at all. Housekeeper Manning introduced him to me in the kitchen. Both she and Cook Farber have been very appreciative of his ready willingness to help them, especially in heavy tasks requiring man-sized muscle. When I invited him to sit, he remained standing, begging my forgiveness because he said he had things needing to be done before dinner. I simply asked him where he came from and did he have family? He told me that he was from the village of Elsfield near Oxford, and his parents were dead. After those few words of exchange, he returned to his work."

"You found nothing to be displeased with in his manner, his obedience, or his abilities?" the Lady pressed her.

"The people of Sir Chad's lower stairs have found Glebb to be anxious to perform whatever is asked of him, my Lady. Mistress Manning is convinced that he desperately wishes to keep his position."

"No one can complain of a hard worker within our service, and he appears for chapel at every morning and evening service," Apollonia noticed. "Continue to seek conversation with him, Nan. I would like you to tell me if you feel he speaks as an Oxfordshire man."

"First, I must find a way to have a real conversation with him. Till now, I have only been able to elicit one or two word responses from Glebb, ever polite and full of courtesy but minimal."

"How have Mistress Manning and Cook Farber found his conversation? Did they say that he speaks with the accents of Oxfordshire?"

"Their comments are similar to mine, my Lady. Throughout the day when the staff are working near each other or even as they are sharing their evening meal, he says little or nothing. Even limited of speech Gareth complains that Glebb has no conversation."

Chapter Seventeen

Vicious Spies

Apollonia could see that young Paul was distressed. His hands and his mind had been busy during the weeks that he spent carving the wooden figure of Saint Apollonia as his gift to her. Then he was focused upon the completion of his surprise. Since the lovely saint now stood regularly in the household chapel, Apollonia noticed that Paul was frequently found there seated alone. The Lady would find Paul in the chapel whenever he was not serving in the household, sent on errands, or working out with Jeremy in the tilting yard. He did not seek out the counsel of Brother William. He was uncomplaining and always brightly willing. The Lady could tell that his mind was troubled, and he could not walk away from it.

This morning, when Nan left her to go to the kitchen to speak with Mistress Farber, Apollonia also left her solar and walked downstairs towards the back of the household where the chapel was located. She could see Paul sitting alone, looking carefully at his new carving. Her entry was so quiet that the lad was not aware of her presence until she sat beside him. He jumped to his feet and began to make apologies.

"I am truly sorry, my Lady. I was unaware that you needed me. How may I serve you?"

"I have no request of you, Paul. In fact I believe it is I who should be serving you."

"How can that be?" Paul asked, somewhat confused by her comment.

"I hope you will not find my questions impertinent, Paul, but I can not help noticing that you have been distracted in recent days, perhaps a bit worried of late. Will you be willing to share with me what is troubling you?"

Paul did not weep, but the Lady could see tears fill his eyes. The lad did not wish to be seen to cry in her presence. He paused to achieve self-control before speaking. When he felt he could speak, he simply said, "My Lady, I can not help but think about my mother, and the dreadful fact that more than seven months have passed and nothing has been done to discover who killed her."

The Lady did not respond at first, for she saw that Paul's honesty cost him further mental and emotional distress. "I have no desire to make a great fuss over my loss, my Lady, but my mother was murdered. Her body was left on display for the entire town to see, and there is no on-going search for the murderer or the reasons for her death."

"Of course," the Lady nodded. "I should have known, Paul, and I must beg your pardon that nothing has been accomplished. There has been no further evidence discovered, no witness has come forward, and nothing new has appeared for us to follow up."

"But, my Lady, we stopped looking. After I was attacked on the street, you refused to allow me to be seen asking questions from the townspeople."

"Only because I was legitimately frightened for your safety," Apollonia protested. "You were threatened with death, Paul. I had to keep you out of harm's way."

"It was you who said that we must be collecting facts, my Lady. When we had facts from those shopkeepers, from anyone who might tell us what they had seen my mother doing on the streets, we might be able to build a description of the culprit. I know that mother felt there was a connexion between the robberies in Glastonbury and the church. You said that we must follow that lead and continue to listen to anyone who might have something to tell us. All these weeks have passed, and we only know that each of the robberies was well planned. The robbers knew what they were doing. So, what was my mother trying to do, and why did she feel threatened? Can you not see, my Lady? I feel that I have been the reason that nothing has been done in her behalf."

Apollonia's shoulders dropped as she sighed deeply and put her hand to her head. "I am so very sorry, Paul. You are right to call me out. We will begin again in spite of the very cold trail. However, I insist that you will not make inquiries on your own. We will re-design our investigation, and you will always work in the company of our household guard. It is late, but we can start again. Summon Jeremy to meet with us in my solar, and then you will remain whilst we lay new plans."

* * *

Jeremy was somewhat surprised to be called to the Lady's solar. Apollonia could see that he and Paul felt uncomfortable retreating to this chamber that the entire household knew had become her private place of retreat since the death of Sir Chad's wife. Nan was with the Lady, as always, so the maid's presence added some balance to their gathering.

Aware of the young men's discomfort, Apollonia decided to focus everyone's mind on the purpose at hand. "Jeremy, we are meeting here because it guarantees us privacy. I am turning to you to lead us as my son's designated guardian of his household. You have made it a point to help us be more careful of our speech in public. You told Nan and me that you wish to accompany us when we must be away from the household. You very carefully check every lock each evening before we retire. Since you were made aware that young Paul was attacked and threatened in the town, you have done a marvelous job training him to grow more powerful in his own self-defence. I have called us together because it is necessary for us to keep the investigation into Paul's mother's death active and on-going. Paul is rightly concerned that no one in the town has done so. He fears that, as the months slip by, his mother's brutal murder is being forgotten."

"Not by your affinity, my Lady," Nan told her. "Only yesterday, Gareth asked me what was being done because two of his stable lads were suggesting that some powerful people in the town were trying to hush interest in the murder."

"This brings us to our purpose, Jeremy. Paul is convinced that his mother's murder was related in some way to the recent spate of robberies in Glastonbury. He also believes that his mother had discovered that the robberies were in some way connected to the church."

"One certain connexion with the robberies was made plain to me," Paul said. "When I went out to speak with those merchants and shopkeepers who were robbed, I was attacked and my life threatened if I did not stop asking questions."

"It is entirely thanks to Paul," the Lady emphasised as she ticked facts off her fingers, "that we know: 1. the robberies were very carefully planned, 2. based on inside information, and 3. had some connexion with the church. Finally, we have been led to see a connexion between the robberies and Paul's mother's death."

"Well," Jeremy's face lighted as his interest was stirred. "This is far more complicated than a simple assault, Paul. I am sorry for your loss, and I can surely understand why you need to find who did this."

"It is not because I desire vengeance, Jeremy," Paul said shaking his head. "Regardless of how badly my parents were both treated by the citizens of Glastonbury, I hope to put an end to the rash of crime that has occurred here and bring my mother's murderer to justice. I am convinced that mother discovered someone who was involved and how the robberies were being informed. The thefts and her death are connected in some way."

"So, we have our work cut out for us, Jeremy," the Lady said. "Where do you suggest we begin?"

"We shall begin by never going anywhere in the town alone," Jeremy grinned. "Also, my Lady, I think we must learn what is being said in the town. If, as Mistress Nan says, there is comment and question among the lads in the barn, we shall surely encounter a great deal more in the public houses of Glastonbury. With your permission, my Lady, I will ask sturdy Gareth to join us."

Paul could see from the Lady's expression she was ready for them to be on the trail once again and was pleased by Jeremy's suggestions. "I will be more comfortable knowing that you make this venture in force. Gareth is a good companion when seeking information, Jeremy. He says little but listens carefully. John will surely be willing to accompany you as well," the Lady added. "Giles and Carrick will remain here with me."

Apollonia obviously continued to express her wish for caution. "Before I send you out, each of you will promise me that you will keep together and take no unnecessary risks. It appears that Glastonbury has eyes and ears tuned to taking advantage of people's weaknesses."

"Let us away to the barn, Paul," Jeremy told him. "We will collect John, and the men of the household to tell them of our plan."

"Before you go," the Lady made them pause, "I have one other thing of which I wish you will make inquiries for me. It may not be at all related to our quest, but I should like to know. My dear Nan has become devoted to Glastonbury's anchorite, Brother Johanus, attached to Saint John the Baptist Church. He has become her spiritual guide and one whom she finds to be truly devout. When I visited Johanus' window, however, I was seeking to learn his reasons for coming to Glastonbury and his sense of mission as an anchorite. He answered all of my questions straightforwardly and without hesitation. He also told me that his dwelling at the church was the gift of one person of the town. He did not know who the person was. Brother Johanus assumes that the donor may be some sort of a recluse. See if you can discreetly learn anything about this person: where he lives, if he has a family, and what is the source of his significant income?"

"Aye, my Lady, we shall do our best this evening and report back to you when we return," Jeremy said.

"But you will take no risks," the Lady commanded.

"There will be no risks taken, my Lady. My head remembers well the last time I ventured too far," Paul said with a sheepish grin.

* * *

After the young men were gone, Nan noticed that Apollonia continued to fuss about her solar, obviously distracted and unable to settle. She had no doubt that her mistress was concerned for the safety of each of her men, especially after the brutal attack on Paul, several months earlier. Nan finally walked near the table where Apollonia mindlessly continued to re-arrange notes she was not reading. "My Lady, pray do not distress yourself so. All of your men are conscious of their responsibility for Paul, and I dare say that Gareth, as the eldest of them on this mission, will assume his responsibility for the rest of your affinity."

"You know I have great respect for Gareth, Nan, and I know well his courage and readiness to protect my household. Truly, I have confidence in all of them, including young Paul. Still, I find that I must keep trying to convince myself that sending them out as a group is adequate protection for them." Apollonia continued to pace all the while she spoke.

"It is the unknown that I fear, Nan, and against which I do not know how to proceed. There is an evil force abroad in this town. Some are watching our activities because they felt threatened by Paul's questioning of the burgled shopkeepers. I want to do everything we can to help Paul come to some conclusions regarding the cause of his mother's death. Still, we must continue to be on our guard for Paul. He was the object of their threat, and he is now part of my household. I suspect that his mother must have discovered some criminal activity that is still resident in Glastonbury. Worst of all, whoever they are may well suspect that Paul knows what his mother knew."

"Oh, my Lady, are you saying that there will be further attacks upon Paul?"

"I wish I knew, Nan. The robberies have ceased within recent weeks. Perhaps those responsible have gone from Glastonbury, but they may have only ceased temporarily whilst those responsible retreat into positions more watchful. First and foremost, I think that we must learn who is watching us. Then, we shall be better prepared to discover how they can be stopped."

"Do you continue to suspect Brother Johanus, my Lady? Why were you so keen to question him?"

"No, Nan dear, I can honestly tell you that I do not suspect the good brother. He was completely forthcoming in his answers to my questions and shared with me very intimate life experiences which I do not feel I may reveal to others, even to you."

"May I ask why you felt you must question him?"

"Let me just say that I hoped to learn where he came from originally, and his reasons for coming to Glastonbury."

"Is Johanus' background suspicious, my Lady?"

"No, Nan. His background was troubled, and he has dealt with its problems kindly and lovingly. I am not able to share anything more with you because it is his very private story. I do assure you that you have every reason to have faith in Johanus. He is a good and pious man. At this point, I only want to be certain that he is not being used by those who have evil motives."

* * *

The Lady and her maid were waiting by the main fireplace in the hall when Jeremy, John, Paul, and Gareth returned from their night on the town. Apollonia invited them all to sit together round the table dormant. Nan brought flagons of ale, and the Lady asked Jeremy if they had been able to learn any new information or even gossip about the death of Paul's mother.

"It was particularly interesting to me, my Lady. Though several of the men recognised Paul as a local lad and some expressed their sympathy with him, no one seemed to wish to talk about his mother's death. Nor would they speak of the on-going robberies in the town, or any possibility that there might be a relationship between those events." Jeremy scratched the back of his head and added, "It is as if no one wanted to be seen speaking of any of it with us."

"I felt the same sense of avoiding the subject by those who know me as a local," John told her.

"John is right, my Lady," Paul added. "When I approached two of my school fellows, they expressed friendship with me and good memories of my pa but did not wish to be seen speaking of my mother's death."

"How would you interpret this reception, Paul?" Apollonia was puzzled by, what was to her, an unexpected reaction.

"My Lady, there is a sense of threat abroad in Glastonbury, but we could learn nothing about its source."

"Indeed, my Lady," Jeremy added, "people are not unfriendly with us at the inn, but knowing that Gareth is your servant, local folk stayed away. Few of them offered the slightest conversation with us after exchanging cursory greetings."

"Well, Gareth, this is disappointing," Apollonia told her stablemaster. "I had hoped that the lads in the barn suggested there was on-going gossip about the murder. What say you? It was you who heard the comments first."

"Oi think they keeps their distance cause we be foreigners to Glastonbury, m'Lady. Per'aps if we become reg'lars at the inn, folk will begin to speak more freely with us."

"Then you must seek to become regulars, Jeremy," the Lady said. "Return to the inn during the nights ahead. Do not press the folk with questions, but allow them to come to know you. Possibly, they will suggest some gossip to you. With Paul at your side, people will instantly understand your motives."

"Well, certainly no one wished to discuss the local person who contributed the funds to have Brother Johanus's dwelling built, my Lady," Paul told her. "Everyone stopped talking whenever the question of such a person in the town came up."

"Once again, stop asking for the moment," the Lady said, "and hope that someone will understand the reasons for our interest and volunteer to help us more privately."

* * *

Ronan had been idling about the fish house at Meare for the past two days. There was nothing for him to do, and he hated being around when Jestin Mallot was in the house. Cadoc's uncle was a disgusting creature from Ronan's perspective, endlessly spouting foul-mouthed comments about priests and monks, even though his only avenue of financial support came from the abbey. Every week, a monk and several lay brothers came to collect a supply of eels and fish for the abbey kitchen. Jestin had to be out on the pond for hours to supervise the netting of the daily catch and be prepared to fill their baskets.

Ronan remained hidden in the upper level of the fish house to avoid any notice by the monk or lay brothers when they came. He knew some of them and feared that they might still recognise him, even with his bearded face and worldly dress. When Jestin went outside to serve them, Ronan would crawl behind the huge bed and remain there until they were gone. He knew that he must stay out of sight, but once again, he found himself irritably bored out of his mind.

Jestin's servant girl was also told that she must remain hidden inside when the monks of the abbey came. Arild was a small young peasant woman, barely larger than a schoolgirl. She was able to hide in a corner cupboard near the bed. On this morning Ronan had been watching her intently after Jestin left, and when she moved towards her corner, Ronan reached from the bed and clasped her wrist. There was nothing she could do, and she knew she had to remain silent. She bent down and whispered to him, "Pray master, release me. Oi too must ide."

He said nothing but refused to let her go, all the while pulling her towards the bed. At first, he did not hurt her, but as she continued to struggle, he grew more demanding. She could tell that his motives towards her were more threatening than discourteous and grew more and more aggressive as he pushed her onto the bed. Suddenly he reached beneath her skirts and up between her legs.

"Pray, master, ye must let me go," she said crying softly as she struggled to back away.

Ronan's physical arousal grew evident and ever more insistent until at last he forgot any need to remain hidden and climbed on top of her. She could see that he intended to rape her, and she twisted wildly to get away. No matter how she struggled, she was helpless to resist him. Erild had no strength equal to Ronan's manhandling of her. He grabbed her chin, and pushed her head onto the bed with his left hand. All the while he pulled up her skirts with his right hand and pressed his legs between hers to force them open, while he thrust his rigid male member deeply into her. The girl tried to scream, but Ronan's hand closed over her mouth and nearly suffocated her. In desperation for breath, she ceased to fight him while her limp body only excited her attacker further.

"Oh, yes," he whispered into her ear, "I knew you wanted it; I know you've been lusting after me, you whore. You will continue to pleasure me, do you understand? Whenever Jestin is busy, we shall be as well," he said with a voice full of menace.

The girl lay quietly moaning until at last he emptied himself into her. He stood to pull on his trousers and pushed her prone body to the far side of the bed. "Get up and wash yourself. You will say nothing of this to Jestin. Do you hear, whore? If you cry to him, I shall accuse you of lustful behaviour towards me, asking for money. He may hate me, but I shall tell him that I merely responded as would any normal man. Your price was cheap. Of course, for your prostitution, he will kill you."

Chapter Eighteen

Discreet Entrapment

Nan Tanner was an excellent judge of people. Despite the Lady's questioning of the motives of Brother Johanus, she felt she could trust him implicitly as her Christian counsellor. Nan was aware of those whose basic goodness lay behind a rough outer skin or, as in the case of Gareth, a painfully shy withdrawal from society. She could also see the distrustfulness of those, even in the upper classes, whose pride and covetousness encouraged them into questionable behaviour. In the case of Sir Chad's servants of Aust House, she enjoyed working with all of them. Nan found a sense of good-natured dedication to Sir Chad in each of them. She did her best to encourage and praise them for their service to his household and especially to his children. Yet, Nan had not been able to come to any conclusions regarding Glebb, the newest servant in the household, recently hired by Steward John. Nan could not make up her mind because Glebb made no conversation with others and always stood somewhat apart. He expressed no interest in joining the men of the household during their evening visits to the public house.

There was no doubt that Glebb was consistently willing to do anything asked of him, that he did his work well, and that he was never found idling about. He even volunteered to help Martha Manning when she required some extra muscle in her housekeeping chores.

It was Glebb's silence that bothered Nan the most. He took no part in the conversations among the household staff. He never made comments to her in passing regarding the weather, the changing of the seasons, or the slightest reference to his past. Whenever she asked him a direct question, he always responded politely but with a single word or phrase. It was not that the Lady's maid was nosy; Nan was disturbed by the arbitrary distance that Glebb kept from everyone. He did not seem to want to be part of the Lady's affinity. She raised her concern to the Lady as they sat together in the solar.

"I find that our new servant, Glebb, maintains an unseen wall about his person, my Lady," Nan told her. "He works hard and serves the household well, so I can have no complaints. Still, he chooses not to be close with any member of your staff. I have tried every possible question within the bounds of courtesy to know more of his background and have learned nothing more than his birthplace."

Apollonia put her book to one side and spoke to Nan's point directly. "Perhaps Glebb is a particularly private person who does not wish to share any of his personal thoughts with others. For some people, maintaining their privacy can be a precious expression of one's personhood. On the other hand," the Lady said wondering aloud, "for some, silence can be necessary to hide their true purpose. Perhaps you should continue to ask various things of him, Nan, but try questions that relate to his household duties. For example, does he know his way around Glastonbury well enough to be able to run errands for me? Is he familiar with anyone in the abbey to expand my contacts there? Most importantly, ask if he can he help Gareth, who is new to the town, find his way to the best local iron maker?"

"I shall try, my Lady, and I will ask Gareth to help us."

"Good idea. Gareth will understand why we are hoping to hear Glebb's accents. It is not merely to determine where Glebb is from but also to verify his class. Especially, if Glebb speaks among the lads in the barn, Gareth will tune in to help us."

"I will speak with Gareth now, my Lady. He will send the stable lads out so that we can speak privately," Nan said cheerily as she walked towards the door. Apollonia smiled inwardly at her dear maid in response. She knew that Nan welcomed every opportunity to speak with Gareth personally. The Lady had treasured warm feelings for Nan and Gareth since their earliest days in Apollonia's service together. Nan had never spoken of her love for Gareth, but the Lady was certain of it. She knew that Nan and Gareth's devotion to each other was never fulfilled by marriage only because of Nan's absolute devotion to her.

* * *

Not long after Nan left, Paul knocked upon the Lady's door. Without her servant to answer, Apollonia simply called out, "Enter." Seeing that it was Paul, she urged him to sit with her near the fire and told him immediately that Nan had gone to the barn. Paul hesitated to be seated at first.

"I am truly sorry to interrupt your solitude, my Lady. I should never have done so if I had known that Mistress Nan was not with you. I only came because I felt I must share some news with you."

"You are not to worry, Paul. Nan will return shortly, and I am always anxious to learn any news you may have. From whom did it come? Does it speak to our investigation of your mother's death?"

"It was one of the locals whom I met in the public house last evening, my Lady. Jeremy and I were in the tilting yard this morning when I noticed him signalling me to come to him where he stood outside the gates of Aust House."

"How do you know this man, Paul?"

"One of his sons was with me at the abbey school. He said that he wanted to speak with me alone, and he did not wish to be seen entering the grounds of Aust House."

"What did he want to tell you?"

"He spoke quickly and said only that there continues to be gossip abroad in the town. People are saying that the week before her death, my mother was seen in the dark of night following the lay brothers from the abbey into the town, loudly accusing them of being untrustworthy. In response, one of the lay brothers attempted to stop her public accusations against him by calling her a woman of ill repute."

"Oh Paul, this is dreadful. Do you believe that you can trust this man? Do you think he really has your best interests at heart, or is he merely trying to add to the dreadful accusations of the town against your parents?"

"I have known this man since childhood, my Lady. He was one of my father's patients, and I think he wishes to be forthcoming. Some of the locals are not certain how to express their friendship to me since I have become part of your household. This man meant to be helpful, I am certain of it."

"Could he tell you the names of the lay brothers?"

"No, my Lady, but he said that they were thought to be those who ran away from the abbey earlier in the year."

"Let us keep this to ourselves, Paul. Do not seek to ask anyone for information. Let people come to you as this man has done in a desire to help you. I hope you will continue to visit the inn with Jeremy and the men of Aust Household. Hopefully, you and John as locals can help members of my affinity become familiar to the townsfolk. What you have told me is convincing me that there are people in Glastonbury who know you and wish to be helpful in your search for your mother's murderer. Thanks to your school friend's father, we now have an important lead."

"When we return to the inn this evening, I shall urge Giles and Carrick, as well as Gareth, to sit among the locals, my Lady. I will make certain that their names are known and their positions within your household. We will all make an effort to help the local folk begin to know members of your affinity."

"Yes, I like that," Apollonia told him. "Good thinking, Paul, but promise me that you will all continue to stay together."

"I promise, my Lady, but how can we learn more about the identities of the lay brothers whom my mother publically accused? Must we only wait until some other person feels drawn to speak with me?"

"No, Paul, first we will act. I will send a message to my friend, Prior Compton, at the abbey asking him for their names. Further, I shall try to learn anything that he may be willing to tell me about their backgrounds. There is no doubt that the prior wishes to have them found if they remain in Glastonbury. I know why they ran away from the abbey, and I know how one of them, in particular, got into trouble. But I don't know anything about the other except that they entered the abbey together and remained close companions."

* * *

Glebb was truly frustrated. He had not done so much physical labour in his life as he had forced himself to do in service at Aust House. During the weeks he had been here, he was no closer to learning where the Lady Apollonia hid her son's family treasure during Sir Chad's absence. He knew where the Lady's bedchamber was located, and he also knew that her most secure and private space was her solar. He did not feel that he could speak in confidence with any of the servants, for they were devoted to the Aust household. Most especially, Glebb knew that he could not question the Lady's maid, Nan. He thought her loyalty to the Lady seemed religiously inspired.

Glebb decided when he came to Aust House that he could not converse with anyone in the household. He knew that his usual speech would betray his advanced education as well as his upper class birth. That would not only destroy his anonymity it would raise questions about who he really was and why he had come to work here.

Another thorn in his side was his partner in crime. Ronan was growing increasingly impatient at the amount of time Cadoc as Glebb needed to plan their final robbery. He never missed an opportunity to express his resentment to Cadoc.

They found a place to meet behind the privy outside the back wall of Aust House. Glebb knew that the household stablemaster, Gareth, slept in the barn, but he also knew that Gareth was an early riser and a very sound sleeper. Everyone in the household spoke of it. Gareth's thunderous snoring could be heard whenever they went near the barn in the evening. The space behind the privy made a good meeting place after dark. Glebb had the perfect excuse to go outdoors at night for there was no garderobe in the servants' bedchamber.

Ronan began his swearing complaints as soon as Cadoc arrived to meet him. "Dammit, Cadoc, your disgusting uncle is driving me mad. He acts as if only his opinons are of value and that I must serve him as long as I stay in the fish house. Worse yet, he ridicules me endlessly for being a defrocked priest. I can not take this much longer. We must finish the job, get whatever money and jewels we can, and be gone from this place."

"You will stay where you are, Ron. It is the perfect hiding place to keep you out of Calevera's clutches. I am to help the housekeeper in the Lady's solar this week and will surely be able to discover where things of great value are kept. I promise you we will be ready to do this soon. Then we shall be off."

"I live for the day, Cadoc. You must take a look at this missive that you received at Jestin's place. It comes from the Bishop of Lincoln."

Cadoc held his candle over the letter and read its contents to himself. Before blowing out its flame, he checked the seal and then slipped into his own series of cursing anger. "That whoreson of a bitch has found my uncle but he will never find me. When we leave Glastonbury, we shall go north to the other archdiocese. We shall have new names and appearances and will never be found in York. What say you, Ronan? York is a lovely city and fortunately located for us. The church may wish to deprive us of our holy orders, but we can always declare ourselves to be clergy in York until we are found out."

"Just get us out of Glastonbury, Cadoc. I want to get away from Meare."

"It will happen, Ron, and I will see that your patience is well rewarded. Be prepared to return to me on Friday next."

* * *

Gareth appeared in the kitchen of Aust House very early on the following morning. He was obviously driven by his own purpose. "Nan, ye must elp me. Oi need to speak with the Lady. There be somethin Oi must tell to er."

"The Lady's maid looked into Gareth's eyes and could not remember seeing him so obviously concerned. She asked for no explanation, simply left him in the kitchen, and went directly to the Lady's chamber. Apollonia assumed that Nan had returned to assist her to dress for the day and met her with a smiling greeting. "Good morrow, Nan, I believe we shall have a sunny if cold day."

"My Lady, I can give you no reason for Gareth's early morning appearance, but he says he must speak with you. He has news of some sort that you must know, he says."

"Then we shall waste no time dressing; simply pull this robe about my shoulders and I shall receive him *deshabille* with my hair down."

Nan made no excuses for the Lady's appearance when she led Gareth into the solar. "Our Lady wishes to see you immediately, Gareth," Nan told him. "Would you please share your news with her?"

Gareth knew that he had taken an extraordinary liberty to call at this early hour. He was also confident that the Lady needed to know what he had to tell her, no matter the hour or her state of undress.

Gareth would not lift his eyes at first and struggled to avoid looking at her. "Oi do beg your pardon, m'Lady. Pray, forgive me."

"We have been friends for many years, Gareth. You do not require my forgiveness nor my pardon. Pray tell me what it is that you have discovered?"

"M'Lady, Oi ad to go to the privy before the sun came up this mornin. As I were walkin to the stalls, Oi suddenly became aware that your servant Glebb were talkin with is friend be'ind the wall. Oi would ne'er ave done this except that ye told me to be watchful of this man, Glebb."

"Did you recognise with whom he was speaking, Gareth?" Apollonia asked him.

"No, m'Lady. Ee were a bearded man bout the same size as Glebb, but Oi could not see im well."

"What did you do next?"

"Oi walked outside the privy and went to the end of the buildings where Oi could ear im better."

"What were they saying, Gareth? What did you hear?"

"They was talkin about somebody stayin at Meare till Friday week when it would be done."

"What would be done?" the Lady pressed him.

"Oi can't say, m'Lady. Oi could only tell they be plannin somethin on Friday week."

"If you could not hear what they were planning, why did you feel their conference was threatening to us?"

"M'Lady, it weren't what they was sayin. The other fella gave Glebb a letter that ee said come from the Bishop of Lincoln."

"Why did that strike you as dangerous?"

"It weren't dangerous by itself, m'Lady, but Oi could see that it were in the ands of a man who can read. Glebb be not an unschooled labourer. Ee were readin it. Oi be certain."

Apollonia took his point immediately. "You are telling me that our newest servant is not a common labourer at all but some sort of clerk who is educated?"

"M'Lady, ee took the letter and eld it beneath the light of a candle until ee finished readin it. Then ee tells is friend that they will do the job soon. Once they done it, they will be off to York."

"Gareth, I believe you have discovered a thief within our gates. My sincere thanks to you, dear friend. I wish you to remain here whilst Nan goes to collect John, Jeremy, and Paul. Forgive my state of undress, but we must act now and gather to prepare our defences. Everything must seem to remain normal for the moment. We will give no indication that any of us suspects Glebb. It appears that we have only until Friday next to make the household ready. I am determined that we shall catch them in the act."

* * *

Early in the morning Wort rushed back to Calevera's house on Archers Way. He seemed unable to contain himself as he rushed into the hall. "We got im, Mistress Calevera. That shite, the runaway monk, be back just as ya said ee would. We was watchin when ee were seen in the darkness of last night at Aust Ouse."

"Are you certain, Wort? Did you follow him? Where did the bastard go when he left Aust House?"

"Ee's still there. The lads an me been watchin the ouse for weeks and finally found out that Cadoc be workin inside Aust Ouse. Oi weren't certain it were im at first. Ee's sportin a darker colour in is air and as growed a beard. Calls imself Glebb. When we be watchin last night, ee come out of the ouse and walked to the privy. It were then Oi sees is piss-eatin friend standin with is orse, waitin for im outside the back wall of Aust Ouse."

"You mean you saw both of them: Cadoc and Ronan?" Calevera's interests were fired by Wort's announcement."

"Aye, mistress, they was both there, but Ronan rode away. Cadoc stayed inside the walls."

"When Ronan rode away, did you have him followed?"

"Oi did, an Oi knows where their ideout is now. They not be idin in Glastonbury. We followed that Ronan out to the Meare Fish Ouse."

"Oh, this grows better and better," Calevera said, as if all of her scheming hopes were coming together at last. "Cadoc obviously believes that we think he has run away from Glastonbury, Wort, and that I am unaware of where he is or what he is doing. He must think he has successfully disguised himself from me and is setting up his own robbery scheme from inside Aust House. We shall reveal nothing; indeed we will remain silent, but ever observant. When he and Ronan actually pull off their theft, we shall be waiting to take them after the robbery. Then, you will kill both of them for me as painfully as possible. When they are dead, we shall take the booty and disappear into the night. We could not have designed this more perfectly, Wort. All the loose ends will be tidied away, so to speak, and I can freely resume command. Soon I shall have all of Glastonbury at my feet!" She laughed with the fierce hatred of a betrayed woman.

Chapter Nineteen

Thieves in Pursuit

Prior Compton halted his day to respond immediately to the Lady Apollonia's messenger. He wrote a quick note in answer to hers, sealed it, and placed it carefully into Jeremy's hands. "Pray, tell her ladyship that I shall need to know if she encounters either of these runaways. As leader of the abbey, I have very personal reasons to find them and to see that they are punished for their abuse of our abbey and one of our scholarly monks."

"Yes, my Lord Prior." Jeremy nodded his understanding and left the prior's chambers to collect his horse from the stable. Jeremy had ridden to the abbey because he knew the Lady expected him to return to Aust House as quickly as he could. He had crossed Lambrook Street and passed the turning onto Bove Town Road. Riding directly into the walled enclosure of Aust House he put his horse's reins into the stable boy's hands, and rushed into the hall where the Lady waited. Jeremy placed the prior's message into her hands and told her "Prior Compton emphasised that you must tell him if you encounter these lay brothers, my Lady. He is determined to see that they are punished."

Apollonia broke the prior's seal immediately to read his message:

My Dear Lady Apollonia,

The two lay brothers, Cadoc Winters and Ronan Willoughby, came to us as penitents, having been deprived of their ecclesiastical status as priests. The Bishop of Lincoln sent them to us because of their youth and fine education. He hoped to reinstate them to the priesthood if they fulfilled their penitential promise. Tragically, I have learned that shortly after coming to Glastonbury, they returned to a life of crime. They regularly left the abbey whilst they were resident here, going into the town to offer themselves as priests ready to take citizens' confessions and offer absolution. In truth, they took confessions to gain private and personal information which informed those who robbed our local burghers. These men must be stopped, but we of the monastery have been unable to locate either of them. Pray let me hear if you discover anything of their whereabouts.

Your friend in Christ's service,

Henry Compton, Prior

"At least we have their names, Jeremy. The one who bullied Brother James is Cadoc Winters. The other is called Ronan Willoughby. It turns out that they are defrocked priests who, soon after they came to Glastonbury Abbey, became involved in criminal activities here. This is important," the Lady told him, "because we know the identities of those who informed the series of thefts in Glastonbury and how they did it. Likely it was Cadoc and Ronan who proved to be the connexion that Paul's mother discovered between the robberies and the church. Now, we must discover with whom they were working."

* * *

Later in the day, Nan told Jeremy that she wished to walk into town to visit with her counsellor, Brother Johanus. Jeremy assured her that he was pleased to accompany her and would wait quietly in the church while she spoke with the anchorite. Nan did not bring questions of faith or Holy Scripture on this occasion. She was determined to learn what the Lady Apollonia had asked him.

The space in front of Johanus' window was empty, so Nan went directly towards it while Jeremy entered the church. She knocked gently on the shutters and was greeted enthusiastically by her friend when he opened them.

"Dear Foreigner Nan, how glad I am to see you. Do let us pray together." After they had repeated the Lord's Prayer, Johanus asked Nan how he could help her.

"Brother Johanus, you know how I rely upon you," Nan began, "and I believe that you know how completely I trust your word. Still, I can not rest knowing that my Lady Apollonia felt a need to question you, your calling, and especially why you came to Glastonbury. Will you share your answers to her with me? I ask you as my friend because she says that she can not tell me. She says her information is private and personally yours."

Johanus' shoulders rose as he inhaled a huge breath. "Of course, Nan," he sighed, "I will tell you everything, and you must judge me as you see fit."

Nan moved more closely to the window and listened respectfully as he spoke.

"I came from Bristol and knew I was born to the church at a very early age," Johannus began. "My father was a sailor and frequently away at sea. My mother is an excellent woman, very caring and concerned for anyone needing help. After I had completed my studies and been ordained to the priesthood, I went to serve in a parish church not far from our home on the docks of Bristol. It was a good assignment for me because I understood sailors' lives and felt a keen desire to support their families during their long absences and dangers at sea. At first, the church welcomed me and seemed grateful for my background. However, after my father died, my mother came to live with me. Then everything changed. The people of my parish did not like her and began to make sneering charges against her."

"Good heavens, Johanus, why should anyone be so cruel to your mother?"

"I am convinced that it was simply because she is such a huge woman. My father was unusually tall and broad. He always joked that my mother and he were built to be a perfect fit. Two of my parishioners accused her of being a depraved giant. Even when she attempted to go into the community to visit the sick, take food to the hungry, or share in my ministry, people would run from her. They shut their doors against her and said terrible things about her."

"That is worse than ungrateful, Johanus. You are telling me that the people in your parish judged her viciously without ever taking time to know her."

"Well, it was more than that, I think. In less than a year after I began as their priest, there was a terrible fire in the Lady Chapel of the church. A valuable reliquary containing a fingernail of Saint Brigid was completely destroyed. My mother was blamed. In short, Nan, we were forced to leave Saint Oswald's Church in disgrace because my mother was charged with witchcraft. It was all completely unjust superstition, but I was given no opportunity to defend mother or myself. I thought my work as a priest was finished."

"Surely not," Nan insisted. "You have come to Glastonbury to serve us."

"You must know that it has been a long road, Nan, and a bitter one for my mother."

"How so?"

"I went to serve in the Abbey of Kingswood and struggled to become a good monk. My mother remained in touch with me by messenger and only told me that she had found a position which suited her here in Glastonbury. Things seemed to be going well, but it soon became clear to me that I was not suited to the monastery. Abbot Theodore of Kingswood was first to notice my struggle. He spoke with me several times, and he too could see that I was not called to be a monk."

"'Johanus,' he told me, 'I have no doubt that yours is a calling to serve people in the world, not to withdraw from it.' Abbot Theodore arranged with Glastonbury Abbey's Brother Parker to have me presented to the priest of Saint John the Baptist Church so that I could become an anchorite attached to this church."

"Is that what brought you to Glastonbury, to be near your mother? What a beautiful story, Johanus. I am so pleased for you," Nan enthused.

"Being united with my mother can not happen, Nan, because I am unable to leave my anchorage. I am always near her and know that she is well. We are able to send messages to each other regularly."

"I should like to call upon your mother, Johanus, and tell her how faithfully you have helped me."

"No, dear friend, you do not wish to call upon my mother, but I am grateful for your kind thoughts," Johanus said as his head dropped slightly.

"I will go safely to her, accompanied by Jeremy, if she is here in Glastonbury. It is the least I can do, Johanus."

"Nan, you will not go to visit my mother, nor will you invite her to visit Aust House," Johanus told her quietly. "My mother runs a successful house of prostitution on Wells Road. Everyone in Glastonbury knows of it and refers to the prostitutes in it as Faith's girls. My mother is Faith Morgan."

* * *

Nan was still aghast when she walked into Saint John's Church to find Jeremy and begin their walk home together. Jeremy noticed how unusually quiet the Lady's maid had become, but he said nothing to her. It was a rainy early November day and Nan pulled her hood down over her face. The Lady's maid was a diminutive woman now walking with her head bowed in thought. Jeremy nearly felt he should take her hand to sustain her against the blowing winds, as he would have done a child. Nan remained withdrawn into herself all the way home. Jeremy decided he must stay silent as well.

Nan did not wait to speak with the Lady Apollonia when they arrived back at Aust House. She rushed up the stairs to the Lady's solar, only pausing at the door to compose herself before knocking. When the Lady called for her to enter, she walked into the chamber and began talking as soon as the door closed behind her.

"My Lady, I can not believe what Brother Johanus has just told me about his mother. Forgive me, but when I visited him this afternoon, I tried to learn from him what you had told me were the troublesome experiences of his life. Just as you described, he was completely honest and forthright and told me that his mother is the owner of a house of prostitution in Glastonbury."

Apollonia answered Nan calmly, "I have heard that it is the most successful house of prostitution in Glastonbury."

"My Lady, how can you be so undisturbed by this news?"

"I have no choice, dearheart, because it is true. I also believe Johanus' description of the motherly way in which Faith sees her role as that of protector and carer for her girls. She maintains the house and pays all its expenses whilst sharing a fair return with each of the women on their profits. She sees to it that they are clean, well fed, nicely clothed, and cared for by a doctor of physic if they are ill."

"Johanus is a devout man of God, my Lady. Surely, he can not accept what his mother is doing."

"Johanus does not accept anything, Nan. He simply continues to love his mother who is taking part in the oldest profession in the world. He knows that she was cruelly and unfairly judged as a witch when they lived in Bristol, probably only because of her unusual size. Finally, he refuses to judge her as our Lord Christ has forbidden us to judge."

"I am still unable to understand, my Lady. Are you telling me that we must accept what Faith Morgan does for her living?"

"Nan, you know that I have never told you to accept anything that you can change for the better. We must always see what can be done to improve peoples' lives. What will you change? Will you close down this house and put the women on the streets? Will that make things better? Faith Morgan struggles to care for her girls. What are her other options? Prostitution would not exist in this community if hundreds of its citizens did not choose to use Faith's girls' services regularly."

"My Lady, how can you defend these women who must be regarded as outcasts?"

"I am not defending them, dearheart. I am unable to define as outcasts any who must be seen as serving the needs of their community. Most importantly, I can not accept that our loving God and Father in Heaven loves me and my sinful nature as a titled woman any more or less than He loves Faith and her girls."

* * *

Apollonia had Nan bring Glebb into her solar after the evening meal. The Lady told their new servant that she had a very heavy chest which she wished to store on a tall shelf hidden behind her desk. "As you can see, Glebb, it is far too heavy for Nan to lift it, so I want you to place it there."

She pointed out to him where he must put it and said that there was a small stool for him to stand upon. Glebb smiled his thanks but said that he did not need the stool. He lifted the chest easily and placed it onto its covered place on the shelf near a collection of the Lady's furs.

Glebb, with an inward smirk, stepped backward, bowed, and began to leave the Lady's solar. He was certain at last that he had discovered the family jewel chest and where it was kept next to the

Lady's chamber when her son, the master of the household, was away. He had just been shown its place of safe-keeping. Most importantly, he knew he could now easily return to the Lady's solar in the dark of night and find it. He made a mental calculation of the size of the solar and especially noted where the hidden shelf was located opposite the door into the chamber. He was an accomplished thief, confident that he could find the chest easily and silently.

As he prepared to leave, the Lady called to him, "Glebb, would you kindly bring Mistress Manning to me? I have some lovely news to share with her. My son Chad is returning to Glastonbury."

Glebb left the solar to speak with the housekeeper. He did not return to his chores in the kitchen after delivering his message. Instead, he followed from a distance as Mistress Manning went to the solar. The housekeeper, suspecting nothing, went in to speak with the Lady while Glebb remained outside the door and pressed it open slightly. He felt he must know of the change in plans and remained near to hear what the Lady was telling her housekeeper.

Their conversation was brief, and the Lady seemed quite excited. "Sir Chad will be returning to us on Thursday next, Mistress Manning. Will you kindly ready his chamber and speak with Mistress Farber? I should like the cook to prepare special evening meals with all of Chad's favourite foods." Glebb left the door quickly to return to the kitchen, swearing all the way.

"Damn and blast," he muttered to himself. "If the master of the house is returning on Thursday, I must get word to Ronan that the robbery has to be done by Wednesday night." As Cadoc continued to think on it, however, he began to be encouraged. "No matter, I am now well enough informed. I can show Ronan where to steal the fine silver on the main floor whilst I slip up the stairs to grab the household jewels and furs from the Lady's solar. Surely, Ron will be pleased to have this job done sooner and will cease his whining about his hateful need to hide away at the fish house."

* * *

When Nan re-entered the Lady's solar, Apollonia met her greeting with an inquisitive grin. "Ah, yes, my Lady, I was watching from the top of the stairs and could see that Glebb did not leave the door to your solar after he had brought Mistress Manning to speak with you. I saw him nudge the door open very slightly and lean his ear to it until he could hear your instructions to the housekeeper."

"If he now understands that he must complete the robbery before Thursday, then we should be prepared to help him, Nan. It is very likely that he will need time free from his duties here to contact his partners in crime. Pray be sensible to an unexpected request from him to be away from Aust House. Enable him with time off when he asks for it and be sure to have Jeremy follow him. For the moment, please send Steward John with Jeremy, Giles, and Carrick to me, and ask Paul to accompany them."

* * *

The men of Aust household gathered in the Lady's solar, and Nan encouraged them to sit together because the Lady needed to speak with them. Apollonia began by saying that she had been given reason to think that Aust House would be robbed later in the week. "We do not know precisely when, but it is likely to be attempted late Wednesday night of this week."

The Lady's announcement was met with an audible gasp, but they were not surprised by her calm approach because it seemed typical of her in times of crisis. John and Jeremy could not hide their sense of responsibility in the master's absence. "We must be ready to deal with this threat, my Lady. How are we to prepare?" Jeremy asked her.

"Let me share with you my suspicions at this point. Our newest servant, Glebb, has come to work here for the purpose of learning the interior of Aust House to organise the theft. We must do nothing to alert him of our suspicions. In preparation, Jeremy, I will outline each of your defensive assignments. John, you must share information with Gareth and with Brother William. I confess that I am operating on suspicion, but I think that I have been able to move up the scheduled robbery to next Wednesday night. I managed to tell Glebb a lie in a roundabout way by speaking with Mistress Manning within Glebb's hearing. I told her to prepare for Sir Chad's return to Aust House on Thursday next. Glebb is intelligent enough to realise that when Chad returns with his men, the masculine strength of the household will increase to ten. He surely wants to achieve the robbery whilst the master is away."

Apollonia began to assign specific tasks for everyone sitting round her. "John, please tell Brother William that he is to remain in the nursery with Nan on Wednesday evening to guard Mistress Eleanor and the children. At the same time, John and Jeremy, you will take up guard hidden inside my solar. Giles, you and Carrick will be on concealed watch through the rest of the house. Paul, you will join Gareth in patrolling the outer walls, keeping watch against the arrival of Glebb's accomplices who will surely come to help him. You should all be armed because I want to take these men with their spoils in hand. I intend to question them before they are turned over to the sheriff's men."

* * *

Early the following morning, Glebb appeared in the kitchen to ask Mistress Nan if he could be allowed to borrow a horse from the stables. He had received a message telling him that his sister was ill, he told her. He begged permission to ride to the village of Street and visit with her.

"I am very sorry to hear of your sister's illness, Glebb, and I will speak with Gareth for you. I can allow you to be gone today, but you must be returned by the evening. Why not take several of these storage apples from our orchard with you?"

"Gramercy, Mistress Nan," Glebb told her feigning humble gratitude.

"Then, come with me to the stables, and I shall send you on your way."

Inside the barn, Nan could see that Gareth was not happy to place one of the Aust household mounts into the hands of this servant whom he now knew to be a potential thief. Nan made a point to tell Gareth that the Lady Apollonia had approved of Glebb's visit with his sister in Street.

Gareth brought one sturdy mare from the stables and showed Glebb where to find saddle and harness. Afterwards, Nan noticed a rather disgruntled Gareth walk out from the barn and not return. She stayed in the barn long enough to store the sack of apples in his wallet and wish Glebb a safe journey before she returned to the house.

What Nan did not know was that when Gareth left the barn, he jogged from Bove Town Road to the centre of the High Street while Glebb was busy saddling the mare and making his preparations to be underway. The stablemaster's intention was to be in the Market Place where he would be able to see which turning Glebb made on his supposed journey out of town towards Street. Within the hour, Gareth returned to Aust House and marched into the hall where Nan sat with the Lady Apollonia.

"Well, ee not be goin where ee said, m'Lady."

"What do you mean, Gareth?" Apollonia asked him.

"Oi watched im from the Market Place, and ee turned up Northload Street to leave Glastonbury. If is sister be in Street, ee should ave made the turnin off Magdalene onto Street Road. Ee ne'er got that far."

"Good work, Gareth," Apollonia encouraged him. "Where do you think he might really be going?"

"Oi can ave no trust in this fellow, m'Lady, but e'en Oi knows that where ee took the turnin, ee were on the road to Meare."

"Then, once the robbery has occurred, perhaps we should be prepared to seek out the location of their hideout. I intend to discover the full number of those responsible for these crimes," Apollonia insisted. "Please have our horses saddled that evening, Gareth. They must be ready whenever they are needed."

When Gareth begged leave of the Lady to return to the barn, he walked past Nan and bent down to whisper into her ear, "Oi just ope ee brings the Lady's orse back."

* * *

Cadoc's ride to Meare went very quickly, but before he could arrive at his destination, he was forced to stop abruptly. It was obvious to him that the wagon of one of the monks and a lay brother had come from the abbey. They were being excessively chatty with his Uncle Jestin, so Cadoc took refuge in a grove of trees near the road where he could remain mounted and watch until the monks finally left. Even with his disguised face, he could not risk being seen, certainly not by the lay brother who accompanied the monk. Cadoc knew this lay brother heartily resented him and his intimidation during their days together in the abbey.

Cadoc rode out from the grove when he was certain that they were well on their way back towards Glastonbury and galloped on to the entrance of the fish house. He quickly tethered the horse he was riding aand bounded up the stairs to the upper level living space where he burst through the door.

"Ron, the time has come to lay our plans. We have to do the robbery on Wednesday night."

"Thanks be, Cadoc," Ronan said as he stood up from his stool near the fireplace. "I am ready to leave this place."

"Uncle Jestin, your help in this matter will make you a rich man. Only today I was able to lift the large chest containing the Aust family treasure. It weighs enough to fill all our pockets with gold once we are able to sell its contents."

Jestin merely grunted as if to say he would believe it once he could count his profits.

"So what shall we do next, Cadoc?" Ronan's questions emphasised his enthusiasm to be underway. "Where do you want me to meet you on Wednesday?"

"You must be ready to ride into Glastonbury with my horse in tow by early evening. Tether our horses near the Slipper Chapel of Saint James, down the road from Aust House, and remain there in the shadows. Begin your walk to Aust House after dark, stopping outside the walled back garden gate behind the privy where we usually meet. I shall let you into the garden, but we shan't actually enter the house until later, in the hours after midnight when I am certain everyone is asleep. Once inside the house, I shall show you where to find the silver whilst I steal up to the solar to take the jewellery chest and the furs. Have you carefully studied the map of the interior of the house that I gave you, Ronan?" On this point, Cadoc pressed him.

"Well, of course I have," Ronan lied. "I shall be more than ready."

"Then, uncle, from Aust House we will return to Meare, divide the loot, and be on our way in the early hours after dawn."

"Oh, aye," Jestin spit back, "just be sure I gets my share."

* * *

Cadoc as Glebb rode his borrowed mare into the barn of Aust House after his return at sunset but while there was still light in the western sky. He handed the reins to one of Gareth's stable lads and walked towards the rear entry to the house. Once inside, he made a dramatic point of finding Nan before he did anything else.

"Gramercy, Mistress Nan, my sister sends her thanks."

"May we hope that she has begun to improve, Glebb?"

"Yes, mistress," Glebb said, returning to his single-word answers.

"Has she been able to find healing skills to help her?"

"Yes, mistress."

"Shall I see you at our evening meal, then?"

"Yes, mistress." With that, Glebb bowed to Nan and returned to the kitchen.

Nan, however, went directly to the Lady's solar. "Glebb has returned, my Lady," she announced to Apollonia as she closed the door.

"Our drama has begun, would you say, Nan?" Apollonia asked.

"Well, at least part of it did not happen," Nan grinned.

"How can you know that, dearheart?"

"Gareth was fully expecting Glebb to steal one of your horses, my Lady. In fact, he returned to us and the mare to Sir Chad's barn as well."

Chapter Twenty

Criminals Exposed

The situation at Meare grew increasingly tense. Ronan hated Cadoc's uncle, and Jestin Mallot had grown ever more annoying to his nephew's friend. After all, it was he, Jestin, who provided the food and shelter for this pompous arse from Oxford, whose only word of thanks proved to be another complaint. Worse yet, Jestin was certain there was something else going on. His little wench followed him for the past week whenever he went down to the pond to net the catch for the abbey. She said nothing but kept a constant distance between Ronan and herself. She refused to stay in the fish house when Jestin was outdoors. The fish master hung up his nets for the last time this afternoon and pulled the girl from the clump of bushes at the side of the pond where she had been hiding while he worked.

"What be wrong stupid girl? Ya should be inside cleanin and cookin."

The girl said nothing, only continued to shake her head, "No". She would not return to the fish house until Jestin went ahead of her. He raised his hand to strike her, but she did not move. Jestin lifted her head to look at him, but she would not raise her eyes. "Look at me eyes, wench," he shouted.

When she lifted her eyes to meet his stare, Mallot could see there were tears in them. "Why be ya cryin? What ave ya done, Arild?"

She dropped her eyes and remained silent. At last, Jestin's twisted mouth grimaced into a different question. "So what as ee been doin to ya?"

At this, she dropped her head into her hands and began to sob.

"As ee touched ya?" he shouted towards her.

She kept her head down but nodded, "Yes."

"Where as ee touched ya?"

The girl slowly lifted her skirt and exposed the bruising between her legs.

"God damn lecher!" Jestin shouted all the way back to the house and up the stairs to the upper floor where Ronan was lying on the bed.

"Get out of me ouse, ye lecherous pig!" Jestin shouted at him, threatening all the while with his club in hand.

Ronan sat up on the bed and began to crawl to the other side towards the wall, away from Mallot. He could see the fury in Jestin's eyes and understood that Cadoc's uncle knew everything.

"It was not my fault, Master Mallot," Ronan said, at first trying to speak calmly as one man to another. "She tempted me and offered herself to me for money. I did as any normal man would do, nothing more."

"Arild knows nothin of money, you shitefaced priest. Get out," Jestin roared, lifting his club as he continued to approach.

Ronan now moved more quickly, backward from Mallot along the walls of the chamber towards the door, all the while looking at the powerful arms with the massive weapon threatening him. The little wench stood behind Jestin and would not leave his side. "Surely, we can discuss this as reasonable men? Do you not see? She did it."

"Out!" Jestin rushed towards Ronan who left off any defence and dashed through the door as Jestin's club crashed against the upper door frame.

Ronan ran down the steps to the rail where he had left their horses saddled and waiting. He grabbed the reins of Cadoc's mount and leapt into his saddle, kicking his horse into a startled gallop. Ronan never looked back while he raced down the lane towards the road to Glastonbury.

* * *

Ronan knew he was riding to Glastonbury earlier than had been the plan. He had made a muddle of things that must be explained somehow. He reasoned to himself, "I can keep out of sight until later tonight. I have Cadoc's horse in hand; everything is ready, just a bit earlier than we thought."

Ronan's ride back slowed to an easier pace while he tried to think of ways to change Cadoc's original ideas and, especially, to think of a good way to get even with Jestin. Ronan did not care about the girl; he never knew she had a name. He had merely used her to ease the boredom of having to remain at the fish house. There was no need for Cadoc to know about the pleasures he had taken with his uncle's wench.

"I have it," Ronan schemed to himself as he rode. "I shall suggest to Cadoc that we keep all of the loot. There is no need to share anything with Mallot. Instead of riding to Meare, I will suggest to Cadoc that we can each have a much larger share if we forget about Meare and simply continue out Bove Town Road towards Wells." In that way, Ronan thought, they could be on their way to York immediately, and Cadoc need never know of the little scuffle he had with his friend's Uncle Jestin. For now, Ronan decided to spend the rest of the day in comfort. After tethering their horses in the assigned spot near the slipper chapel on Bove Town Road, he walked back into Glastonbury to his favourite public house.

* * *

Well after dark had fallen, Ronan returned to the place where he promised to meet Cadoc. He waited there for a matter of minutes until Cadoc opened the gate and let him inside the wall. Quietly they walked through the garden at the back of Aust House and entered the kitchen. Everyone in the household had gone to bed, Cadoc told him. "You must stay here in silence until I can be certain that everyone is asleep; then, I will return."

Ronan was grateful to wait for him. He knew that he had not studied the drawing, as he promised Cadoc he would, and remained uncertain of the inner layout of the house. He needed to have Cadoc show him where to go.

* * *

As usual, time went by annoyingly slowly for Ronan. He found himself lighting a candle to prowl around the kitchen looking for whatever he might find in the larder. Jestin Mallot had thrown him out at Meare hours before the main evening meal, and he was feeling famished. There was plenty of food stored in the larder. Ronan simply helped himself to various pieces of ham, cheese, and bread. He was feeling much better about how this was going until suddenly he managed to knock a platter onto the floor with a crash. He froze, blew out the candle, and hurried back into the kitchen where Cadoc had left him. After what seemed endless minutes, Cadoc came into the kitchen furiously looking for him.

"What are you doing, you fool? Everyone must be sleeping soundly. Otherwise you would have them all awake and searching for us," he hissed in an angry whisper. "Sit down and do nothing until I give the signal."

At last, when Cadoc was certain that no one had been disturbed by Ronan's noise, he brought him from the kitchen and led him into the hall. There, he silently pointed out the collection of silver and indicated that Ronan should take it all while he quickly ran upstairs to the Lady's solar.

Once inside the Lady's chambers, Cadoc moved like a cat, silently, cautiously, but going directly to the hidden shelf where he had placed the Lady's jewellery chest. It was heavy but no struggle for a man as strong as he. He slid the chest from the shelf, pulled it into his arms, and also took all of the valuable furs from the shelf, stuffing them into a large sack he carried. Finally, he left the solar as quickly as he had come.

Cadoc found Ronan waiting for him in the darkness of the main floor hall. He had gathered a significant collection of silver plate, silver service, some vessels of gold and fine quality linens which he had in the sack, now flung over his shoulder. Cadoc led the way from the house through the kitchen and into the garden towards the back gate. Ronan followed him.

Cadoc picked up the pace once they were outside the garden wall. The two men hurried down Bove Town Road on foot to the Slipper Chapel of Saint James where their horses were waiting for them. Cadoc began to tie the huge sacks of their spoil to his saddle. "That was easy, Ron," Cadoc said very pleased with himself. Before they climbed into their saddles, Ronan walked closer to his friend, suggesting they would be smart to begin their ride to Wells now.

"We have no reason to ride back to Meare, Cadoc. You said yourself that your uncle Jestin is a greedy bastard. Meare is out of our way and a waste of our time. Why should we not go inside the chapel, make our split here, and then be on the road to Wells before dawn breaks. There will be that much more for each of us. Jestin has done nothing to help with this robbery except for some lousy food and to sleep on his floor."

Cadoc seemed to like his idea; instead of objecting to Ronan's plan, he added his own thoughts. "There is no doubt that none of this could have happened if I had not inserted myself into the Aust household. I lived and worked like a dog there. No one offered any help to me, not even you, Ronan. All right, Ron, let's forget Meare. We will take the booty and make our split. It will not take us long."

The two thieves hoisted their bags of stolen goods from their saddles and walked into the darkened chapel. Carrying their loot to the altar, Cadoc took out everything and began to spread it before them while Ronan lighted a collection of candles.

Cadoc was about to open the large chest when a strong female voice interrupted their plans. "Stand back and put your hands to your heads!" she commanded the two lay brothers. Calevera walked into the chapel and stood in front of Wort with six of her henchmen around them, all with swords drawn.

"We shall take what you have for our use, gentlemen," she demanded. "Do you see how pitiful it is, Wort? There is no loyalty to class amongst these gentles and truly no honour among thieves."

Cadoc turned round abruptly trying to keep his right hand near the dagger in his belt. Wort slipped into the darkness and remained unseen. The lay brother could see how desperate their situation was but attempted to create the best explanation that he could. "Come now, Calevera," he said pretending friendship with her. "We will do the split among us all. I have no desire to keep a third from you."

At that, Calavera gave out a huge guffaw of disbelief. "Can you believe it, Wort? He pretends friendship with us."

"Why do ye put up with this shite, Calevera?" Wort spoke as he grabbed Cadoc's arm and pulled it behind his back. "Ya know ee be a liar and a cheat. Let me kill em both."

"Consider, Calevera," Cadoc looked up at her pleading, "you know that I have been of great help to you in the past. Surely we can repair our friendship and continue in business together?" Cadoc's voice attempted to express fondness for her but was unable to conceal his real fear. "Do let me return to your side. I can be your right hand man, an intelligent one, able and experienced to design your schemes. I shall not need to be seen in the town. I shan't need to be a priest to plan your robberies for you."

"What about me, Cadoc?" Ronan shouted at him peevishly. "I thought we were friends. Will you abandon me for this bitch?"

Wort dropped Cadoc's arm and lashed out in a mighty blow towards Ronan's face. Ronan swiftly sank beneath the altar where he stood, and Wort's blow flew over him.

"Mistress Calevera," Ronan whined as he turned to look up to her from under the altar, "pray forgive me. You must not believe the betrayal of my so-called friend. Cadoc is attempting to manoeuver himself back into your good graces. Truly, he has never ceased calling you every foul and disgusting name for womankind."

"Ah, no," Cadoc said as he tried to move away from Ronan. "Calevera, you must see the truth. This man is the murderer of that Medford woman. She began to accuse him in public. To shut her up, he attacked her in the darkness of an alley and strangled her."

"You filthy cheat," Ronan shouted. "You know that I did not strangle her. You held her by her neck whilst I raped her. There was no doubt that she wanted it. No reputable woman would follow men in the dark of night unless they are whores. You were laughing at her feeble struggle and obviously enjoyed it all the while she fought against you. It was you who twisted her head until you broke her neck. I raped her, you killed her."

"Ah, Wort," Calevera said with bitter humour, "are we not hearing the best of entertainment? These two will stop at nothing to expose each other. Can you imagine what they will report to the sheriff about us, my friend?"

Calevera decided that she had seen and heard enough. She signalled to the collection of her henchmen, and they began to close in a tight circle around Cadoc and Ronan. Wort led the rest with his dagger in hand.

When he began to lift it above the head of Cadoc, another strong female voice shouted at them, "Drop your weapons, all of you!"

Calevera turned round sharply and saw behind her in the little chancel of the chapel an even larger circle of men, all with weapons drawn.

"I am the Lady Apollonia of Aust, Calevera. Cadoc Winters and Ronan Willoughby have robbed me this night. If you wish to avoid being charged with robbery, you will tell your men to obey."

"Why should I fear such as you?" Calevera smirked. "Do you think my men will surrender to an old woman and a few clerks?"

"Keep a civil tongue in your mouth when you address my sister, woman." A knightly figure walked through the door of the chapel declaring, "I am the Earl Ferdinand of Marshfield, acting in behalf of the sheriff of Gloucestershire. My men have this chapel surrounded. You are all under arrest."

* * *

The sun was rising when Ferdinand's men finished tying each of the thieves to their horses' saddles to lead them back into Glastonbury and the abbey gaol. Cadoc and Ronan ceased to speak with each other as each seemed determined to find ways to place blame on the other. Ronan constantly whined that he had done nothing; he only followed Cadoc's instructions.

Calevera did not utter a word but silently planned to summon her man of law to her defence as soon as they returned into the centre of town. After all, she told herself, it was Cadoc and Ronan who had been caught in the act of robbing Aust House. She would say that she had captured them with their booty in hand.

Wort knew that she was thinking through her rational excuse for being present at the time of the robbery. He struggled to ride as near to her as he could so that whatever she said, he would agree with her and second her as she provided justification for him.

The Lady Apollonia purposefully manoeuvred her horse next to Calevera's mount in an effort to speak with her. "I have hoped to meet you, Mistress Calevera, though surprised by the circumstances."

Calevera said nothing, merely indicated that she knew very well who the Lady was.

"Would you be willing to tell me if you were the benefactress of Brother Johanus, the anchorite whose cell is attached to Saint John the Baptist Church?"

Calevera refused to respond to the Lady's question. She looked straight ahead and simply said, "There is no reason for my arrest. My men and I interrupted the robbery of your household. It was we who made this capture of the true criminals possible."

"I do thank you for whatever assistance you have provided," Apollonia said slightly skeptically, "but I should like to know more about you. Are you a native of Glastonbury? Does your family live here?"

Again, Calevera refused to respond to her, so Apollonia tried a different question. "Are you a woman of the West Country, mistress?"

"I come from Devon," she said abruptly.

"Ah," the Lady responded enthusiastically, "I have many friends in Devon. Perhaps we have acquaintances in common."

Calevera returned to a state of stony silence, so Apollonia tried a different approach.

"If you are Devon born, what has brought you to Somerset?"

"A man," she seemed to spit the words from her mouth, "an unfaithful, disloyal, inconstant, perfidious man."

"Are you saying that you came to Glastonbury to be married?"

"Indeed, I came here in good faith, prepared to become a loving wife. As our wedding approached, I discovered that the man whom I thought had declared his love for me rejected me, justifying his perfidy by insisting that his life must be dedicated to the service of God. I offered everything to him: my dowry, my love, my body. He rejected it all," she said in a hateful tone, "and I will never allow him to forget it. There will be no life in a nunnery for me. He can remain behind abbey walls, but I will never forget his betrayal and will be certain that he is never allowed to forget it either."

"Is this man still living here in Glastonbury? Is he one of the Benedictines?"

"Oh, yes," Calevera said bitterly, "he does his good deeds every day: feeds the hungry, gives to the poor, protects the innocent. He puts on his show of holiness, but he has never fulfilled his promises to me and never accepted his responsibility for destroying my life."

"Who is this man, Calevera?"

"Everyone in Glastonbury knows him," she shrugged.

"Can you tell me his name?"

"If it matters to you," she said, "question the bloody prior."

"Are you are speaking of Henry Compton?" Apollonia was taken aback, especially because she thought she knew the prior well and could not believe her friend capable of such betrayal. "The prior of Glastonbury Abbey is Henry Compton. Was it he who abandoned you?"

"Think what you like," Calevera said bitterly, and turned away.

At that point, Wort forced his mount between Calevera's horse and the Lady's palfrey. The Lady Apollonia's conversation with Calevera could not be continued.

Chapter Twenty-one

Betrayal Confirmed

Early the following morning, Prior Compton accompanied the Earl Ferdinand into the abbey gaol to confront the captured thieves. The prior was anxious to interview Cadoc and Ronan to learn as much as he could about the extent of the robberies committed in Glastonbury while they had been lay brothers at the abbey. They went directly to the cell where Cadoc and Ronan were being held, but the prior was shocked to realise that the cell contained more than just the two lay brothers. One brute of a man called Wort was on the floor of the left side of the cell with several of his henchmen. The two lay brothers obviously kept to themselves on the opposite side of the cell, but when the prior entered the gaol, each of them leapt to the bars of the cell.

"You will tell me how you organised these foul robberies, Cadoc," the prior demanded. "I know now that you abused our monks and deceitfully used our abbey as your cover. How many of the townspeople's homes and shops did you plunder?"

Ronan began to shout his response, all the while pointing his finger at Cadoc. "My lord prior, this is not my fault. I only did what Cadoc required me to do. I would never betray the privacy of the confessional, and I certainly never robbed those whose homes we visited. It was Cadoc who was determined to become rich and run away to York. He threatened to beat me if I did not help him. You know what a bully he is. Look what he did to Brother James."

Cadoc's pretence of humility returned in the presence of the prior. He knelt at Compton's feet inside the bars of their cell and said humbly, "My lord prior, I pray you will ignore all that Ronan says. He pretends innocence, but he has hidden away every bit of his share of the money and treasure that was stolen. I, on the other hand, was badly used by that evil woman. It was she," he pointed at her, "Calevera, as leader of the local gang, who planned and took charge of the robberies. It was she who had the listening hole built into the anchorite's cell, and she who used our ministry in the confessional to gain personal information to enable and inform her henchmen."

Cadoc was pointing towards the female figure sitting on a bench in the shadows. "She did it, father prior. Ronan and I robbed no one. We ne'er stole a ha'penny. She is the leader and organiser of all the robberies in Glastonbury. She said she was determined to humiliate a leader of the abbey whom she knew to be a hypocrite." The woman did not move, and Prior Henry ignored her.

"You and Ronan lied to us when you came to Glastonbury. You are both defrocked priests who were thrown out of your home diocese. You misused your positions as lay brothers to hide your crimes in Glastonbury. And you, Cadoc, tortured and bullied Brother James all the while he was writing the new history of our abbey. Most egregious of all, I have learned that you corrupted and debased the confessional. Dear God, forgive us. You elicited personal and private information from those whom you then arranged to rob. Can you deny any of these heinous sins against God and your fellow men?"

"Oh, no, my lord prior, I shall confess my guilt, but you must know that I was led astray by the sexual temptation of that woman in the cell. She promised she would make us rich. I was a poor young priest living a celibate life, father prior. I was unable to defend myself against her aggressive seduction."

At this, the woman in the shadow behind him howled with laughter. "You could not manage to excite a dog in heat, Cadoc. You are neither young nor a man. In God's Truth, you are a filthy sodomite."

"Do not listen to her, my lord prior. Our abuse of the confessional was her idea. Ronan and I did not take part in the robberies. We merely shared information with her and her henchman, Wort. It is they who are the criminals. We were used by them under threat of death if we did not cooperate. I pray that you will have us released from this prison straightaway. We claim our rights to trial under canon law."

"Before you claim any right, Cadoc, or Glebb, as you have made yourself known to my household, you will answer my questions," Apollonia said as she walked from the side of her brother, Ferdinand.

"Ah, my Lady Apollonia, I am truly sorry," Prior Compton said, obviously ashamed of the attack upon her household. "All of us in the abbey were completely taken in by these evil clerics. I was unaware how they used their residence with us against the burghers of Glastonbury and even attempted the robbery of your son's home."

"If you will allow me, Prior Henry," Apollonia said accusingly, "I have come to charge them as responsible for a more brutal crime than robbery. Christina Medford was murdered earlier in the year. The gossip of the community suggests that she was killed because of her public accusations against these two lay brothers. Christina discovered what they were doing and how they were misusing their priestly role."

"Hold, my Lady," Cadoc said snidely, "that is, as you say, mere gossip. You can prove no element of truth in it. There are no witnesses to such lies."

"On the contrary, Cadoc Winters, or whoever you truly are, we have a witness. A local beggar has come to speak with Paul Medford, Christina's son and a member of my household. He gave us his word that he was begging near the Market Place on the night of her murder. This witness says that he saw both of you, Cadoc and Ronan, drag Christina into an alley behind the Pilgrims Inn."

"That is beneath you, my Lady of Aust," Cadoc insisted self-righteously. "How can you accept the word of a beggar against a gentleman of the church?"

"Caedmon the Beggar is desperately poor but known by everyone Glastonbury as an honest fellow who has fallen on hard times. I know you only as a deceitful and cunning servant who sought to rob me. Caedmon's word will be accepted in a court of law," Apollonia added quickly.

Ronan had been listening to everything Cadoc said up to this point but now suddenly began to howl, "My Lady, I did not kill her, Cadoc did. Yes, we needed to shut her up because her accusations were bound to be noticed by people on the street. We dragged her into the alley to shut her up. That is all."

"Well, it was not quite all, was it Ron?" Cadoc smirked. "It was you who insisted on having your way with her."

"It was you who seized her round the neck. I only did what any virile man would do when tempted, nothing more. She refused to lie still, and you put too much pressure on her slender neck. It snapped. You killed her, Cadoc. I am not guilty of murder."

"Oh, shut up, Ronan. No matter what the charges, my Lady, you can do nothing. We claim our rights as members of the clergy, once ordained, always ordained. You can not try us under civil law. We are subject only to canon law."

"Truly, my Lady, they are correct," the prior told her. "We are all witnesses to these confessions, however, and I shall see that they are written down and signed. We must transport these men to the Bishop of Bath and Wells for trial."

Now, the woman stepped forward out from the shadows at the back of the cell towards the bars. "Is it not extraordinary what the wealth of the church can purchase for itself? Its own version of the law enables its criminals to avoid hanging."

Prior Henry was startled. Apollonia thought that he seemed stricken as he looked upon the woman's face. It was as if he could not believe what he was seeing. He moved closer to the cell and stood directly before her. "Vera, is it you?"

"Surprise, Henry. I prefer to remain in the shadows, but I am always prepared to exact my personal revenge upon you."

* * *

The Earl Ferdinand prepared to take Cadoc and Ronan from Glastonbury to the cathedral town of Wells later that week. Apollonia noticed that he stayed at Aust House longer than expected. The Lady was pleased that her brother seemed to wish to spend more time with her. They had been sitting together before the large fireplace in the hall and, she thought happily, were sharing a rare occasion for conversation. Ferdinand was sickened by the foul behaviour of the clerics and their abuse of the church against the merchants of the town.

"This has been a disgusting business, Polly, and I do hate to leave you here whilst Chad remains away with the king."

"Dear brother, Nan and I are well protected within Chad's household and very comfortable. Best of all, I am glad to be here with my grandchildren. I have seen a sense of recovery in them since the dreadful loss of their mother last year. Juliana grows to look more like her mother each day. Young Geoffrey has become an excellent horseman. Even baby George is able to handle himself on his pony. During Chad's absence, each of his children has learned well, not only in school but also by spending time with my servant, Gareth. Pray, grant them some small acknowledgement of their achievements before you must leave."

"I shall be a proper great-uncle, Polly," Ferdinand sighed, "but I am forced to complete my shrieval tasks and deliver Cadoc and Ronan to the Bishop's gaol in Wells. I will see to it that charges of robbery, sexual assault, and murder will be pressed against them both. I confess it is difficult for me to regard either as a churchman, much less a whole human being. They have degraded to the level of slime, foul evil substance with no grace or goodness in their characters. What is happening to our world, sister? I can not fathom the church's need for pardoners, summoners, and those whose only mission as clerics is the pursuit of personal wealth."

"My lord brother," Apollonia smiled warmly at Ferdinand, "we must not allow ourselves to be overwhelmed by such creatures as Cadoc and Ronan. I try to think instead of the many faithful and truly devoted priests, monks, and nuns in our English church. I prefer to focus on the life of my friend, Mother Julian of Norwich. She has inspired the faith of many through her writing in our English tongue. It is beautiful, Ferdinand. Mother Julian has been able to express her personal near-death experience as an experience of divine love."

"You know I am no scholar, Polly. I have not read Mother Julian's treatise. I see my role in life to protect those who live on my lands, to serve my king when called, and to worship my God. I can find no gallantry, courtesy, or honour in any man, lay or cleric, who flaunts any position to grow rich and abuse power. Ah, well, shan't fix it I suppose. I must be off to bed. The morrow comes early."

Apollonia moved towards her brother to plant a large kiss on his blushing cheek. "Indeed, Ferdinand, you are a good man. I thank God you are my brother."

After she bid Ferdinand good night, Apollonia sent Nan to bring Paul to her private chamber. When the lad came into her solar, the Lady begged him to join her near the fire while she pulled a warm shawl round her shoulders. "Come and sit with us, Paul. Pray, forgive an old woman, but I find as the days grow colder, my bones seem to grow more stiff."

"Indeed, my Lady, I am grateful to be allowed to speak with you. Can you tell me what you were able to learn? I have heard that both of the runaway lay brothers of the abbey were arrested for my mother's murder."

"You have heard correctly, lad. Because they are clergy and must be subject to canon law, my brother, the Earl of Marshfield, will take them as his prisoners to the Bishop of Wells' gaol on the morrow. They will be prosecuted, Paul."

"Thank God, I pray that mother will finally rest in peace." Paul put his head down as tears slid down his cheeks.

Apollonia saw the tears and dared to hope that Paul could be able, at last, to release the grief and anger he had locked in his heart during the months since Christina was killed.

"Remember that it was you who made this arrest possible, Paul. We were only put on the right trail when you told me of your mother's charges against someone in the church. That helped me focus our search first on the Church of Saint John the Baptist and its anchorite, then upon the abbey. And it was you who pointed to a likely connexion between her death and the robberies going on in Glastonbury." Apollonia could see that Paul was trying to keep his composure. She hoped to help him find positive meanings from a wholly evil event in his life.

"You must also be grateful for the help given you by the good people of Glastonbury, Paul. If they seemed fearful to be seen speaking with you, it was only because of possible retaliation by Calevera's gang against them. Wort's attack on you near the almshouses was precisely that, meant to force you into silence. I do not think that Wort wished to kill you but frighten you enough to stop your inquiries. Pray, remember the good people in Glastonbury who reached out to you. It is because you are a local lad and the son of a physician admired by some, not because you happened to become attached to my household."

"Why did those two lay brothers want to kill her, my Lady?"

"She accused them openly and loudly on the streets of being involved in the robberies, Paul. Both Cadoc and Ronan said that they did not intend to kill her, but they had to do something to silence her. Each of them says the other is the guilty party. I am truly sorry, lad.

During her sleepless nights exploring the town, your mother made the connexion between the lay brothers' visits to various merchants' homes to take confessions and then feed that highly personal information to Calevera's gang to use."

"How could they have been so brutal? They actually broke her neck." Paul's eyes were still full of tears, but he felt he must ask.

"I am not able to answer your question, Paul. I can only say that those who abuse others, especially a single woman, are worse than bullies. Cadoc and Ronan are vicious, unprincipled men who have stooped to great evil in satisfying their greed."

There was a slight smile on Paul's face when he prepared to leave the Lady's solar. "Gramercy, my Lady Apollonia, for everything you have done to help me deal with my loss. I especially thank you for your reminder of the help given to me by the townsfolk. They have been good friends to me. As Brother William has promised, my parents are rejoined in death and rest in peace. Now I am able to believe it."

"Brother William will offer a mass for the dead on Friday of this week, Paul. All of my household will join you in sharing their prayers for those whom we have lost."

"Gramercy, my Lady, my sincerest thanks," Paul told her as he left the solar.

"Our young Paul is handling his grief in a very mature and admirable way, my Lady."

"Oh, I do hope so, Nan, dear. It is not easy for one left alone in life to heal his losses. I could not describe to him the bestial brutality of his mother's murder. Some things need not be known."

"My Lady, it will be best if he can return to some normality and hope in his future life," Nan said.

"I am planning a surprise for him in the months ahead," the Lady said with a large smile and a wink at her maid.

"May I know of it, my Lady? I promise not to reveal a word."

Apollonia was pleased to share happy thoughts with Nan; words simply poured out of her. "Surely you will remember William of Wedmore, the builder of our chapel in Exeter House, Nan?"

"Indeed, my Lady, that was more than fifteen years ago, was it not?"

"It was, and our friend, William of Wedmore, has become a very successful master mason. Presently he is working on new carvings for the west front of the cathedral of Wells."

"That is an impressive position," Nan put her hand to her cheek. "It would be a great pleasure to meet with Master William again after all these years. Will we be able to see him again?"

"Yes, Nan, and I confess to you that I have asked him to come to Glastonbury for a purpose. I plan to show Paul's carving of Saint Apollonia to him. If he is impressed by Paul's art, and I believe he will be, I shall introduce him to the newest member of my household who designed and completed it."

* * *

After Cadoc and Ronan were taken off to Wells by the Earl Ferdinand and his men on their return journey to Marshfield, Calevera, Wort, and her henchmen remained the only occupants of the abbey gaol. Prior Compton found himself going daily to visit with Calevera. The days were growing shorter and the weather colder as autumn grew into winter. Henry could see that conditions in the gaol were miserable: damp, cold, and not always clean. Calevera never hesitated to point them out to him.

The prior begged God to lead him. He spent hours on his knees in personal prayer earnestly seeking divine guidance. Henry Compton knew he must do something to help this woman who had been an important part of his young life. He knew there was no option for her within the law. She and Wort had been accused of organising all of the robberies and the townspeople were certain of her guilt.

When he tried to speak with her privately, she would only turn from him and demand that he bring her man of law to the gaol. She would not allow herself to be treated as a defenceless woman once again, she shouted. The man of law was summoned to her, but Prior Compton could see that he had no desire to take her defence. In the eyes of the community, she and her men deserved of hanging.

Calevera was told that the town claimed her house on Archers Way and that all of her possessions were being sold off to pay back those from whom she and her gang had stolen. Still, she smirked to herself that she had significant monies hidden away if she could just get free. When Compton arrived on this morning, he tried to deal compassionately with her. "You must see that I can do nothing for you, Vera."

Her only response was to grow hysterical in his presence. "You know you are the beast who destroyed my life," she continued to shout at him. "I was but a girl, holy man. You took what you wanted from me and abandoned me."

When, at last, the prior could bear it no longer, he instructed the gaoler to release Calevera to his custody, and he installed her in one of the abbey guest apartments. She railed against him again and again, insisting that he must also release Wort.

The prior could not recognise the girl he had once known. Calevera had become a vicious and nefarious woman but an intelligent one, highly skilled in manipulation. She could sense the growing guilt and weakness expressed in the prior's behaviour towards her. She was determined to use it.

Prior Henry ceased going to confession. He could find no answer to his prayers, and he could think of no one to counsel him within the abbey. He finally decided that there was only one way to bring this chaos in his life to a close. Late in the last evening of her residence, he walked silently to the guest house and knocked quietly on the door to Calevera's chamber.

When she opened the door to him, she grinned wickedly. "I knew you would come. I hope I have destroyed your self-righteous faith. I can feel you are full of doubt."

The prior entered her room. After she closed the door, he sat on a bench and told her simply, "I give up, Vera; I surrender. What is it you wish me to do for you?"

She arrogantly approached him, listed all of her demands, and when she finished, Henry left her chamber.

Later that night when the hour of midnight passed and the monastery was asleep, the prior returned to the guest house bringing Wort with him. He did not speak with either of them except to gesture that they must follow him. Compton led the couple across the abbey park land, past the fishpond to a deserted back gate in the abbey wall facing Bere Lane. He opened the gate which faced the abbey barn. Calevera and Wort went quickly through it, and the prior slammed it closed behind them. In the silence of the night, Henry Compton fell to his knees and wept. "My God, my God, forgive me. Grant me Your Grace."

* * *

The following morning, Apollonia rose early and busied herself in the hall with Nan and Giles. Unknown to her, a familiar visitor approached Aust House, walking on Bove Town Road. It was Henry Compton, Prior of Glastonbury Abbey, but a seriously diminished person. His face was familiar but his shoulders bent, and his body leant heavily upon a walking stick. The Lady was taken back when he was shown into the hall, but she rose immediately to meet him.

"Dear Prior Compton, I am surprised to see you. Pray come in. I never hoped to be able to invite you to my home."

"My Lady Apolonia," Prior Henry told her sincerely, "I truly feared that you would never wish to receive me into your home after you learned the truth of my life's story."

"Friendship is life's most precious gift, Prior Henry. Since we have been in Glastonbury, I have treasured yours. Welcome to Aust House. Pray come and meet the men of my household." The Lady and the prior walked together to the table dormant where Apollonia introduced Henry to her steward, Giles, then to John and Jeremy who stood on either side of her work table. Each of them expressed a warm welcome to the Lady's guest.

Henry's face relaxed amidst their congenial greetings. He was seated with the Lady and Nan and soon flagons of ale were poured for everyone. The Lady raised her drink in welcome to their guest but would go no further in her questions of him. She knew something unusual must have happened, but she would wait until the prior decided to tell her.

"Your arrival is perfectly timed, Prior Henry. We have a bright and sunny morning to begin this new day."

"Indeed, my Lady, it was a great relief for me to realise that in the absence of your son, the Earl Ferdinand had come to Glastonbury to protect you and his nephew's household. I am unable to tell you how sorry I am that the abbey enabled the ongoing crimes of Cadoc and Ronan against the good people of Glastonbury."

"Ferdinand's arrival was merely a bit of good fortune, Henry," the Lady said. "Early on the day of the robbery, which all of us were anticipating, I received a messenger from my brother. He told me that he wished to stop with us on his way home to Marshfield from Exeter. My household was very well prepared to deal with Cadoc's plans against us, prior, but it is always helpful to have an extra bit of muscle."

"You need not address me as prior, my Lady," Henry said quietly. "I am no longer Glastonbury abbot's deputy. Sub-prior Wilkins has taken charge of the abbey. I am returning to my home monastery of Canterbury as a disgraced penitent."

"Henry, may I invite you to sit with me in my solar?" Apollonia interrupted him gently. Chiefly she hoped he would feel more comfortable speaking with her in private.

He put down his wallet containing a few belongings, along with his walking stick, and followed the Lady from the hall up the stairs. When they were seated on either side of the fireplace, Apollonia continued to wait quietly.

"I know that you are aware of my relationship with Calevera Morton, my Lady. I wish to tell you that I released her and her devoted guardian, Wort, from the abbey gaol yesterday. It was the only positive thing that I could do for her, and I hope that those Glastonbury merchants whom she robbed have felt repaid by the sale of her home and goods. I pray that she will give up her destructive life of crime. She has left Glastonbury and promised me that she will never return."

Apollonia was shocked by his news, but she said nothing, simply encouraged him to continue.

"Whilst you have been in Glastonbury, I have been very glad of your friendship, my Lady, and I hope that you know I continue to respect your intelligence and advice as my friend. If you will, pray allow me to share my story with you before I continue on my journey. I prefer to know that you have heard it from my lips."

"Of course, Henry, I am grateful for your confidence."

"My story begins more than twenty years ago, when I was a young squire living in Templecombe. My family arranged my marriage to a young woman from a good family in Devon. You know her as Calevera Morton, but I knew her as Vera Montfort, the daughter of a knight. I can not say that we fell in love immediately. Vera was only fourteen years old, but she was mature for her years, very bright and well read. We loved to talk together, share new ideas and speculation that interested us. As we grew to know each other better, there was no doubt that I was drawn to her, and we began to look forward to the day when we would marry."

Henry could be seen, at this point in his tale, forcing himself to recall painful memories. He sighed deeply but went on, "I was a rash young buck then and prone to take risks. On one afternoon in the tilting yard, I challenged an older veteran of the wars in France to a sword fight. As you might guess, my arrogance was met with a master swordsman. I do not believe he wished to take advantage of me, but when I foolishly lunged at his chest, he stepped back and struck towards my sword arm leaving me with a badly wounded right hand.

"I was devastated. There was a real possibility that I would lose my right hand, and I could not face life as a cripple. Every day I begged God's forgiveness for my haughty pride, imploring Him to grant me healing and save me from amputation. For weeks, it seemed as if the wound merely festered and refused to close. I knew that my parents called upon the best physician in our town, but even he seemed doubtful of saving my hand. I was bled regularly and the physician interpreted the stars every evening, searching for direction to bring healing to a person of my humour." Henry paused. Apollonia could tell that this period in his young life was difficult for him to recall.

"Vera was wonderful. She remained at my side daily, tried to encourage me out of my bouts of depression, read to me, brought me each of my favourite fruits when she could find them. Still, my wound did not heal.

"I began walking daily to our parish church to offer my prayers of confession and repentance. I promised God that I would go on Crusade, if only He would save my right hand. Our parish priest was aware of my wound and my constant presence kneeling before the altar. On one occasion, he remained to speak with me, for he could see how I was struggling.

"When I revealed my fears of loss to him and my unanswered prayers for healing, he simply asked me what I believed God wanted from me. I confessed to him that I had never given it any thought. In short, my Lady, when I finally asked God what His Will was for me, I began to see that He was calling me to serve Him."

"I decided to declare my life to the Benedictines, first as a lay brother, but then I offered to serve God in every way that I could. I stopped praying for healing; I simply prayed daily for guidance. This is God's truth, my Lady. Slowly, my wounded hand healed, and although I have less dexterity in my right hand, it remains in place on my arm."

Apollonia could see that Henry had no doubt that he had been given a miracle of healing, but there was much more to his story.

"My family with Vera and her family rejoiced at first, until the day came when I told them of the vow I had made to give my life to the Benedictines of Canterbury. My mother broke into tears of joy, but Vera looked at me as if I had struck her. She would not speak with me; she left the room and refused to see me again. It was as if she literally sliced me out of her life. I told myself that she chose to treat me in this way so that she could get on with other plans. She was young and attractive. I was certain that she would always have men seeking her hand in marriage. Surely, she would marry someone else and forget me. I did not realise how cruelly I had wounded her. She says that I destroyed her life."

"Oh, Henry," Apollonia objected, "each of us experiences some romantic disappointments in our youth. Though we are convinced at the time that we shall never recover, our lives go on, and we find new avenues open to us." Apollonia felt she must offer some understanding to him because it was clear that the former prior had grown painfully overwhelmed by regret and guilt.

"No, my Lady, I know now that I did wound her tragically. She has told me."

"It was you who had been the wounded one, my friend, and you who felt you must respond to God's call."

But, Compton would not allow any expressions of sympathy to him. "Pray allow me to tell the whole story, my Lady. In a moment of passion several months before, Vera had given herself to me wholly, body and soul." Henry spoke the words very quietly, but Apollonia knew what he meant. This was obviously the basis for his sense of very personal guilt.

"You mean that you cohabited before marriage?"

"I did have affection for her, my Lady, and at the time, it did not seem an evil thing to do. My body wished to love her body, and we gave ourselves to each other."

"So, when did you tell her of your vow to enter the monastery?"

"When I was certain of my call, when I was convinced that I must give my life to the church, I told Vera. We had been so close to each other, I truly thought she would understand. Instead, she turned from me, refused to speak or have anything to do with me. She curses me to this day and regards me only as a deceiver to her, never a true lover. Even worse, she says that I am the lowest of thieves, for I am he who despoiled her. My Lady, I can not deny that I did any of these things."

Chapter Twenty-two

The Prior's Disgrace

The former prior prepared to leave the Lady's household and Apollonia feared that she was seeing a transformation in her friend towards a life bereft of self-respect and hope. She tried to encourage Henry to rest awhile with them at Aust House and not continue on his journey immediately. He insisted that he must keep going. Winter was coming on, he said; the days were definitely shorter. He could no longer face life in Glastonbury. Apollonia begged him to stop as he was gathering his things, just long enough for prayer with her in the family chapel before his departure. When he agreed, she left Henry briefly to speak with her almoner, Brother William.

"William, when Henry leaves us, I beg you will walk with him on the early part of his journey. I fear for his state of mind. He is haunted by accusations of guilt that I believe have been unjust but none the less destructive to him. Would you walk with him during the beginning of his journey? Grant him your company, but also give him your good counsel as you walk together."

"Of course I shall, my Lady," William assured her. "Can you recommend any helpful emphases I might add to our conversations?"

"Only one, William. Henry must be helped to see that God truly loves him and has forgiven him. He has to be urged to continue listening to God's direction, not the accusations of others. Accepting God's grace is not always easy and he must learn to forgive himself."

* * *

Cunomorus Amairogen rejoiced to be home in Ireland and returned to his work as Seer and Brehon of the King O'Donnell of Tyrconnell. His life reverted swiftly to that of honoured and respected member of the court, and his painful memories of suspicion, loss, and error experienced in Glastonbury were beginning to fade. However, the Druid felt a strong sense of responsibility to one elderly English woman whom he remembered fondly. Cunomorus was hopeful that he might find a way to maintain some friendship between them.

He used his evenings for study and contemplation but also began composing a letter to the Lady Apollonia. His purpose was to offer his thanks for her expressions of friendship to him while he stayed in Somerset as an alien and a foreigner. He was determined to be forthright with her in describing who and what he really was and why he and his departed mother had travelled to Glastonbury. The Lady Apollonia was not only a noble woman, she had impressed him as intelligent and well educated. He could not be sure that she was aware of the role of Druids in Celtic society, but he was certain that she would make intelligent inquiry and not merely dismiss him as a pagan.

Cunomorus had been aware, when he met her, that the Lady knew he was hiding the complete truth of his reasons for being in Glastonbury. Still she respected his privacy and never asked for more detail.

He found it a difficult letter to write, especially because as a Druid, he knew he must be completely honest with her and offer explanations of those things not part of her culture. He decided, therefore, to begin by describing the true purpose of his journey:

> To my friend, the Lady Apollonia of Aust:
>
> Greetings and all good wishes from your new friend of Erin: I, Cunomorus Amairogen, servant of the King O'Donnell of Tyrconnell, wish to introduce myself to you fully and in complete honesty. I am a Druid, a member of the intellectual class of men held in special honour by all Celtic peoples. Druids are natural philosophers and those who study the science of nature as well as moral philosophy. We are regarded as the most just of men in our culture, and are entrusted as judges for individuals and the public. In ancient times we also served as arbitrators in war.
>
> It was clear that you did not believe my stated purpose for travelling to Glastonbury. I said nothing to you that was untrue. Now I will state the fullness of truth.
>
> My mother, Eponina Amairogen, and I travelled to Glastonbury from Ireland because we were informed and directed by an oracle declared by my sister, the renowned seer,

Velada. It was our desire to fulfill the promises of the oracle as we understood them because my deceased father, Archdruid Artur Amairogen, had begun to fulfill them earlier in this present age.

We made every effort to enlist the blessings of the gods upon our task and in many ways were assured that we received divine guidance in all that we thought we must do. My mother was struck down by a mortal sickness immediately after completing our task. As she lay dying, Eponina told me that we had misinterpreted it, that I must undo all that we had done on Glastonbury Tor.

I completed the correction necessary on the Tor only to be taken captive by the monks of Saint Michael's and kept under guard in their monastery. My great blessing whilst in England was to be sent to the prior of the Abbey by Saint Michael's monks. Prior Compton interpreted my visit to Glastonbury as that of a visiting foreign dignitary. Best of all gifts, he introduced me to your grace and saw to it that I was royally entertained for the remainder of my visit.

Now I rejoice to be returned to Tyrconnell, and I hope to hear from you. I value your friendship and long to continue our correspondence. I shall answer any question you may have of me or our task in Glastonbury.

The blessings of the gods be with you,

Cunomorus Amairogen

* * *

The following day when Cunomorus was satisfied that he had written all that he could in this first message to the Lady, he simply put the missive into the hands of a messenger now on his way to England and hoped for the best. He knew it would be weeks before the journey to Somerset could be complete and the letter delivered. Cunomorus could not be certain that the Lady might not be put off by the declaration of his true station in life, but his intuition told him that her curiosity would be stimulated and she would wish to know more. He looked to the future hopefully.

* * *

Encroaching winter brought significant chill to their days, and Apollonia found herself glad to remain close to Chad's home working on her needlework in the mornings and helping the children gather any late-season apples to store them for the winter ahead. They were in the orchard late in the afternoon when Nan pointed out that she could see Sir Chad and his companion, Sir Walter, riding towards the house from the heart of town.

"Oh, Juliana, come with me and bring your brothers to the entrance gate. We shall be there to welcome your father and his friend home to Glastonbury. Nan, do speak with Mistress Farber and order a celebratory dinner for the household this evening. Tell Gareth to come round to take their horses."

Everyone was excited because they could see Sir Chad, Sir Walter, and Sir Walter's servant, Phillip, riding along Bove Town Road. The children were first to reach the front gate, but Apollonia was in place to take part in the boisterous welcome home.

Chad was obviously pleased to see his family waiting for them, and he leapt from his horse to pull the children into his arms. Gareth was standing ready to take the masters' horses back into the stable, but the Lady could not help noticing that Chad's friend, Walter, was uncomfortable as he climbed from his horse even though he had ridden to the block for an easier dismount.

Once on the ground, Sir Walter walked towards her, and she extended her hand to him in welcome. "Sir Walter, how glad I am to see you."

"My Lady, it is my pleasure to be with you again," he spoke as he bowed slightly, and his rigid body continued to move with obvious discomfort.

The Lady walked to his side and took his arm without saying more. "Pray, Sir Walter, do come into the hall and sit with me. Certainly we have much to discuss as we catch up. You must tell me all the news from court."

A great fire had been stirred in the main fireplace in the hall, and Apollonia walked with Walter to the chairs nearest its warmth. "Pray, forgive my awkward movement, my Lady," he said as he collapsed into the chair. "I am now in the middle of my sixth decade of life, and I find that my body proves to be somewhat disabled after a long ride."

"I shall speak as one older person to another, Walter. Such rigidity and stiffness requires no apologies. I begin each day with its symptoms." Apollonia smiled.

"Chad and I have been discussing some anticipated changes in my life, my Lady," Walter told her. "He and I have been grateful to serve together this year. Even though I must acknowledge that I am no longer the vigorous person I once was, I have one more mission I must fulfill."

"How do you see these changes, Walter? Can you tell me more specifically what your plans are?"

"My Lady, do you remember the action of King Richard against a number of English noblemen during last September's Parliament?"

"I am certain that no one in England can forget," the Lady said quietly.

"You will remember that only one of the former members of the Lords Appellant was saved from death."

"Indeed, everyone knows that the Earl of Warwick, Thomas Beauchamp, was able to save himself by his complete confession of wrongdoing, to the king's delight."

"The extravagance of the king's delight has been commented upon again and again. For many, Beauchamp's pardon has been ridiculed as the actions of a coward. He is described as having broken down like a wretched old woman and incriminated others."

"I can make no judgement of the earl, Walter. I have never met him."

"Well, my Lady, I can and I must. Thomas Beauchamp was my commander in arms in the days of my youth. I have been told that he has grown weak and sickly in his later years. I also suspect that King Richard and his favourites must have terrified this confession from him. Recently, I found out that King Richard has exiled Warwick to the Isle of Man under the guard of William Scrope. I must go to the Isle and continue my friendship as an exile with him.

"Walter, you can not be certain that you will be allowed any contact with the earl," Apollonia said. The Lady worried that such an expression of friendship might bring trumped up charges of being a traitor."

The knight shrugged his shoulders. "There is little that can be done to me; I am an old man and threat to no one. Before I leave I wish to tell you how much I admire you and your son, Chad. I will always be grateful to have spent time, however brief, with you. I shall leave early in the morning, but I want you to know that I carry with me fond memories of our conversations together."

Apollonia was silent. She could think of no adequate response to him at first. Even worse, she found herself required to face loss again. The Lady had been widowed three times and had to endure the death of one of her sons. Her family was very dear to her but so also were special friends whom she admired and she knew admired her. Life must go on, but she had only just said goodbye to Henry Compton. Now she was being forced to say goodbye to Walter.

"Pray, forgive me, Walter. I am silent only because I do not wish to see you go, and I selfishly prefer to beg you to stay with us. Brief as it has been, I am grateful to have known you and shared your friendship with my son. I feel that your willing devotion to Beauchamp in exile speaks volumes of the strength of your friendship for him. God go with you, dear friend; we shall keep you and Phillip with us in our prayers."

* * *

It was more than two weeks before the Lady's almoner, William Fallows, returned to Aust House and asked to speak with the Lady Apollonia privately in her solar. He entered the chamber where the Lady was seated with Nan. Greeting both of them, William appeared to be somewhat uncertain that the value of his journey with the former Prior Henry was all the Lady had hoped for.

"Henry Compton is a sincere Christian, my Lady. I respect him very much, but as you suggested when you expressed your concerns for his state of mind, I am not sure that I helped him restore a strong sense of value and self-respect."

"How far were you able to travel with him, William?"

"I am pleased to say that I walked with him to Salisbury, my Lady. That journey and my return are not bad for one of my years," her almoner told her with a slight shaft of pride in his eyes. "When we parted, Henry promised me that he would let me know when he reached Canterbury. His plan is to go first to London and then join the Pilgrims' Trail at Southwark. He is hoping to speak with pilgrims as he walks with them. The prior wants to share their stories and see if he can offer ministry to them. He does this not as one who presumes to guide them, but as one who has sinned and also seeks redemption."

"Did Henry tell you his story?" Apollonia asked.

"Only that when he was young, he had carnal relations with a woman and did not marry her," William said. "Henry was obviously full of guilt for having done that."

"What did you say to him, William?"

"As you suggested, my Lady, I reminded him that as Christians, we must all acknowledge our sin, but we must also rejoice that God through Christ forgives us. His grace is never earned but must be accepted with thankful hearts."

"Do you think that Henry is able to acknowledge God's Grace as freely given to him, William?"

"At first, I thought that he responded positively, but it was a kind of, 'Oh, yes, I know it,' in an academic sense."

"Do you think he has been willing to release any portion of his overwhelming sense of guilt?"

"Well, I tried a slightly different approach, my Lady," William said quietly. "I began to tell him my story."

Apollonia remembered well how William had come to serve her household after having been disgraced and expelled from his Gilbertine monastery.

"You see, my Lady, I felt Henry should know that as a young canon regular, I was thrown out of the Gilbertines in Lincolnshire but never allowed to learn why. I was judged guilty of mortal sin but never told what my sin had been."

"Still, you always suspected that one of the nuns of the order had acted against you out of jealousy and accused you falsely," the Lady defended him.

"Yes, my Lady, but you especially must see that I can never be certain of this explanation. I only know that I was accused of something for which I was judged guilty and acted against immediately. My question to Henry was how do I deal with this guilt? I shall never know what I am guilty of, simply that I was judged, condemned, and thrown out of my order."

"What did Henry say? Surely, he could see the injustice acted against you."

"In short, my Lady, he did not say anything. He grew quiet and we continued to walk. But, I am certain that my questions remained in his thoughts."

"William, I know this is a painful episode in your life for you to recall, but it was very good of you to do this for Henry. Hopefully, in sharing your story, you have opened his mind to new questions of how he must re-examine his extraordinary burden of guilt. It must be seen in the assurance that God's grace is offered even before he begs forgiveness."

When William left the solar, Nan was moved to say how sorry she was to have the story of the Gilbertines' injustice towards their almoner raked up again. "William was treated cruelly and unfairly, my Lady. We all know that."

"Yes, Nan, William was, but it made a stronger, more Christ-like man of him. He was the best person to take counsel to Henry in his present state of mind, and I thank God for it."

* * *

Chad's steward, John, came in the middle of the afternoon to announce to the Lady that a man had appeared at the front entrance asking to see the Lady Apollonia of Aust. "He says that his name is William of Wedmore, my Lady, and that he is a friend of yours."

"Gramercy, John, I am so glad that he has come. Pray, do show him in."

When William entered the hall, Apollonia saw that he now wore his prosperity very well. His tall, muscular body had grown older in the past decade and a bit more paunchy round his middle. He was very well dressed, however, and his eyes were brightly inquisitive as ever.

"My Lady of Aust, this is a great pleasure to see you once again," he greeted her with honest enthusiasm.

"Ah, William, you are welcome as the flowers of May, in spite of its being late November. I am so pleased that you are able to come to Glastonbury to visit with me. Pray, sit with me by the fire."

Apollonia and William seemed to burst into conversation as soon as they were seated. Both were obviously pleased to renew their friendship and speak together, sharing recent changes in their lives. The Lady was especially glad to hear of William's steady advancement to the position of master mason, now in charge of the completion of sculpture on the front of Wells Cathedral.

"I will be very frank with you, William. I am truly thrilled to see you again, but I do have a favour to ask of you."

"Name it, my Lady. I shall do my utmost to grant it to you."

"Please come with me into our household chapel. I would like you to see a gift of carving of my patron, Saint Apollonia. that I recently received."

The master of Wedmore continued to chatter away as they walked, bringing up the names of mutual friends remembered in Exeter and his continued work on the sculpture of the west front there.

When they entered the Aust family chapel, William stopped abruptly inside the door. He saw Paul's carving placed near the holy water stoup, and it captured his attention immediately.

"Hmmm, this must be the work of a young mason, my Lady, and one who displays real gifts of capturing living human figures with movement, originality, and imagination." William continued to walk around the pillar on which the saint stood to look at it from every angle. "This carver has talent."

"William, I am so glad to have your comments. The statue was carved for me by a teenage member of my household who is completely untrained and looks upon himself as merely the carver of toys for children."

"May I be allowed to meet this young man, my Lady? I am always looking for young carvers of promise."

"Indeed, I was hoping you would. His name is Paul Medford. He is the son of a Glastonbury physician, though by this time both of his parents are dead."

Nan was sent to find Paul while the Lady and the master mason remained sitting together in the chapel, sharing their memories. They had enjoyed working together, designing and building a family chapel in Exeter House when the Lady was living there with her second husband and growing family.

Nan returned to say that she found Paul in the barn helping Gareth and that he would be with them as soon as he had managed to wash up.

It was not long before Paul loped into the chapel. He stopped to straighten his jerkin in the entrance and then bowed politely to the Lady.

"My Lady Apollonia, how may I serve you?"

"I want you to meet a long-time acquaintance of mine who is now resident in the city of Wells, Paul. This is my friend, William of Wedmore, a master mason working on sculpture for the west front of Wells cathedral."

"Greetings, Paul. I have been admiring your carving of Saint Apollonia. It is truly original."

"Good day, sir. It is my privilege to meet you. Thank you for your kind remarks. I simply tried to carve the saint as a personal gift to the Lady for all that she has done for me. I must tell you that I have never had instruction from a professional craftsman as you are."

"It is clear to me that you are already a gifted carver, lad. I am impressed by the lifelike body you have created for the saint, as well as the lovely young face and the graceful gesture of her extended arm offering the pincers holding a tooth."

"It was just an idea, Master Wedmore. I wanted to create the saint in the act of offering relief to all those who suffer from toothache."

"You achieved it, Paul, and have created a saint's figure full of life. As I told the Lady, I am always looking for young carvers with talent to be part of my workshop. Would you be willing to return to Wells with me and begin your training?"

For the first time in their acquaintance, Apollonia could see that Paul Medford was stunned, completely taken aback by William's offer. He did not say anything at first, and she began to worry that leaving Glastonbury just now might be too difficult for him after the recent loss of his mother.

"Perhaps you would like more time to think about Master Wedmore's offer, Paul?" she asked him.

"Oh, no, my Lady. With your permission, I shall be ready whenever the master mason wishes to leave. I could not be certain that you were willing to release me from your service."

"Well, then, you have my heartfelt permission. I hope you will take Saint Apollonia with you as well--not my lovely carving of her, of course. Instead, I pray you will remember the saint's blessings of freedom from pain and blessings of peace to those who have faith. Whenever your master will allow it, however, I hope that you will return to us. You have become an important part of our lives in Glastonbury, Paul, and a beloved member of my household."

"Gramercy, my Lady. I truly do not know what to say. You must know that I shall always be grateful for your encouragement. I can never forget your kindness and all of the ways that you have been my guide back to wholeness." The Lady extended her hand to the lad, and Paul took it gently while bowing to kiss it. When he looked up towards her face once again, Apollonia was thrilled by his smile. The boy was filled with excitement about his new possibilities for the future. He obviously credited her as his benefactress.

"God go with you, Paul. Everyone at Aust House is glad to be your friend," she told him quietly. Within her silent thoughts, however, the Lady prayed as if for one of her own sons. "Gracious Father, bless Paul in all that he does. If it be your will, help him remember his residence at Aust House in Glastonbury with rejoicing for his future."

Chapter Twenty-three

Brehon of Tyrconnell

Apollonia was surprised when early in the morning Nan brought a well-travelled letter to her. "This was just delivered, my Lady— from Ireland. It appears to be from that man whose name I am unable to pronounce."

"You are right, Nan," Apollonia said delightedly. "It is from Cunomorus Amairogen. Do look at the impressive seal upon it. He is servant to the King of Tyrconnell and a man of status in the royal court. I could only hope when he left Glastonbury that I might hear from him again some day."

When Nan looked more closely at Cunomorus' seal, she noticed that it was designed with those swirling lines that told her it was Celtic. "It is a dramatically designed seal, my Lady, but is it Christian?"

"I have only seen such things in drawings," Apollonia said to her. "Ireland is a very Christian country, dearheart."

Apollonia began to read its contents after tearing through the beautiful seal. "Oh, Nan, Cunomorus tells me that he is a Druid."

"Good gracious, my Lady, does that mean that he is not a Christian at all but an Irish pagan?"

"I knew him to be of a different culture from ours, Nan, but let me read on."

Apollonia discovered Cunomorus' purpose in writing to her when she came to the second paragraph in his letter. He said that he wished to tell her the full truth of his reasons for coming to Glastonbury. She read silently through the rest of the letter and then folded it back.

"I am going to take this upstairs into my solar, Nan. I shall want to read it again before writing my response."

Nan looked somewhat skeptically at her mistress and then put her question into words. "My Lady, are you seriously considering corresponding with this man? Do you think it proper to communicate with a confessed heathen?"

"Of course, Nan. You will remember that Cunomorus was a guest in this house. We shared meals together as Christian and Druid. I enjoyed a great deal of fascinating conversation with him. He is so intelligent and well informed; I still hope to learn more from him."

"Surely, you could not have known then that he was a Druid. Brother William, as your confessor, will not approve of your continued correspondence with him."

Apollonia could see that Nan was growing unnecessarily troubled; the tremor in her voice betrayed the depth of it. The Lady spoke to her point immediately. "My precious Nan," she said in her most calming voice, "Brother William knows that I have no desire to convert or alter my faith in any way. He also knows that I am driven to learn, and this is a once-in-a-lifetime opportunity for me. I have never known anyone from this mysterious upper class of the Celts. Julius Caesar wrote of them in his Gallic Wars. Of course, I will write to Cunomorus. He promises to answer any questions that I may have."

Nan was not convinced of this "chance of a lifetime" that the Lady was so keen to pursue, but she said no more. She simply placed her spectacles on her nose and turned to focus on her knitting as the Lady left the hall to go up the stairs to her solar. Apollonia was anxious to write to Cunomorus, to let him know that she had received his letter, and tell him that she, too, hoped that they might create an ongoing correspondence. It was clear to her that the Druid was inviting it and indicating that he intended now to tell her the whole truth. In her heart of hearts, Apollonia had many questions of Cunomorus, but she wanted to plan the text of her letter carefully.

* * *

In the privacy of her solar, Apollonia re-read the Druid's letter and began to compose her answer:

> I send greetings to my honoured friend, Cunomorus Amairogen.

My sincere thanks and warm wishes from Aust House in Somerset to you in far away Tyrconnell. I am grateful to know that you are safely returned to your homeland and complimented by your expressions of friendship and respect to me. Indeed, I shall be pleased to continue our correspondence. I am especially grateful to you for your promise that you will be willing to answer my questions. I hope to learn more from you about the persons who are called Druids.

My knowledge of what you do is painfully limited, but I assume that you fulfill the roles of priest, educator, judge, or administrator. Can you describe for me your special role in serving the King O'Donnell?

Thank you for offering to explain to me your real purpose in coming to Glastonbury. It appears from your letter that you are the son of parents who were both Druids. Can you tell me what Velada's oracle was? If it was that which brought you to Glastonbury, can you share with me how you misinterpreted it? I will maintain your confidence in all things.

The blessings of the Trinity, God the Father, Son, and Holy Spirit be with you,

The Lady Mary Apollonia of Aust

* * *

In the early afternoon of the same day, the Lady's letter had been given into the hands of a messenger on his way to Ireland. Apollonia asked Nan to bring Jeremy to them because she wished to walk into the town and visit with Brother Johanus once again. One further detail needed to be explained, she said.

Nan was always ready to speak with Johanus and hurried off to collect their cloaks and find Jeremy. The weather was sharply chilly; the afternoon skies hung with darkly grey threatening clouds. It was not a long walk from Aust House to the church, and Brother Johanus was delighted to see them when he opened his shutters to their knock.

"Ah, my Lady of Aust and Mistress Nan, I am so pleased to see you," he said as he pulled his hood up to protect his head from the chill wind. "Let us pray together, and then I shall welcome any question you may have of me."

He led the Lady and her maid in repeating the Lord's Prayer together. After their "Amen", he felt moved to ask Apollonia why she had come. She was not the regular visitor to his cell that Nan was. "How may I serve you, my Lady of Aust?"

"Brother Johanus, I am fully aware that you can not reveal anything shared with you in the confessional, but can you tell me anything about the person who built this cell for you after your burial mass and permanent installation here?"

"Ah, my Lady," Johanus said happily, "you do understand my role as an anchorite. I remember the mass well, lying prostrate in the Church of Saint John through the scripture reading, being sprinkled with holy water, and then standing to declare my vow to remain here, dead to the world, alive only to God." Johanus obviously enjoyed remembering the ceremony but also sharing the description of the rest of his life being an anchorite.

"Yes, Brother Johanus, I have been mightily impressed by the extraordinary devotion of anchorites and the service they provide to their communities, Apollonia told him. "I was wondering if I might ask you to confirm for me who in Glastonbury provided the funds to build your cell? In some ways it is a small cottage attached to Saint John's Church, but I should like to understand its unusual shape."

"It is a generous cell, my Lady, but as I have not been outdoors since the day the prayers of the dead were said over me and the door was closed permanently behind me, I can only tell you that the donor was a local person. I remember being surprised that the man whom I saw as the donor's representative appeared to be a rude sort of ruffian, but I could only thank God for the gift and respect the donor's desire for anonymity."

"Would you allow me to speak of it with the priest of Saint John, brother? I should like to be allowed to take a careful walk around the exterior of your cell."

"Of course, pray do, my Lady. I hope you will feel free to find answers to any of your questions. The parish priest is in the church at the moment. He will surely be glad to answer any question you may have."

Apollonia went into the nave of the church with Jeremy and found the priest still in the chancel.

He seemed somewhat puzzled by the Lady's request, but he encouraged her interest. "Do allow me to walk with you. Frankly, I have never investigated the slightly strange shape of the anchorite's cell."

They began at the side of the cell where Brother Johanus' window opened to the world. Then, they walked together past the door which had been permanently closed at the time of the Johanus' installation. "This is the entrance the anchorite used to go into the sepulcher as it is called in the liturgy," the priest pointed out to Apollonia. "Brother Johanus entered the cell singing the antiphon, 'Here I will stay forever; this is the home I have chosen,' Then, the door was closed and locked leaving the recluse alone inside."

The Lady had never witnessed such an enclosure service but could understand its dramatic declaration of purpose for the anchorite as well as members of the congregation of Saint John the Baptist Church. She and the priest continued walking to the other side of the cell towards an unusually angular-shaped portion of the wall of the cell built against the wall of the church with yet another narrow door. "I have no idea what this portion of the cell is used for. Perhaps it is some sort of storage," the priest added.

"May I open the door?" the Lady asked him.

"Allow me," the priest told her, and he pulled it open, only to discover that nothing was stored there. The space was large enough for a single person to enter and stand inside next to a small hole in the wall, covered by a curtain, which opened directly into the anchorite's cell. "What can the purpose of this space be, my Lady?" the priest asked. "I have never seen such a construction before."

"I have a suggestion, father, that its purpose was not meant to be a positive one," Apollonia told him. "It is likely that this was the listening hole used by those who were organising the robberies in Glastonbury. It was built for them and probably used by them. We have recently learned that the same gang leader was able to abuse the confessional as well."

"Oh, dear God," the priest gasped, "what sort of unscrupulous creature would use the counsel of the anchorite in such an unholy manner? I shall have this spy hole closed immediately and the whole perfidious closet bricked over," he said as they began to walk back into the church together.

"Do you know the identity of the anonymous donor who arranged to have Brother Johanus' cell built?"

"No, my Lady, the donor's name was never given to me, but the man who made the arrangements for its construction had a strange name. I think he was called Wort."

"I shall donate the cost of the demolition of this space to your church, father," Apollonia told the priest, "but I pray you will not tell Brother Johanus any details of its insidious abuse of him or the good people of Glastonbury."

When the priest left, the Lady continued to sit with Jeremy in the nave of the church, waiting for Nan to finish her conversation with the good brother. Apollonia was completely drawn into her own thoughts and remained silent. Jeremy, too, said nothing, for he assumed the Lady was praying. Instead, the Lady was madly piecing together confirming details she had learned this morning with others she already knew.

"The priest was very helpful," she told Jeremy. In her own thoughts she was reconstructing Calevera's scheme, working through Wort to build this secret access to highly personal information. There was no doubt in her mind that Calevera's gang used Johanus' conversations for their own purposes. Her henchman could easily have slipped into the closet and listened to everything wealthy people of the town would tell Johanus. "I must say nothing of this to dear Nan either," the Lady thought. "The robbery of Aust House may well have been informed by something that she mentioned to the anchorite."

* * *

"Grandmamma," Juliana called as she crashed through the door into Apollonia's solar that evening. "I had the most wonderful walk up the Tor this afternoon. Jeremy walks with us whilst I drive my pony cart to the abbey barn. We leave my cart with him, and Mistress Albert and I walk on to the Tor. I have grown able to climb to the top in record time."

"I am proud of you, Juliana, but you must be careful not to push Mistress Albert to such strenuous heights regularly."

"No, grandmamma. It is Mistress Albert who insisted that this is her favourite exercise. She says that she is always full of peace after we have been able to pause in the church of Saint Michael for prayer before our return walk down the Pilgrims' Trail."

"Mistress Albert is the best of servants, Juliana. I hope you remember to thank her regularly."

"Truly I do, grandmamma, I make a special point to thank her and Jeremy, too, because I am much stronger now. As many times as I have climbed the Tor, I have never felt a need to use my walking stick. How grateful it makes me to see my stick hanging with those of other healed pilgrims in Saint Michael's porch."

Apollonia's heart swelled to hear Juliana say such things. There could be no doubt that the little girl was able to walk with a balanced stride in her special shoes and that she stood straight and tall since giving up the use of her crutch.

"Grandmamma, it seems to me that I can see different levels on the sides of the Tor. It is as if they were carved by a huge hand to help pilgrims make the climb. Do you believe that God created the Tor to be that way?"

Apollonia was caught up by Juliana's question. The Lady was glad to see her granddaughter curious and stimulated to learn, but she had no answer.

"When I asked Papa about that, he could only say that he had never noticed," Juliana said.

"All things are possible to God, Juliana, but I have a new friend in Ireland who may be able to tell us a great deal more of the legends of the Tor. When next I write to him, I promise I shall ask him if he can help us."

* * *

Early the following morning, Chad appeared at his mother's chamber door bursting with news. "Mamam, I have just received a messenger from my friend, Sir Walter Heath. Walter specifically asks me to share his news with you, for he says that he knows you will want to be aware of what has been happening."

"Indeed I shall, Chad. Pray be seated. You make me sense anxiety in the air. What has Sir Walter told you?"

"This was a little confusing for me, Mamam. Walter says in his letter that I must tell you that you were correct in your description of what might happen when he arrived at the Isle of Man. He was not allowed to visit with his friend, Beauchamp, and was interrogated by the earl's captors. They did question the reliability of his loyalty to King Richard if he could be so devoted to his friend, the Earl of Warwick, a confessed traitor. He was told to return to England and demonstrate his fealty to the king."

"Oh, dear God," the Lady said quietly. "This is precisely what I feared might happen, Chad. Where is Walter, son, and what is taking place now?"

"He is at his home in Templecombe, Mamam, with his loyal Phillip. I fear that he is not well," Chad told her.

"Perhaps it is best that he remain at home. I pray that by staying out of the saddle, he may begin to help his body recover," Apollonia told Chad with a cautioning smile.

"Honestly, Mamam, I was not aware that Walter was struggling until we reached Aust House. He is always in good spirits and ready to support me in any adventure."

"There is no doubt that he regards you as dear to him as a son, Chad," Apollonia assured him. "You must know that he is older than I by ten years, and frankly, dearheart, our age does catch us up."

* * *

Later in the day, Apollonia was walking with Nan and Jeremy towards the abbey gate to take advantage of her regular visits to their excellent library when a well-dressed young driver approached her party and asked if he might speak with the Lady of Aust. Nan and Jeremy immediately moved closer in case there might be any threat against her. The Lady, however, indicated that she would speak with him.

"My Lady, I bring you this message from my mistress." He put a small note into her hands and stepped back courteously. The note was well written in an excellent hand, but Apollonia was most surprised by its message:

My dear Lady of Aust,

Would you be so kind as to sit within my carriage? I can see no other way for us to have a conversation, and I should very much like to thank you in person.

Faith Morgan

Apollonia looked to the driver. "I will speak with her. How shall I find your mistress?"

"If you will follow me," he said as he turned and led her party through the Market Place, up Benedict Street. When they came near the church, a large expensive carriage was parked, and the driver pointed to its door.

When the Lady began to walk towards it, Jeremy objected. "I pray you, my Lady, do not enter this carriage. I fear that you might be driven away by these strangers, and I could do nothing to save you."

"You must not worry, Jeremy. I believe I know this woman, and I do hope to speak with her. I have not met her before, but I should like to converse with her. Will you kindly remain here with Nan whilst we speak?" To Nan she said very quietly, "This is Faith Morgan, Nan, Brother Johanus' mother. I am in no danger of being kidnapped. I pray you will read her note."

The Lady walked to the coach and stepped inside its open door. Only the wealthiest people of the town could afford such a convenience. It was obvious to Apollonia that this one was especially built to hide those who rode within it from public view.

Once inside, the door closed behind her, and she was greeted by its single occupant. "My Lady of Aust, I am Faith Morgan. You are very gracious to meet with me."

"Mistress Morgan, I am glad to know you. Members of my household and I have been especially grateful for the ministry of your son, Johanus. You must be very proud of his spiritual gifts to all of Glastonbury."

Faith Morgan was a huge woman whose presence seemed to fill more than half the interior of the coach. Apollonia reached out to offer her hand in greeting, and Faith broke into tears. "You must know, my Lady, that you are the only person in Glastonbury who would offer me such greeting. Many know me well but would never acknowledge me in a public place."

"I am sorry that society places arbitrary walls between us, Mistress Morgan, but I have been hoping to meet you and simply could not think of a way to do it."

Faith wiped her eyes, blew her nose, and then simply said, "First, let me tell you how grateful I am for your household's friendship with Johanus. He has told me of the trust and faith that you have expressed to him. I know that we must not be seen to spend time together but you must know how grateful I am to you for ridding our community of Calevera Morton. Sadly, because of the similarity in our names, many folk presumed that she might be my daughter. Lord knows, it is not easy to imagine that she had a human mother. She used me as desperately as she used the church and the community."

"How so, mistress? How could she?"

"My Lady, she has taken hundreds of pounds of protection money from me over the years. She called it protection, but it simply meant that as long as I paid her, she would not burn our house down or do injury to my girls. She was an evil woman. I can say that, even as one who is regarded as disreputable in the town of Glastonbury. I have never been an evil member of my community."

"How long have you known Calevera, Mistress Morgan?"

"She came to me with her brutal henchman, Wort, when they first arrived in the town. She told me that she was setting up her gang to control Glastonbury, and the first thing that I must do was submit to her. I had no choice for there is no force here to whom I could turn for help. The abbey tries to shut us down every now and again, but mainly through preaching against us. No one in Glastonbury was willing to be seen as defending me, certainly not the mayor or city officers."

"Then, you must know that Calevera has been released from gaol, mistress."

"Indeed I was told of it, my Lady…," Faith said as if she wished to say more.

"The town is now fully aware of her villainy," Apollonia told her, "and will not allow her to return. I have been told that she has promised to go far away by the person who was her reason for coming to Glastonbury. He, too, is no longer resident here, Faith. Take comfort in that."

"Calevera can never return to Glastonbury, my Lady."

"How do you know, Faith?"

"Because she is dead, my Lady."

"Dear God, what has happened? I was only told that she was released from Glastonbury Abbey's gaol and set free. I know this from the man who personally gave her freedom in spite of her criminal past."

Faith was not comfortable speaking of this, but she decided that the Lady must know the truth. "I recently learned of her death in a letter from an old friend in Bristol who knew of my struggles with her. The story has dominated the gossip of Bristol. Calevera escaped to the city with her henchman, Wort. She must have decided to return to her home in Devon. It is believed that she attempted to dismiss Wort and told him that he could not go with her. She said that she had gained his freedom for him and would pay him handsomely for his services. However, she declared that she was returning to her home under her maiden name and planned to start a new life. She told Wort that he could not be part of it."

"Faith, even I knew that Wort had devoted his life to Calevera. How did he receive such casual dismissal?"

"It is said that he stabbed her eighteen times, my Lady, and then remained holding her body in his arms until the sheriff's men came to arrest him. His only words of explanation were to insist that she was his. No one else would ever have her."

"Oh, Faith, what a dreadful end. I had heard nothing of this. Still, it tells us that even sincere devotion can be based upon violent possession.

"Forgive me, my Lady," Faith interrupted her, "you must leave now, and I shall drive on. I am donating the monies I would have paid Calevera to the church of Saint John the Baptist to support prayers for her soul."

"You are a good woman, Faith, and I, too, will pray for her soul. Pray God we shall never see her like again," the Lady said while crossing herself as she stepped down from the coach.

Apollonia returned to her friends as the coach drove off, and the Lady knew then she would never see Faith again.

Nan went to her side, still holding Faith's note. "Thank God, you are out of that carriage, my Lady. Surely you should never have agreed to such a meeting." Nan was near to tears of worry but could say no more in front of Jeremy.

"You must know, dearheart, I am not only certain that I needed to speak with her, I will tell Johanus that having met his mother, she is a very good woman."

Jeremy could make no sense of their conversation but walked quietly with them as they returned to Aust House.

When they entered the hall, Chad was waiting for them. "Mamam, a letter has come to you from Ireland of all places. I confess I am bursting with curiosity. Can you tell me more about your contacts in Ireland? I am surprised to learn that you have acquaintances there."

It was obvious to Chad that his mother was excited to find the letter waiting for her. "Oh, Chad dear, it is a long story but begins with my meeting a visitor from Northern Ireland here in Glastonbury. His name is Cunomorus Amairogen, and he serves the King of Tyrconnell. You would have enjoyed meeting him, but he came to Glastonbury whilst you were resident at court. He is a man near in age to you and extraordinarily well educated. You will be fascinated by all that I have learned about the significance of Celtic culture in Glastonbury."

She sat down immediately to read Cunomorus' letter aloud to Chad, hopeful that her son would find her new acquaintance in Ireland as fascinating as she did. "Oh Chad, just listen to this: 'My dear Lady Apollonia of Aust, whom I regard as my English friend, thank you for your letter. I am grateful for your willingness to continue our correspondence. I can understand your interest in my mother's and my real goals when we lived briefly in Glastonbury. Indeed, we did have an ulterior purpose in coming, as you surmised. I give you my assurance that we had no evil design upon the town or your country.'"

"Mamam, what have you discovered regarding this visitor from Ireland? What sort of evil design did you suspect him planning?"

"I suspected him of planning something unusual, not evil, Chad. His honesty with me has been completely forthright since he returned to Ireland, but I felt he was required to withhold specific facts from us whilst he was here."

"Why should he have come for such a mysterious purpose that he could not speak of it with you whilst he was here?" Chad grew more suspicious of the Irishman as his mother spoke of him.

"Let me read the rest of his letter to you, my son. I believe that you will find him to be not only honest and forthright, but also willing to share insight into the truths of his personal Celtic culture with us." Apollonia continued reading aloud: "'My sister, Velada, is a member of our family of Druids, and she is known throughout Tyrconnell as an inspired Seer. Velada was granted an oracle more than two years ago. My father, Artur, had intended to come to Glastonbury to achieve her vision, but he died shortly after her receipt of it. My mother, Eponina, insisted that we must come to Glastonbury so that we might assist the Great Earth Mother in making a powerful change.

"'My mother interpreted Velada's oracle to say that Druids would return in strength to all of Britain when the monastery of Saint Michael on the Tor was no more. Just before my mother's death, however, I learned that the proper interpretation of the oracle was as follows: There could be no return of Druids to Britain until the end of Christianity in Glastonbury.

"'I do hope my words will not seem threatening to you but will ease your excellent curiosity. I pray that you will never hesitate to ask further questions. May the blessings of the gods be with you, Cunomorus Amairogen.'"

Chapter Twenty-four

The Druids' Tor

Early in November, Apollonia received another letter from Ireland. The Lady decided she would read it first and very carefully, so that she would be certain to understand Cunomorus' answers to Juliana's questions about the Tor. She could tell from Chad's inquiring glance that he hoped to learn more about this most unusual official whom his mother knew. Instead of commenting before reading it aloud, this time Apollonia kept the letter in her hand and asked Chad to retreat with her to her solar.

They stole away quickly and were up the stairs behind her closed door when she finally opened the seal and began to read it to him: "'My dear Lady of Aust, I am always pleased to find your questions of me and our faith. I hope you will feel free to continue to ask them. Obviously, your granddaughter is as observant as her grandmother.

"'The Tor, which Glastonbury Abbey and the Monastery of Saint Michael now claim as their own, is far more ancient than Christianity. Tor is a Celtic name meaning a high place. Although the Christians have extended some of the levels of the Tor to use as fields for sowing their crops, the original levels carved into the Tor's sides are of Celtic design. The Druids' goal on the Tor was to create a maze made for ritual purposes essential to our faith. The levels spiral around the Tor seven times, and though its path does not lead directly to the top of the Tor, it ends at the summit where the present Christian Church of Saint Michael dominates. A stone marks the beginning, and a later stone on the path marks your first turning to the left. May the gods go with you, dear Lady. I am certain that you will wish to trace the levels of the maze. Pray let me know more of your adventure. Your faithful friend, Cunomorus.'"

Apollonia hit the letter with her finger, as if she were tapping her head. "Oh Chad, how could I have missed this? Will you walk with us to the top of the Tor? Though the days are now very short, Juliana always enjoys the climb, and this time we shan't follow the Pilgrims' Trail. I will take parchment and pen with me whilst we walk following the path along the levels round the sides of the Tor. If we can follow them to the very top, I hope to complete tracing the path of this maze."

"Are you certain that you wish to do this, Mamam? I confess I have never heard of such a thing."

Nan entered the Lady's solar and Apollonia immediately offered her apologies. "Dearheart, I am more than ever sorry to have made such a fuss about my age on our last walk up the Tor. My old woman's mind was too distracted to be intellectually alert, and I missed so much."

"In what way were you distracted, my Lady?"

"Well, I confess to you that I was more worried about exposing my heavy breathing in your presence. I completely missed noticing the unusual shape of the Tor as a truly ancient place dedicated to religious ceremony."

"My Lady, I also confess to a bit of heavy breathing on our climb," Nan grinned.

Apollonia turned to Chad, "Dearheart, shall we do our walk early in the morning of the morrow?"

"I have never done it, Mamam, but I hear the views from the climb are beautiful."

"I do not intend for us to remain on the Pilgrims' Path, Chad," Apollonia reminded him. "We shall walk the levels carved into its sides, and you will help me make a map of them."

"All right, Mamam, out with it. What have you learned from your letter today that makes you feel so determined to explore the Tor in this manner? Why do you wish to confirm all the Druid has told you of a maze on its sides?"

"You are my most inquisitive son, Chad, always full of questions. In this case, you must credit your precious daughter for her keen observations. She called it to my attention." Apollonia handed Chad the letter she had just received and told him, "Cunomorus is the best-informed person of our island's ancient history that I have ever known. If only you could have met him whilst he was here in Glastonbury, your curiosity would be as fired as mine. I want very much to understand the Tor, not merely as a steep hill but a monumental achievement of the religion of an ancient people."

* * *

Juliana was ready and impatient to begin their walk at first light the following day. "The days are so much shorter now, grandmamma. We must be on our way."

Apollonia was also ready to proceed when Chad arrived with Jeremy. They went to the stables first to collect their mounts and rode together to the abbey tithe barn. There, they left the horses in Jeremy's care and began a different climb on an overgrown path off Well House Lane. On this occasion, it was the Lady Apollonia who used a walking stick, and when Chad noticed it in her hand, he was slightly taken aback.

"Are you certain you should be doing this, Mamam? I can walk with Juliana to the top. I am certain that we can find a lovely place for you to sit comfortably until we return."

"Gracious, no, Chad. I have my drawing parchment, pen and ink in my wallet. We must stay off the Pilgrims' Path, and you must help me remain on the trail of the levels of the Tor. Ah, there is the first standing stone which marks our beginning. Let us look for the next, and we shall be certain that we are on the first level the Celtic maze."

Chad was not certain of the sense of this, but he always enjoyed a good walk and began immediately to take in the lovely Somerset countryside surrounding the Tor. Juliana led the group as always and hurried ahead. "Remember, Juliana," her grandmother called, "stay with this level. Do not be tempted to walk up hill."

They remained on the first level until they walked entirely round the Tor and returned to the stone where they began. There, the path seemed to go down slightly and turned to go round the Tor again in the opposite direction on this slightly lower level. "This is a strange way to progress, Mamam," Chad told her, somewhat frustrated.

"This is not a direct path, Chad. Remember, we are following a maze cut into the sides of the Tor."

Juliana called out to urge them to go faster, but Apollonia persisted in her slower pace. With each of their seven circles of the

Tor, Apollonia paused to draw their route round the Tor, complete with arrows indicating which direction they had gone.

Chad helped his mother verify the path on each level but also decided that he would take time to enjoy the views as they progressed, sometimes up a level, sometimes lower down. The sun continued to rise, and the beautiful shades of autumn against the blue sky enhanced the surrounding glories of the valley. Chad loved the views as they progressed but couldn't help noticing that his mother remained intent on her drawing. When he pointed out the glorious landscape to her, she simply nodded.

Juliana, on the other hand, was delighted when she discovered each new turning of their level and hurried on ahead to lead them. Chad was thrilled to see Juliana's body growing straight and tall while she walked unaided with no visible limp. When they finally turned onto the level of the monastery at the very top of the Tor and walked toward the tower of the church, the sun had nearly reached its noontime peak. They went into the sanctuary. On their way through the porch, Juliana quietly pointed to her stick hanging there and smiled shyly at her father. He knew it had belonged to her, and he could feel tears fill his eyes, tears of a father's earnest prayers begging God to allow his dear wife in heaven to rejoice in the sight as well.

No service was in progress when they entered the church as the monks were at their one meal of the day. The church was still full of pilgrims, however, many struggling with different handicaps, and all here to gain some hope of healing. Chad stayed especially long on his knees before the altar. He knew in his heart he had many reasons to thank God.

Chad was pleased to be able to wear his pilgrim's badge announcing his achievement when they finally left Saint Michael's. Once outdoors again, he paused to allow his eyes to feast on the view surrounding them. This vision of Glastonbury from the Tor looking across to Wearyall Hill was enough to take his breath away. He made no audible comment, but he felt, for the first time in his life, an overwhelming sense of the blessings of God's creation.

They returned to Glastonbury on the Pilgrims' Path downhill, and now Apollonia was especially pleased that she had brought her walking stick. "Juliana was right," she thought to herself, "it is sometimes better to have a third leg, and it surely provides better balance as I walk." Stored away in her wallet was her drawing of their path along the levels of the Tor. They had not always been certain that they remained on a path. Things frequently were overgrown on the various levels, and occasionally there had seemed to be no path as such. They had meticulously followed the levels carved into the sides of the Tor and ultimately found themselves at the top. In the Lady's mind, this was not of nature's creation. It had to be one of ancient mankind's expressions of his faith.

* * *

They had barely returned home that afternoon when Juliana was suggesting another walk. "Papa, I think we must walk up Wearyall Hill. The view of the Tor from Wearyall is said to be one of the best in the county."

Apollonia felt she must speak before Chad could respond. "It is a lovely idea, Juliana, and I shall be pleased to go with you, but not tomorrow. You must allow your aging grandmamma to rest."

"I hope you will please excuse me as well, Juliana," Chad told her. "I must prepare to leave on the morrow to visit my friend, Sir Walter, in Templecombe. I do not think I shall be gone long, Mamam, but I am concerned for him. I fear Walter has become more depressed since he returned home. It was a blow to him not to be allowed to visit his old friend in exile."

"I was fearful for him when he left us, Chad. Our King Richard has become keen to subordinate everything to his royal will, especially the nobility. Dear Ferdinand writes to me simply saying that it is best to stay in one's home county out of sight, whilst taking every opportunity to express one's loyalty to the sovereign."

"When Walter and I were at court, Mamam, we could remain largely unnoticed. The king has his favourites, and one must be full of courtesy towards them. It is the favourites upon whom the king lavishes his concern. All of the forfeited lands of the destroyed so-called Appellants have been given to the king's new dukes and earls. Yet, even they know that one can not trust the king if ever he feels his royal prerogative is being challenged."

"This is a frightening state of affairs, Chad. I discouraged Walter to seek to visit Warwick in exile precisely because, from the king's perspective, friends of his enemies are his enemies."

"I will be off to Templecombe and hope to find Walter restored. As Uncle Ferdinand says, 'I shall remain in my home county, far beyond the king's suspicious notice.'"

"I hope you will take my greetings to Walter, Chad. Pray tell him how much I enjoyed each of our conversations, and I hope that they will be able to continue soon. In short, ask Walter if he will be willing to return to us in Glastonbury? Assure him that the worst of the criminals here has been chased away. King Richard's focus is upon Gloucester where he struggles to have his ancestor, Edward the Second, made a saint. And, I know that Glastonbury has a very fine doctor of physic."

* * *

Chad was only gone from his Glastonbury household for a matter of weeks. When he and Jeremy returned to Aust House at the beginning of December, Apollonia could see at once that her son was altered. He walked into the hall where she and Giles were working and begged her to retreat with him to her solar.

"I pray you, Chad, please go upstairs," Apollonia urged him. "I shall join you there, straightaway." Chad greeted Giles, but seemed anxious to avoid other members of his household or even greet his children until he could speak with his mother. His spirit was troubled.

When Apollonia entered her solar, she found him sitting on a bench near the fire, holding his head in his hands. Closing the door quickly, she went to take him into her arms. "Chad, dearest heart, what has happened?"

"Sir Walter Heath, my friend, counsellor, and comrade is dead, Mamam," Chad told her as he lifted his face to hers. "I am past tears for his loss, but I do feel again a desperate emptiness in my life, not unlike that with which I struggled after Cynthia died. I must compose myself before I go to visit with the children."

Apollonia continued to hold her son all the while she, too, felt a painful sense of loss in her own heart. "I have no words to tell you how sorry I am, Chad. I know that Walter was dear to you, that you were kindred spirits, and valued each other's company. I admired him as your mentor but as a good friend to me as well."

Chad took his mother's hand, his voice trembling. "Pray tell me again what you said to me about our 'wounds' when Cynthia died, Mamam."

"I only told you what I felt, Chad. When Cynthia died, we had all been wounded because a precious part of our hearts was torn from us. I also remember telling you that if you endured such a wound in battle, there could be no way to avoid expressing horrible pain. Is it too difficult for you to tell me what happened? I will surely wait if it might be easier for you later."

"No, Mamam, there are some things that can not wait, and I will need your help to achieve them."

"I shall do anything you ask, Chad."

"By the time I reached Templecombe, Mamam, Walter was very weak. He tried to welcome me, man to man, but he was not able to stand for any length of time. We sat together in silence at first. When he spoke, I could hear a kind of breathlessness in his voice. I told him that we are old friends; we could easily sit and enjoy each other's company just being together. He smiled and said that I must know that he did not have time to waste. It was urgent, he said, that we discuss arrangements which had to be made soon. Then he pulled a large roll of parchment from beside his great chair."

"Chad," Apollonia asked him, "are you telling me that Walter knew he was near death when you arrived?"

"Yes, Mamam, but his sense of urgency was not related to any sort of fear of death. He told me that he had an important task that must be done. He begged me to help him achieve it, for he knew he could not."

"Pray, go on, Chad." Apollonia could see that this was painful for her son, but the Lady also knew that it was better for him to continue to talk with her.

"The parchment that he shared with me was his will. He told me that it included all of his last bequests, and he urged me to read it. I saw the expected gifts to his personal servant, Phillip, to his steward, and so on. It was the last name that was a complete surprise to me. The rest of his estate at Templecombe he left to a young lad named Owen of Tintern in Wales."

"How does he know this boy, Chad? Did he tell you?"

"Yes, Mamam, Owen is Walter's son."

"Oh," the Lady said, but added nothing more.

"The boy is now seven years old and in school at Tintern Abbey. He was born to Walter and a Welsh maid who served Walter's household. There is no doubt in my mind that Walter's sense of guilt at having broken his personal vow of celibacy was immense but multiplied by the death of the maid who died from a festering cut on her foot when Owen was an infant. The boy believed that he was the son of a wandering Welsh poet whom he never saw because the father lived on the road, entertaining in the halls of the great with his bardic songs and tales. Walter wanted Owen to remain in care in Wales to perfect his mother's Welsh speech and to grow up within the culture of his birth."

"What did Walter ask of you, Chad?"

"It is relatively simple, Mamam, he asked me to bring his son to England and help prepare him now for his inheritance as an English gentleman's son."

"Ah," Apollonia said again, still somewhat speechless after Chad's revelations.

"At the time of Walter's death, I not only promised him a burial mass in his parish church, I also promised that I would assume responsibility for his son, Mamam. I hope you will not mind remaining here in Glastonbury with the children whilst I go on to Tintern to collect the lad."

"What are your plans for Owen, Chad?"

"Well, I decided that I will bring him here to Glastonbury and raise him with my children."

"Whilst you are completing your promised errand for Walter, would you consider one other option for young Owen?"

"Of course, Mamam, what do you have in mind?"

"Would you allow me to take him into my household? You know of my desire to nurture young people of promise. I shall continue his education and see that he learns the gentlemanly courtesies as well as how to be part of a noble English household, serving as my page."

Chad did not answer her immediately. As he reconsidered his promises to Walter, he remembered happily his home, his education, and especially growing up in Aust with his mother and father.

"I remember you as a strict but loving mother, far less willing to allow our foibles and pranks than father ever was, Mamam." Chad paused again and looked into his mother's eyes. "Perhaps that would be best for Owen, to live in a noble household led by a forceful motherly image."

"Forceful grandmotherly image," Apollonia corrected him, "whom you know will seek the very best for Owen and keep him at my side."

"Oh, Mamam, it is because I know how Walter admired you that I can be certain he would be glad to have his son become part of your affinity."

"Before you must leave us on the morrow, Chad, let us retire to the chapel. We will ask Brother William to offer our special prayers for the soul of Sir Walter Heath, not only as a dear friend and confident, but also our brother…in Christ."

When Apollonia led the family into the chapel that evening, she could not help beginning her silent prayers long before she seated herself. Her prayers were in fervent thanks for her family, but especially now she prayed that she would be able to bring a sense of loving family to Walter's son, Owen.

* * *

When Chad and Jeremy returned to Glastonbury with Owen, the boy at first seemed dreadfully ill at ease. He was uncomfortable in such a grand house but even more frightened to be in the Lady's presence. He had lived with the Cistercians most of his life, and although he had encountered women and girls in the town, he simply did not know how to behave in Apollonia's presence. He had never known a lady, much less known how to speak with a titled lady.

Juliana came to his rescue immediately. She went towards him in her usual forthright manner. "Hello, Owen, I am Juliana Aust. Do you like to ride?"

Juliana was smaller than Owen though older than he by a year. Owen was not certain how to respond to her. "Forgive me, mistress, I have never been allowed to be near a horse."

"We shall fix that. Come along with me to the barn. Gareth will tell you everything you need to know, and you can try George's pony. George will not mind, long as you treat the beast well."

The children left the hall together, and Apollonia sent for Eleanor Albert to come to her from the nursery. "Gramercy, Mistress Albert," the Lady said, "I need to speak with you about a temporary new addition to the nursery whilst I remain in Glastonbury."

"How may I serve you, my Lady?"

"My son has brought to us a young lad from Wales. I believe he has been well educated by the monks at Tintern, but he has not experienced the love of family. His mother died when he was very young, and his father has recently passed away. Juliana has taken him out to the barn to become acquainted with Gareth, and when they come back to the house, I am certain that she will introduce him to you. I pray you will make a special point to help Owen feel at home with us."

"I shall do my best, my Lady."

"His name is Owen, and though born in Wales, he is the son of an English gentleman who will inherit his father's lands when he comes of age. At the present, I am taking him into my household to continue his education. He will serve as my page. I would like to speak with him before he retires this evening. After you have finished your supper, would you bring him to my solar?"

"Of course, I shall, my Lady. Do you have any further instructions for me whilst Owen remains with us?"

"I know that Juliana adores you, and you have been a great comfort to her since the loss of her mother. If you can find ways through which you are able to help Owen begin to know what it means to be part of a family, Mistress Albert, I shall be very grateful to you."

"Then, I shall begin by asking young master Owen to take charge and lead us in grace before supper. Everyone in a family needs to assume responsibility," Mistress Albert told the Lady. "Juliana has always said grace, but she will understand that it should be Owen who does it as the eldest male in the nursery."

* * *

When Owen was shown into the Lady's solar that evening, Nan moved to take his hand and led him to meet her mistress. "Greetings, Owen, I am Nan, the Lady's maid," she said. "Welcome to our household. This is my Lady Apollonia of Aust."

The boy merely nodded, then walked forward quietly to bow before Apollonia.

"Greetings, my Lady of Aust."

"Owen, I am glad to know you. What can you tell me about yourself?"

"Pray forgive me, my Lady, but I have only just learned who I truly am. I feel a bit confused. I knew Sir Walter, for he came regularly to Wales to visit with me, and I was always grateful to him. He told me that my father was a Welsh poet who was forced to be on the road to earn his keep. He said that it was because of my father's absence and my mother's death when I was very young that he had taken over my care."

Apollonia saw that Owen was struggling to understand these profound revelations to him. He was only seven years old and feeling overwhelmed just to define himself. Apollonia was determined to express sympathy with his struggle, but she especially wished to give him a new goal in life. Deciding to change the subject slightly, she began again, "I, too, have just learned that Sir Walter had a son in Wales, and you are he, Owen. There is no doubt that Sir Walter was a very good man, a valiant knight who served his king and country. I admired him and will always remember our acquaintance with pride. As his son, I should like you to enter my service. Will you be willing to join my household as my page?"

"Gramercy, my Lady, it is my dream to become a knight," Owen told her excitedly.

The mention of his real father and the Lady's acquaintance with Walter seemed to help the boy feel more at ease, so Apollonia decided to encourage his comfort level. "I must confess that I did not know Sir Walter very long, Owen, but I did know him as a good friend to me and a mentor to my son, Sir Chad. Now, as you are to become part of my affinity, I shall send you to the barn to spend more time with one of my oldest and most faithful servants, Gareth Trimble. You have already met my Nan."

"Your servant, Mistress Nan," he said courteously. Then, turning to Apollonia, he said, "I shall go gladly, my Lady. Your stablemaster knows more about horses than any man I have ever met. He even allowed me to ride round the garden on one of the ponies. I promise you that I shall work hard to learn from him."

Apollonia found Owen's enthusiasm encouraging, but even more, she could sense his growing relaxation in her presence. "Whilst we are in Glastonbury, Owen, you will sleep in the nursery with Juliana and the little boys under the direction of Mistress Albert. However, you will have different quarters when we return to my home in Aust. There you will grow to know the Gloucestershire side of the Severn and learn to serve as my page in training for your own status as a knight."

Epilogue

Saint Joseph's Treasure

It was after Christmas when Juliana was finally able to get her grandmother and father to agree to climb Wearyall Hill with her. The Lady especially asked Owen if he would care to go with them and Juliana seconded her invitation. "You must come, Owen. I am told it is the very best view of the Tor, the town, and the entire valley. Although it is a cold day and the winds will be brisk, climbing the hill will keep us warm."

Owen was always ready for a new adventure with Juliana, so he said that he would very much like to join them. Apollonia rode in the pony cart with Juliana for this occasion, while Chad, Jeremy, and Owen, each in the saddle, rode behind them. It was a bit of a trip from Aust House on such a chilly day. Once they made the turning onto Street Road, they soon came to a place where they were able to leave their horses and cart with Jeremy and begin their walk up Wearyall Hill.

Chad gave his arm to help his mother from the cart. She pulled her warmest woollen cloak tightly around her. Taking her stick in hand, she walked with her son while the two children ran on ahead to begin their climb to the top of the hill.

"I am glad that you are willing to do this with Juliana, Chad. She has a wonderful curiosity and in many ways reminds me of your enthusiasm when you were a boy."

"I have to tell you, Mamam, the children think this is great adventure, but I am making this walk especially to be with you." Chad paused for a moment and then began again, "I have never asked your forgiveness for the coldly despicable manner in which I treated you when first you came to us in Glastonbury. I was truly sorry then, even as I continued to maintain an artificial distance from you. I am truly regretful now when I remember the cold distance I kept whenever in your presence."

Apollonia wanted to tell Chad that she did not want him to feel blame or regret. She simply rejoiced that they had been able to restore their closeness as mother and son once again. His voice lowered to continue to speak intimately with her while they walked. The Lady decided to remain silent, to listen, and encourage him to put his thoughts into words.

"You remember how I ran away at the time of Papa's death, Mamam. I was already in my teens then, and I was so afraid that I would be seen to be unable to stop crying. I have always been prone to cry easily, and I knew I would not be able to maintain a manly pretence during the mass, and especially during the burial in Aust church yard. I remained hidden in the barn until Papa's funeral was over and other people had gone away."

Apollonia smiled and kissed his cheek before she answered him, "I remember it well, Chad. At first, I was frightened by your sudden disappearance until Gareth told me where you were in the loft and promised that he would watch over you."

Chad smiled back to acknowledge her awareness of his boyish weakness. "Gareth is a good man. Thank God for his service to you and to our family. Still, as I have had to deal with the deaths of persons dear to me three times in my life, I believe that I am finally learning to face it honestly, thanks to you, your patience, and your strength. I see my tears now as the expression of depth of feeling even if they are unmanly."

"Our bodies cry to express painful injury, Chad. We can not prepare for the death of any one dear to us. One simply must endure it for the sake of the living. I shall admit to you that I beg God to allow me to die before you or your brothers. Our loss of your brother, Alban, has been a tear in the fabric of my life. One does not expect one's children to die before their parents. You have proven yourself a valiant servant of the king, a loving and faithful husband, and a devoted father to your children. I shall always be proud of you." The Lady took her son's hand and held it as they continued to climb.

"Come along," Juliana shouted at them, "grandmamma, papa, hurry up! We will never reach the top at this pace." She and Owen were nearly halfway up the hill and pushing on steadily.

They all gathered at last at the top of Wearyall Hill. Juliana began looking immediately for the Holy Thorn. "There it is! It is blossoming, grandmamma, so beautifully. Can you believe it, Owen? This bush has grown since Saint Joseph of Arimathea planted his staff here after having come all the way to England from the Holy Land."

"Why should he have done that, Juliana?" Owen asked her skeptically.

"Why did he, grandmamma? Can you tell us?"

"No one can be certain, Juliana, but I think we must put ourselves back into the days after the crucifixion of our Lord Jesus. Joseph of Arimathea was an important councillor in Jerusalem. He was also a secret disciple of Jesus who asked to take the Lord's body for burial after His death on the cross."

"Why would that make Saint Joseph want to leave his country, grandmamma?"

"When Jesus rose from the dead, dearheart, I suspect that the Pharisees who were strong in Jerusalem might have made charges against Joseph. After all, it was he who provided his own tomb for the body of Christ. The Pharisees may have thought that Joseph hid the Lord's body away to make it look as if Jesus had risen from the dead, as He said he would."

"I know that Jesus did not like the Pharisees or the Sadducees, my Lady, and they did not like him," Owen said. "When we were reading in the Gospels at Tintern, Jesus called them hypocrites."

"That is an important point, Owen, because after Jesus' resurrection, the Pharisees and Sadducees were probably very angry to learn that Joseph was a secret disciple of our Lord. It is possible that Joseph left his home in Jerusalem to escape from their charges against him. All we can know certainly is that his legend tells us that he came to England with his disciples and founded the Abbey of Glastonbury in his new life as a Christian. He landed here on Wearyall Hill and planted his staff in the ground where it miraculously burst into leaf showing him that it was here he must settle and build a church. The staff continued to grow as this thorn bush which blossoms every year at Christmas time."

"What a beautiful Christmas story, grandmamma. I am especially happy that we came now. Papa, is this not the best time to be here?"

"Yes, Juliana, indeed it is. It tells us the story of a good man who was forced to travel a very long way to begin his life anew. I will try to do the same, little one, and I shan't have to travel a very long way. I shall do it in my home with my enthusiastic children to help me."

All the way down from the hill top, Apollonia's mind tried desperately to hold and absorb every memory she had experienced in Glastonbury. The winds grew stronger and she pulled her hood to cover her head, using her stick to steady her footsteps. Nothing, she told herself, could chill the warm gratitude she felt in her heart. These days in Glastonbury had meant grief and struggle for her family. Yet, as they prepared to leave, Saint Joseph brought to all of them the hope of a blessed new beginning, she told herself. "Surely this has been a gift to us of Joseph of Arimathea's real treasure."

The End

Glossary

Abbey: monastery supervised by an abbot.

Affinity: medieval concept of loyal household, wearing the livery or heraldic badge of one's lord and granting full allegiance and acceptance of his rule in one's life.

Anchorite: a religious recluse frequently attached to a parish church in England.

Appolonia, Saint: Deaconess and martyr of Alexandria, died c 249. She was seized and had all her teeth broken out with blows on her jaws, then threatened to put her onto a bonfire if she refused to recite blasphemous sayings. Without flinching, she leapt onto the bonfire and was consumed.

Augustinian: a member of the religious order observing a rule derived from St. Augustine's teachings.

Benedicite: fourteenth century usage, meaning (the Lord) blesses you.

Benedictine: member of the order of monks founded by St. Benedict at Monte Casino, about AD 530.

Bishop: member of the clergy who supervises a diocese, governing many parish churches and whose main seat or throne is found in his cathedral.

Canon: member of the clergy chapter that live communally like monks.

Canon law: the body of ecclesiastical or church law which applied to all officers of the clergy and administration.

Carrel: a small enclosure or study in a cloister.

Celts: Indo-European tribal peoples occupying England at the time of the Roman invasions and before the arrival of the Anglo-Saxons. Now Celts are represented chiefly by the Cornish, Irish, Gaels, Welsh and Bretons.

Chivalry: rules and ideal qualifications of a medieval knight: courage, courtesy, generosity, valour, and dexterity in arms.

Churl: a peasant or rustic or a rude, boorish, or surly person.

Cloister: a covered walk, usually opening onto a courtyard, within a religious institution, monastery, or convent.

Commons: commonality, the common people, as distinguished from those with authority, rank, and station.

Compline: the final service of the round of daily prayer took place around 7:00 p.m. See *opus dei*, round of daily prayer.

Courtesy: in the understanding of those followers of Julian of Norwich from about 1400, courtesy is not meant to be understood as excellence of manners or polite behaviour. Courtesy means loving respect implying not only indulgence of another but also goodness granted freely regardless of sinful behaviour. Mother Julian describes God as our "Courteous Lord".

Crossing: the intersection of the nave and transcepts in a cruciform church building.

Curate: any ecclesiastic entrusted with the cure of souls.

Destrier: a medieval knight's warhorse.

Diocese: ecclesiastical district under the jurisdiction of a bishop.

Druids: after 800 BCE and throughout the Iron Age, British society was transforming into the European Celtic culture led by the Druids, a priestly class. The learned and respected Druids' spiritual practices focused on the teaching and initiation of individuals and on honouring the local spirits of place.

Franciscans:	members of the mendicant order founded by St Francis of Assisi, also called the Grey Friars.
Friary:	a monastery of friars of a mendicant order, such as the Franciscans or the Dominicans.
Gaol:	British variant spelling of jail.
Garderobe:	medieval privy often built into the walls of a castle or manor house.
Garter knight:	a member of the Order of the Garter, founded by King Edward III.
Gentry:	well-born, well-bred people, an aristocracy; in England, the class under the nobility.
Gramercy:	an expression of thanks meaning "grand merci".
Grey Friar:	a brother of the Franciscan order.
Henchman:	in the middle ages a trusted attendant, a supporter, or a follower.
Holy Orders:	the rank or status of ordained Christian ministry.
Indulgence:	a document of the church containing a partial remission of punishment in purgatory still due for sin after absolution.
Lady Chapel:	a chapel dedicated to the Virgin Mary attached to a church at the eastern extremity, usually behind the high altar. In Glastonbury, however, it was attached to the monastic church at the west.
Lauds:	a service of the church marked especially by psalms of praise; in monastic life, Lauds is the first daytime office of the daily round of prayer called the *opus dei*.
Liripipe:	the tail or pendant part of the back of a hood or hat of the 14th century.
Livery:	a distinctive dress, badge, or device formerly provided by someone of rank or title for his retainers.
Man of law:	14th century barrister or lawyer.
Minion:	a follower or subordinate of some person in power.

Missal:	book of prayers or devotions.
Nave:	the principal longitudinal area of a church extending from main entrance to the chancel.
Nave aisle:	in a major church, the architectural longitudinal division of the public space, extending from the main entrance to the chancel. The nave aisle is the central aisle. In the 14th century, the nave had two aisles, separated by the colonnade.
Noble:	distinguished by birth, rank, or title.
Noblesse oblige	the moral obligation of the rich or highborn to display honourable or charitable conduct.
Noblewoman:	a woman of noble birth or rank.
Normans:	natives of Normandy.
Opus dei:	literally the "work of God" but referring specifically to the services for the divine offices of the church; eight services or offices required by St Benedict including Matins, Lauds, Prime, Terce, Sext, None, Vespers, and Compline.
Page:	a boy in training for knighthood, ranking next below a squire in the personal service of a knight.
Palfrey:	a saddle horse, not a war horse.
Pardoner:	an ecclesiastical official charged with the granting of indulgences.
Physic:	in the 14th century, any medicine, or drug, especially one that purges.
Plague:	epidemic disease of high mortality, pestilence.
Prie-dieu:	piece of furniture especially designed for kneeling upon during prayer.
Priory:	monastery governed by a prior or prioress.
Quaestores:	Latin word used as title for church official known as a pardoner.
Quire:	archaic spelling of 14th century area in a medieval

church for the choir stalls.

Quire aisle:	main space between the rows of choir stalls.
Quire screen:	a stone or wooden screen or structure of division separating the choir from the nave of a great church.
Relic	ecclesiastical term referring to the body, a part of the body, or a personal memorial of a saint or members of the Holy Family and worthy of veneration.
Reliquary:	beautifully crafted receptacle for a relic.
Sanctuary:	(the place) the part of a church around the altar.
Sanctuary:	(the act) a church or other sacred place where fugitives were formerly entitled to immunity from arrest.
Saxons:	Germanic tribes, a group of which invaded and occupied parts of Britain in the 5th and 6th centuries.
Sext:	service of the church, the fourth of seven canonical hours.
Solar:	a private or upper chamber in a medieval English house or castle.
Somerset Levels:	an area in the northeast corner of the County of Somerset, known to have had settlement from as early as 4000 BCE. It was marked by raised track ways, ancient earthworks, and water courses, as well as some drainage sites and several roads constructed during the Roman occupation of England.
Sovereignty:	the status of authority and independence.
Squire:	the first degree of knighthood, squire as servant to a knight; a country gentleman, especially the chief landed proprietor in a district.
Steward:	one who serves as manager of financial and business affairs, serving as manager or agent for another.
Table dormant:	a table permanently in place.
Table tomb:	a sepulchral structure with a flat, slab-like top.

Tor:	a hill or rocky high place. Tor is a word of Celtic origin. Glastonbury Tor rises 520 feet (158 metres).
Tor Burr or Egg stone:	an unusual feature of the Tor sandstone is the presense within it of much harder round, oval or egg-shaped boulders. Known as 'Tor burrs,' they are anything from a faction of an inch to a few feet in diameter. The exact cause of their formation is unknown, but it may be that iron rich water percolating through the sand began to accrete around small nodules that eventually grew into eggstones.
Tracery:	ornamental work within a Gothic window.
Transept:	the cross-like arms of a major church extending out from the intersection of nave and choir.
Treasury of Merit:	a treasury of the goodness, the merits of Christ and the saints, left to the keeping of the Church and which is the source of Indulgences. In the later Middle Ages, the sale of Indulgences became a significant means of raising funds.
Tunic:	an outer garment with or without sleeves and sometimes worn belted.
Villein:	a member of the class of partially free persons in a feudal system who serves his lord but has some rights and privileges.
Vowess:	dedication of a woman to the service of God without requiring her to go into a nunnery.
Wallet:	14th century expression of a bag for carrying small articles.
Wimple:	a 14th century woman's headcloth drawn in folds about the chin, still worn by some nuns.